PRAISE FOR
Bride's Children- Worlds Apart

Don and Marcia Wilson's praise for Bride's Children- 8 June 2019

Don is a retired creative writing professor. Marcia is an Asian studies scholar. They graduated from Georgetown University in 1964. They are 84 years old.

"Incredible," Don said before picking up the manuscript and hefting it a few times. "No matter what happens to this going forward, you have provided your sons with the template decent people use to become successful in a troubled world."

Marcia asked, "May I see everything else you've written? Your story telling, grasp of detail, and characterization were a revelation. I never learned how pervasive the Americans were in the opium trade, or what roles the diplomats and traders may have had in destabilizing 1850's Japan. Your portrayal of what the secessionists were doing in California came as a surprise. I think that I should mention what happened while our daughter and son-in-law were visiting from Honolulu. Our son-in-law saw the manuscript on the counter. I didn't think he would be much interested in it. He's a techie who passes the time reading journals and entertains himself doing math puzzles. He read the manuscript from cover to cover and summed up his impressions with one word: mesmerizing."

Don asked Marcia who her favorite character was. She thought a moment and said, "There are so many to choose from. I liked Willard the most. He's fascinating."

That figures. Willard is the character who most resembles her son-in-law.

"A thoroughly enjoyable read!" Tom Dodsworth, millennial, homebuilder

"I loved the story, but the feeling that sticks is the sense of motion I felt in every shipboard scene." Amber Lidstone, yachtswoman

"I don't usually read historical fiction, but I found your narrative fully formed and engrossing, something I rarely say on any book I review." Christoph Koniczek, Friesen Press

"This book is a triumph. I felt honored to work on it. The rich detail, authentic historical settings, layered characters and ever shifting exotic locations, were fascinating and quite a feat to pull off." Rebecca Hendry, editor, Friesen Press

WORLDS APART

Bride's Children: Book One

ROBERT J. JOSEPH

Novels by
Robert James Joseph

Books in the Trilogy:
Worlds Apart- 1 January 1860 thru 30 June 1860
Collison Course- 4 July thru 31 December 1860
Retribution- 1 January 1861 thru 12 April 1861

 FriesenPress

Suite 300 - 990 Fort St
Victoria, BC, V8V 3K2
Canada

www.friesenpress.com

robertjjoseph.com

Portrait photographer: Jamie Reichert, reichertphotography.com

Cover graphics: Will Taylor, willoid.com

Interior Design: Teresita Hernández-Quesada

ISBN
978-1-5255-6120-7 (Hardcover)
978-1-5255-6121-4 (Paperback)
978-1-5255-6122-1 (eBook)

Fiction, Historical

Distributed to the trade by The Ingram Book Company

DEDICATION

This work is dedicated to James Bishop, my mentor, Early Evans, my bride, and Patricia Richards, the first friend I made when I arrived in Canada all those years ago.

QUOTES

"...when we're dancing with the angels, we'll be asked, what did we do in 2019 to keep our democracy intact?"

Representative Elijah Cummings (January 1951-October 2019), the first black Congressman to lie in state in the US Capitol, a structure built by slaves in 1793.

"The cost of doing nothing isn't nothing. Our children are the living messengers to a future we'll never see. Our time is too short to not fight for what is good, true, and best in America."

President, Barack Obama, quoting Cummings while delivering Elijah's eulogy on 25 October 2019.

ACKNOWLEDGEMENTS

The author wishes to thank the following people, authors, and agencies for their assistance in making this book possible.

I owe a great debt of gratitude to my sons, Florian and David for foregoing hunting and fishing trips with me while I focused on producing this work. Thank you. I thank my sister, Gale LaPlante for reading and formatting several drafts. Thanks to numerous readers, including Joel Russ, Dianne Goldsmith, John Candy, Thomas Dodsworth, Will Taylor, Nicola Flossbach, Celine Cluff, Nancy Lee Evans, Becky Johnson, Cousin George Joseph, his friend, the renowned Maine outdoor writer, George Smith, Lavinia Lidstone, and her mother, Amber. William L. Crothers (*The American-Built Clipper Ship*) and Dr. John Harland (*Seamanship in the Age of Sail*) put me aboard the Bride and showed me how to sail her. Several agencies and individuals participated in editing the book's 20 drafts. Special thanks must go to Michael Alpert, Director of the University of Maine Press, without whose assistance I never would have met the man who became an indispensable guide on this journey, James Bishop. Thanks to Renni Browne, author of *Self Editing for Fiction Writers*. I read her book straight through four times and referred to it so often, I knew exactly where to look whenever I needed inspiration on how to show rather than tell readers what was happening in each and every scene. I would like to thank, Jane Ryder, former office manager of Renni's company, The Editorial Department. Jane passed me to their senior editor, Peter Gelfan who edited draft six. Thank you, Peter. Your suggestions, comments, and criticisms made the book come alive, especially after I followed your advice and cut the first four chapters! I'll always be indebted to Ann Morris, director of the Rockland Historical Society; her encouragement got me through a difficult period. Don Wilson, a retired collegiate writing instructor, and his wife, Marcia, an Asian Studies scholar, read draft 15. This work is better for having passed through their hands. Genie Daly of Maine Authors Publishing provided a thoughtful thematic edit that resonates throughout the tale. Last, but certainly, not the least to deserve recognition, are Christoph Koniczek, Astra Crompton, Jessica Bonney, Rebecca Hendry, Kevin Miller, Teresita Hernandez, and James Stewart of Friesen Press. They are my publishing team. To these and so many well-wishers, I say thank you.

TO THE READER

I never would have guessed that the release of this book would occur after a failed Presidential Impeachment or during civil unrest in the midst of a global pandemic.

Writing a book on how the Americans got into a Civil War takes time. Years. The *Bride's Children* tale began on 15 March 2003, the day after John Yoo, a George W. Bush Justice Department lawyer revealed his infamous memo, "…federal laws against torture, assault, and maiming would not apply to the interrogation of terror suspects…," i.e., enemies of the state. I'd been thinking about writing a novel since the Watergate Scandal and that memo got me started.

Gerald Ford may have planted the seed for this book as far back as 8 September 1974, the day he pardoned Richard Nixon. Instead of using the pardon as originally intended (to correct travesties of justice), Ford used it to expand the concept of *unitary executive theory*. He went beyond any previous interpretation, and by so doing, provided a remedy for how future presidents may escape prosecution for their criminal behavior. The Reagan Administration's mean spirited application of this theory set in motion a series of cascading calamities that gave us the likes of Geo. W. Bush, Dick Cheney, and Robert Rumsfeld.

The practice of putting criminals in the White House has left us with a degenerate presiding over a divided republic on the verge of Constitutional collapse.

If presidents can be exonerated by a complicit Senate for enlisting the aid of foreign governments in defeating their political foes, what is to prevent them from using John Yoo's terror memo as a convenient precedent should they decide to expand their punitive reach into the homes of their domestic rivals?

The tale you have in your hands should provide you with an entertaining diversion from these thoughts. I've tried to make this diversion worth your while by offering insights into the roles our ancestors may have played in getting us to where we are today. Get comfortable if you decide to see what lies inside, because if you do, you'll be joining Earl Yeaton and his crew on a turbulent voyage through the soul of Darkness.

And yes, to those of you who thought to ask, I am a Yeaton. And yes, I do come from a long line of patriots, the most famous being Hopley Yeaton who George Washington and Thomas Jefferson tapped to be the first commissioned military officer in the new republic. Captain Yeaton's remains are interred at the gates to the US Coast Guard Academy.

PROLOGUE

Yeaton Wharf, San Francisco, California, 1 January 1860, 5:30 a.m.

Ol' Bud Mawer got a whiff of what lay ahead long before the pennant began to stir. "I've a feelin' we're in for a whole lot more than a dose of heavy weather."

An hour or so later, he drove home a hatch's last wedge and leaned on the skylight. Pushing the red pom-pom on his battered tam o' shanter to windward, he straightened and had another peek at his surroundings. Squinting at the fitful pennant, he poked a split match into the space between two molars and picked at a piece of pork. Sucking the nugget free, he tossed the mallet in a tool locker and decided to take a load off. Spreading a scrap of sailcloth on the damp lid, he sat and dug out the fixins. Tamping burley into a clay bowl, his wise, old eyes scanned the dreary sky and came to rest on a group of ship's boys huddled by the rail. The boys were exchanging nervous glances beneath restless halyards slapping tall masts. Bud and the boys were coping as best they could with the apprehensions reserved for those about to spend the first day of the New Year on the open ocean.

At the other end of the wharf and out on Spears, a couple of late-night spillovers shuffled into their own case of the jitters. The cold stares they received from the armed men opening a pair of massive warehouse doors set their nerves on edge. Moving closer to the middle of the gas-lit street, they picked up the pace and stepped into the path of a closed carriage coming from the rear. Caution turned to fear as several of the waiting men came toward them to take up positions on the other side of the street beside a matching set of doors. Hurrying past the opening, they got a glimpse of what lay beyond the loaded guns. Feeling eyes on their backs, the pair separated and kept their hands in plain sight.

They heard the carriage turn, enter the cavernous gallery, and rumble straight through to the midpoint of the moored ship. The two drunks were nearly out of earshot by the time the driver pulled on the reins and called. "Whoa!" from the other side of the wall.

Captain Earl Yeaton and his men were there to greet the carriage. Satisfied with what he saw around him, he reached up and opened the door. Two women dressed in traveling clothes stepped onto the wharf. He noticed they had the good sense to be wearing flat-heeled shoes. Earl glanced at the pair and addressed his men. "Permit me to introduce our passengers, Evelyn Griffin and Myra Landers."

Evelyn's intelligent green eyes politely met the appreciative nods and paused on an attractive pair of hazel eyes. She lowered her blond lashes and turned to meet Earl's gaze.

Hmm, he mused, having met her the previous day, *my first impression is still intact. She's retained the rare gift of being likable on sight; quite the feat, since along with everyone else standing here, she's been up all night.*

Shifting his attention to her traveling companion—escort, really—he saw a woman who made no excuses for being unattractive, tired, or distant. The self-righteous stare he received after glancing at the loose ribbon marker sticking out of the King James Bible in her purse told him all he needed to know about Myra Landers. Keeping his face neutral in the presence of the brittle moral rectitude of this piously devout spinster, he said nothing. Didn't stop him from thinking, however. *This one would prefer to arrive in Los Angeles on the next tide without having anything to do with the uncouth seamen responsible for getting her there safely. That pinched hatchet face has the mien of an ill-tempered hen, and the sooner we're rid of her, the better.*

The men standing with Earl were used to hosting all manner of passengers and were able to avoid the awkward silence the less prepared would have experienced in the presence of the hostile Myra.

Although the women had traveled on clippers before, they still felt a sense of awe standing near a ship that appeared so large in port but could be so small on the vastness of the ocean. Earl sensed their misgivings. *There's at least one thing we have in common.* Offering a reassuring smile, he turned to a companion. "Ladies, if you will permit, this gentleman will see you to your cabins while we complete our business here."

Bill Hobbs stepped forward and bowed to the women. He appeared ordinary in every sense of the word. His unobtrusive manners would serve the women's needs to perfection; he would blandly deposit them where they could shut the doors to their suites and sleep for as long as their tired bodies wished. Bill gestured to the gangway. "Follow me, ladies, and I will show you to your cabins."

Earl nodded at the men waiting to assist with the baggage. Seeing the last of the women's things removed from the carriage, he motioned to the driver and twirled a finger above his head. The carriage came about, passed through the warehouse once more, and entered a similar building across the street. Closing the doors walled off the two Yeaton Brothers buildings.

Two men in the second building took seats at a table set in the narrow space between a pair of upstairs windows. The soft yellow light of several wall lamps reflected off rifles and shotguns mounted nearby. One of the men flipped an ace and scanned the street. His companion cut a deuce and lined up the pegs.

Earl led his group to a pine-paneled office. The group consisted of his nephew, Adam, the first mate, and the wharf manager. Earl waved a finger, and Adam closed curtains on windows that offered views of the gallery, the ship, and harbor. The large room contained a couple of desks, a cash register on a glass-fronted display case, navigational aids, a small library, a large table, chairs, file cabinets, charts, marine oils, maps of San Francisco, the known world, and two large safes. One was for the manager, and the other was for Earl and his brother, Nathan. A Seth Thomas station clock ticked off the minutes on the wall behind the register. Earl removed a leather-bound folder from a safe. "Have the crewmen who were out last night returned?" he asked.

"Yes." Adam took a seat with the others. "They engaged in the usual indulgences. Two of the ship's boys tied one on last night. Don't expect them to be of much use today. An incident with James is worth mentioning. He and Elmer were followed for most of the night by two of Alan Wittington's agents."

Wittington, area supervisor of the US Customs Service, made it his personal mission to follow the strict definition of the law. Little went on in San Francisco that he did not know about. Over the course of his career, he had cultivated an array of snitches spanning every social stratum of the city, from the lowest housecleaners to the mayor's advisors. He suspected, but could never prove, that Earl Yeaton and his crew skirted the law. One of his snitches had told him Earl was avoiding customs duties on undeclared cargo.

Earl knew Wittington's men wouldn't approach James Marshall and said as much. He also knew his men would not carry anything to incriminate them or make contact with anyone who might arouse suspicion. Wittington and his agents had no way of knowing they were wasting their time. The goods in question had been smuggled aboard the night the agents were at home sleeping off their Christmas dinners.

Adam nodded to his uncle. "Kato and Munenori have returned from the Japanese consulate. The trunks they brought with them are in the hold. The hatches are sealed and everyone's accounted for."

WORLDS APART

Bride's Children: Book One

ROBERT J. JOSEPH

TABLE OF CONTENTS

Praise for Bride's Children- Worlds Apart i

Dedication vii

Quotes ix

Acknowledgements xi

To the Reader xiii

Prologue xv
Yeaton Wharf, San Francisco, California, 1 January 1860,
5:30 a.m.

Chapter 1 1
Stanford Mansion, San Francisco, 1 January 1860, shortly
after midnight

Chapter 2 10
Stanford Mansion, Drawing Room, 1 January, 1:30 a.m.

Chapter 3 15
Stanford Mansion Ballroom, 1 January, 1:45 a.m.

Chapter 4 27
Nob Hill, San Francisco, 1 January, 2:15 a.m.

Chapter 5 34
Warehouse Office, 1 January, 6:00 a.m.

Chapter 6 40
Yeaton Wharf, San Francisco, 1 January, 6:30 a.m., ebb
tide stirring

Chapter 7 45
Off the Coast of California, 2 January, 11:15 a.m.

Chapter 8 61
Midway between San Francisco and Los Angeles, 2 January,
1:20 p.m.

Chapter 9 81
Banning's Landing, San Pedro, 3 January, 10 a.m.

Chapter 10 89
Santa Fe Trail, El Monte, 3 January, 4:00 p.m.

Chapter 11 103
Lake Vineyard, San Gabriel, 4 January, 10:30 a.m.

Chapter 12 128
Rancho La Brea, 5 January, 6:00 a.m.

Chapter 13 133
Off Santa Catalina Island, Los Angeles Bay, 5 January,
5:30 p.m.

Chapter 14 155
23°26' N, 21°29' E, Tropic of Cancer, 11 January 1860,
12:30 p.m.

Chapter 15 166
Queen Emma Kamehameha's Hospital Reception, 5 March
1860, 6:00 p.m.

Chapter 16 185
Off the Southern Shore of I Wo To, 24° N, 141° E, 18
March, 7:00 a.m.

Chapter 17 194
Edo Harbor Anchorage, 36° N, 138° E, 28 March, 8:45
a.m., high slack tide.

Chapter 18 220
Renji Yi Hospital, British Legation, Shanghai, China, 30
April 1860, 11 a.m.

Chapter 19 231
Dajing Ge Pavilion, Shanghai, China, 30 April, 6:00 p.m.

Chapter 20 246
Kowloon Harbor, China, 12 May, 5:00 a.m.

Chapter 21 272
Kolkata, India, 24 May, four bells of the morning watch
(10:00 a.m.)

Chapter 22 286
Sahibzada Muhammad Mardan Palace, 25 May, 6:00 p.m.

Chapter 23 311
Off the Coast of South Africa, 7 June, daybreak

Chapter 24 333
Blandy's Wharf, Port of Funchal, Madeira, 20 June, first bell
of the dog watch

Chapter 25 352
Open Ocean south of Cadiz, Spain, 30 June, four bells of
the forenoon watch

About the Author 363

CHAPTER 1

Stanford Mansion, San Francisco, 1 January
1860, shortly after midnight

"Happy New Year, Adam," Earl said, raising a glass of champagne over the babble surrounding them.

"Same to you, Uncle; wouldn't miss it for the world," Adam deadpanned while giving Earl's glass a tap. "And we're sticking together no matter what happens, right?"

"Yes. Now go on with ya. Greet your friends, and be ready to leave in an hour."

The celebration they were attending at the Nob Hill mansion of Jane and Leland Stanford represented the upper crust of San Francisco society. Earl was there to see one attendee, and it wasn't the one who got his attention first. Unable to avoid Alan Wittington's salute from across the room, he stifled a frown, nodded and took a sip. "Hell of a way to begin the New Year," he muttered behind the rim of his glass. "Adam starts it off with a reminder of what we are in for, my second toast is with a wharf rat, and we're sailing into a nor'wester."

His host's approach took the edge off his fixed smile and forced him to drop his ill humor. She wore a pale-yellow evening gown beneath a white crocheted shawl draped across bare shoulders. Emeralds and pearls glittered off most of her exposed flesh. The diamond-studded tiara holding her auburn hair in place sparkled above an infectious smile. Still thawing, he spoke to a passing waiter. "Zhe hai chiabudo." ("Now this is more like it.")

"Captain Yeaton, thank you for coming to my house to ring in the New Year," she said, slipping an arm over his and lowering her voice. "Since you're the only man I can truly trust, the moments we share are precious." She paused and smiled at the admiring glances she and her handsome companion received. "I know my time with you is short, and the only reason you are here is to say goodbye. I haven't seen you since Christmas, and we have catching up to do before I let you go for another twelve months. Let's be by ourselves for a bit. We won't be missed in this crowd."

Steering him through the congestion, she led him to a room in a quiet section of the house. A large bay window offered a panoramic view of the harbor from a pair of winged chairs flanked by side tables. The hill beneath the window gave way to a gentle slope plateauing out along the shoreline. Cooler air lifted fog clinging to the dark, oak-lined hills across the bay. A thinning moon cast its pale reflection on the water. The lampposts strung along Broadway and Spear lit the way to the harbor. Earl could see the faint outline of his ship rubbing against the wharf.

"Soon you will be free of this place," she said, noticing how his gaze lingered over the view. She fired up a gas lamp by the open door and turned the flame as low as propriety would permit.

"Yes. I've done this so many times that I've grown accustomed to farewells. I was thinking of other things just now." He stopped beside a wheeled table laden with spirits, selected a liqueur called Tia Maria, and poured a few shots into a couple of tumblers.

"That ship down there," she said, pointing a glittering finger, "has taken your attention away from me. What's got you thinking, Earl Yeaton?"

"I was thinking of many things. Stepping into a room like this with one of the few people of privilege I admire is one of them. I like being here and am grateful we've become such good friends. And humbled too."

He skipped over what she already knew and avoided what he left unsaid. There was no mistaking the disappointment he saw her eyes every time he shied away from revisiting a desperate period in his life. He was adamant in his refusal to discuss with her what had happened in the spring of '36, even though she was aware that he had graduated from Harvard Medical School as a penniless doctor after his father had lost his lumber business in a banking scandal. He suspected she'd been told no one would hire him because of his role in a fatal accident that may have precipitated the disappearance of a classmate.

Having no prospects and coming from a family of mariners, he decided to flee the source of his sorrows. He'd managed to avoid the folly of sailing with a master who saw him as a necessary inconvenience and chose instead to sail with a captain who saw him as a young man in need of sound guidance.

Earl put the cork back in the bottle. "So much of my good fortune has relied upon skirting disaster and being shown how to wisely grasp life's golden rings. Captain Pinkham, now dead, once said becoming successful is a lot of work. How well we know. I'm still puzzling over another thing he said. Had to do with avoiding the inherent pitfalls associated with surviving success."

"Umm," he heard her say.

Earl picked up the tumblers and saw Jane looking toward the harbor.

"If I'd been less successful, how would I cope with the cumulative effects of lost opportunities as I age? How would I handle the dismay of entering my final years feeling as if my life hadn't amounted to much and discovering I'd become the man I least wished to be?"

"Ahh," she said to the image gazing back at her in the window.

"That got me thinking of the contrast between the majority of your guests and three people who came west with a dream too. I hired them in Vancouver. I was imagining what they were up to. But we're not here to discuss new crew members or how they came aboard. I apologize for not paying attention to you." He handed her a glass.

"Listen to me, Earl; you're my friend in large part because I find you so interesting! You know why I brought you in here and it can wait. Go on."

She refrained from mentioning how much she relished being in the presence of a man who made her feel as if she was the only woman in his life each time they were together. She found his urbane manners, arresting characteristics, and capacity for being intimate in the absence of desire quite compelling. She trusted him without reservation. Waving him to a chair where he could see through his reflection, she adjusted herself in the seat facing him. She took a sip and placed her drink on a side table.

He sat across from her and holding his drink in one hand, leaned back. "We were three men short by the time we entered Vancouver Harbor to pick up a load of river ice," he said taking a sip. "We'd been up the coast to Haida

G'wai trading with the natives, exchanging medical supplies, tools, saws, knives, fishing nets, and tackle for furs, clothing, jewelry, and art objects." He raised his eyebrows and nodded as she waved a silver Haida bracelet he'd given her on another occasion.

"We lost a boy off Terra del Fuego, and by the time we got to British Columbia, two crew members had decided to stay ashore and try their hand at prospecting. The three replacements are down at the wharf getting ready to leave. They've been out west for the past five years. They're a mixed bag. An old-timer, a young man, and a boy. The old-timer's companions are from Peggy's Cove, Nova Scotia. We came across them while they were working for the Fraser River ice cutters. They asked to come aboard and offered to work their passage Down East."

Earl swirled the liquid in his glass, sighed and had another sip.

"They had a tragedy in area this side of the Rockies called the Kootenays. The boy is the orphaned son of a dead partner. His father was working a quartz vein in an unstable wall. The rock face collapsed and buried him. By the time they dug him out, the only thing left to do was clean out his pockets, say a few words over the corpse, and cover him back up. They decided to quit the country and headed for the coast. Those men wouldn't be down there if we hadn't stopped in Vancouver to get ice for your party."

The lamp's yellow flame softened his sober expression. "This year is going to be like no other. I'll be sailing west away from a country in turmoil and will be returning from the east to a country that could be at war with itself."

"Yes," she said. "Leland says those who wish to protect the individual through laws and reason could become the carrion of vultures if the special interests trying to tear this country apart aren't dealt with mighty soon."

He met her gaze. "I still hold to the belief that there are enough patriots among us to put a stop to the perpetrators of so much discord."

"Yes and no. Your optimism could put you in peril," she responded with undisguised doubt. "Thank you for being a friend I can count on."

"You're welcome," he said, tipping his glass and taking a companionable swallow of the sweet brown aperitif. A moment later, he experienced a caffeine-infused boost. *Pleasant, but I need to get food in me if I want to keep my wits sharp for the rest of the night.* He gave his attention back to Jane.

"Thank you for introducing me to Dr. Yee," she said. "I saw him again two days ago. His remedies have settled my stomach."

Earl became more alert. Leland Stanford called the Chinese the "scourge of Asia" and supported laws to restrict these "degraded people, who if unchecked, would have a deleterious effect on the superior white race." *A Chinaman could be saving his wife's life, and she probably keeps her visits to the good doctor secret.*

"Earl, do you think me a meddler because I'm not afraid to speak up in the presence of Leland and his friends? Friends who I believe are trying to silence me?"

"Perhaps. You may be seen as an obstacle to those who wish to influence Leland in ways you find objectionable." He waited for her to bring up what he thought she had brought him there to discuss.

"The more I want us to extricate ourselves from his enterprises, the more his partners expect Leland to participate. I'm sure they are a big part of his decision to become the next governor of California. I feel as if my voice in these affairs is growing fainter. I also feel it's time to share our wealth and stop accumulating more."

He heard exasperation in her voice as she shifted in her chair. "How can I get him to reduce his involvement with Crocker, Hopkins, and Huntington, so we can get on with our lives?"

People referred to her husband and his associates as the Big Four; the most influential power brokers in California.

She dropped the subject. "Earl is there anything I can do for you?"

"Hold it a second, Jane," he said, showing her a hand. "You're going to have to be extra careful from now on, and I'm not going to be here to look after you. You can't help me, but Dr. Yee can help you. See him regularly. Asking you for assistance in any of the activities I'm engaged in would put you at more risk than you already find yourself. Thanks anyway."

She nodded. "There is one last thing to mention before we rejoin the party." Earl sat a little straighter. "You're aware the military courier who arrived on the Empire was murdered, and his pouch was taken."

"Yes. General Clarke's aide, Lieutenant Anderson, is in custody. Apparently, the courier, Lieutenant Whipple, and Lieutenant Anderson had a violent disagreement over which of them is better suited to marry Dr. John S.

Griffin's niece, Evelyn Griffin." Earl leaned forward and put his glass on the table. "Let me see your hands."

Jane put her elbows on her knees and offered her hands. She watched him closely while he turned them this way and that. "Dr. Griffin is an influential Los Angeles resident," she said. "He happens to be the brother-in-law of the renowned General Sidney Johnston, General Clarke's replacement as the next general of the Pacific. Johnston is spending the holidays in Los Angeles with Dr. Griffin. Their wives are sisters. General Johnston is about to become the most powerful military man in California." Not daring to ask why he continued to squeeze her right palm after releasing the left, she continued. "Are you aware that Dr. Griffin's brother leads a team of mechanical engineers in New York? They're working for a consortium intent on producing a petroleum-fueled internal combustion engine. Many applications exist for engines that don't require a boiler. Evelyn could become an heiress if her father's successful." Her voice trailed off with her breath as she fumbled for her drink with her free hand.

"Yes, I'm aware." The lines around his eyes drew tighter. "I'm familiar with her uncle and the generals. From what you've said about her father, it seems there are reasons beyond her beauty to make Evelyn attractive," he added, squinting at a crosshatch in Jane's lifeline. It had not been there the last time he'd examined the hand. Wrestling with the merits of telling her what he was seeing, he released her hand and sat up. Hoping he would not regret it, he decided to reveal what he had seen only if she asked. He felt she had enough on her mind without having to endure the specter of a premature death.

Clearing his throat, he shifted in his seat. "Evelyn is a catch capable of getting fools excited enough to do the unthinkable. I doubt she's the reason Lieutenant Whipple's dead, though. I met her yesterday at the Clarkes. She's a guest of the general's daughter and will be returning to Los Angles with us," he said watching Jane absorb that bit of unexpected news.

"Huh. Did the Clarkes introduce you to Evelyn's cousin, Myra?"

"Yes. Do you know anything about her?"

"Not much. Myra is the daughter of Ezra Cole, a strict Congregationalist minister in Boston. Ezra's sermons damn anyone who challenges his literal interpretation of the Old Testament. Friends are calling him and his ilk evangelicals, whatever that means. Militant Christians maybe? Myra is a chip off the old block, apparently. You may have heard of her grandfather, Emmet Cole, of Cole Firearms New Haven."

"Yeah, I know who Emmet Cole is. I'll try not to ruffle his granddaughter's feathers." Earl leaned back. "It's an open secret the federal government intends to audit the records of all shippers, banks, and gold and silver producers. The government wants to identify Southern sympathizers and their financial supporters. Authorization to conduct those audits was in the stolen pouch."

"Yes, I heard," she said, perplexed by the web of intrigue surrounding her. She let him continue, feeling swamped by her growing concern.

"Unfortunately, we are forced to contend with nefarious compatriots who are openly sympathizing with the Union and quietly supporting the secessionists," he said, making her head spin even more. "I'm sure these men would prefer to keep their allegiances private for obvious reasons. The audit could ensnare judges, Governor Weller, his cabinet, military commanders, and for sure, many of the more well-heeled snollygosters out there." He waved an open hand toward her party.

Jane shook her head. "Evelyn's Uncle John is a vocal Southern sympathizer who would like nothing better than to see California join the secessionists. The California oil fields he and his friends are purchasing could become quite valuable if his brother is successful."

"Just the same, I don't think Evelyn Griffin or an audit were enough to motivate Lieutenant Anderson to murder a fellow officer," Earl said, lifting his drink. He swirled the glass and watched the oily residue retreat into the remaining dark liquid. "I could be wrong. I often am. Just ask my sail master."

Earl pinched the bridge of his nose. "I'm in a quandary regarding land transfers. I'm not sure I'm that much different from these California colonials. My family lives on land once occupied by natives. Our docking facilities are on land once owned by natives and Mexicans. I have no idea whether or not they were fraudulently taken from their original owners before I purchased them." His voice trailed off with the unpleasant thought that he too could be a colonial of sorts, even though he supported an aunt who was married the son of an Algonquin chief. Not allowing his thoughts to drift any further, he stopped and listened.

"True, but you would never participate in branding the people who object to giving up their lands 'native troublemakers' or support laws sanctioning bounties on their heads and murdering them, as we do. As for the families left behind, state law has extended white supremacy by preventing non-whites from filing complaints for any crime committed in the absence of a white witness. You would never agree to those practices, Earl."

"No," he agreed, "nor would I support laws making it nearly impossible for the current occupiers of those lands to prove ownership or allow Governor Weller to go around promoting the secessionists without charging him with sedition."

Jane nodded. "Leland says too many elected officials are using the power of the state to seize the more desirable parcels and transferring them over to their friends. The whole exercise would be made moot should civil war break out before a new set of instructions arrive."

"That would be a whole different matter," Earl responded, a part of him wondering if the topics they were discussing had anything to do with why the crosshatch appeared in her lifeline. "Jane, if you have incriminating information, you're in more danger than I thought." *And your enemies may be willing to go beyond poison to silence you.*

Chilled by the menace in his tone, she drew the shawl higher on her shoulders. "I know Arthur Harrington has been involved."

"Umm, yes." Earl avoided eye contact, but she knew him too well for him to be able to disguise the hurt he still felt from the role Arthur's father played in the loss of the Yeaton family fortune.

"The greed of California land speculators, northern industrialists, southern cotton growers, and the secessionists has pushed the country to the brink of civil war," he added, chilling her even more. The icy edge that cut through his calm demeanor caused her to shudder. "You know the Harringtons and I go back a long way."

"Yes," she murmured, fearfully aware of how touchy he was about discussing the Harringtons.

"Arthur has done quite well for himself since he arrived with the first wave of forty-niners," he continued. "He's shrewdly running his family's California branch office. He's a Yale Law graduate, a member of the secretive Skull and Bones Society, and is married to Anna Peabody, the daughter of a Boston Brahmin. I heard he has his eye on the White House once we get through what he is calling 'the current fuss.' The Harrington family dates back to the colonial period, so he claims to be a Son of the Revolution, yet for all of his patriotic platitudes, he exhibits the character of a titled aristocrat. Friends in New York tell me that the family's loyalty isn't to the Constitution but the British Crown, with whom they have maintained close ties since the Revolution. His father is Clinton Harrington, an eastern industrialist, railroad magnate, shipper, and land speculator. Clinton and his friends have made fortunes from the inflationary bubbles Arthur is orchestrating here. Arthur's son, Palmer, a recent graduate of Yale Law, arrived yesterday aboard a Harrington clipper, the Shadow. He's here to join his father's firm. I saw Arthur milling among your guests and will probably have to speak with him before I leave."

The malevolence residing in his delivery caused a shiver to run up Jane's spine and she reached for her glass with an unsteady hand. She lowered her gaze to the liquid's quaking surface and in so doing exposed the wet beads of worry forming beneath her crown. Unnoticed, a trickle of cold sweat slipped from the nape of her neck into the fine threads of her shawl when she tipped her head back and tossed off her drink.

CHAPTER 2

Stanford Mansion, Drawing Room, 1 January, 1:30 a.m.

Vexed by Earl's sour expression, Jane rose from her seat and frowned at him. Her tiara dipped and sparkled as she picked up the empty glasses and mimed a refill.

He declined with a shake of his head. "Water, please."

She did as he asked and poured herself a few more ounces of Jamaica.

"Thanks," he said taking a drink while she rearranged herself in the chair. "The separatists are consolidating their gains, and if they get their way, the Pico Act will divide California into two territories. Through numerous partners, they recently financed ten million dollars in bearer bonds for distribution among their sympathizers. A small price to pay for securing the secessionist majority votes in the state legislature. And the only reason we know about this is because an aide in the governor's office blabbed after drinking too many Christmas cocktails," Earl added with a grim smile.

"And Arthur Harrington?" she asked, knowing she was walking on thin ice.

"Arthur and his friends reside in a social stratum whose members are constantly posturing for advantage and prestige. Through guile, creative debt financing and calculated daring, they've accumulated a vast amount of wealth and political influence.

"Their protégés speak as if they understand and appreciate what most people have to endure in this life, yet have no compunctions about ignoring a homeless person begging for the price of a meal. Woe to those who disagree with them, stand up for minority rights, or are members of religious groups contrary to their definition of what constitutes a good Christian. Secure in the belief they've inoculated themselves from public censure, they then pursue their true objective: personal gain at the expense of the people who've come to depend on them for economic security. We call the more egregious among them tyrants. History is replete with people of this sort.

"These are the same people who buy their way into the White House on promises to 'drain the swamp'. The only thing they end up draining is the public purse. This is usually accompanied by an unabashed propensity to get into armed squabbles with their neighbors.

"In times past, their followers came to their senses, revolted and placed the heads of their deposed leaders on pikes. A part of me wants to skip the carnage and go directly to the pike stage!"

Jane squirmed in her seat. "Have a heart, Earl; I'm trying to enjoy my New Year's celebration! I must say I'm frightened by the way you flex your fingers and stare at me. I had other reasons for inviting you in here."

Her innocent gesture produced a response in Earl that he was unable to squelch before she saw him try. *Hum,* she mused, *the thought of closing and locking the door does have its attractions.*

"I'm sorry," Earl said. "I get carried away sometimes. But those people are really starting to get on my nerves. The reason I've told you so much is because I'm going away, and there are people out there who intend to make it difficult for us to see each other again."

"That's true," she said. "I don't know why wars are started or what happens to the leaders who fail, but I'm familiar with how the scoundrels who get us into these messes operate. The pittance you referred to happens to be more than the combined wealth of Leland's Big Four! Whoever is in possession of those bonds is the wealthiest person in California!"

His reply was an indifferent shrug accompanied by a flat stare.

The tiara glistened once again as she shook her head in confusion. "A lot has happened since the Shadow and her sister ship, the Empire, arrived yesterday. The bond courier was aboard the Empire with Lieutenant Whipple. Now they're both dead. The courier was murdered in his Fairmont Hotel room and the bonds stolen. Earl, do you know where those bonds are?"

"No," he answered, holding her eyes. "Do you or Leland?"

His unguarded expression sent a welcome shiver of delight through her. "You're the only person I know who is unfazed by the prospect of having so much money. Everyone else would move heaven and earth if they thought by doing so they could get their hands on those bonds."

His shrug reminded her of a comment Leland had made: "Aside from what happened in his past, Dr. Earl Yeaton is the luckiest man I've ever met."

It's true, she thought. *Earl is an example of what happens to people who do not let their misfortunes get in the way of their decency. He is lucky. Fortune may smile on him because he believes there's such a thing as being obsessed with money.* Feeling too good to become distracted any further, she pushed aside a troubling thought that lingered: The more her husband and his friends accumulated, the further removed they seemed to be from generosity, tolerance, compassion, and so many other behaviors she found attractive—behaviors they *expected* to receive from underlings.

His response to her observations caused his eyes to turn a darker shade of blue, thrilling her. In the silence that followed, she watched and waited, hoping he would reveal one of his deepest secrets. The moment passed, and as if on cue, she saw the shutters close on another opportunity to hear him put to rest a complicated rumor, a rumor involving Earl's role in the death of a young woman and the disappearance of his classmate, Black Jack Harrington, Arthur's elder brother. She decided not to prod him.

"No, if we did we would certainly use the bonds for the opposite of their intended purpose," she said. "Leland wants no part in what those instruments are supposed to accomplish. We want this country to remain united. I would, however, like to have the bonds! A university, libraries, and hospitals!"

"Hmm," he murmured, watching the warmth of her smile spread into her dancing eyes. "I count you, Jane Stanford, among the exceptions in this odd world. There are few among us who get more pleasure out of sharing wealth than accumulating it."

Feeling giddy from the effects of the alcohol, she laughed and shook her head at the absurdity of having her wishes praised by a man whose generosity filled the holds of his ship. "Thank you, Earl." She readjusted her tiara and raised her glass with a firmer hand. "Merry Christmas!"

"Yes!" he exclaimed. "And a prosperous New Year!" The sound of two adults laughing like children burst from the room and echoed down the wide hall.

"You've invited quite an eclectic group of people," Earl said, "most of whom will have wildly differing views on what we've been discussing. The only opinion of interest that's missing is Joshua Norton the First, Emperor of the United States."

"You missed him because, last I heard, he was in the servant's dining room. I'm told he's regaling my staff while he samples our buffet. Let's go indulge him if he's still in there," she said cheerfully.

He sobered and held up a hand. "Now, before we go, I want to give you this." He reached into his vest pocket and passed her a jewel box.

She opened the lid and removed a thumbnail-size piece of amber resin set in silver. "This is a beautiful amulet," she said, removing the separate silver chain from the box.

"Yes. The resin contains the flower and root of the angelica plant. The Franciscan monk who gave it to me said its purpose is to ward off evil spirits and protect the wearer from a variety of maladies. Perhaps it will help protect you from harm. Wear it in good health."

"Thank you, Earl. I'll start right now." She put the amulet on the chain and nestled them beneath her pearls.

They knew it was time to go. Taking her hands in his, Earl sighed. "I'll be heading south on the tide. I won't be here to keep an eye on you, so you'll have to get through the next twelve months on your own. I plan to be back in December. You're a friend I wouldn't wish to lose in the meantime. There's still much to do before departure. " He grinned widely. "Hate to eat and run, but that's what I intend to do once we return to the ballroom!"

"Will you join me in the staff dining room on your way to the front?" she asked. "I could use a bit of help with Norton!"

"I would be honored," he said with a bow.

Joshua Norton, the self-proclaimed Emperor of the United States and Protector of Mexico, sat at a table regaling his "subjects." The cooks and a couple of carriage drivers were laughing merrily at the comments their "king" was directing toward the people they served.

Jane could hear his remarks in the hall. Her unexpected arrival added to the merriment when she entered the room and said, "I agree! But for the grace of God, my husband and I could be one of you!

"Sit if you wish. You're welcome here! Continue enjoying yourselves," she said, making an elaborate mock bow to her emperor.

Her "king" let out a hoot, leaped out of his chair, and bowed to kiss her hand. "My Queen!" His eyes darted to Earl, who became a little unnerved by the sight of the fellow's slightly mad expression and gaudy, dated clothes.

Taking Jane's arm in his, Norton permitted her to lead him to the festivities.

"Thank you for coming to my party tonight, Joshua," she said, knowing how this unique individual had become emperor over the court of San Francisco.

Earl trailed along behind the self-declared king and reluctant queen of Nob Hill. He smiled and kept to himself the origin of "nabob" and how it came to be bastardized into the word Nob. *This is one of those times where it is best to be quiet and listen*, he mused, thinking about Nob Hill, its residents, and how troubled he'd become about his role in their lives. San Francisco's aristocratic enclave blessed its occupants with great views of the harbor and easy access to the financial district. Earl had more than a passing acquaintance with the Hill's residents. Their insatiable appetite for exotic trappings provided him with an entertaining and profitable entry into their magnificent dwellings. *Yes*, he thought, watching the pair, *but at what cost to my self-respect?*

CHAPTER 3

Stanford Mansion Ballroom, 1 January, 1:45 a.m.

Rose-tinted wall sconces glowed beneath the splendid crystal ormolu suspended from the domed ceiling. Couples danced in a circle of light surrounded by onlookers. Stuffed in an alcove, a string quartet played a sonata above the clamor of conversation and laughter. Although it appeared neither group was aware of the other, the volume occasionally rose and fell with the notes. Most of the women in attendance were married, and the few willing to dance with men other than their husbands were much in demand. The majority of the men were in San Francisco for one reason: to make their fortunes and get back to their own women as soon as possible.

Tables groaned with silver and crystal platters bearing a wide variety of foods. Oregon smoked salmon competed with cuts of beef, pork, and fowl carted up from the Stanford farm. A selection of prepared fruits and vegetables shipped at great expense from Mexico filled the remaining spaces on the buffets.

Concealing his amusement, Earl listened to the banter of Chinese servants who were finding it increasingly difficult to keep the tables' contents in order as the guests consumed ever more spirits. The waiters did not know he could understand the insincere servility they expressed to people who, for the most part, treated them as if they were an inferior race. Although the waiters could speak English, their masters laughed at the notion of learning to converse in Chinese.

Well aware of the contempt the *gwei lo* (white devils) had for them, the servants also knew how two words, *coo* (rent) and *lee* (muscle), had become a pejorative aimed at them. The joke was on the gwei lo. Few gwei lo understood that the indignities they visited on these "coolies" in the Land of the Golden Mountain were nothing compared to what their ancestors had endured for centuries under one oppressive regime after another. They converted the bulk of their meager wages into gold wafers and shipped the gold to destitute families in a China wracked by civil war and imperialist conquest.

Racist laws levied a 40 percent export tax on gold bound for China. Severe penalties deterred most captains from smuggling the gold past customs agents. As for the coolies willing to pay the tax and shipping fees, they gave up the fruits of their labor with no assurances the intended recipients would ever see the gold.

Most of the Chinese workers who found their way to North America had come from Guangdong Province in southern China. They'd embarked from the port city of Guangzhou, whose name Portuguese traders changed to Canton. Earl's cook, Ming To, and his helpers taught Earl and his nephew how to speak the language of Guangzhou, commonly referred to as Cantonese.

Earl stood under a wall sconce behind a serving table half listening to servants bustling in and out through the serving doors. He ate standing up and gazed at the milling mob. He saw vintage wines tossed off with no more appreciation for the bottle's contents than would be given to a wine a few seasons removed from grape juice.

Waiters carrying trays of champagne through the swaying throng found their passage becoming increasingly perilous. He stepped aside as they scurried to the kitchen with empty containers and returned with more trays laden with food and drink. The two-way doors between the ballroom and the serving corridor were never still for long.

He watched Jane and Norton make their way into the crowd until all he could see was her tiara shining beneath the chandelier. The crown soon merged with the sea of top hats, bejeweled turbans, pomades, and feathered caps. Adam was in the mix. He heard Norton's booming voice as he addressed what Earl assumed to be a disparaging comment from an unfaithful subject. "As a madman is apt to think himself grown suddenly great, he that grows suddenly great is apt to borrow a little from the madman! Think on that, dear sir, the next time you gaze upon your conceited reflection!"

"Phew," Earl exclaimed under his breath. "The room is full of 'great men' who could benefit from Norton quoting the sentiments of Samuel Johnson!" *Yes*, a little voice whispered between his ears, *and if you misplay your cards, you could end up just like him.*

Shrugging off cautionary thoughts, Earl completed a tasty dinner and rinsed his palate with a drink of water. He decided to top his meal off with a dollop of caviar spread over a small cracker. He placed the treat in his mouth and felt assailed by the scent of patchouli oil.

A rather imperious voice accompanied the pervasive odor. "I find the Columbia River caviar to be comparable to the finest golden sterlet beluga, and I see that the serving spoons are mother of pearl. Silver and salt leave a disagreeable metallic taste on one's palate, n'est ce pas?"

Suppressing a sigh, Earl chewed, swallowed, and had a drink. "Mais oui, naturellement," Earl answered, feeling trapped and unable to escape without causing a scene.

His lips tightened before he returned Arthur Harrington's guarded expression. *What new challenge will he present this time? Well, I'll soon know*, Earl thought. "Good evening, Arthur. How are you?"

Earl viewed a pair of pale blue eyes that were doing their best to conceal the latent intent to dominate the will of the man who dared meet their gaze. Little flecks of yellow bloomed in his irises, revealing the soul of a predator. Earl thought the handsome combination of dark-black hair, unlined forehead, patrician nose, and tight flesh spread over the man's well-defined bone structure combined to create what many would call an aristocratic mien. The man's lithe body lent itself well to the regular fencing exercises to which he subjected himself. Arthur Harrington was in his early fifties, but his finely tailored suit accentuated the carriage of a much younger man. He exuded the confidence of a person used to having the best of everything and secure in the belief that he was entitled to more of the same.

Deftly plucking two glasses of champagne off the tray of a passing waiter, Arthur offered one to Earl. "To a successful New Year, Dr. Yeaton."

Earl raised his glass. "And you, Arthur Harrington, Esquire." Assuming an amused expression, Earl took a sip while watching those peculiar eyes and waited for Arthur to display his penchant for steering the conversation to his advantage. He almost felt pity for a man so transparent in his efforts to hide a reptilian gleam every time he saw an opportunity to pounce.

Earl had known the Harringtons too long to have any thought of pity for such an offensive familial predisposition. Earl also knew that although he had the measure of the person in front of him, the opposite was not true. Arthur believed he was superior, a sentiment that suited Earl just fine.

"I saw you leave with Jane Stanford right after you arrived. You were alone for quite a while. What made you stop?" Arthur asked with a smirk.

"She hurt my feelings, and I wanted to be alone," Earl quipped, hoping Arthur would get the message and leave.

"Hmm," Arthur observed, "this is a fine tete de cuvee. I've not seen the bottle, but I'm guessing this is the Pol Roger '49. Dry enough to be the Brut Reserve, although I prefer the Brut Vintage."

"Right you are," Earl said casually. On guard and knowing the perils of getting too familiar with this character, he refrained from telling Arthur that the *Brut Vintage* was in his hand. Nor did Earl think it necessary to tell the man he had given the Stanfords six cases of each for Christmas.

"Adam here?" Arthur asked, patting his cravat before flexing his wrist and adjusting the cuff.

"Yes," Earl said. Out of courtesy, he asked if Arthur's son, Palmer, was present too.

Arthur shook his head and showed Earl the tip of his tongue. "Not now."

"Ah," Earl said, unable to move aside before a passing waiter bumped Arthur.

An annoyed scowl replaced Harrington's false good humor as he balanced the remains of his drink over a wet cuff. Earl handed Arthur a napkin and heard the waiter mumble in an apologetic tone. "Bai shazi dai zai nali, wo xia ci ni hao." ("White fool, I get you good next time.") Earl retreated a little more.

"Word has it you'll be sailing on the tide," Arthur said, wiping his hand with more vigor than Earl thought necessary.

"Yes," Earl said, gazing at the bubbles and thinking of Andreas Eisch, the producer of these fine glasses.

He heard Arthur ask where he was heading. "South," Earl said before an electric shiver of caution jolted him out of his musings. *This is not the time to be taking pleasure in satisfying an order for glassware,* he thought. *I'm in the presence of a man who interprets any lapses in concentration as an opportunity to gain an advantage.*

"Oh, come, come, Earl. We all know that. No need to be cagey with me. You've had cultural exchange Jappos sailing with you for a year. I dare say it's time for them to return to their Nipponese dojos," Arthur said, accenting his comment with an exaggerated sniff.

Earl frowned over his urge to correct Arthur on how to say the proper word for "home" in Japanese.

"You sail to the east by way of the equatorial trade winds via Hawaii, no doubt," Arthur continued.

"Since you know my itinerary, there's no need to discuss it," Earl said in what he hoped was an even tone. *True to form,* Earl thought, *Arthur Harrington is beginning to tick me off.*

"Good man, always best to keep one's intentions private. Never can tell what the consequences of candor will be over the horizon and out of sight," Arthur said with undisguised irony.

What have his spies told him? Earl wondered. *Does he have anything to do with why my brother is a month late?*

"You plan to be in Camden for the Harrington-Winthrop wedding in August, n'est ce pas?" Arthur asked, studying Earl over the rim of his glass.

"Oui," Earl said, wondering how much more Arthur knew of his family and his affairs. "The wedding of the summer on the Maine coast."

Years earlier, Earl had invited his sister, Vera, to the Harvard class of 1836 commencement ceremonies. Earl had completed his medical degree and Stanhope Winthrop his finance degree. The thought that he, Earl, had been the one who brought the two of them together still rankled. His sister possessed the vitality of two women, the wit and intelligence of a roomful, and the beauty of a goddess. He pressed his lips together. *She could have married anyone,* he thought for the hundredth time. *Why did it have to be Standhope Winthrop, the repository of all that exemplified the worst of the Boston Brahmins? His family might not live on Louisburg Square, but they're Beacon Hill neighbors who move in the same circles. Arrragh, my sister is married to an implacable snob.*

19

Standhope and Vera fell in love, married, and had children. Their oldest daughter, Olivia, was engaged to Arthur's nephew, Jules Harrington, who expected to graduate from West Point in May.

"As you know, my brother Sidney and his wife, Josie, will be hosting the wedding at our father's oceanside estate. A rather convoluted way for our families to be related, wouldn't you say?" Arthur asked.

"So it would appear," Earl said, trying to fashion a graceful exit from the conversation. *How much does he know of what happened twenty-four years ago?* He could feel the pretense of civility giving way beneath the weight of his efforts to put a clamp on thoughts of the past and his desire to get away. *I can't take much more of this.*

"Did you know Sidney is a lawyer in Washington, D.C.? He prepares government procurement contracts in the Department of Commerce."

"Yes," Earl said, feeling his temperature rising. "He'll be busy soon."

"The federal government has already started the tendering process in anticipation of the coming conflict. Sidney has a lot on his plate already. My father has positioned himself to be of assistance by providing the government with armaments, sundry military equipment, and supply trains. We see no reason to restrain ourselves from profiting from the rush to defend principled ideology at all costs, including taking up arms and using them."

"I'm sure," Earl said in the most level tone he could muster, loathing the man's arrogant disregard for the consequences of his greed.

Earl observed his unwelcome companion assume an arched squint before lowering his voice and leaning forward. "Since we are going to be like family, I could assist you in participating in our endeavors. I suggest you start now while we can still benefit from aiding both sides."

As Earl struggled to compose a reply, the serving door swung open and rammed Arthur in the backside.

Wheeling like a cat, Arthur cursed a waiter who held a steaming platter of curried chicken. A second waiter bumped into the first, causing the platter's hot contents to be plastered against Arthur's chest. The cursing turned into a scream of horror as hot juices found their way through his clothing.

Surprised, Earl held off on lending a hand, preferring to savor the moment. His pause was short.

Breathing rapidly, Arthur poured a pitcher of water over his wounded pride. The incomprehensible utterances coming from the waiters were more than the man could bear. Sputtering and cursing, Arthur's rage got the better of him. Dropping the pitcher, he reached for a large serving fork.

Earl quickly stepped between Arthur and the waiters, whom he shoved back through the doors. Their retreating chatter put a severe test on Earl's ability to keep his face straight. Grabbing a handful of napkins, he traded them for the fork. Grumbling through his pain, Arthur let Earl attempt to calm him.

The headwaiter appeared with his helpers and began cleaning up the mess. Much to Earl's thinly disguised delight, they too were mumbling among themselves. Hoping to avoid eye contact, he draped an arm across Arthur's shoulders. "Let's go to a more private place."

Earl steered Arthur to the room that he and Jane had used. The Stanfords arrived and apologized before Earl sent them away. Jane returned with damp towels and a clean shirt. She left without uttering a sound.

"Let me give you a hand," Earl said, helping Arthur out of his soggy shirt. A crimson glow extended from chest to belly button. Earl wrapped the shirt in a towel while Arthur daubed greasy bits of tomatoes, chicken, and onions. Earl's lips curled at the sight. *A boiled lobster sporting a well-deserved case of the measles*, he mused with indifference. "Don't pop the blisters. You'll be sore for a few days."

Shirtless, Arthur stepped over to the liquor caddy, selected cut-crystal tumblers, and filled them with Jim Beam. "Thank you. Stings like hell," he said, handing Earl a glass. "Right now I'd like to gather up all the Chinese, residual Mexicans, and Yuki Indians. I'd stuff 'em aboard those abandoned clippers in the harbor, have them towed out to sea, and sink 'em with red-hot cannon fire!"

"Sounds rather drastic," Earl said, beginning to fret over how much longer he could disguise his feelings. He sat in a chair facing a couch. A low table separated the two.

A pained and determined grimace of undisguised hatred replaced the flickering lights in Arthur's eyes. Taking a couple of long swallows, he waved the empty glass. "There'll come a time, Earl Yeaton. The races of the world will be competing for fewer and fewer resources. We must strive to be the only surviving race. Thanks to Andrew Jackson, we've started by removing those currently at our disposal here in North America. Associates of ours are setting in place the process to complete the task globally. We both know what lies ahead."

Earl suppressed a growl, placed his untouched drink on a coaster, sat back, and watched Arthur pour a second helping of liquid fire down the chute. *He'll be hot all over pretty soon*, Earl thought as he waited for the alcohol to loosen the fool's tongue. He did not have long to wait, especially after Arthur downed a third.

Arthur refilled the glass, crossed to the couch, and slopped a little on his lap while seating himself. He wiped the area with a discarded towel and tossed the soggy mess on the leather-covered table. "People will think I pissed myself." Earl picked up the towel and added it to the pile on a glass-covered tray.

The pause gave Arthur time to prepare for his next outburst. "In case you hadn't noticed, Earl, there is a mass mobilization of the tribes taking place. The North is against the South, the East is against the West. Whites are at war with the other races. Our side has the upper hand. I want to see it stay that way, and the sooner we exterminate them all the better. We will not allow our white contemporaries to constrain us either. Those same people would tax away our wealth, regulate our methods, and interfere with our right to engage in commerce as we see fit."

Arthur snorted. "We have ways of dealing with them, too."

Unaware he'd pushed Earl to the limits of his patience in the first rant, he missed how he'd taken Earl's capacity to disguise his emotions in the second, so Arthur carried on and blundered into the realization that he was in danger. He stopped his tirade and stared through red-rimmed eyes at a man he no longer recognized. The cold gray eyes staring back reminded him of how frightened he'd felt many years earlier at the sight of a wolf gazing at him from inside a cage. This time there were no bars between him and the feral eyes. The iron will those eyes projected shook his self-confidence in a way he hadn't experienced since he was that child.

"If you breathe a word of this conversation to anyone," Arthur sputtered, "I'll deny it." He lifted the hand holding the refill as if he didn't know how it got there, gave Earl what he hoped would pass for a meaningful dismissal, and returned to the caddy.

Earl narrowed his eyes and said nothing while Arthur's surprisingly steady hand poured the untouched refill back into the bottle. It occurred to him that the silly man no longer wished to drink with a man who did not share his worldview.

"What I say to people is for me to decide," Earl said, filling the void. "All you have done is tell me where your sentiments lie. I do not agree with you—that much is plain. The country you and Andrew Jackson wish to rule is not the one envisioned by Washington, Jefferson and Franklin. *And if this bastard ever gets to sit in the Oval Office, he'll surely hang a portrait of his murderous hero in plain sight!*

"In view of what you just said, I have to ask, were you privy to the plan to kill Lieutenant Whipple and steal General Clarke's instructions to implement the audit?"

"I'll not answer that. I'm putting you on notice. If you interfere with me or anyone with whom I am associated, I cannot protect you."

"I don't seek your protection," Earl answered with a glint in his eyes that Arthur failed to notice. "I'm sure the offer to participate in your endeavors is withdrawn. You've probably figured out by now how I feel about profiting from the misery your investments are going to visit on us all.

"You must be among those who were dismayed to discover the courier was murdered and the bonds stolen before he could deliver them. More's the pity his reason for possessing them has become public knowledge. Ah, the best-laid schemes of mice and men often go awry, eh?"

"We have finished our business here," Arthur said, slipping into the clean shirt.

"Yes, and we'll be in Maine the next time we see each other. I intend to be civil, and I expect the same from you."

Arthur sneered. "I can give you no assurances we'll meet in August. A lot can happen between now and then," he said, malice dancing in his eyes. "You've been making enquiries about why your brother Nathan is not here. Sticking his nose into places where it doesn't belong may be a family trait that has finally caught up with him. I was prepared to let bygones be bygones and put what happened in the past behind us. Not now," Arthur added with contempt.

A menacing rumble escaped through Earl's clenched teeth before a single word forced an icy calm to control his desire to strike: patience. *This is neither the time nor the place to settle our differences,* a voice in his head cautioned, so he watched in silence as Arthur dressed and departed.

Filing what he had learned and getting himself back under control, Earl picked up his drink and held the glass in front of a mirthless smile. *People like him never stop to think that their belligerence is precisely why so many hate them. His attitude will prove to be his undoing, and I intend to be there the day he is undone.* The smile turned to stone beneath flint-gray eyes gazing at distant memories.

Pausing to sniff the whiskey's honey and vanilla highlights, he tipped the glass and took a healthy swallow. He extended a finger and probed a spot below his left shoulder while the dark liquid burned a fiery path past the dull thuds sending tremors through the chambers of his heart.

Arthur's parting snub reminded Earl of an evening spent near Harvard Square. He was playing poker with a group of medical students in one of Holyoke Tavern's upstairs rooms. A player had cashed in and poured himself a parting drink. Being pretty inebriated, he changed his mind and decided to return his drink to the bottle. A classmate placed his hand over the opening. "I wouldn't do that if I were you. Never put spirits back in the bottle—brings bad luck. Drink it, or better yet, give it to me, and I'll finish it off."

"Bah," the drunk grumbled, pushing the hand away and pouring. "Just another one of your mariner's superstitions."

Then instead of departing the tavern, the dunce approached the bar and ordered a hot flip—a combination of ale, rum, and molasses. Stirring the concoction with a red-hot swizzle caramelized the sugar and gave the potent drink a rich, toasty flavor.

A lively debate took place among the students a short while later. They couldn't agree on which factor contributed the most to their classmate's demise. One camp sided with the ship owner's son who'd warned of a curse so willingly assumed. Another camp blamed it on the flip. They all agreed the unfortunate fellow died soon after leaving the tavern. He was tardy while crossing Brattle Street ahead of a passing coach.

The irony of how the past and present often merged amused Earl in a perverse sort of way, and while anticipating what might be in store for Mr. Harrington, his equilibrium returned. Feeling confident he and the Fates were in agreement regarding Arthur Harrington, he had another belt of the amber fluid.

"We'll meet again," Earl muttered to himself. *And yeah, we'll meet on my terms. Not that it matters much, but, if I ever see Arthur Harrington again, it'll be too soon.*

Stopping at the buffet for a drink of water, he surprised the waiters by using the correct bow, followed by a wink at the headwaiter. "Wo zantong ni gwei lo" ("I agree with what you say about the white devil").

The table area was back in order, the waiters who caused the disturbance were out of sight, and the party was going strong. Earl decided it was time to go and wove his way toward the door.

He made noncommittal replies to the various remarks he received while passing through the press of people who wanted to know how Arthur was doing. He tolerated comments on the impertinence and ineptitude of the Chinese waiters. His eyes scanning the crowd, he listened to opinions on what to do with the perpetrators of such an outrage if only one could identify them. Many observers were of the opinion that this was "impossible, of course, because they all look alike."

Noticing Adam from across the room, Earl pointed to the cloakroom. The Stanfords were there waiting for them.

"I do hope Mr. Harrington isn't in too much pain," Jane said, feigning concern. "He left a few minutes ago by a side door. He didn't even stop to grab his coat and say goodnight!"

"He'll be back in fine fettle soon," Earl said, donning his riding cape. He rewarded Jane's false sincerity with a shake of the head, a small frown, and a raised eyebrow. "This has been an enlightening evening," he added for the benefit of their observers. "Go easy on the waiters. They were just doing their job. I gave Arthur an opportunity to step away from the door. He chose not to do so and suffered an unfortunate consequence. His role in the incident may be of more concern to him than his injuries. I suspected he might be in a hurry to leave." Her suppressed giggle nearly gave away their secret.

Shaking Leland's hand, Earl got the distinct impression that Stanford actually took pleasure in having seen Arthur's blisters. *I wonder why*, he thought.

Sobering, Jane took Earl's hand in hers and drew him close. "Be careful out there," she whispered in his ear. "Sides have already been chosen, and people of goodwill are in danger."

CHAPTER 4

Nob Hill, San Francisco, 1 January, 2:15 a.m.

Conveyances of every description lined the street in front of the mansion. Drivers leaned on the sides of carriages or circled in the middle of Fulton Street smoking pipes and sharing nips from flasks. Earl and Adam entered the congestion and exchanged greetings with the men Earl had seen in the kitchen.

Oliver Maxwell, a Yeaton shore man, appeared, followed by Fred Johnson leading four saddled horses. Both wore pistols on a night most people had chosen to go unarmed. Fred's greeting was unusually curt as he passed over the reins. Coachmen and grooms parted with puzzled "goodnights" as the group rode past.

A minute or two later, Oliver pulled up beneath a streetlamp and handed Earl a note. "You stepped outside just as we were coming to get you, Capt'n. Ah Toy's runner found us, handed it over, and ran off. All he said was, 'Doctor Earl quick come.' Hope you can read it, 'cause it's all Greek to me."

Earl frowned and held the note up to the light. His frown deepened as he read the Chinese script. Stuffing the note in a vest pocket, he said, "Arthur Harrington's son, Palmer, and a few of the Shadow crew members got into a scuffle with the Mendocino County Lamars in Ah Toy's brothel. The Lamars got there first and raped several of her women before all hell broke loose."

At the mention of the Lamars, Adam's head jerked around. He and Earl had taken a load of medical supplies up to the Indian camp north of San Francisco a week before Christmas. They'd seen what the Lamars and their friends had been doing to the defenseless natives. He could well imagine what they had done in Ah Toy's home.

Ah Toy, madam of the most successful brothel in San Francisco, counted Earl among her friends. She had many "friends." Arguably the most attractive woman in the city, she commanded attention not only with her beauty but also because she possessed a keen business acumen. She had amassed a fortune in a line of work Earl equated with slavery. Her fortune had grown as she put to good use the political and investment information her clients provided while she pleasured them in her chambers. Rumor had it she knew more about the various business dealings in San Francisco than any other person alive.

As the Chinese sex-trade tongs became more influential, her share of the market decreased in equal proportion. She went from maintaining hundreds of hookers in many squalid locations to housing a dozen sophisticated prostitutes in her new Dupont Street mansion. Ever the clever executive, Ah Toy not only had the most influential business and political leaders as her personal clients, her staff of beautiful courtesans also gleaned valuable information from their own johns. Ah Toy had made the extremely difficult transition from sex-trade worker to San Francisco power broker.

She and Earl had become acquainted a few years back after he assisted her gardener, Lac San. Whites had beaten him severely on the street in front of the Yeaton Brothers warehouse before the workers could drive them off. Earl was there at the time and had the injured man carried to the apartments above the stables. Earl kept Lac San in bed until he recovered enough to walk on his own. At no time during his ordeal did Lac San speak to Earl or his cooks, even though he knew the level of assistance he received from a dreaded gwei lo was a rare occurrence in the Asian community. Most whites would have left Lac San lying in the street. They'd give the injured man no more thought than they would to one of their own, with a possible exception: a few pedestrians might be inclined to drag a white man out of the traffic and dump him in a gutter or against a wall.

Several days after Lac San left, a runner arrived with a bolt of silk printed with an exquisite floral pattern. The accompanying note written on fine bond contained a request. Would Earl care to visit her for tea? Ah Toy wished to thank him personally.

They met in her private quarters a few blocks up from the Yeaton warehouses. Ah Toy was in for a surprise. Earl Yeaton treated her like a lady, made no overtures toward her, and politely refused to bed any of her women. She became even more interested in this unusual man on finding he actually cared enough about her culture to have learned how to converse and write in her language. Much to their mutual delight, they enjoyed each other's company and became friends.

"Let's go see what we can do to give her a hand," Earl said, lifting the reins and nudging his horse in the ribs.

The night became louder and louder the closer they got to the Chinese area around Broadway and Pacific. Alcohol-fueled revelers filled the intersection. The swirl of men milling around the gas-lit area reminded Earl of dishwater sloshing around in a bowl. He'd seen flocks of birds acting this way. Knots of twenty or more would flow in one direction until dispersing into another group or bouncing off a congested opening, only to change directions, reassemble, and start the process all over again. Earl waded in, thinking he and his men were cutting a wake through a puddle of dementia.

The crowd parted before Oliver's big black stud and the maple cudgel he held across the saddle horn. A tap on the head or shoulder did the trick to get the less willing to move. Earl and Adam followed close behind. Fred kept a watchful eye from the rear. His expression was more than enough to discourage any who wished to pilfer the gear strapped to the horses.

Oliver led the riders to a quiet area behind Ah Toy's house. A stable hand was waiting. "Wanshang hao" ("Good evening"), Earl said, and thanked the man for being there to greet them.

"Ni zhonghu zhengzai gaishan, Zhou" ("Your Chinese is improving, master"), the man said with a glance at the bordello's rear entrance.

"Dwo je" ("Thank you"), Earl answered, handing over the reins. He gestured to Oliver and Fred. "You two stay here and keep an eye on things. Adam, come with me, and bring your bag."

Adam removed his bag by feel after seeing what awaited them on the porch. The angelic face he saw nearly caused him to forget why he was there.

Earl planted an elbow in his nephew's ribs. "Keep your wits about you, young man. You will soon be meeting the clearest mind I've ever met."

"My mistress to greet you wishes in parlor see. Preese, this way to come."

Earl nodded. "Ai Kee."

Adam followed and found himself praying he could hear the sound of her voice again. Enchanted, he closed his eyes to mere slits and followed her scent to a room shipped from a Beijing *dasha*. Red, black, and gold accents highlighted a tapestry of light and texture whose overall effect created a sense of awe in Adam and continued to impress Earl each time he entered Ah Toy's parlor.

"You've been holding out on me, Uncle," Adam whispered as his gaze shifted from the lovely maiden to the most beautiful woman he'd ever seen.

Ah Toy rose from a group of chairs arranged around a low lacquered table. She bowed and greeted them in simplified Cantonese. "Huanying lai dao woja." ("Welcome to my home"). She switched to English. "Thank you for coming here tonight. You honor me. I know your time is precious, and you sail on the tide. There has been a disturbance. The Lamars gang-raped three women and destroyed their rooms. Palmer Harrington and several Shadow crewmen arrived while the Lamars were beating the women. The men started fighting and Palmer's crew chased the Lamars off. Palmer's threats didn't get him what he wanted either, so he and his crew raped the women too. They left without finding what they were after. I'm sorry to ask for your help, but I have no one else to turn to who can save their lives. This is the first time anyone has dared behave this way in my home. Palmer's father is associated with powerful people who will not take kindly to what happened—people I also have business relationships with in this city. They will be unhappy with the Harringtons. The Lamars I only know by their foul reputation. Aie, I have to put those worries in a box for now. Come."

Ah Toy led the pair to the first of three rooms. The room was spotless, with a single bed, a night table, lamps, chairs, and a basin. Servants had bathed the injured woman and covered her with a clean sheet. "This one, Sun Morning, is hurt the most. The Lamars attacked her first. She has been unconscious since they got here."

Ah Toy left the room soon after her solemn eyes watched the doctors and two of her serving women get to work. Earl arranged the contents of their medical bags on trays covered with clean towels while Adam examined Sun Morning.

"Lots to do here, Uncle. I see a broken arm, loose molars, and a couple of cracked ribs. And there's more," he said, pointing at the red stain below her abdomen.

"Yes, I noticed," Earl said, loading two syringes with morphine. "Her face is unrecognizable. The damage to her nose is so severe it probably won't hold its shape. The amount of morphine she'll require to keep her still could either kill her or turn her into an addict."

Adam pulled the sheet back some more.

"The nose will have to wait, Uncle. She could bleed to death before we finish suturing the vaginal and rectal tears."

They began treating Sun Morning a little after two, and it was close to dawn by the time they tied off the last bandage on the third patient. Ah Toy saw how they braced themselves as they reentered her parlor, but not before she caught a glimpse of how the women's injuries had affected them. Although their feelings were close to the surface, they assumed the dispassionate masks of trained professionals.

"We've done everything we can do for tonight," Earl said. "We left all of the laudanum we brought with us. You can get more, and I don't need to tell you of its effects with prolonged usage. I know you will ask Dr. Yee to assist you. He will have alternate sedatives, salves, and sterile dressings. The women will need care around the clock until they can sit up on their own." Try as he might, he could not tell what was occurring behind the eyes of a friend he had known for years. "I doubt Sun Morning will make it through the night. I'm sorry to say, the blows she took on the face may have caused brain damage."

Ah Toy's habitual response to stress was to reveal nothing of what she was thinking or feeling. Her experiences with deceitful people had taught her to conceal her emotions quite well in the presence of gwei lo. This night was proving to be an exception. The speed with which these honest men hid the pain in their faces put her protective detachment to an unusual test. *So Chinese*, she thought. The realization demanded a concerted effort on her part to maintain her composure. Waving them to seats and taking her own, she turned her attention to the tea service arranged on the table. Willing the hand pouring tea to remain steady, she felt an unfamiliar jolt of compassion and glanced at Earl. She lifted the spout and poured another cup, thinking she had never seen gwei lo behave this way. By allowing him to see the brief flare in her eyes, she conveyed to him how much her opinion of him and his nephew just went up.

Settling into a companionable silence while her guests drank their tea, the studiously observant Ah Toy realized these men had come to her aid without any expectation of reward. The realization tickled a secret emotion packed away in her heart of hearts: desire.

"I do not know how to thank you," she said, allowing them to hear the discernable tremor in her voice. "You have done my house a great honor tonight. I will always be indebted to you."

"Thank you, Ah Toy, but we will not hold you to it. You may wish to assist us in the future if you can do so without harm to yourself." Earl placed his empty cup on a saucer and reached for his bag.

All three stood and bowed. She reached for Earl's hand.

"You have revealed yourself to be more than a calculating executive tonight, Ah Toy," he said. She gave him a small twist of her lips. "Your secret is safe," he added in a low voice.

"Secret," she whispered, enjoying her own private pleasure even more. Still holding Earl's hand, she noticed his gaze become a penetrating stare. She held on as he tried to let go. "So much of what we do here is satisfy men who cannot find pleasure in their lives outside these walls," she said. "They often come here to have a fantasy. Palmer Harrington's father, Arthur, visits from time to time. One of my ladies heard him exclaim 'Josie!' at the height of his passion. She soothed him like a sobbing child and asked who Josie was. Arthur said she is a love he must have, or he will go mad. I think he is already mad," she hissed, dripping venom.

"Aye," he nodded. His outward calm may have remained the same, but Ah Toy's delicate fingers felt his quickening pulse.

"You know who he is talking about," she said, releasing his hand.

"Yes," he said, keeping eye contact while shaking his head. "Men and their inability to control their secret desires. The idiot covets his brother's wife."

"You would not behave this way because you know the value of discretion, Earl. You are among the rarest of men. You can think like a woman."

"Dwo je, Ah Toy," Earl said through tight lips. "I'll be back."

Nodding into his stare, she led them to the rear and said goodnight.

Walking alone down the dimly lit hallway, she tried to put thoughts of Earl aside and compose a list of priorities. Halfway to her parlor, she stopped and shivered. She was also privy to the Earl Yeaton rumors and knew a great deal more than the average gwei lo did about this man and his warrior ancestors.

She took a deep breath and lifted her head. "Lao Shifu shi bian you." ("Old Master is right again.") "The Yeatons are us."

Her almond eyes turning hard as agates, she paused to consider what Earl might do to the men who dared violate the peaceful *wa* of her home. "Sss . . .," she hissed, until her thin red lips turned upwards. "My man will be back."

Oliver and Fred had not been idle. They moved around to the front and spent the past several hours on the street. Oliver handed Earl his reins. "We should stay close. The Lamars and Palmer Harrington's people may still be nearby. Harrington men were watching the brothel when we arrived. We shooed off the ones we recognized, but in this crowd, there could be more we don't know. I think you should buckle up."

The ride down Dupont and over to Spear went without incident. One glance at four armed men was enough to get the revelers in their path to move aside. The group stopped on the street in front of the Yeaton buildings. Earl and Adam kept their guns and removed the medical bags. Oliver and Fred led the horses into the stables.

Earl and his nephew entered the chandler's office, climbed the stairs, and went to their rooms to clean up, change, and get ready for the arrival of the coach bearing Evelyn and Myra.

CHAPTER 5

Warehouse Office, 1 January, 6:00 a.m.

Adam, Ryan Ames, the first mate, and Earl's warehouse manager, Ward Davis, tracked the leather-bound pouch from the safe to Earl's place at the head of the table. Earl flexed the pouch. "We have Walter to thank for making it possible for us to get this." He was referring to Walter Tuttle, a childhood friend whose steam tug, the *Ajax*, made it much easier to get ships in and out of the harbor. "Lieutenant Whipple found a way to get this pouch aboard the Ajax while Walter was setting up to tow the Empire over to Harrington's wharf." Earl put the pouch on the table. "This could have disappeared right along with the stolen audit instructions destined for General Clarke."

He cleared his throat and changed the subject. "I met with General Winfield Scott and Attorney General Edwin Stanton in New York last summer. I've been waiting for these to arrive." Earl opened the pouch and spread a pile of papers in front of him. "It's time you saw these. Two of them are documents that provide us with military and diplomatic directives as officers of the Union. The third is a letter from General Scott outlining his reasons for giving these to us. You should know General Scott and Attorney General Stanton had to prevail upon Secretary of State Cass to sign these counselor appointments over to us. We believe Cass is a Southern sympathizer. He could be involved in the murder of Whipple and the disappearance of the audit directives. His allies and spies could be anywhere by now, including here. The fourth is a document from Secretary of the Navy, Isaac Toucey, tasking us with taking the measure of American political and commercial interests abroad. Wide latitude in interpreting the activities of our fellow citizens in Asia and Europe has been assigned to us."

Earl told the group of his encounter with Arthur Harrington. "Safe to say, we're already at war, and there are people on the other side who didn't want us to receive these orders. Arthur's insinuations gave me the impression he knew about these papers. We must assume he and others suspect we have them. We must also assume they see us as an enemy and will use every means at their disposal to prevent us from representing the Union. They do not want us to thwart their efforts or report what we discover.

"Protecting us on paper is one thing. From an armed adversary is an entirely different matter. That is why we secretly sailed to New Haven with a skeleton crew to meet with Oliver Winchester, Benjamin Henry, Christopher Spencer, and John Griffin of Griffin Guns. The fewer people who know what we are doing the better. The Union supplied us with five hundred preproduction Spencer lever-action rifles. All the shooter has to do is load a seven-shot package of .56-.56 rim-fire cartridges into the stock receptacle, chamber a round, and fire. We can now deliver fifteen to twenty rounds in the minute required to load a percussion rifle. They gave us five thousand rounds and the approval to pass them on to our friends. The Spencers will go nicely with the long-range German rifles stored in the holds.

"I was unsuccessful in getting a sample brace of .44-caliber Henry repeaters. None will be available until next year. What we do have though are the newest rim-fired Smith and Wesson .22 Model 1 six-shot revolvers. Have to admit, they're peashooters. But if you ask me, I still wouldn't want a hot pea bouncing around in my brain pan.

"They also equipped us with the capacity to deliver a most devastating charge—exploding shells fired from cannons located beneath the foc'sl. These cannons are the latest Griffin three-inch carriage-mounted artillery pieces. What the cannons give up in weight they make up in accuracy. The barrels are rifled. We have a thousand shells."

Earl was about to conclude the meeting when there was a knock at the door. "Hold on," he said. Gathering the papers, he put them back in the pouch, stuck them in the safe, and closed the door. "Enter!" he called as he returned to his seat.

One of the men keeping an eye on the street stepped into the office. "There's a Chinaman outside insisting he see you, Capt'n. He's in the gallery holding a flour sack."

Earl nodded. "Adam, you stay. Ryan and Ward, go to places where you can keep an eye on this room." He turned back to the man at the door. "Bring him in."

Moments later, a frightened man entered the room and appeared to be relieved to see Earl and Adam. Earl addressed him in Cantonese. "Thank you for coming to see us. You're Ah Toy's gardener, Lac San. What can we do for ya?"

Lac San placed the sack on the table and handed Earl a folded sheet of paper. "Ah Toy sent me. I am to return now," he mumbled.

Earl held the man's gaze with his cool blue eyes. "How have you been since you were our guest awhile back?"

Lac San's pupils dilated in his otherwise impassive face. He probed his ribs. "I am alive and much better, thanks to you. The last time I was here, my face was a mess. I did not expect you to recognize me."

The memory saddened Earl. He'd seen Lac San once or twice but hadn't spoken with him until now. "I try to see the person behind the mask," he murmured. The brief exchange of mutual respect they shared often startled those not used to seeing what lay behind the unguarded eyes of kindred souls. Exchanging bows with Lac San, Earl saw him to the door and told Ward to make sure their guest got back to Ah Toy safely.

"Now what?" Adam asked, watching Earl close the door and empty the sack. A package wrapped in common butcher paper landed on the table.

"Let's find out. Come closer and lower your voice. I'll read this to you." Earl waved a note written in Chinese.

> "Thank you for coming by here tonight. Lac San gave me the package after Sun Morning died. He is my most trusted servant and holds many secrets. Sun Morning confided in him and swore him to secrecy. The man who gave her the package was a client of hers, a manager of one of the banks. Arthur Harrington was supposed to meet the manager at the bank, sign off on the bonds, and pass them to one of the Big Four. The manager and a Shadow crewman decided

to steal the bonds. They went to the hotel room, killed the courier, and stole the bonds. They split up after they were seen leaving. The banker told his accomplice he was going to give the bonds to Sun Morning for safekeeping. The crewman was caught by shipmates who were there to keep an eye on the courier. The banker came here. He told Sun Morning she was the only person he could trust. He said friends would protect him from Harrington's men and he would return with them to pick up the package. Sun Morning hid the package in a flour bin after the banker left. I think the Shadow's crew got what they wanted out of the thief, killed him, and came here. The Lamars probably killed the banker too after they found out what he had done. They got here first. Sun Morning saw them coming and told Lac San where to find the package. The Lamars were too rough with her. The other women who were there said the men became angry with the man who beat her. Things got bad after Palmer Harrington and Shadow's first mate, Dwight Grant, arrived. They did terrible things to the helpless women. I am fearful they will return. I told Lac San to bring the package to you. He and I are the only ones who know where it is. I have not seen what is in the package and do not want to. No one else knows I sent the package to you."

"Hmm," Earl said. He placed Ah Toy's note on a metal tray, struck a match, and burned it.

"She knows what she gave you, Uncle."

"Yes, I do not need to open the package either to know what's inside. This has been the number-one topic of conversation everywhere we have been these past twenty-four hours."

But for the ticking of the clock, the room was silent. Pondering what to do next, Earl moved the tray to the glass countertop and glanced at Adam. "Watch and learn, Nephew." Earl removed the string and paper from the bonds and set them aside. Then he put an equal amount of blank stationery from the office supply on the wrapping paper. Refolding the package, he tied it off with the string and put it on the flour sack.

He wrote a short note, stuck it in with the bonds, and picked them up. He passed around the counter and knelt on the floor. To Adam's astonishment, he removed the display items and pushed on the bottom shelf. A pressure-release latch popped and freed the shelf. Setting the shelf aside, he removed a section of flooring to reveal a safe hidden in a box joist. Earl rotated the dial to a series of numbers and opened the lid. He placed the note and bonds inside, locked the lid, and spun the dial. He then put everything back.

Standing, he pulled Adam in close. "The combination is easy to remember," he whispered. "Think multiples of three: twenty-seven, nine, twenty-seven. You, Nathan, and I are the only ones who know about the safe. Can't be seen from below."

Earl pointed at the floor. "As if you need to be reminded, ten million dollars are down there. Should anything happen to Nathan and me, you get the bonds. Put a substantial portion aside for yourself. Give Jane Stanford three million dollars' worth. Should be enough to endow her university. Talk with Dr. Yee, and give him whatever he needs to build and staff a new hospital. Pass the rest to people with whom you can share your good fortune. Don't make the mistake of thinking you can take the money with you when you die.

"The bonds are redeemable at face value. Whoever bears the bonds is the legitimate owner. That is why they attract so much attention. Anyone can own them, and anyone can spend them."

Earl dumped the ashes in a trashcan, opened the door, and asked the others to come back in. "We don't need this around here," he said, putting the package in the flour sack and sliding it over to Adam. "Take it up to the Freemont Hotel. Try leaving it on the front steps without anyone seeing you. Hurry, we've a tide to catch." He turned to Ryan. "Walter should be here soon. Go make sure we're ready for him."

"Yes, sir." Ryan shook Ward's hand. "We'll see you on the other side of the calendar. Take care."

"You too."

Earl locked his safe after retrieving the leather pouch. He opened the curtains, surveyed the room, and then turned to the man in whom he placed so much trust. "You're going to have an interesting twelve months while we're away. You could be under siege from powerful people in this town. Are you prepared to protect our interests, even at great personal risk?"

"Of course," Ward answered without hesitation. "You've taken care of me and my folks and have given me a job no hardscrabble dirt farmer could ever expect to earn. This place'll still be here in December." He handed Earl an envelope. "This contains a bank draft for most of the earnings I've received from you and my share of last year's profits. Please pass it on to my mother."

"I will," Earl said. "Thank you for staying put. One less thing to worry about."

Ward smiled for the first time that morning. "You carry the burdens of a village with the carefree ease of a wandering minstrel, Doctor Yeaton."

Earl's return smile expressed a great deal more than Ward expected. "I wish it were true. Adam shouldn't be gone long. Let's go outside and get us underway."

CHAPTER 6

Yeaton Wharf, San Francisco, 1 January,
6:30 a.m., ebb tide stirring

Earl slipped Ward's envelope into a breast pocket and patted his coat. "I'll see your mother and put this in her hands myself."

"Thank you. She'll like that."

Earl sorted out the government documents and resealed the pouch while his office manager tidied up and turned out the lights. He handed Ward a dockworker's cap, slipped a black watch cap on his own head, picked up the pouch, and led the way to the pier side of the open gallery.

Stopping to sniff the air and check the drift of the clouds, they heard the gurgle of water swirling past the pilings, a subtle counterpoint to the rhythmic creak of timbers straining against the ship's motion. Foggy tendrils streamed through rigging strung among the swaying masts and spars. At the tip of the mainmast, the green-and-yellow pennant snapped in the breeze.

"We're a long way from home," Ward murmured.

Earl nodded and said, "We sure are." He placed an arm across his friend's shoulders, patted his head, and pointed at the gilded script painted across the sweeping curve of the ships stern:

MAINE BRIDE
ROCKLAND

Walter Tuttle arrived and slewed the *Ajax* to a stop in front of the *Bride's* bowsprit. Two men jumped onto the wharf and cleated lines fore and aft.

Walter emerged from the wheelhouse wearing a sou'wester and hopped on the wharf. Men from both vessels started setting up the tow. Light lines attached to hawsers passed through the ship's bulkheads and into the hands of men waiting to haul the heavier ropes aboard and tie them off on stout bollards.

Adam joined the group while Walter was still shaking hands with Earl and Ward. Exchanging greetings, the four walked to the end of the wharf to huddle by themselves. Walter fired up a bent briar. "Quite the night we've had around heah."

"Ayah," Earl replied and waited for his long-winded friend to begin. Tut, as he was often called, hadn't changed much since they were children. The grizzled old man was years removed from the scrawny kid who allowed Earl to tag along, but he was still a chatterbox near to bursting with useful information. Earl smiled despite the worries plaguing him. He knew the conversation he was about to have would be one-sided, and, as usual, he'd be lucky to get a word in edgewise. Walter's father once said he'd thought of a way to get the boy to stop talking: bundle him in a grain sack and toss him in a river.

Nodding as if he knew what Earl was thinking, Walter licked his lip, and squinted through a streaming cloud of smoke at the wharfs, ships, and men emerging in the cool dawn. "Should be ovah fairly soon. Many eyes'll be lookin' this way." Turning upwind, Walter locked his bright browns on Earl's blues.

The men watching the pair thought nothing of Walter's reassuring nod, but Earl did and felt relief. Years earlier, Earl helped Walter land a job in the boiler room of Massachusetts General Hospital. Times were tough in the Tuttle household after the collapse of Maine's lumber industry, so Walter took a night shift that no one else wanted. He tossed bandages, body parts, unclaimed corpses, and medical school dissections into the incinerator. The stench and popping fats were more than most people were willing to bear. Walter worked Sunday through Thursday. He reserved Friday and Saturday nights for Boston's North End "bardellos where the darkies and me stomp to the beat of jungle music 'til we git the rollers a rockin' in their cribs!"

Walter was on duty the night Black Jack Harrington went missing. That was also the night Earl and Oliver Holmes delivered a Harvard Medical School cadaver. "All the disposal papers appeared to be in order," Walter told a police detective investigating the disappearance. "Nooo, I do not know what became of the school's copies." He responded to another question by removing his crossed fingers from a trouser pocket and opening a file cabinet. He found what he was after and waved a sheaf of papers. "Mine're right here." Walter came close to giggling every time he thought about how delighted he'd felt while shoving the corpse into a furnace fired by Clinton Harrington's Virginia coal. The eyes returning Earl's hooded gaze on this particular morning were not smiling.

"I think we've managed to keep you out of it, Tut," Earl said, through slitted lids.

"Far as I know. Can't be sure no one saw young Whipple pass me the packet. As for the rest, got nothin' to do wid me," he added, tossing the spent match in the water. "I do 'ave news for ya. Theyz to be a quick turnaround for the Shadow. They asked me to be prepared to tow 'er out latah this mawnin', aftah noon at the latest. Rumah has it there may be anothah vessel gittin' an early stahat too."

The others had given up trying to get a word in, so they just stood there waiting for what came next.

"Some're sayin' ya took the bonds away with ya," Tut said, before taking a drag and studying his companions through a red spray of popping sparks. The fireworks display garnered several blank stares and a barely perceptible wink from Earl.

Snorting two streams of smoke past his nostrils, he grinned. "Arthur Harrington's people would like ta examine the Bride out on the open ocean where no one can question their search methods. The skinflints armed their fleet with nine-pound cannons and a few swivel guns. Not that they'll be much good in a pinch. The captains think live-fire drills are overrated. Say it's a waste of time and money. They expect the sight of the guns bein' run out to be more'n enough to get the other side to heave to." He tut-tutted as if to say that tangling with his friends would cost the Harringtons a whole lot more than powder and shot.

He gestured with a smudged thumb toward the *Bride*'s forecastle. "I'm sure those little squares aft of the anchor hawse holes ovah theya do more than open to let fresh air aboard at the first sign of trouble. The Harrington boys may be willin' to hold off 'till ya've left Los Angeles. Might want the Griffin gal to git back safe and sound. Word has it she's heah on her uncle's behalf to petition Gen'l Clarke to join the secessionists." He shook his sou'wester from side to side. "I've studied wimmin all my life and can't say I know any more about 'em than I did the first time my ma put me on her titty. What ya see ain't always what ya git," he said with a thoughtful puff. "I heah there's an added inducement to trail along behind ya. They suspect ya may be smugglin' a ton o' gold back to China—an obligation of which the Harringtons would like to relieve ya. They'll do their best to maim ya, git what they want, and then sink ya, of course." He stuffed a thumb into the hot coals to tamp down what was left of his tobacco.

"Hmm," was all Walter heard from Earl.

"People love to talk, Earl," Walter said, taking a final hit.

"Hmm," Earl said again. "Hell of a situation."

Walter's keen eyes scanned the faces around him, saw only quiet confidence, and concluded Earl Yeaton still had a few tricks up his sleeve.

Gulls cawed and circled in the growing light. A raft of mergansers drifted past. A resting cormorant made a rude deposit on the *Ajax*'s wheelhouse and flew off.

"Well, time to get a move on," Walter said, frowning at the bowl and exhaling enough smoke to make most people cough for a week. He turned back to Earl. "I'll tow the Bride through the cemet'ry of our eastern forests 'till ya can git into open watah. Likely to be stiff winds this mawnin'. Wet air'll be out of the nor'west once ya clear Alcatraz. Theyz a storm comin'. Should produce quite the cross chop for ya passengers to enjoy. Keep the slop buckets handy."

"Always the card," Earl deadpanned with a tired smile.

"Soon's the towline goes slack, leggo my hawse, and ya on ya own."

Walter climbed aboard and entered his dripping pilothouse. His men slipped the lines, hopped onto the stern deck, and were ready to play out the hawse by the time Tut tapped the throttle.

The mergansers made way as the *Ajax* slowly maneuvered into towing position. The moon, a forgotten presence, faded away into nothing among the lowering clouds.

Earl and Adam said their goodbyes to Ward and stepped over the gangway onto the *Bride*'s weather deck. Waiting men closed and threw the bolts on the entry port. Ryan nodded, and the ship's last tether was tossed onto the wharf.

"She's ready for sea, full fifty-man complement, Capt'n. Shorelines have been released, our best riggers are manning the hawse, and the Ajax is taking up the slack. The sail master is in the wheelhouse. We're seaworthy."

The deck slid forward as the *Ajax* pulled the *Bride* into a passage lined with row upon row of deserted sisters, ships abandoned by crews heeding the siren call of gold. Earl gazed at men watching their last chance to join their peers slipping away. "More than a few will be peering aft in the teeth of a gale seeking to be reassured that the choice they made to ride on the Bride will lead to their El Dorado." His eyes turned to the forecastle as a grinning ship's boy, Charley Polanowski, slammed the clapper against the bell six times to mark the hour, 7:00 a.m.

James, who was standing beside a wheelhouse door at the other end of the ship, shook his head. "Not much of a pause between the three sets of rings," he muttered. "One hour to go in the morning watch." He stepped in to turn the glass. "A bell's worth of knot practice on the quarter deck this aftanoon oughta smaaten him up," he said and reached for a pen to mark the departure time in the log.

Nodding from his place by the wheel, Elmer lifted weary eyes to a bank of clouds rounding Fort Point. "Should hit just about the time we release the lines, and of course by then the only thing left to see will be the Ajax's flickering tail lamp."

CHAPTER 7

Off the Coast of California, 2 January, 11:15 a.m.

Adam rose out of the depths of sleep into a world of muted light and shipboard sounds. Snuggling deeper into the pillow, he awoke with the dull awareness that whatever he had been dreaming about was not coming back. "My cabin," he croaked watching the wainscoting rise and fall with each roll of the ship. Numb and disoriented, he resisted the urge to go back to sleep and groped to peel away his cocoon. Propping himself on an elbow required an unexpected test of will and didn't get him any closer to the answer his squint sought on the other side of the curtain. *What time of day is it? My legs feel like lead.*

Forcing his legs to move, he let his feet fall to the deck and managed to stop the rocking without tumbling out of the gimballed bed. Sitting on the edge with his head in his hands, he addressed a small portrait screwed to the wall. *What ails me? It must be late morning. How long have I slept?* After fumbling through the clutter on a side table, he came away with his pocket watch. The second hand was not moving. Useless. "Huh," was all he had to say about that. He put on a pair of trousers and shuffled aft to use the head, remembering in time to use the one on his side of the companionway. The one across the hall was reserved for the passengers.

He managed to clean up, shave, brush his teeth, finish dressing, and comb his hair without succumbing to the temptation to climb back in bed. Still feeling groggy, he donned a watch cap, slipped the cabin key thong over his head, pulled the door to, and listened for the lock's satisfying click. He also heard a sound coming from a guest cabin, a sound that he knew preceded a most offensive odor. *Myra*, he mouthed, creeping for the exit. He pushed on the door, stepped over the coaming, and held the door open a little longer than usual.

Wind shear greeted him while he struggled to get his bearings. Leaning against the door, he compared the angle of the massive mainmast with the horizon. "We'll be walking sideways today. Late morning," he said aloud. "Oh," he groaned, noticing how the deck pitched and yawed, "I'm not ready for this."

Feeling thickheaded, he hardly noticed the constant stream of cool air flowing beneath the tattered gray clouds or the wet sails they left behind. He paid no heed to the fact that the ship was pointed south and sailing as close to the northwesterly winds as possible or that the bow cleaved through ten-foot waves as if they were ripples in a faraway pond. The sheets of spray flying over the starboard rails received a passing glance. Nobody stood on the quarter-deck above his head. He had no desire to be standing on one of his favorite spots. Nor did he wish to be up there taking in the sights while seated nearby on an overturned quarter boat. He did notice the melody produced by the hiss of foaming churn, the whine of stays, and the calls of men working aloft. Preferring to hear those soothing sounds from between the sheets, he nearly caved and went back to bed.

Not relishing the idea of crossing the open deck on unsteady legs, he girded himself for the trek to the midship deckhouse. The smoking galley stack helped to overcome his reluctance by giving rise to thoughts of what might be available inside. The sight caused his mouth to water and stiffened his resolve, if not his spine.

His destination housed the dining salon, galley, cook, and crew berths. The salon, as its users called the dining room, was aft with the galley and berths forward. The deckhouse served as the communal area for all aboard. Two parallel rows of tables and benches lined the interior walls. A central aisle led directly from the door to the serving counter. The passageway made a portside detour around the counter to a door set in the partition separating the galley from the crew berth.

The men could come and go from the sleeping area to the salon as long as they stayed on their side of the yellow line painted on the deck. The line separated the short corridor from the galley, which was off limits to anyone but the cooks.

Two doors were set in the sidewalls. One was in the passageway wall; the second was on the starboard side of the crew berth. Resting men did not take kindly to the door opening while they were trying to sleep, especially during inclement weather.

The stove backed on the partition separating the galley from the crew berth. A long cutting table occupied the space between the stove and the serving counter. A trapdoor located between the serving counter and the cutting table led to the second deck. The stairway gave the cooks easy access to the huge icebox, water tank, and pantry. The cooks slept with the crew.

Large round portholes lined the walls beside each of the dining tables. Kerosene lanterns were set between the portholes. Wide knotty-pine paneling rose above the narrow black-walnut wainscoting. Bird's-eye maple trimmed the portholes and doors, and cherry crown moldings accented the curved ceiling's pumpkin-pine panels. The combination of light and dark woods made for a welcoming dining area. The crew berth, wheelhouse, and aft deckhouse suites received the same attention to detail in varying degrees depending on their location in the ship's hierarchy. The captain's suite exhibited the most ornate treatment and the crew berths the least.

Adam skirted the aft hatch, the mainmast, and the large main hatch on his precarious way forward. Three weeks ashore and hours of sleep had a dampening effect on how confident he felt about walking outside. He made it through the salon door without embarrassing himself by tripping over the coaming.

He had expected to see men eating their lunches. He did not expect to hear loud voices coming out of the galley so soon after being ashore. It usually took a week or two for the cooks to get on each other's nerves. A listener did not have to speak their language to draw conclusions on how two of them felt about each other. Adam and the diners heard a mixture of colloquial Cantonese and Mandarin seasoned with a sprinkling of the most offensive epithets imaginable. Their listeners had no way of knowing the spat was pure theater. Walking the length of the room, Adam said hello to men shaking their heads and raising their eyebrows over what was going on in the galley. Adam addressed a group sitting with the mild-mannered Bill Hobbs.

"Do you suppose they're aware people may be trying to sleep on the other side of the wall?"

Stopping at the serving counter, he helped himself to a glass of water. Three men with knives were staring at a short, wiry man with long graying hair tied in a queue. His goatee was bobbing up and down as his contorted lips prepared to release the next outburst to pass from his sharp tongue. Ming To, the head cook, brandished a knife in the air above his head as he confronted another cook who had stopped slicing a roast to glower at his tormentor. The other two cooks shook their heads and resumed chopping vegetables. Adam emptied the glass and sympathized with the source of Ming's anger, Chin Lo, second cook.

Chin's native tongue was Mandarin, the official court language of the Chinese capital, Beijing. The cooks spoke both languages so often that all four could easily understand anything said. The subtleties were beyond the reach of Adam and his uncle.

Adam bowed, greeting Ming with his usual honorific. "Jo sun, Lao Shifu." ("Good morning, Old Master.") "What has Chin Lo done to upset you so much?" he asked in basic Cantonese.

Including Adam in the same scowl of contempt he directed at Chin, Ming returned the younger man's bow with a dismissive nod. "This fool from the sewers of Shanghai dares to suggest I always lose at mahjong. He knows he lies. I lost for a reason," Ming snorted, lowering his knife and viciously cutting slices off a second roast.

"You will be telling us next you lost because the heavenly Ai Kee would be more willing to bed you because she won and the cost of her affections would be less this way than if you paid in full," Chin said with a ferocious stare, waving the bloody point of his knife at Ming.

Up came Ming's razor-sharp blade from across the table. "No, you idiot, she was happy to have my sacred stalk and my money. She lost track of time and in addition gave me the pleasure of September Moon, Face Wash, and Horse and Carriage for free! You know nothing of how to make the pleasure of your company more important than time and money to young women. Bah, talking with you is the same as speaking into a well! All I hear is what I've heard before! Easy to see why they charge you more than me! The only thing you want from them is to get that piss adder of yours to squirt sticky juice quicky-quick into their honey pots. Arggh, what can be expected of a moron who was left on a dung heap the night he was born?"

Ming slapped a slice on the board with his blade and continued talking, demonstrating to Chin that he too could communicate in the more cultivated Mandarin, even if the delivery was a tad juvenile for Adam's sake. "The coffee is fresh, and muffins are in the box over the stove. You may enter and take a few. I suppose you want us to prepare poached eggs with a lemon sauce over toast. Well, you are not your uncle. Besides, he would never ask for such a thing from an old man after seven bells of the forenoon watch. You young people think we are here to serve you at all hours. Wrong again, my beloved grandson."

Frowning at his blade, Ming wiped the blood on a piece of sailcloth and, staring at Chin, rasped the edge back and forth on a steel. "They're all jealous of me because I was getting my pleasure pistol lubricated for free while they had to pay like common sailors!" he cackled, losing his balance and swaying with the motion of the ship. His observers thought the little man intentionally exaggerated his recovery by the way he suggestively shoved his hips against the table.

Ming stuck his blade in the mutilated roast and, with a sly grin, asked a question in guttural Cantonese. "Hey, Grandson, did you bed the skinny redhead who met you at the dock the day we arrived at her Golden Gate?"

Pretending not to understand, Adam grabbed a muffin, poured a mug of coffee, and took a window seat on the port side. His head was spinning from drowsiness, constant movement, hunger, and the mixing of the two Chinese languages. The name Ai Kee sounded familiar, but he couldn't recall where he'd heard it.

Sitting by himself, he was too preoccupied to count out noon's eight bells or pay much attention to the leaping waves rushing toward the fog-shrouded coast.

He offered indifferent nods to the men taking turns putting plates and silverware in tubs of warm water set on fenced counters below the serving shelf. Raised strips, called fiddles, lined the table and counter edges to keep things from sliding off with the motion of the ship.

Allowing his thoughts to settle, Adam answered Ming's question in his own mind. *The redhead's name is Emily Parsons, and if she is still in San Francisco on my return, we'll be doing the Horse and Carriage again. She's certainly not skinny!* Adam smiled to himself and took a bite of the delicious muffin. He nearly choked at the thought of Ming ever knowing what he did with Emily. There would be no end to the ribald jokes he would have to endure.

The tedious task of learning the Chinese languages does have its rewards, Adam mused. Prior to their arrival in San Francisco, and in the spirit of staying attentive, he'd asked Ming to describe how to do the Horse and Carriage. Emily's enthusiasm during the encounter suggested that she found it to be a particularly satisfying experience.

The men in the galley were laughing by the time Adam dumped his mug in with the plates. "Thanks, Ming. Time to exit the scene and go check out what's happening in the wheelhouse," he said, unable to escape without hearing indecent comments about what was in store for the young woman who had come aboard the previous morning.

"What did you just say?" Adam asked, glancing over his shoulder. Ming was transferring a slice of roast onto a plate.

"You heard me correctly," the cook said, turning to a simmering pot and ladling a healthy dollop of creamed French onion sauce over the meat. "You've been in your cabin since we cleared the Presidio," he continued, adding *legumes rotis mirepoix* to the dish.

"You'll need more than the oomph contained in a muffin to put lead in your pencil when you visit the blond across the hall from you," Ming said, handing over a steaming plateful of food.

Adam was feeling much better by the time he got up to leave and said hello to the off-watch crew entering the salon for their noon meal.

Closing the door, he felt a current of warm air sweep over the bulkhead. The tattered clouds had given way to patches of blue, and the fog was lifting to reveal a thin strip of land in the distance. Walking aft on the weather side of the cabin house, he stopped beside the starboard rail. There was nothing but Pacific Ocean between him and Japan. Approaching the half poop, he heard feminine laughter coming from the wheelhouse.

Leaning over the side, he saw dark clouds and churning seas receding in the *Bride*'s wake. Sobering, he thought of the women in the brothel and their long road to recovery. "Could be the reason for why the cooks are so testy. Rest assured, dear cooks, Uncle and I will be checking in on those women," he vowed, "and soon after, we're going to have a few get-togethers with the Lamars, Palmer Harrington, and his boys."

Adam's thoughts returned to what Earl had said in the companionway after he handed the ship over to the sail master. Stopping at Adam's door, Earl glanced at the guest cabins and whispered, "Thank you for being with me tonight. We did all we could for Sun Morning. I'm sorry she didn't make it. We saved the lives of her two friends, and for that you deserve a lot of credit. You did well. What happened last night is only the beginning. I know I can count on you. Get some rest because I've a feeling your surgical skills are going to be needed again in the near future. We'll settle the score with the Harringtons and Lamars the next time we're in San Francisco." His uncle's words triggered an intoxicating memory. He blinked and remembered following Ai Kee's scent into Ah Toy's parlor.

Taking a firm grip on a mizzenmast backstay, he swiveled and saw the ship rise and plunge over a large roller. The sight nearly took his breath away. The sun had broken through the clouds to reveal clear skies all the way to the Channel Islands. The decks glistened as the *Bride* passed through streaming bands of gossamer spray thrown up by the bow wave.

From her elliptical counter to the figurehead holding a glowing globe, all 240 feet of ship was alive with thrumming propulsion. Vibrating cordage, thundering canvas, the voices of men aloft, and the squeal and clack of blocks complemented the constant hissing surge flowing along her sides. At such moments Adam saw the ship as a living creature. *Could she speak*, he thought, *she would tell me she keeps fast company, since they are the only ones who get anywhere!*

The bow plunged into another roller. Adam watched spume fly along the bulwarks, through the monkey rails, cross the deck, and disappear on the way to the lee-side scuppers. Canted as the ship was, Adam's eyes could follow the arc of the black hull. The red streak painted along the water line rose above the sea. He followed the line back to the tastefully scripted gilt painted on the hull, *Maine Bride*. He turned to see more gilt accenting all of the contrasting lines between the various fasteners, shroud banks, hatch covers, doors, and crown moldings. The aft and midship deckhouses gleamed in white, as did all of the inboard vertical surfaces, including bulwarks, the forecastle, hatches, davits, and boats.

The last of the streaming clouds parted, allowing the sun to bathe the ship in golden light. He reveled in every feature revealed in the sun's rays. Adam stared at the rich woodgrain accents in the spar-varnished fir masts and yards. The natural matte finish of the teak decks, stairs, and rails provided a subtle counterpoint to all the other gleaming surfaces. High above on the mainmast's tip, the pennant's long finger snapped in the stiff breeze. The contrasting colors pointed out the wind's south-by-east path.

"We'll be breaking out more colors in a day or so," Adam said, referring to the American and Yeaton House flags, colors packed in a locker near the wheel with numerous other flags and banners. The flags announced the ship's nationality and owners whenever they entered ports or were in the presence of unfamiliar ships at sea.

The *Bride* ran up the house colors each time she hoisted Old Glory. The Yeaton flag bore the family crest sewn on a field of green canvas. The crest consisted of a medieval knight's helmet resting on a bright yellow shield transected left to right by a black diagonal line. The family's origins traced back to a twelfth-century coastal principality in Yorkshire, England. The Yeatons had sailed to Portsmouth, New Hampshire, in the eighteenth century. They arrived in much the same way—as legend would have it—their Viking ancestors stepped ashore during the ninth century: penniless and full of dreams for the future. The Yeatons may have immigrated to North America via England, but their loyalties were to the republic under whose flag they sailed.

Feeling puny beside the towering mizzenmast stretching over a hundred feet above the deckhouse, Adam lowered his eyes and tapped the glass on the other side of his curtains. *My safe haven*, he thought. Only an hour or so removed from sleep, he noticed his hips and legs already flexing with the rolling deck. Pausing in his inventory of what made sailing so special, he thought of ancient mariners whose dragon boats had carried dreamers across northern seas. He squinted at the men reaching for the shrouds and wondered, *Can we still count on our ancestral spirits to guide us through turbulent seas?*

Adam extended his gaze to the men scaling the foremast ratlines. They were on their way to check the rigging, make repairs, and replace worn equipment. There was always a list of things to do aboard a ship under way.

The forecastle deck covered a large area, and the capstan tower rose out of the middle of the forward section. The capstan served a variety of purposes. Most notably, it was there to turn the massive screw on the windlass mounted two decks below. The anchor chain passed through a hawsehole, over the windlass, and through the lower decks into the chain locker in the bowels of the ship. The windlass raised and lowered two anchors, each weighing over two tons. Shackles attached 130 fathoms of chain to each anchor. At 6 feet per fathom, the two lockers held nearly 1600 feet of chain. Stairs mounted on either side accessed the foc'sl. Sliding doors hung between the stairs. Walter Tuttle had assumed that Earl had a few tricks up his sleeve, but he had no idea how right he was. Earl had hidden his cannons behind closed doors and ports. The ship's bell hung above the doors. Inscribed in the brass was *Maine Bride* and her date of commissioning, 1853.

Forward of the foc'sl, extending out beyond the bows, was the plunging bowsprit. Farther still were the jib boom and flying jib bow features, held in place by the seemingly indestructible martingale. The booms served as fasteners for a variety of winged jibs, halyards, and stays. The *Bride* figurehead adorned the upper bow beneath the bowsprit, a graceful female form wrapped in gold foil. The large crystal globe she bore gathered light and reflected the rays out over the water like a beacon.

The creak of the mizzen brought Adam out of his reverie. *So much pressure exerted on that massive trunk*, he thought, eyeing the stout timber. Each mast had three sections, each section forward fidded to the one below. The bottom two yards on each mast lowered to set the sails; the upper yards rose. The *Bride* was capable of setting nearly fifty different sails. The amount of skill and coordination required to get each sail set took years of practice. Having all possible combinations out at once was a feat of seamanship that defied comprehension.

Adam noticed that the sail master had chosen a moderate cruising speed. They were gliding over the ocean in the most comfortable fashion possible. *Probably why I slept as well as I did*, he thought. Running close to the wind, the *Bride* had the jib, a couple of staysails, the topgallants, and the upper and lower topsails out on each mast. He experienced a familiar feeling while examining the towering bank of canvas, masts, and spars rising above him. If humans were capable of doing this, they could accomplish anything.

Another peal of laughter attracted his attention. He turned to the wheelhouse rising out of the half poop deck. The small cabin sat on the poop aft of the deckhouse. Ever mindful of getting the most sail on the mizzen boom, the wheelhouse profile was only four feet above the quarterdeck. Traditionalists told Earl the structure was superfluous, arguing that the helmsman should be out in the open. How else could he adjust the wheel and take advantage of the winds? Earl had many long conversations with two of the foremost naval architects of their generation, Samuel Pook and Donald McKay. They discussed the pros and cons of having a covered space over the wheel. Earl decided to follow McKay's reasoning. The protection afforded the helmsman outweighed the limits placed on his ability to view the wind in the sails. The architects knew that the helmsman rarely acted alone in guiding a ship on her course anyway. The decisive factor came with the realization that the covered space also provided an ideal command location. Reasons for going ahead with the wheelhouse won out over the reasons not to.

Adam climbed the short set of stairs and stood on the poop facing the wheelhouse. To his right another short set of stairs attached to the deckhouse accessed the roof deck, called the quarterdeck. Adam's suite was one of many lining the passage below this deck.

The helmsman was standing at the wheel. Several people stood or sat in the small room. He saw Elmer returning to his seat after having stepped outside to check the sails and see what lay ahead.

The wheelhouse entry was over a coaming and through sliding doors mounted along the sides. A narrow space between the doors allowed for easy passage through the structure. Sliding windows provided fresh air and access to a small bell mounted on the outer wall. The binnacle or compass card holder sat under a glass dome atop a pedestal mounted in the middle of the deck below the helmsman's gaze. The ship's log nestled on a ledge beneath a window behind the wheel. Rain gear rocked back and forth on pegs strung around the back corners.

Forward of the wheel were benches and a narrow table bolted to the deck. A ship's clock and barometer filled the space between two starboard-side windows. Numerous retractable telescopes and binoculars were in holders mounted between the port-side windows. Overhead racks held navigational aids, charts, books, and well-thumbed copies of the *Old Farmer's Almanac*.

The hourglass fit into a sleeve on the table in front of the helmsman. *Calling it an hourglass was really a misnomer*, Adam thought, *as there is only a half hours' worth of sand in the glass.* They rang the bell at each turn of the glass.

Elmer and several others were watching Evelyn Griffin and James Marshall play a game of cribbage. Evelyn had woven her honey-colored hair into a French braid. Her unassuming manners and open, cheery disposition affected everyone. The contours of her lovely face and body were a welcome addition to a space seldom occupied by women. Adam could see she felt at ease in the presence of her admirers.

James could not have been more different, although he too displayed a companionable disposition most of the time. The way they were both confidently playing cribbage suggested they had another thing in common—a competitive will to win.

Where Evelyn was svelte, James was round. His large head housed a prodigious intellect. The dome of his skull seemed to rise out of his thinning black hair the way a mountain lifts above tree line. His alert brown eyes could not see a thing without the thick pair of rimless spectacles that were his constant companions. The glasses amplified the size of his inquisitive eyes and appeared to make them much more observant. His nose reminded Adam of those he had seen in Napoleonic paintings—elegant and full, like his lips, which covered large, even white teeth. As with most of the men aboard, he knew how to use a toothbrush, and his broad smile showed it. A full graying beard gave James the appearance of a cave-dwelling dwarf one might encounter in Norse legend. There was no mistaking James for a cave dweller, however; years of standing on an open deck had given his exposed skin the texture of fine leather.

He interpreted the moods of the ship, winds, and seas. He knew where they were on the surface of the planet at all times and could generally tell what the weather was going to be for the foreseeable future. His was the voice all wanted to hear over the howling winds and the thunder of bows crashing through rising seas. His was the hand controlling pressed iron shells towering over deserted decks.

James's broad shoulders sloped over a large-boned frame. He was of average height and remarkably agile for a man of his build. He knew his worth and could become acerbic at times. He now found himself in the awkward position of having to keep up appearances while being challenged by an especially disconcerting young woman.

Entering the cabin, Adam got a nod from James as Evelyn slapped a card on the table.

"Take that, Sail Master," she cried in delight. "Thirty-one for two!"

"My crib," James grumbled as he watched her move a peg a little farther down the board and reach for her pone cards.

"True, but I get to count first," she said primly. "Let's see, fifteen-two, fifteen-four, fifteen-six, fifteen-eight, fifteen-ten, a pair for twelve, and three of a kind for eighteen." She deftly moved another peg down the last row.

James watched her fold the cards and place them in front of her.

"Fifteen-two, fifteen-four, and a pair for six," he said moving a peg. "Now the crib." He lay a hand on four more cards.

"She's going to win," said a quiet, confident voice.

James slapped a crib devoid of points on the table. His consternation was momentary, and he managed to speak in a civil tone. "Willard, wouldn't you rather be elsewhere, like in your suite toying with Fermat's Last Theorem or memorizing Gaussian geometrics, moon tables, star charts, and the contents of the holds?"

"She will win because there are a miniscule number of card-point combinations capable of giving you a favorable outcome," Willard said with a grin. "You do not have room on the board to catch up."

"The uncertainty is one of the reasons we call it a *game*," James snapped. He was fully aware that Willard Coombs was the only person who could confront him on the subject of tides, latitude calculations, sailing notes for different waters, or, in this case, probability theory.

"Yes. You'll see," Willard said and kept to himself his reason for smiling. Fermat's equation was included on a book of math puzzles his mother had givin him on his tenth birthday. He wasn't about to tell James he'd seen the solution the moment he laid eyes on the formula. Unless asked, of course.

Willard's slight build supported a round head whose wispy brown hair appeared to float above his scalp. He always wore long-sleeved shirts buttoned at the cuffs and all the way up to and including the collar button. His clean-shaven face was the color of fresh cream and although easy to look upon had no distinguishing features. His light-gray eyes were prone to ready acceptance, and his innocent expectation of cooperative candor was genuine.

His appearance may have been unremarkable, but what went on inside his head was a wholly different matter. Take his fascination for languages as an example. He happened to hear his mother conversing in Quebecois with a traveling tinker while the man repaired one of her pots. Willard, for reasons incomprehensible even to him, was able to interpret most of the conversation by the time the man had brazed the leak. Later, his mother gave him an English-to-French dictionary, and soon after memorizing its contents, he too was conversing with her in French.

He received a watchful eye each time he was on the weather deck. Being adverse to physical exertion, he had no idea what was going on around him.

He was, however, paying huge dividends on Earl's investment in him. He kept meticulous records of everything that went through the *Bride*'s holds. He knew the monetary value of the ship's cargo. He had memorized the contents of ships' logs and registries, books on the history of wine, spirits, art, furniture making, music, medicine, finance, tools, and a variety of esoteric books covering Earth's arcana. All he asked in return was that his mother be well cared for in Rockport and that he be treated kindly.

Earl set up a trust for Willard and his mother with a lawyer in Camden— enough to cover the Coombs family's expenses for the rest of their lives. It pleased Willard immensely that his mother need not ever worry about how to pay the tinker.

"Hi, Adam," Willard said before anyone else could greet him.

"Good afternoon, Willard, everyone," Adam replied, nodding to those present. "Where's Uncle?"

Willard pointed at the floor. Adam pursed his lips and leaned against a doorjamb.

Evelyn collected the cards, shuffled, and dealt out twelve to James and herself.

"How are you, Adam?" she asked, putting two cards in her crib.

"I'm fine," Adam said, crossing to the binnacle and checking the compass. The big S was directly under the forward line. He exchanged nods with Elmer and then addressed Evelyn.

"Did you sleep well?"

"Yes," she answered, smiling at him. "All night. Myra did not and is indisposed. Her closest friend became a porcelain bowl once we entered open water. Captain Yeaton has been with her off and on. He's been giving her drops from a tincture he made consisting of morphine and a belladonna extract. I think her stomach has settled down a bit today. She is understandably drowsy though. I'm sure she would be content to sleep all the way to our destination."

"Ahh," Adam said with false sincerity, "how unfortunate."

James cleared his throat and tossed two cards into Evelyn's crib. He cut the deck, and she turned over a five of hearts. "Were you sleeping all this time, Adam?" he asked, dropping a five of clubs. "Five."

"Yes, I think I slept nearly twenty-eight hours. Passed out a few minutes after I heard your order to release the jib and loose the tops'ls."

"Um-hmm," James said, concentrating on the cards. "You slept the sleep of the just, no doubt, because your heart is pure." He raised his eyes just enough to make eye contact with Evelyn.

Her blush was brief before she put down an eight and deadpanned, "Thirteen."

Arching an eyebrow toward Willard, James countered with a jack of hearts. "Twenty-three. Should be in Los Angles tomorrow morning," he said with a short sniff. "High tide is at ten a.m.," he added.

Willard grinned. The others pretended not to notice. Everyone except Evelyn knew that under James's gruff demeanor, he was fond of Willard. The feeling was mutual.

"Thirty," Evelyn said, putting down a seven.

"Go," he responded, watching her move a peg.

"Five," James said, laying a diamond away from the club already out there.

"Twelve," she countered, dropping another seven.

"Grrr," he rumbled while rapping the edge of his remaining card on the table.

She said nothing as she watched him place a five of spades beside the others. "Seventeen."

"Last card," she breathed, dropping a deuce on the pile and moving another peg.

"The master has twenty-nine," Elmer murmured, his eyes darting between James and Willard.

"One in 216,580." Willard wisely chose to say nothing about what the odds were on James's chances of pegging out.

There was stirring around the table as everyone watched James arrange his three fives and the suited jack. Experienced players all, the group took a moment to admire the highest hand in cribbage. Then everyone's gaze went to the board to see how many holes left to go on James's side.

"Keep a firm hand on the wheel and your eye on the compass," James warned the helmsman with just a bit of testiness.

They all could see that James's twenty-nine points had put him in the stink hole—one measly hole away from winning. He put a peg in the hole. "What've you got?"

"Fifteen-two, fifteen-four," she said tapping the two sevens with the eight, "and a pair for six," she added, moving a peg.

She gave a delicate shudder after placing the peg five short holes away from her stink hole. James's upper lip moved down, and he managed to refrain from having another sniff.

She picked up the crib and turned the cards over. She had discarded a pair of fours. James had given her a four and a king. "Three of a kind for six!" she exclaimed as she moved the last peg into the winner's hole.

Several pairs of eyes flitted between Willard and James.

"Thanks for the four, Mr. Marshall, because without that, who knows what would have happened? This has been a most enjoyable game of cribbage," she said, leveling her merry eyes on him.

"That was fun," James said, his eyes smiling in return. "Let's play again," he offered, unable to maintain a silent laugh with her over how she'd deadpanned his "purity of heart" quip.

Enjoying the sound of her laughter, he glanced at the clock, reached for the hourglass, and addressed Hopley Yeaton, a ship's boy. "Please go forward and ring in two bells of the afternoon watch. You appear to be a little slack today, young man."

The clock said 1:05. Hopley rolled his eyes and ran off.

Evelyn stopped laughing, and her voice dropped an octave. "Thank you for inviting me up here and giving me this entertaining diversion. I would like to come back and play again. And now I think I should go check on Myra." She paused, "I was having so much fun, I forgot to eat. Would it be possible to have lunch in my suite?"

"Yes," James said, noticing the subtle change in her demeanor. *Go easy on her,* he thought. *She's still recovering from what happened in San Francisco.* He gestured to Adam.

"I'd be happy to see you below and bring a tray to your cabin," Adam said, stepping outside and girding himself for another round of galley humor. "This way." The call from aloft came while he was reaching for her elbow.

"Deck there! Sail fine on the weather counter!"

CHAPTER 8

Midway between San Francisco and Los Angeles, 2 January, 1:20 p.m.

Earl joined the group leaning on the aft rail. Adam and Ryan were with James, who was trying to get a fix on the vessel in their wake. The northern horizon was a brassy sheen of rolling crests washing deep recesses in slate-gray cloudbanks.

Earl gave his nephew's greeting a curt nod and ignored Ryan's worried frown. The hard stare he directed at the following sea was enough to make James bite his tongue. No one dared to ask their captain why they hadn't seen him since leaving San Francisco.

James lowered his binoculars. "Can't see her from here. I sent Mike up with a signals telescope. He's seated on the skysail yard with Maynard."

Everyone raised their heads. James's shudder at the sight of the swaying legs summed up their feelings. Long way to fall.

Maynard Kimble, aware of and indifferent to their apprehensions, preferred to be aloft most of the time. He exhibited the much-sought-after quality of being a fearless main-top man. Unlike most people, Maynard loved being up high and would have been happy to have his hammock hung from the mainmast crosstrees and his food sent up in a bosun's chair.

Seeing his first clipper cruising off Owls Head settled it for Maynard. From that moment on, he knew what he wanted to be. He would have to wait ten years, however, before he joined the first crew to come aboard.

He was a favorite of the boys, especially Mike Stanley, the only one who shared Maynard's passion for heights.

Maynard had been enduring a lot of kidding lately from the current crop of boys. They'd started calling him an old-timer on his twenty-third birthday. "Yes," he said, reminding them, "but I can still see better'n most."

Maynard's skin was the color of bronze. The only part of him that was white went from his waist to the knees of his cut-offs. Like most of his breed, he ran around barefoot in all weather. His tan extended all the way to the tips of his toes. His sandy-blond hair grew long, and his lithe body attracted women like moths to a flame. His teeth were perfect, and his clean-shaven face looked like polished marble. Few could resist the allure of his bright-blue eyes and long blond lashes.

"Deck there," he called, "she's the Polar Bear out of Baltimore." Grabbing a backstay, he slid to the bulwark, hopped onto the poop, and joined the group by the counter. Mike landed right behind him.

Earl led them into the wheelhouse where they could talk without having to raise their voices. Willard and Elmer sat at the table playing double solitaire.

Excusing himself, Earl asked Willard to put his cards down and pay attention. He wanted Willard to fill everyone in on the *Polar Bear*.

Closing his hand and placing it on the table, Willard summarized what he knew of the vessel in the *Bride*'s wake. "She's owned by a New York mercantile consortium. They're involved in banking, finance, real estate, and arms manufacturing. They have a black birding operation that ships slaves to the Newport auctions. The Bear also ships armaments and opium to China. She recently arrived in San Francisco with plunder from the China conflicts. She's well-armed."

Maynard tapped Willard on the shoulder and picked up the thread. "She was in the harbor for three or four days before we left. The crewmen I spoke with said they made a stop on the way to China—first time any of them had been to a Japanese port. Weren't supposed to talk about it," he said with a twist of the lips. "Yeah, right. Secrets and alcohol shouldn't be in the same room with seamen. Sailed into the harbor under the guns of a British frigate and offloaded a shipment of weapons. They were planning to sail for New York at the end of the week. You may've heard of her captain, Carlton Lang."

The men in the wheelhouse exchanged startled glances. "Yup," Maynard said, seeing recognition dawn on each face.

Four years earlier, Lang had hanged and thrown overboard several members of his crew. Apparently, they were guilty of refusing to reef topsails Lang had left out too long in his haste to drive his men and his ship to their limits. His reason: Get to San Francisco several days sooner than his closest rival, so he could reap a tidy bonus for coming in first. At the subsequent trial, the jury acquitted Lang of all charges. They could not reach a verdict.

Time passed, and unbeknownst to the *Bride's* crew, Lang assumed command of the *Polar Bear*. The ship's owners allowed him to choose his own crew, and, as expected, this crew was composed of hard, deep-water men willing to do anything for the right price.

Rubbing his temples, Earl narrowed his eyes. "How're her sails set?" he asked. He would have rubbed his temples even harder had he known that several of Lang's crewmen were gunner's mates prior to being cashiered out of the Navy for insubordination.

Maynard cocked his head and studied the ceiling racks. "She's carrying nearly all of the canvas possible. They could put out the weather studs'ls, I suppose. You'd turn me back into a head cleaner if I suggested trying to use the sail rig he has out there." He heard a grunt and nodded to the sail master. "It's a wonder she hasn't dismasted or torn her sails to ribbons by now. I think I saw her main yards brushing the water—be quite the feat considering how close-hauled she is. Appears to me Lang's in a mighty big hurry to get down here."

"Hmm," Earl murmured. "His reason for haste is obvious. He knows we have the gold and thinks we have the bonds. He wants to catch us before we panic and offload them in Los Angeles. Want to hazard a guess on how long it'll take to overhaul us, James?"

"Six hours." James turned the empty glass as four bells of the afternoon watch rang out. "Be full dark by then. I doubt if he'll try anything tonight."

"Ayah," Earl said, leaning against the doorjamb. "She's under warrant to Arthur Harrington's group, so Lang isn't necessarily acting on his own. She'll be armed with nine-pounders, langrage, chain-shot, grape, and maybe even a carronade packed with canister. Lang will attempt to dismast us in the morning and try boarding us. Arthur Harrington has decided money's more important than Evelyn's safety, apparently. No surprise there, I guess."

"As it stands now, he has the wind gauge," James said, watching Earl.

"The wind has been holding a northwesterly pattern. Will it continue?" Earl asked, meeting his gaze.

"Yes, it'll be steady for most of the way to San Pedro. The warm swirl in the atmosphere will give us a boost. The farther south we go, the more predictable it will get. For the time being," he added, tightening his lips and furrowing his brow, "we're just coming out of the turbulent air into a steadier southwesterly. The tide'll be coming in around five p.m. Right now we're at slack tide. San Diego and the change in current are a long way off."

"So the tide could have a negative effect on our progress if we alter course and sail west," Earl finished for him.

"Right. Are you proposing we try to gain the weather gauge overnight? Tricky exercise because we'd be sailing much closer to the wind. New moon, so we'd be sailing by starlight," he stated, giving Earl a questioning tilt of his head.

"Just thinking." Earl moved to the bench under the forward window where he could sit facing the room. "How many knots do you suppose that wretch is doing back there?"

"Can't be much more'n fifteen, I'd say. We're doing a little less, probably closer to twelve. We're in the neighborhood of a hundred and fifty miles out of Los Angeles," James answered. "The Bride could easily wear more canvas, but we decided to have a leisurely trip south. Under the circumstances, I'd prefer beating them at their own game. There's time to pick up the pace and be in Los Angles hours before them," he grumbled as each thought spilled out. He did not have to say how he felt about the idea of sailing at night with lots of canvas exposed to the wind.

Earl glanced at Willard. "I agree," Willard said. Shifting to Ryan, Earl squinted at the man's vague nod. A wary stillness descended on the men as they watched their captain. They were all thinking the same thing. The captain's smiles seemed to be in short supply of late. The stare he laid on each pair of eyes conveyed the same message: How long you stay aboard this ship will depend on how well you do the job assigned to you.

Finally, Earl spoke. "We're not going to try to back-door Capt'n Lang just yet. Wind, current, tide, and the opposite shore don't favor us enough to challenge the Bear right now. We'll sink her with all aboard if Lang chooses to press us further, but not today or tomorrow. I'm not ready for our guests to be in a position to tell others how we're armed. It's way too soon for that tidbit to find its way to our enemies, if it hasn't already. The less they know of our affairs, the better. So, no. If possible, we will choose our own time and place to confront the Bear. The Shadow will be along directly as well. I'd prefer not to contend with them both at the same time. But we will if push comes to shove."

The message in Earl's manner left little doubt about how he felt about the level of assistance he expected to receive in overcoming their adversaries. "So, Mr. Marshall, I'll leave it to you to arrange a sail pattern that will get us fifteen knots on the double. I expect you to do so without dismasting us and turning this fine ship into fodder for another one of Longfellow's tragic Hesperus-themed poems. We aren't about to let Ol' Mr. Lang out-sail us, are we?" Earl asked of his childhood friend. "I want us in Los Angeles tomorrow morning before the tide turns, James. Lang will have to cool his heels until we're ready to face him on our terms."

"Aye, aye, Captain," James replied in dismay, all too aware that this was not the time to confront his captain. *I haven't seen that expression in his eyes for over twenty years*, he thought, becoming worried.

Duly noted, Earl thought, and headed for the stairs, Myra, and solitude.

James cleared his throat, glanced at the departing captain, and addressed Willard before issuing orders to the others. "Thank you for your support."

Willard's hair shifted back and forth above his nod. He and Elmer picked up their cards.

"Maynard, get a bite to eat, help with the skysail, return to the crosstrees, and keep a weather eye on our tail. Bring the Stanley boy with you," James said, giving Mike a quizzical glance. *What is it about this boy's eagerness to be in danger?* "The fore and main topgallants will be bunted up enough for you to see where we're pointed. The mizzen topgallant will come off in a little while, giving you an open view of our wake. Keep Mike on the crosstrees.

"Ryan, go forward and call all hands. Get the watch crew to put out the flying jib right away. Tie the men to separate lifelines before they step onto the bowsprit. Be impossible to find a lost man in these conditions. We're going to heel and may take on water, so net the lee rails before we set the sails." He peered at the boy, liking the way Mike's eyes remained calm while under scrutiny.

James stepped behind the helmsman. "Once the sails are set, no one goes to the foc'sl until we adjust the trim. We'll ring the watch bells from here for the time being. Those rollers may have a surprise or two among them. Be best to err on the side of caution and know where everyone is at all times, especially if we're running under full sail at night. The tops'ls and topgallants we have out now we'll trim again. Tell the men I think the wind will hold steady, and with a little luck, we may be able to stay the course all night if we rig everything properly now. We're going to be sailing on a bowline for the next while. Spiral trim all the way up each mast."

James reached for a sou'wester, and Adam addressed him while he adjusted the strap under his chin and slipped into one of the full-length waxed canvas coats. "I can stay with the helmsman."

James stepped over the coaming and turned. "Won't be necessary. By the time I have the Bride trimmed the way I want, the spokes will feel like feathers in the helmsman's fingers, even if we are canted a little more to port than we are now! Cover yourself with rain gear, and join me at the rail. I want to talk with you while we wait."

As the men went off to do their various tasks, one question prevailed in the back of their minds: what would the following sea contain at four bells of the first dogwatch?

Adam donned the rain gear and followed James to the deckhouse rail. They were still huddled together when Ryan called to say everyone was in position to execute the sail drill. Ryan stood amidships holding the mainmast shrouds and watching the men release the flying jib, sheet her home, and take their places by the foremast. His eyes appeared to be darting everywhere at once. He checked to see that the bosuns responsible for each mast's crew were in position and ready once he gave the go-ahead to release and sheet the sails, raise and haul the upper yards, man the braces, and set the trim.

James pointed at Elmer and the helmsman. Elmer nodded their readiness for the changes about to take place on the rudder. "Fore, main royal and skys'ls, release the gaskets!" James called to Ryan, who repeated the call to the men aloft. Turning aft again, he nudged Adam and threw a thumb over his shoulder. Evelyn was grinning through the wheelhouse window as she slipped her arms in the weather coat Elmer held open for her. Elmer plunked a sou'wester over her golden locks, and with a quick tug on the drawstring, she was out the door.

Getting a good grip with their bare feet on the foot lines strung below the royal and skysail yards, the topmen freed the sails, tied off the gaskets, and headed for the ratlines. After helping to release the skysail, Maynard raced Mike to the crosstrees. High above the deck they turned aft, sat, and leaned against the topgallant mast. Lifting brass telescopes, they scanned the northern expanse through a gap between two sails. Bobbing in and out of sight, the *Bear*'s white canvas stood in stark relief against the dark clouds blanketing the far horizon. Several miles beyond the enemy, Maynard thought he saw the *Shadow*'s canvas begin to separate itself from the distant crests. Taking his eye off the lens, he looked down in time to see Evelyn crossing the deckhouse.

A moment later, she was standing with Adam and James at the rail. She arrived dressed for the spray, with blue canvas pants, a woolen sweater, and a pair of borrowed sea boots. "I hope you gentlemen won't think me crass for wearing men's pants aboard your elegant ship," she said, standing between them and getting what she hoped was a good grip on the rail.

"Quite the contrary," Adam replied. "We approve. By the way, I noticed those pants earlier. The material's familiar. We delivered a small mountain of bales to a tailor in San Francisco last month. We shipped the fabric all the way from India."

"Why, thank you," she said, laughing. "I like the blue color, and it goes well with almost all my blouses. I prefer to wear trousers instead of dresses out of doors." She did a slightly off-balance half pirouette.

Putting his cares aside for a moment, James shared a grin with her. "Hang on, young lady, and be prepared to get a little damp!"

"I would rather be up here instead of alone in my cabin listening to Myra retching!" she burbled as the ship hit a roller. Losing her grip on the rail, she sat with a thump on a quarter boat. "Oh!" she exclaimed. "This is probably where I should be right now anyway." Smiling gamely, she adjusted herself and spread her feet on the deck.

Adam and James exchanged appreciative nods before James returned to the task at hand. Adam sat down beside her. "Having three points of contact may not always be enough to keep us upright out here. Believe me, I found out the hard way. Try to remember, one hand is for your safety, and the other is for the ship. Besides, this is as good a place as any to watch what is going on around us."

"Hmm," she said, placing her hands on her knees and taking in the scene. Her eyes grew wide at the speed with which the mainmast skysail topmen came down the ratlines and scooted past the men freeing the royals from their yards.

"Mains'l skysail halyards up lively!" James called to Ryan, who raised a circling index finger. High above, Maynard and Mike put down the scopes and held on for dear life. Adam and Evelyn watched as men on deck hauled on the skys'l halyards. Up went the yard. The loose sail snapped loudly before filling with air.

"Sheet the skys'l home!" James watched the flapping skysail pulled tight by men on one set of lines, then trimmed by additional men hauling on braces attached to the swaying yard. "Fore, main royal yards up lively," he called out, and Ryan rapidly circled his index finger. Up went the fore and main royal yards.

"Wow!" Evelyn said as she watched two lines of men pass in opposite directions on either side of the ship. As soon as the men hauling a line on one side came to the end, they crossed the deck to lend a hand on a line going in the opposite direction. Up and up went the fore and mainmast royals on their yards. The snapping and popping of released canvas turned to duller thumps.

"Fore, main, sheet the royal's home." The men on the sheets stretched the royals to the limit.

"Man the braces. Fore, main, royal release and haul!" Ryan called over the squealing blocks, thumping canvas, and protesting yards.

"I've sailed on many ships," Evelyn said, "but no one has explained how the sails are set. Would you mind?" she asked, waving her hand.

"Of course," he said. "Did you know, the sails mounted on the masts are all reasonably square with the exception of the spanker located over the wheelhouse?"

"Yes."

"Did you know that the names of all the sails are the same on each mast, starting from the bottom?"

"Um-hm, and I also know they're the course, lower topsail, upper topsail, topgallant, royal, and skysail. The mainmast is the only mast with the skysail. The foremast has only the course, lower topsail, topgallant, and royal, no upper topsail. The furled sails are held against the yards by ropes called gaskets."

"Aha," he said, pointing at the mizzenmast. "Tell me what you know."

"Well," she said, "this mast has the course, upper and lower topsails, topgallant, and spanker. Halyards raise and lower the upper yards from the deck."

"So, I guess the only thing left to do is tell you what James and the men are up to as we go along."

Evelyn's expression turned to wonder as she felt the surge caused by the additional canvas. The bow was cleaving the waves at a shallower angle, and the spray washing over the weather deck flew through the rigging in sheets. The shirtless upper bodies of the men glistened in the warm California sun. She experienced an unexpected flutter in her heart and placed a hand over her breast. James caught her eye and winked. "We will deal with that directly, Miss." She had no idea what he was referring to.

"Douse the mizzen topgallant!" he called out.

The mizzenmast crew untied the sheets from the pins and let the lines run through the blocks. The air spilled out of the sail as other men hauled on clew and buntlines, pulling the sail up to the yard. Men scrambled out on the yard and began fisting and pulling the canvas into a manageable bundle. Working above Evelyn's rocking head, they soon had the sail gasketed in place. While they were working to bundle up the sail, others pulled the yard around until it was level and perpendicular to the ship. Maynard and Mike now had an unobstructed view to the rear.

"Ahh," Evelyn said. "Why are those two looking aft?"

Adam felt unprepared for the question and unsure how much he should tell her. "There's a ship following us."

"Why would they be doing that?" she asked, becoming serious.

Adam could not tell if she knew the reason a ship was back there or if she was only curious, so he told the truth. "They think we have the stolen bonds and want to take them from us."

"Oh. Do you have them?"

"No, but they don't know it. The men on that ship will go to any lengths to determine for themselves whether we are telling the truth, even to the extent that they are willing to disable us, come aboard, and tear the ship apart."

"Am I in danger?"

"Only if we cannot get to Banning's Wharf before they overhaul us. That's why we're putting on more canvas. We plan to outrun them and get you to safety before they try anything else."

"Huh. Can you do it?"

"Yes."

"Topgallant braces, Ryan!" they heard James say as the boom of canvas and the squeal of blocks subsided.

She adjusted her bottom and cocked her head. "I've seen this done before," she said, watching James turn his attention to the fore and main lower top-sails. "The men at the foremast are larger than the ones on the mainmast."

"They are," Adam said. "The foremast crews have to be out here in all weathers, often work on a wetter deck, absorb the waves coming over the side, and still must be able to set the sails. The mainmast crews are nearly the same size because the sails tend to be larger. The smaller mizzenmast crewmen get the most ribbing for a lot of reasons, even though their task is a vital one."

She pointed at a giant, who, like his mates, was shirtless. "He's one of the most muscular men I've ever seen. He must be well over six feet tall. The man's skin is so black it has a blue sheen."

"Senegal. We found him off the west coast of Africa last spring. We were on our way to Casablanca and sailed into a debris field. The men spotted a body lying on a hatch cover. Uncle had a boat lowered and sent the men to fetch the body. He was more dead than alive, the sole survivor of a slaver capsized in a storm. Uncle Earl and I cared for his wounds, but it was Hopley who cared for his will to live. They spent many hours together while Senegal recovered and learned English. The boy is hopeless with languages. I think he has managed to learn greetings in French, Arabic, and Wolof. Senegal says he does not know where on the continent his family originated or where they are now. He has no memory of his life prior to us finding him. I guess we're his family now. We named him after a slave owned by Hopley's famous namesake.

"You may or may not know Hopley Yeaton was the first commissioned military officer in the United States, and like most of the men in our family, he was a mariner. He received his appointment from Washington and Jefferson soon after independence. Gets a little complicated here, so please bear with me. His grandson, our Hopley's father, is a frigate captain stationed at the Washington Navy Yard. This Hopley is my third cousin. He's Uncle Earl's second cousin once removed. To keep things simple, he calls him Uncle Earl."

"How interesting," she said. "I have a famous relative too. My great-uncle, William Clark, mapped a trail across the continent with Meriwether Lewis."

Adam nodded. "I know who those brave men were. One of the ship's boys is a Lewis. I have no idea whether or not he's related to Meriwether," he said, taking note of Evelyn Griffin's beauty. He decided to reassess his aversion to freckles and drew closer to the ones sprinkled across the bridge of her nose.

"I have a brother too," she said. "He's not famous, but he's a military man. He will be graduating from West Point in May. A classmate of his has invited our family to a wedding in Camden, Maine, this summer. Are you going to be there by any chance?"

Adam recoiled and could not prevent a furrow from forming between his eyes. Willing his eyes off the freckles, he turned away and noticed a knot tied on one of the quarter boats. Whoever tied the knot had used a highwayman's hitch. Having found the distraction he was seeking, he knelt by the boat and undid the knot while examining the implications of this unexpected and potentially disagreeable topic of conversation. *Evelyn's brother may have befriended a Harrington*, he thought, *and I may be developing an attraction for her, but it doesn't change the fact that I don't want my cousin marrying a Harrington*. Drawing the line through a ringbolt, he squeezed the loop and retied the lash using the much easier to release mooring hitch.

He tugged the snatch loop with a grunt and sat beside her. "We've touched on a matter I would rather pursue once we get to know each other a little better. But your question deserves an answer. Yes, I'll be there. The wedding we'll be attending is between my cousin, Olivia Winthrop, and your brother's classmate, Jules Harrington."

"Have I offended you?" she asked.

"No, but for reasons best left for another day, I think we should drop the subject," he said, glancing aft.

She nodded. "Four other boys around the same age, fifteen or so?"

"Yes," he said, liking how well she took the hint. "They all just happen to be fifteen. Mike Stanley will be the first to turn sixteen."

"Munenori Suzuki, the Japanese boy, is the youngest. He came aboard a year ago with his cousin Kato Kawasaki, who is twenty-six. They come from old and honored samurai families. Kato is on the mizzenmast crew," he said, pointing to the men standing below them. "Surnames precede given names in Japan. Kato and Munenori are their last names. We westerners ignore the distinction for reasons I have yet to understand. Munenori's father and Kato's mother are siblings. That's why they have different surnames."

He may have found her apparent confusion humorous but he was unprepared for how quickly she said, "I get it!" *She has a mind like a steel trap,* he thought, *and if I'm not careful, I could find myself under her spell without even knowing how I got there.*

As they conversed, the men on deck moved into position for the next set of orders.

"The other ship's boys are Charlie Polanowski, Mike Stanley, and Colton Lewis, who came aboard in Vancouver. Charlie and Mike come from family friends of Uncle Earl. Mike is sitting on the crosstrees with Maynard right now." Adam raised a finger and pointed at the dangling feet swaying far above them.

"Dizzying," she said, leaning into him as the ship rose up and over a large roller.

Throughout the whole exercise, James's commanding voice carried over the booming canvas, squealing blocks, and thrumming stays. Around came the yards until James called out, "Make fast!" Each sail was set a few degrees farther abeam of the one above. So it went until all the sails had been trimmed to the new pattern.

"Two sails to go on each mast," Evelyn said, placing a steadying hand on his thigh and craning her neck to get a better view of the towering mass of canvas scraping blue skies.

"Not quite," Adam rumbled, imagining he could feel the heat of her hand. *What is she seeking? Reassurance? Companionship? Or something else?* "The mizzen course will stay where it is for now. You'll see why in a few minutes. They'll release the fore and main courses after the lower tops'ls. These sails are on yards fixed to the mast. They do not lift but can swing."

"Ah," Evelyn said with a laugh. She gave his thigh a light squeeze, removed her hand, and grinned, "Makes sense. It would take a lot of effort to pump such big yards up and down."

"Um-hm," Adam said through tight lips, his mind jamming a series of distracting thoughts into flimsy compartments. Willing his pulse to return to normal took more effort than he anticipated. *Threats on the horizon, and she's toying with me*, he thought. *Where's the greater danger?* Feeling outwitted, he answered her next question without thinking.

"Adam?" she asked, becoming serious, "do you feel it's important to know your family history?"

"In a way."

"How so?"

"Well, I honor the ancestors I admire by remembering who they were. I revere the ones who did their best to rectify the follies of the past. I'm told they tried to leave the world in better shape than it was the day they arrived. Be nice if I'd be remembered the same way long after I'm dead."

"Thank you," she said in tone he could not fathom.

James's call interrupted their thoughts. "Ryan, sheet home the fore and main lower tops'ls!" The huge sails snapped with the crack of gunfire. The men on the sheets and braces were ready. The squeal of tackle changed the clamor into a dull roar as the wind caught the canvas and lifted the bows.

A sudden acceleration rippled through the hull and set the masts to quivering in their vibrating stays. The whistling winds rose above the thunderous clamor of waves crashing against the hull. Evelyn put sober thoughts aside and let her eyes grow wide with the thrill of seeing men mastering such primal forces.

James gestured to the mizzen crew. "Let fall the spanker!" His wink at Evelyn was lost in a welter of spray rising over the side. Elmer and the helmsman saw the wink and knew what it meant. The rudder pressure dropped off the moment the men sheeted the sail home and secured the boom.

Adam shook his head. "Evelyn, did you notice how lowering the spanker caused the bows to lift and reduced the amount of sea coming over the side?"

"Yes!" she exclaimed, raising her voice over the wind. "And the ship feels steadier."

"Yup. This is the change James was referring to a short while ago when he winked at you. We call the trapezoidal spanker the Driver. The spanker drives the stern into the water, lifts the bow, and adds stability to the ship's trim."

Evelyn moved to the rail "Mr. Marshall, the bows are taking the tops off the waves as the ship planes over the water. You really are a master, and your Bride is truly running before the wind!"

"Thank you, Evelyn," James said. He thought she might have returned his wink, but he could not be sure. He was quite impressed, however, by her willingness to be there the whole time in the wind and spray. *Arggh*, he thought. *A younger me might be willing to fight for her favor too!* "This youngster has a lot more to offer than beauty and grace," he mumbled as he watched Adam guide Evelyn down the stairs. *Yes, but . . .,* a voice cautioned inside his head, *don't forget her pedigree. She still bears watching.*

Adam took the wheel, so Elmer could lead a group standing by a device attached to the counter. Evelyn leaned against an open door and watched what the men did next. James stood above them and watched from the aft portion of the roof deck. A few of the mizzen crew were standing with Elmer beside the device. The device, called a chip log, consisted of a freewheeling spool wound with a light rope to which a knot was tied every forty-seven feet, three inches. Several of the boys were moving among the men. "Stand back! Give Elmer room to toss the wedge," James said gruffly to the boys crowding around. "Charlie, git your fingers away from the cranks, for God's sake!"

Evelyn squinted up at James and crossed her arms. The ship rolled, and she lost her balance. To make matters worse, she fumbled her grab at the handrail and recovered with an artless flourish. Her embarrassment vanished the second she saw Adam's unguarded expression. They laughed over her momentary loss of dignity, her inept attempt to make it appear normal, and Adam's subsequent effort to divert her attention from the lust she had seen in his eyes. Smitten by the encouragement he received in her response, he became too excited and started tripping over his words. Instead of stopping to regain his composure, he valiantly babbled on. "Don't worry about me, ahh, James, his bark is you my bite!"

Frowning at the skylarking going on in the ship's control room, James pulled a watch the size of a turnip out of a coat pocket and opened the case. Holding up an index finger, he made eye contact with Elmer and lowered his gaze to the second hand. His expression softened as he paused to contemplate the shirttails hanging below his friend's woolen vest. Elmer's disheveled appearance hadn't changed much over the years, but the area around the kindly gray eyes had. Elmer's aging freckles had mottled into different shades of brown, giving his face a camouflaged appearance. The pair waited for the second hand to get closer to the top of the dial.

Elmer True was of average height, deceptively strong, and one of the oldest members of the crew. He preferred to work the helm. He was a willing hand on the mizzenmast and accepted that it was where the least-skilled started and the ones on the way to retirement ended up. He was most assuredly a member of the latter group. He did not know, and would be flattered if told, he was welcome to stay aboard for as long as he wished to remain a sailor. Elmer's clever hands could fix anything, and he loved fiddling with gadgets. Everyone enjoyed his company.

Elmer squeezed a wooden wedge in a fist. His other hand held a loose coil of rope tied to the wedge. The rope ran onto the spool. The coil in his hand was long enough to reach the water.

James dropped his finger. "Okay, Elmer, toss your wedge."

Elmer tossed the wedge and released the coil. As soon as the wedge's drag began pulling line off the spool, James noted the location of the second hand on his watch. The line rapidly spooled out. All were quiet until they saw the first knot roll off the spool.

"One," the boys called out. More and more knots peeled into the sea.

The boys chanted out the count until James told them to stop.

"Fifteen knots in thirty seconds!" the boys said seeking Evelyn's approval. She smiled. "Bravo!"

James pried his eyes away from Evelyn and shook himself.

"Might get a little more out of her if you put out weather studdin' s'ls," Elmer commented.

"Harrumph," James said. "Good enough for now. Wouldn't want Lang to see what we're capable of if we really put our minds to it now would we?"

Elmer shrugged and watched the boys line up to take turns reeling the cord back onto the spool.

At six bells into the afternoon watch, James, Earl, Willard, and Ryan joined Adam in the wheelhouse. Adam was taking another turn at the wheel while the helmsman ate a cookie beneath the forward window. James stepped over the coaming, checked the compass, tapped the barometer, and glanced at the outside thermometer. The pressure and temperature had risen since he'd last checked. Things were starting to go their way for a change. "How's the wheel feel?" he asked.

"Light as a baby's breath."

"Fifteen knots are all we are going to need just now. More'n enough to keep the Bear in our wake," James commented.

"Fine with me," Earl responded. "I don't want them to see how fast we can travel in these conditions. The wind?"

James glanced forward at the bright, cloudless sky and the serried rank of leaping waves before he said, "I'm sure it'll hold steady. I reckon if we continue under full sail, we're going to be at the approaches to San Pedro between seven and eight a.m. We'll be coming in on the flood tide. Be light enough to see where the Bear is by then. Might be a good idea to start reefing as we approach the shipping lanes anyway, so our timing should be good."

Two hours later, the second bell of the first dogwatch rang out from the foc'sl. The wall clock's hands pointed at 5:00 p.m. The glass was turned, and the helmsman went off to dinner. The on-watch helmsman saw Adam at the wheel, took a seat, and picked up an 1859 copy of the *Old Farmer's Almanac* James had left on the table.

The dogwatches were two hours long—4:00 to 6:00 p.m. and 6:00 to 8:00 p.m. This way the watches shifted forward, so the crews were on deck at different times each day. The first, middle, morning, forenoon, and afternoon watches were each four hours. Since there was a half hour between bells, there were four bells in each dogwatch and eight bells in each four-hour watch.

Two eighteen-man crews worked the ship in four-hour shifts. They dined, loafed, and slept off watch. Earl, James, Ryan, Adam, Willard, and the passengers, having no set watch schedule, ate and slept whenever they felt like it. Willard and the guests were the only ones not expected to take watches from time to time.

A half hour later, Adam turned the glass, feeling hungry. "Dinner time." He handed the wheel over, glanced at the following sea, and headed for the stairs.

Returning to his cabin, he washed, put on dry clothes, and stood in the passageway. He sniffed and listened but did not notice any scents or sounds coming from the other side of Myra's door.

After eating, he relaxed in the salon for a while before going off to see what was happening in the wheelhouse.

Back on deck, he crossed to the weather rail and leaned over the side. The sea was creaming smoothly along the hull. Stretching out over the rail, he saw copper cladding reflecting the late afternoon sun. He pulled his head back as another big roller crashed against the side, sending spume flying over the bows and carrying away the smoke coming out of the galley stack. Sliding a hand along the wet rail, he headed aft. Stepping over the coaming, he nodded to the helmsman, James, and Ryan. "Maynard in the tops?" he asked.

"Yes," Ryan said. "We just sent him up with a glass. Mike is with him."

"Deck there," Maynard called from aloft. "Two sails on the starboard quarter!"

Wary eyes glanced at each other in the enclosed space. A moment later, Maynard stepped into the wheelhouse. Mike stood outside and leaned against the door. Earl arrived in time to hear Maynard's last comment. "The Polar Bear's still out there. They rigged studding sails after we added more canvas. The other ship is gaining on her. Her sails were clearing the horizon several hours ago. She's probably the Shadow." Maynard placed his glass in the rack beside the one Mike had been using. "The storm we out-sailed is driving her."

"Thank you, Maynard. You can go now. We'll take it from here, Mike," Earl said to a boy who couldn't contain his glee at being included in such weighty matters. "We're too far ahead. They can't catch us before we clear Los Angeles. I figure we're off Muru Point Rock and well on our way to being on schedule. Carry on, gentlemen, I have a patient to attend to. As foul as the tincture tastes, I think she would drink the whole bottle if given half a chance."

"Hmm," Adam said, "that would produce quite the sideshow. A madwoman running around partially clothed, sexually active, and hallucinating might be an entertaining diversion for everyone. God knows what she would do in the crew berth if she released a lifetime of desires. Bad, bad, bad," he finished with a mischievous grin.

Everyone shivered at the prospect of such a thing occurring to the spectral Myra. If anyone had Evelyn fantasies, they kept their thoughts to themselves. Going down the lee stairs, Earl heard his nephew's parting shot: "Keep the medicine room securely locked, Uncle Earl!"

The dogwatches ended with four bells into the second. The winter sun's last glow faded into night's gloom. With the exception of the torpid Myra, each of the ship's occupants had finished their dinners. Off-watch crewmen retired to their rocking hammocks while their mates took turns steering clear of other vessels, ringing the bells, and running the rigging from the deck. They lit the forward lantern, and for obvious reasons, the aft light got the night off.

Maynard greeted the men in the wheelhouse and put the glass away after coming down from another search of the sea beyond the ship's phosphorescent wake. He flopped in his hammock thinking of Ming and a star cluster he called the Tianmiao Constellation. The cook wanted to know how brightly the stars known to westerners as Alpha, Beta, Gamma, and T Pyxidis emitted their yellows and oranges. Closing his eyes, Maynard recalled how the old man stroked his goatee after learning that the stars of Tianmiao comprised Jason the Argonaut's mast in the ancient Greek constellation Argo Navis. The last image Maynard saw before he fell asleep was the glimmer in Ming's eyes after he said, "T Pyxidis is turning red."

The cooks were in the galley mocking the habits of gwei lo. They'd finished preparing the morning menu and were about to play an abbreviated round of mahjong before turning in to sleep until the first bell of the morning watch. Ming changed their nightly ritual by pointing to an ancient tome sitting beside a signals telescope. Excusing himself from the game, he said he wished to familiarize himself with the portents emanating from the celestial House of the Emperors.

Evelyn sat by a porthole gazing at her reflection. Half listening to the sound of water passing by the hull, she saw a sad smile and thought about how much she would like to stay aboard, skip the stop in Los Angeles, and sail on. The eyes in the image narrowed as she closed the curtains. "The men aboard this ship are not the people my uncle and his friends want me to spy on," she whispered. She turned out the light, put on her nightdress, and went to bed wondering how Adam would reply to a question that her guilt had not permitted her to ask when she had the opportunity: *How will my children's children remember me and the current crop of Griffins?*

Drifting off, she found herself mulling over what she had seen taking place aboard this mysterious ship. Her last conscious thought provided the answer to a question she had never thought to ask before: *What is the elusive quality that sets Dr. Adam Yeaton apart from all of the other men I have known?* "Ahh," she breathed, "he treats me as an equal."

Hopley was in the boys' cabin two doors down from her. He had received the first magazine installment of Charles Dickens's recently published *A Tale of Two Cities.* He'd no sooner started reading, "It was the best of times, it was the worst of times, it was the age of wisdom, it was the age of," than his eyelids began to droop. He put the rag aside, turned out the lamp, and fell into a dreamless sleep among his off-watch shipmates.

Ryan lay in his bunk across the hall. Yawning widely, he placed a bookmark in a compilation of essays. He blew out the lamp, ran a wet tongue over dry lips, adjusted the covers, and thought, *"Tomorrow I'll be meeting the kind of people Emerson must have been thinking about the day he wrote 'a foolish consistency is the hobgoblin of little minds.'"*

Willard and Adam stood over the table with Earl in the captain's spacious cabin. They were going over customs documents, bills of lading, and the list of items they planned to offload in the morning.

James stood beside a table in the wardroom on the other side of the captain's open door. Adjusting to the image in a large magnifying glass, he bent closer and ran a stubby index finger along a detailed chart of the Peruvian coast. Placing a pair of divider points over an area of interest, he straightened to ease his back and weighed the merits of sailing into a little-known harbor at the lowest tide of the year. Picking up a pencil, he plotted various ways to satisfy Earl's intention to find a sunken Spanish treasure galleon. His pencil scribbled notes while an ever-vigilant part of his brain assessed the sounds and motions that comprised the *Bride*'s current mood.

Above him in the wheelhouse, the binnacle lamp lit the helmsman's shadowed face. Keeping him awake and alert, two mates sat at the table playing crib.

Cabin lights lit the shrouds, bulwarks, and rigging beneath the clipper's great spread of tan canvas.

The dark sea claimed the stars of Argo Navis one by one, but not before the light emitted fifteen thousand years earlier by T Pyxidis reached tiny Earth. Massive solar eruptions had pushed the star's temperatures into the red spectrum, causing the orb's arterial glow to flare in a receptive eye. As T Pyxidis followed the Argonauts over the southern horizon, the glow assumed the color of spilled blood.

Long after the tall ship dwindled in the distance, the vast surface began to sparkle as the globe rotated beneath the speckled lamp of the Milky Way. Hours later, the broken ranks of rollers passing through the patch of sea so recently vacated moved aside as two vessels charged through the indifferent waters.

CHAPTER 9

Banning's Landing, San Pedro, 3 January, 10 a.m.

Phineas Banning stepped forward and extended his hand with a broad smile. "Good morning, gentlemen, welcome to sunny Southern California! I must compliment your master's handling of the Bride's arrival. I've never seen a docking go so smoothly. The sail drill, the hundred-and-eighty degree turn, and the soft landing were flawless!"

"Good morning to you," Earl said, taking Phineas's hand. "James has a flair for the dramatic. Fair breezes and favorable tides can make sailors of us all."

James had executed a maneuver only the most adept sailors dared to perform— turning a ship around in a confined space. The skills required to place the ship at a predetermined spot were enough to dissuade most mariners from attempting such a perilous feat. His landing had placed the ship's bow facing the open ocean, port side against the wharf with the keel in deep water at low tide. She was in position to sail away.

Ol' Bud pried out the wedges, the crew set aside hatch covers, rigged yards, and hauled stores to the hatches in the time it took to tie off the mooring lines. Twenty minutes later, the yards delivered swinging crates and barrels to waiting freight wagons. A soon as a wagon was loaded, another took its place.

Light, warm airs drifted over the starboard quarter. Gulls circled over men furling sails to the yards.

San Pedro Harbor, like most of the shoreline for miles in either direction, possessed wide tidal flats and estuaries providing abundant nutrients for a host of plants and animals.

"Ah, there goes a chevron of tree swallows," Phineas said, pointing to the darting birds.

They heard a clear call through the twittering backdrop. "Townsend's warbler," Earl said with disinterest.

"Not to be confused with that yellow-rumped flitting about over there," Phineas said, noting Earl's lack of enthusiasm for their favorite pastime.

Phineas wore the clothes of a well-dressed teamster and had the bearing of a man used to manual labor. Still in his twenties, he had made the transition from stagecoach driver to one of the most influential men in Southern California. He now owned the stage line, was founding a community, and seemed to be involved in every aspect of the social and commercial life of Los Angeles County.

The wharf that made it possible for ships to offload their cargoes was long and strong. His vision was the driving force that made it possible for ships and wagons to exchange wares from a dock.

Phineas stood apart from many of his contemporaries because he was able to maintain studied neutrality in his dealings with the secessionists. As a Unionist, he accepted that many of the people he traded with had strong beliefs contrary to his own. Making sure he held up his end of any bargain solidified his reputation for trustworthiness and drew people of all persuasions to him.

"Dr. Griffin has sent transportation for the ladies," he said, gesturing to men waiting by a carriage parked off to the side. His eyes narrowed at the mention of Dr. Griffin. Noticing movement nearby, he stopped before he could make a potentially embarrassing comment. Caught under the scrutiny of Evelyn's green eyes, he realized she'd been listening. Her amused expression suggested she knew she was the reason he'd checked himself.

"Ahem, ah, there they are," he said, making an elaborate bow to Evelyn and Myra. "Welcome to San Pedro, ladies. I trust you had a safe passage."

Keeping eye contact with Phineas, Evelyn laughed as she returned his bow. "Thank you, and yes, we had a safe passage."

Her merry eyes told Phineas more than he would have thought possible under the circumstances. She didn't appear to care what Phineas thought of her uncle, and he thought she might even agree with him. He shifted his attention to Myra. "Good morning."

Myra, having returned to form, said nothing. Her haughty stare reminded Phineas of a turkey hen he'd once seen guarding a poult. He shook his head, blinked the image away, and smiled brightly at Evelyn.

She returned his smile with a puzzled expression and glanced at Myra. *What?* her eyes said before she turned to Earl.

"Thank you for being so kind to us. We'll be seeing you again tomorrow at Benjamin Wilson's ranchero."

"Yes, and you're welcome, Evelyn," Earl said with a bow. "We'll see you there." He removed an envelope from his pocket and handed it to her. "Please give this to your Uncle John."

"I will," she said and put it in a purse.

"Miss Landers, I hope you'll be feeling better soon," Earl said with a dignified bow. All he received in return was cold stare.

The warmth in Phineas' smile dropped a few degrees. *I'd wager I'm not the first to fantasize about squeezing that scraggly neck!*

Evelyn directed a fixed smile at Phineas. "Will you be joining us?"

Feeling highly entertained by the unspoken messages being passed around, he nodded. "Yes, I will. I'm curious to see what Earl is putting in those wagons."

He stood aside while Earl and Adam said their goodbyes to the ladies, saw the pair to the carriage, and waved them on their way to Los Angeles.

Phineas led Earl and Adam to the office. The room was bright and offered expansive views of the harbor. Inside were two desks, a station clock, and a Thomas Cole, titled *New York from the Palisades*. The men walked past the clerk's desk, cabinets, a large safe, a small library, and a bulldog stove. Phineas took a seat behind his desk, waited for the Yeatons to arrange themselves in two captain's chairs, and asked how long they planned to stay. Earl answered while placing a Wells Fargo draft on the desk. "Should be enough to cover ten days' moorage fees. I'll write you another if we stay longer. We'll spend the weekend with the Wilsons. We plan to stay for a few days after the shipment is unveiled to his family and friends."

Phineas slipped the check under a polished burl. "The wagons will be going today. They should be there before dinnertime. It'll take the better part of three hours to get them up to the San Gabriels. Two if going by carriage. I have one ready for you."

He'd known Earl for several years and had learned to be patient while listening to Earl's plans. Earl was a man who liked to keep his cards close to his chest and reveal them one at a time. His plans usually had several unanticipated plays.

"Thank you. I'd prefer to have a coach with two teams of sound horses. Adam and two boys will ride with me. I'd also like to have saddle mounts for four outriders."

Folding his hands in his lap, Phineas leaned back and watched Earl put his second card on the table.

"The coach will be carrying the more valuable pieces. One of my men will ride along with your driver for security."

Phineas's eyes narrowed even more as he waited for Earl to tell him what was going on behind the scenes. A shutter closed on his relaxed view of Earl, and another he preferred not to open was showing cracks. Suppressing a sigh, he sat up and listened to what the enigmatic Captain Yeaton had to add.

"The freight wagons we don't plan to keep with us can return in the morning. They'll be carrying six-hundred-litre pipes. Ryan is expecting them. One of the wagons will be staying with us at the Wilsons. The coach driver can return with the wagons.

"I've made arrangements to return by another route, Phineas. I would rather only you and a couple of others know this. I plan to visit Rancho La Brea with Henry Hancock early next week. José Rocha has pulled artifacts out of his tar pits. I think he's had time to clean them off and pack them for me. We should be there for the remainder of the week.

"We'll also need your assistance in delivering a surgical ward and the contents of a field hospital to the Sisters of Charity. Is it possible for us to get that started today too?"

Phineas nodded and wrote notes on a pad. The cards were piling up. *How many more do we have to see before we know how he plans to play the hand?*

"I know this is short notice, Phineas, and I didn't tell you what I have in mind in writing," Earl continued. "There are people in the area who would divert those hospital units to the secessionists. I felt it would be better for you not to know these units were coming. You may wish to send them under armed guard. I'll pay the shipping."

Phineas snapped the pencil on the pad "No, Earl, you will not be paying for the shipping. I'll send them up there under armed guard. Who knows? I may need the contents of those crates too! I haven't been the same since being run over by that freight wagon in San Francisco a few years ago." He shook his head and smiled. "Once Sister Scholastica gets her hands on the contents of those crates, it'll take more than an armed regiment of secessionists to get her to release them! Who's paying for those hospital units, by the way?"

"The Union. Consider the gesture a contribution to your community," Earl said, sitting up straighter and squinting at the harbor.

Phineas followed Earl's gaze and reached for the draft. He crushed the check and dropped it in a quahog shell. Earl and Adam took their eyes off the new arrivals at the sound of Phineas scratching the underside of his desk. He carefully propped the burning match on the crumpled check. "You owe us nothing, Earl. I'll take care of the customs fees, arrange a coach for you, see that the freight wagons arrive safely at the hospital, and arm the wagons headed for the Wilsons. I'll also supply you with a brace of shotguns. Your men will be riding on my best saddle mounts. The Bride can stay right where she is. I've a feeling she'll need armed protection too," he added soberly, his good humor at seeing his friend evaporating. "Now show your last card, and tell me why those Harrington clippers caused you to stiffen."

Hours later, Earl heaved a sigh as he watched the harbor disappear behind the crest of a low hill. The masts had been lost from view for a while. He snorted. *I must be experiencing the same feelings a parent has after leaving a child at home.* He felt slightly comforted knowing *his* child was in Phineas Banning's care. *"Can't control what's out of my hands,"* he mused thinking of his adversaries. The *Bear* and the *Shadow* had dropped their anchors and sent boats ashore long before Earl could complete loading the wagons for the trip to the Wilson ranch. "What mischief are they up to now?" he whispered, feeling disquieted.

The coach made good time along the Bluff Road from San Pedro and into the hills east of Los Angeles. The sun was low on the horizon by the time they approached the Santa Fe Trail junction. The route ran east a ways on the old trail before making the short hop to their destination, Rancho Huerta de Cuati, or, as Wilson preferred to call it, Lake Vineyard.

Earl passed the time thinking of what the next few days had in store. *Thank God for lists*, he added, patting the breast pocket of his traveling coat. He smiled. *My life has become a series of lists, it seems.* He went over the list he'd had to go through before departure. First, he'd arranged with Ryan and Phineas to keep the *Bride* protected while he was away. Next he made sure all the items in two separate lists were stowed on freighters for the trips to Los

Angeles and the San Gabriels. The list and valuables destined for the Wilsons he carried with him on the coach. Stowing them had taken much too long, he felt, dreading the possible consequences.

Returning to the present, he found unexpected comfort in the company of his dozing companions. The sun's dusty rays softened their resting faces and tempered his anxiety. Earl sat on the right side of the rear-facing seat with Munenori. Mike sat across from Earl beside Adam.

Twenty minutes later, the coach leveled off after descending the hill. Tall palms and fragrant shrubs grew in abundance on the lush plain. The landscape felt close. Detecting a change, Earl picked up a moist, earthy scent accompanied by the territorial calls of red-winged blackbirds. Leaning forward, he heard other bird species chirping in the thickening vegetation. He also heard Ralph Crompton, the coach's driver, speaking to Tom Flanagan. "We're heading into the El Monte Island Dip, so you may want to grab a persuader." The island was a marshy area at the lower end of the San Gabriel waterway. The marsh was a welcome relief to travelers who saw the fertile plain as the end of the often-barren Santa Fe Trail. Willow thickets and cattails tall enough to hide mounted riders lined the road.

Tom reached back and removed two coach guns from a case packed among the items lashed to the roof. He placed one beside Ralph and the other between his knees. He also flipped the latches on a second case. Two additional shotguns were now within reach.

The stage driver's caution was worth heeding. El Monte harbored a concentration of the most ardent secessionists, cutthroats, and thieves in California. Georgia crackers and inbred Texans comprised most of the town's residents. Their end of the trail resembled what occurred after spring floods dumped loads of detritus on alluvial fans, and as a result, the ramshackle town of El Monte grew larger with each seasonal deposit of white trash. Anyone who saw the federal government as a nuisance fit right in. The newcomers who enjoyed the most welcome were those who wanted to divide the state and break up the Union. Many saw the robbing of travelers as a legitimate means of raising money for the Confederate cause. Others were secessionists in name only. The creed they adhered to was the one defining humanity's lowest common denominator: the strong take whatever they want from the weak.

Tom was familiar with the type of people the driver was referring to and had seen what poverty did to the human spirit in the depressed villages of coastal Maine. He'd learned how to handle firearms from the son of a Maine Yankee who'd grown up using guns for protection and hunting. The young man had lived through several life-threatening altercations in his twenty-seven years. He was a foremast deckhand who would as soon reeve a block in a gale as in fair weather and had proven to be a steady man. Today he was holding a loaded William Moore double-barreled ten-gauge. The fourteen-inch open choke provided maximum shot spread, and Tom had a pouch beside him that held twenty loads of double-aught buckshot. Each two-ounce load held eighteen .33-caliber pellets. Fired at close range, both barrels were capable of delivering a quick dispersing hail of lead. He deferred the problem of having to reload paper cartridges and primers by leaning the loaded backup on the seat between himself and Ralph. Tom subscribed to the belief that the best form of life insurance resided in his hands.

Earl's lips curled into a mirthless smile on hearing the shotgun's butt plate thump between his shoulder blades. *Tom Flanagan*, he thought, *sent to sea because his father couldn't curb the boy's wild ways and run a Camden building supply company at the same time. Well, he fits right in with the Bride's crew and hasn't been in a knife fight since we left Rockland!*

Earl shook his head and had a peek through the coach windows. He liked what he saw, including the new man who Bill said fit right in. Bill, Kato, Maynard, and Roy Horie flanked the coach on horses. Roy had come aboard with Bud and Colton in Vancouver. With the exception of Kato, they carried the new Spencer repeating rifles, Colt Navy .36's, .44's, and belt knives. Earl and his crew wore tan denim shirts and pants. The shirts had the Yeaton crests sewn on the left breast pockets. Bill started calling the garments "ranger clothes," and the name stuck. Earl's group wore Stetsons, with the exception of Munenori and Kato, who'd opted for colorful bandanas tied as skullcaps. Everyone wore durable, flat-heeled half boots. Thinking they might be able to turn their rifles into carbines, Bill and Roy had run up to Phineas's wagon shop before the party pulled out and set to work with a couple of hacksaws. They clamped the rifles in vises and cut the barrels back six inches for a better scabbard fit.

Kato wore swords. His long sword was in a sheath resting between his shoulders and held upright by a chest harness. His smaller sword was in a sheath clipped to his belt.

Munenori had unclipped his short sword and placed it on the seat beside him. His long sword was in his duffel up on the roof. Earl, Adam, and Mike had .22 revolvers.

Earl eased back in the seat and went over in his mind what Adam had told him while they were waiting for Bill and Roy. He had been standing by himself on the edge of the wharf watching shorebirds. "This is the first time I've had a chance to be alone with you this morning, Uncle."

Must be serious, Earl had thought at the time. He'd seen Adam's expression while the men loaded a crate bound for Wilson's ranch. He waited, expecting Adam to tell him why he was reluctant to let it go.

Instead, Adam surprised him.

"Evelyn's brother is in Jules Harrington's graduation class at the Point, and Jules has invited the Griffins to the wedding in Camden."

Earl smiled despite the added worries that bit of news created. *Should be fun watching Adam introduce Evelyn to the single women who are awaiting his return.* Earl sniffed, glanced outside, and had another look at his nephew. *Handsome fellow*, he thought and smiled again, this time over how much the young man resembled his mother. *As for the crate, he'll either tell me how he feels about what's in it, or he won't.*

Adam came out of a euphoric doze and saw his uncle. He was barely conscious of having just listened to Field's *Nocturne No. 5* playing in his head. He blinked himself awake in time to see Earl's lips curl. "What are you smiling at? Could it be how excited Phineas got after you presented him with a new Singer sewing machine?"

"No, but the memory does make me smile. Did you hear him exclaim that his wife will keep him in butter tarts for the rest of his life now that she's the first person in the Los Angeles basin to have one of those?" Earl said with a laugh.

Adam didn't get a chance to reply before an unfamiliar voice called for the driver to pull up.

CHAPTER 10

Santa Fe Trail, El Monte, 3 January, 4:00 p.m.

Tom laid the gun across his lap and cocked both hammers the moment he saw riders emerging from the roadside willows. His mates sat up a little straighter, kept their hands away from their weapons, and reined in their horses.

Earl, Adam, and Mike palmed their pistols and held them below the coach's windows. Munenori laid the sword across his knees and tried to concentrate on what his sensei had said about mortal combat. Feeling the onset of nausea and praying no one would notice, Mike glanced at Earl and responded to his captain's wink with a sober nod.

Three mounted highwaymen were on either side of the coach. Two on each side of the lead horses, two in the middle, and two more brought up the rear. Two footpads stepped out of the cattails and came around their mounted cohorts to take up positions beside the coach.

Mike's shallow breath ended with a hiccup when he spotted a shiny barrel rounding a horse's flank. The threat posed by the hand holding the .44 became dreadfully personal. Prickles of fear spread from the top of his head to the tips of his fingers. The enormity of the peril posed by the deadly tube's proximity put a severe clamp on the youngster's innards. The prospect of not making it through the next few minutes sprung a leak in his self-control. He felt faint. The little pistol felt heavy all of a sudden and would have become dead weight had he not cast a frightened glance at his leader. Earl's calm gray eye winked once more. Bolstered by his captain's response, Mike realized that if he lived to tell the tale, he'd probably leave out how a wink kept him from wilting. Pushing back on the gut-wrenching burden threatening to crush his will, he took a deep breath, swallowed bile, and fingered his trigger. *We're boxed in and Capt'n Earl's cooler 'n a cucumber.*

The coach came to a stop with Tom's gun pointing at the right knee of a mounted highwaymen. The rider was facing forward and waiting for the signal to shoot Roy in the back. Roy was beside the lead horses. Tom's eyes narrowed at two bandits who rode up and reined their horses to a stop, blocking the road.

"No need for y'all to get excited, now," the lanky rider in front of Roy drawled as he sidled his horse over to a lead mare and grabbed the reins. His lean face held a pair of overly bright eyes rimmed with bushy graying brows. His companion held Maynard in check with a six-shooter resting on the saddle horn.

The talker brought his pistol to bear on Tom. The man's tobacco-stained beard gave Tom the impression that the man's mouth had shit itself. Keeping his face straight, Tom sat and waited.

"You can ease off on the reins, driver. I can take it from here. You may as well set your brake. We could be here for a spell."

From the corner of his eye, Tom watched Ralph set the brake, wrap the reins around the handle, and sit back. Out in the cattails, red-winged blackbirds continued squawking at one another. Dragonfly wings rasped in and out of the tense figures. A horse shook off some flies, and the clink of bridle rings sounded loud in the still air. Mourning doves cooed from branches spreading over the sun-dappled scene. Tom kept his eyes fastened on the man doing all the talking and thought of a name for him.

"What we're going to do here is relieve y'all of your possibles and be on our way. Now don't that sound reasonable?" The .44 in his hand was a black tunnel aimed at Tom's heart.

Tom's reply was a resigned shrug. *If I die today, I die,* he thought, *and that'll be that. Seems odd for it to happen here at the hands of people whose backgrounds probably aren't a whole lot different from my own. If Daddy hadn't a shipped me off with Capt'n Earl, I might have ended up just like the man on the other side of the gun over there. Shootin' a man can't be a whole lot different than killin' wild game. First time for everythin', I suppose.*

Tipping his head and frowning over what he was about to do, Tom shrugged again and waited some more.

"That's better. We can all calm down and get on with what needs doin'," the talker said. Having misread Tom's passive response, he turned to spit a gob of tobacco juice off to the side.

Taking exception to Mr. Mouthy's attitude and the way he puckered his lips, Tom tightened his grip on the shotgun and squeezed one of the triggers. The distance of ten feet was nowhere near enough for buckshot to disperse properly. The rider's thigh took the full load as it bored a wet hole through cloth, meat, bone, saddle fender, and horse ribs. Tom figured the gun's roar would catch Mr. Mouthy in mid-pucker. He was correct. He thought he saw the man gasp and inhale his plug as he snapped his head around. No matter; the last thing the renegade saw was a yellow flame shoving hot lead through everything between his shirt and the back of his vest. He may have noted the gaseous eruption this caused before his life drained away with the liquefied gel burbling out of his shattered backbone.

The next ten seconds defied the survivors' ability to recount what actually happened. Everyone agreed Tom's second shot must have occurred after Kato charged the rider covering him. Tom dropped the gun that killed the leader and grabbed the one beside him. Thumbing back the hammers on his swing to the right, he clipped the side of Ralph's head and fired both barrels.

The rider covering Maynard didn't have time to react to Tom's first shot before the effects of the second showered his right side with blood and gore. The rider lost interest in Maynard long enough for Maynard to pull his gun and say, "Welcome to the surprise of your day." The body shot drilled a .44-caliber dimple just below the man's left nipple. A second later, Maynard found himself sprawled on the ground beside the man he'd just killed. *How'd I get here?* he wondered. He became vaguely aware of men yelling, gunfire close by, and a spreading numbness on his left side. Pushing himself away from the flailing hooves, he felt a sharp pain radiating out of a cracked rib.

Earl's crew seemed to do everything all at once from there. The assault was sudden and lethal. The shocked attackers had no time to recover from Tom's first blast before their supposed victims were attacking with deadly earnest.

Kato had already picked his target and knew what he was going to do if given the opportunity. Tom provided the opening he needed. He kicked his horse into the rider covering him. The man fired. A burning sting seared a fiery path across Kato's abdomen as he cleared the long sword and stood in the stirrups. The gunman's second shot nicked Kato's thigh and smashed the cantle. "Dai akuma!" Kato exclaimed over the sounds of gunfire and whinnying horses. "Die, devil!" he repeated in English. Using all the power in his arms, he swung on the diagonal. Keeping his eyes fastened on those of his dumbfounded opponent, he felt the razor-sharp blade cleave the man's shoulder, upper arm, ribs, heart, lungs, and lower sacks before exiting near the navel. "Hai!" he yelled as the gaping wound released the man's last breath along with the contents of his organs. He tightened his lips at how quickly the bandit's predatory gleam turned into disbelief. Jerking on the reins, he lost eye contact as the head of his helpless foe fell with the severed remains spilling off the saddle.

Bill and the thief covering him saw what Kato had done. Their stares followed the eviscerated body's short trip to the ground. Not knowing it was possible to dismember a body this way, they were too stunned to move or hear the splat of loose entrails landing on the gut pile. Although no sound came out of the gaping hole, the mouth jawed like a fish out of water, opening and closing as if trying to express the torment seen through eyes that flicked back and forth from a twitching leg to the severed arm whose hand still held a smoking gun. Their horses not only saw but were also the first to smell what happened. Their reaction was much swifter. Bill and the bandit were on nearly uncontrollable horses soon after Kato jacked his horse's head around and focused on the gunman standing by the coach. The confused man had raised a hand to wipe the wheel rider's blood spatter off the back of his neck.

Earl and Mike fired several shots through the coach wall before Kato's second flash of steel severed the man's wet hand and sliced his unsuspecting head right off its shoulders. A quick nod to Earl, and Kato was seeking another target. No need. All four men on his side of the coach were down.

Tom's third blast drowned out Adam's first shot. Squeezing off a second round at the man standing beside the coach, Adam heard Munenori yell. The boy jumped past him and planted his sword in the footman's upper chest before the man realized he had been shot twice.

The mounted rider above Munenori had knocked Maynard out of the saddle. He was about to shoot the boy when Tom's swivel introduced him to two loads of double aught. The man was dead before he hit the ditch. Just as well, because his lower jaw, most of his chest, and all of his shredded upper body parts were scattered among the bird nests, willows, horses, and riders in the rear.

Tom's last contribution to the fight compounded the horses' confusion. They tried to flee after the explosive effects of Tom's third blast added a sense of urgency to their desire to get away. They would have too if their riders hadn't kept a firm grip on their reins. The blood-smeared horses were keening, spinning, and crow hopping in their efforts to escape from the painful bits pulling their heads toward the foul remains of Kato's kill.

"I better get busy, or there'll be none left for me!" Bill hollered. He let Mr. Colt join the deadly conversation just as the man covering him fired. Both missed.

Bill and his assailant quickly discovered how difficult it is to shoot from a maddened horse. They added loud cursing to their exchange of gunfire. It was a standoff until the remaining bandit fired off all five rounds in his Baby Dragoon. Driving his horse in close enough for the muzzle flash to scorch the entry hole, Bill dropped his Navy's sixth shot into the other man's brisket.

All the horses had come unhinged by then and were rearing, bucking, and trying to run. Roy slid to the ground and tied the quivering lead horses' heads to the wagon tongue. The wheel teams slipped their traces but weren't going anywhere. The horse Tom had shot wheezed through the hole in its side, and the four riderless ones found each other and ran until the firing stopped.

Maynard got up and felt along his side where the bullet had smacked him on the way by. He spit grit on the dead bandit. "I'll be sore for a few days, but otherwise . . . I'm still standing."

"Sweet Mother of Jesus!" Bill exclaimed, getting his horse back under control and having a look around. "For a moment there I thought I was a goner." Whatever Bill said next Roy drowned out with a shot behind the ear of the wounded horse. "Not worth repeatin'," he sighed to his distracted listeners.

The eight would-be highwaymen were either dead or dying. The dying one was the first hit. He lay where he had fallen. The man's confused whimpering and horrified glances at his amputated limb suggested he was having difficulty comprehending what had become of his leg.

Earl stepped out of the coach and tilted his hat back. "Thanks, Tom."

Tom glanced at Earl and rammed home another load. Ralph appeared to be in a trance and was patting his head as if he expected his hair to be on fire. Tom's last shot had not only removed Ralph's Stetson but his hearing as well. Ralph didn't know he was bleeding until he felt a sticky collar.

"What a mess," Earl complained, wrinkling his nose at the sight of the mutilated bodies, shivering horses, and crookedly smiling crew. "Those smiles'll change to a dull awareness of what *could* have happened to you if I don't keep you busy." He found it odd that the blackbirds continued squabbling among themselves as if nothing had happened. For all he knew, they were testing each other's defenses while the guns were going off.

"Domo arigato, Kato, anata wa watashi no jinse o sukutta." ("Thank you, Kato. Life mine you save"), Earl said, hoping he was using the correct words.

"Do itashi mashite" ("You are welcome"), he received in reply.

Peering through the coach's open door, he saw Mike absently stroking his pistol's handle. "I just shot a man," the boy murmured.

"You did good. Now put the gun away before you shoot yourself. Get off your duff, and make yourself useful. Go fetch—" Earl stopped and caught his breath when he saw a splintered .44-caliber hole on the interior side of the door. Leaning inside, he saw the exit hole on the other side of the coach. "Did you see the footman fire the shot?" he asked Mike.

"No," the boy said, closing the door and staring at how close the bullet had come to rupturing his gut sack.

Munenori came around the back of the coach holding his dripping sword. He bowed to his cousin. "Watashi wa kyo, hite o koroshimashita." ("I killed a man today.")

"Hai," Kato said, returning the bow. Pointing at the sword, he held out his hand. Munenori passed it over. Kato rinsed the blood off in the cattails and cleaned the blade on the clothing of a dead bandit. Returning the sword to Munenori in his open palms, he bowed.

Bowing back, Munenori took the sword and slipped it into its sheath. "Sanzoku Kiri," Munenori said, naming the sword Bandit Killer.

"Hmm, hmm, hmm," Earl said, "Mike. Get out of the coach, and go fetch the horses. Take Munenori with you. We all in one piece?"

"Nope," Tom said, opening a breach. "Maynard and Kato got hit. Ralph is going to need stitches. I clipped his temple with the end of a barrel just before I fired my last shots." Tom turned to Ralph. "His hands are squeezing his knees to keep from shaking. He may see what's on the ground in front of the lead horses, but I don't think the inside of his head has caught up with how Mr. Mouthy got there."

"Huh?" Earl said, glancing at Tom. *How did he come up with that name?* he wondered. He followed Ralph's gaze to the front and saw Maynard spit on Mr. Mouthy's corpse.

"I'll be all right," Maynard said, coming around the lead horses and raising his shirt to expose a furrow of torn flesh.

Kato lifted his shirt too. He had a weeping black-and-blue blister forming on his abdomen. He also had two red holes in a pant leg where a bullet had torn his thigh.

Adam climbed a wheel and rummaged around for his bag.

Bill wasn't ready to stop talking and raised an arm. "After a while there, I don't think we could clearly see each other. Bugger missed the meat." Bill had four smoldering holes—two on an elbow and two next to his ribs.

"Small wonder," Earl said. "Lots of lead flying a moment ago. I see you managed to ruin one of my uniform blouses."

Several pairs of eyes scanned Bill, who was suddenly sheepish and had begun rubbing spittle into the glowing cloth. "I'm not the only one who has holes in his clothes," he mumbled. He flicked his fingers at the blood and pieces of flesh on his shirt. "Did I get any on my face?"

Earl shook his head and walked over to the dying bandit. He checked to see if there were any surprises in the man's hands. It didn't take much to know the fellow would never be holding anything again. *Shock will probably kill him quicker than his injury*, Earl thought. Removing the pistol and belt knife, Earl arranged the injured man in a more comfortable position. He came to rest facing Tom, who was tamping a load of buckshot.

"I seen better days, ain't I?" the thief asked, holding Tom's gaze.

Tom sucked air through a side of his mouth, put the gun down, and started loading a second shotgun.

"Probably," Earl said, folding back damp cloth to get a clearer view of the mangled stump. He saw a trickle of blood dribbling out of the exposed blood vessels. *Too late to stop the flow in time to save him.*

The dying man's eyes suddenly grew frightened. Kato had raised a hand over his shoulder, but instead of grabbing his sword handle, he removed his bandana, dipped it in a roadside puddle, and offered it to Earl.

"Mind telling us who you are?" Earl asked as he wiped away the oily sweat gathering on the man's bloodstained face.

"We're part of Charlie Wilkins's crew. A fast rider told Charlie you were comin' through here with a load of valuables we could convert to Confederate gold," he said, glancing at Tom.

"Really?"

"Uh . . . no, not really. I'll be dead in a few minutes, so may's well tell the truth for once in my sorry life. We don't like Yankees and figured you was fair game."

"You were planning to kill us, weren't you?"

"Yeah," the man grimaced, exposing rotten teeth coated with algae.

"Well, you and your friends didn't do your homework before you decided to hunt Maine Yankees." Earl's voice had more steel in it than his crew were used to hearing.

"What's that?" the man asked with his last breath.

"We can be just as ornery and unpredictable as any goddamned Georgia crackers."

Earl's stony expression remained the same long after death turned the lights out in the man's eyes. He stood up and moved to where he could speak to his men. "If anyone asks about what happened here, tell them we were ambushed and killed the men sent against us. That's it. Nothing more. If the driver talks, so be it. I don't think he saw much. He's deaf, has a headache, appears to be addled, and is not likely to be believed even if he tells the truth." Earl's tone was more than enough to get everyone moving. "Gather up the horses, and tie the bodies across the saddles for the return to El Monte. I want to see where they came from. You're the driver now, Mike. I'll take your seat, and Ralph will sit in the coach. I want to see what's in front of us for a change."

Half listening to the mourning doves cooing from a safe distance, Adam glanced at Earl and saw a man back in command. He finished threading a needle and lifted his eyes. "Ready, Kato?"

Since the ambush had taken place close the village's outskirts, the residents expected to see their men returning after the firing stopped. They did not expect to see them arrive in pieces slung across bloodstained saddles.

Earl and his grim companions led the dead past piles of broken trail gear and hovels made out of wagons stripped of their boards. Women and children dressed in homespun rags pushed hide doors aside and stepped onto the dusty road. Desperate mothers clutched little ones trying to follow the caravan into what passed for the town center. Earl's coach came to a stop beside the thieves and gunslingers lining the slatted walls of seedy saloons. Painted ladies cast nervous glances between the hard faces and hands gripping holstered pistols. The sneaky slunk off to the best places from which to shoot and dive for cover. Shoppers gathered on the boardwalk to gawk. Charlie Wilkins was among them. He leaned on a porch post in front of the general store with a hand resting on his Colt.

Phineas Banning had mentioned El Monte in passing. Not expecting Earl to visit the place, he had described Almira Hale and her useless husband, Nickie. Phineas said she was the oldest living resident of that squalid place because she was the quickest to assess situations and thus managed to avoid becoming another casualty of the town's senseless shootings.

Almira crossed the street and kept darting glances at what Earl assumed to be Charlie Wilkins. Following her gaze, he glanced at Charlie's bitter face and the hand gripping the holstered gun. Opening the coach door, he stepped into the street, keeping one eye on Charlie and the other on Almira. "You must be Almira Hale."

"Yes," she admitted, her eyes skittering between the two men. She'd been around gnarly men for years and knew the ones who were delivering the dead could take fire, not flinch, and give as good as they got. Charlie had met his match, and she had to act right quick before things got any worse.

She felt Earl sizing her up and watched him nod to the bag of bones trailing along behind. He waved a hand. "There are going to be quite a few more funerals if that fellow on the porch gets his way and tries to dry-gulch us for doing you all a favor." He turned to address the stick figure. "And you are Nickie."

She glanced at Charlie in time to see his eyes shift to what was left of Mr. Mouthy. The corpse's head and legs hung out of a saddle blanket draped over a horse. The street grew quiet, and in the stillness that followed, the horse shook off flies and dislodged the man's last chaw. Mr. Mouthy's plug hit the dirt with a moist splat. Blood continued to drip after his tobacco-stained oval vomited a backlog of jellied blood and gore. The mortified widows got no relief when they turned away and noticed bloody puddles forming under the other blankets slung across the dripping saddle gear.

Nickie's Adam's apple was too busy bobbing up and down for him to give Earl more than an acknowledging grunt. He wasn't paying much attention to Earl. He'd come to a stop between Charlie and the strangers, and his frightened eyes were on the hand squeezing the butt of Charlie's pistol. That put a damper on his ability to keep track of what was going on around him. Things were moving too fast for Ol' Nickie, so he missed hearing the shotgun hammers snapping into place. They were plenty loud enough for Charlie to hear them over the leaking corpses, clink of bridles, trace chains, and snorting steeds. Charlie's hand gripped the post faster than Nickie's bewildered brain could follow.

Ignoring Earl's approach, Nickie focused on the inexplicable changes taking place in Charlie. Charlie looked like he'd seen a ghost. Nickie followed Charlie's stunned expression to the pair of snake eyes resting on Tom's lap. The sight of those flat black holes aimed at the bridge of Charlie's nose caused Nickie's stomach to send a squirt of stomach juice past his tonsils.

Oblivious to Charlie's predicament, Almira raised her voice over Nickie's sudden fit of gagging. "What happened out in the Dip?"

"We killed the men sent to ambush us," was all she got for an answer.

She saw the dead men's reins handed over, nodded to Earl's goodbye, and watched him climb in the coach and leave.

Her eyes on Charlie, she addressed her husband. "That, my Nickie, is one hombre peligroso! He's a dangerous man. Anyone who goes hunting him should dig their grave first."

The wagons from the coast caught up with Earl's party while they were in El Monte, so a heavily armed group veered north off the Old Santa Fe Trail. Not wanting any more to do with Earl's party, Ralph rode with the freighters.

The sun was a brass shield hovering over the western horizon.

Earl twisted and tilted his hat brim. "The glare brings your facial features into sharper focus," he said before looking past Adam and Munenori.

Calmed by how the warm yellow rays had the opposite effect on the distant landscape's natural features, he made an observation. "The honey-tinged air reflecting off the San Gabriels forces the shadows to retreat into shadings of lesser light. No wonder the people who've been here for a while live on mañnana time. It's sublime."

"Not for us, Uncle?" Adam asked, dropping a fist on Earl's knee.

"No." Earl's thin smile held no warmth. "I prefer to live elsewhere."

"Harrington's men set up the ambush," Adam said, glancing up and catching his uncle's nod. "They're not going to stop, are they?"

Earl cleared his throat and scanned each pair of clear eyes before speaking to their expectant faces. "No. By rights, today's attack should have ended it for them. We'd be dead and lying in a wet ditch if it weren't for Tom and Kato. We were lucky this time."

Taking a deep breath and savoring another pass at the beautiful setting, he exhaled slowly. "From this point forward, we play each card as they're dealt. I've managed to stay away from the Harringtons and their friends for over twenty years. Now they're raping and killing innocent women, fomenting the dissolution of the Union, and trying to kill us over a supposition. They don't know what became of the bonds," he said with the same steel in his voice he had used on the dying outlaw. He moved his lips into a smile reeking of danger. "There are other things going on that I haven't yet had the pleasure of figuring out," he hissed, "and I doubt if we'll learn what they are before we return to the East Coast. What we went through this afternoon was the opening skirmish in a whole line of battles to come."

"Yes," his nephew stated, raising his voice over the creaking leather springs. "And in the meantime we deal with 'em as we find 'em!"

"Right," Earl said, lapsing into silence.

Ramon Diaz, Benjamin Wilson's ranch supervisor, was present when Earl's party rolled into Lake Vineyard's yard.

"Buenas noches, señores, bienvenitos a Rancho Huertea of the raccoons!" he said by way of greeting. He waited for the coach to come to a stop before opening the door.

"Buenos noches, Señor Diaz," Earl answered with a weary smile. "Siempre un placer a verte otra vez." ("Always a pleasure to see you again.")

Ramón pointed at the bullet holes and thanked Earl for sending a rider ahead with news of what had transpired in the Dip. Ramón's normally cheerful face assumed a mock sober cast. "The coyotes are fewer, and that is a good thing," he said, crossing himself.

Smiling broadly in anticipation of the introductions to come, Ramón was unprepared for what he saw in Tom Flanagan's gray eyes. *This muchacho is a killer.*

Forcing his smile to stay in place, he turned to the Japanese cousins, and with Earl translating, said hello. Ramón let his eyes linger on their unfamiliar faces. *Si*, he observed, *a pair of diamondbacks: still one moment and quick as lightning the next.* He listened while Earl spoke to the pair in Japanese. They bowed with respect to Ramón. "*Christos*," he breathed, and with a glance at Earl, bowed just as deeply. Seeing their surprise, he offered to shake their hands. Asking Earl to translate, Ramón said, "Que hueva joven mas grande!" ("These young men have big balls!") He was delighted to see their smiling acceptance of his good intentions. He switched to heavily accented English, and addressed the Japanese. "You I like!" This time all three bowed together. To Ramón's relief, the rest of the introductions went with a lot less fanfare.

He told Earl that Don Benito, a nickname for Benjamin Wilson, was with his wife, Margaret, and pointed to a vat house nestled into a low hill. "The Wilsons are inside bottling one of the sherry solera casks. They're running behind. Getting ready for the party is taking longer than expected. A dozen six-hundred-liter casks destined for the Bride are sitting on the loading dock. Six will stay aboard the ship for two years."

The practice had become quite common among oenophiles after an eighteenth-century captain had found an errant barrel of Madeira aboard his ship. The cask wasn't offloaded as planned and had traveled through the tropics for several months. Whoever had finally opened the cask and tried the wine had a pleasant surprise. Exposure to tropical temperatures enhanced the unique characteristics that distinguished the wine from others. After that, many captains started carrying wines on voyages around the world, and referred to them as *vina da roda*, loosely translated as "wines of the round voyage."

"We have made arrangements for the mules, horses, and crew," Ramón continued. "You and your nephew will be staying in the house. We cleared a wagon shed for you to use while you are here. The cookhouse has dinner ready for your men. They will sleep in a bunkhouse. I have been asked to take you inside to your rooms, show you your baths, and invite you to dine with Señor Wilson and Señora Margaret. They will be down soon. Leave everything right here. I will take care of your men and the contents of the wagons. The shed is over there," he said pointing to a building off to the side. "The crates will be offloaded and arranged on the floor. My men will see to loading the casks for the return trip. We'll do that tonight. We will feed and stable the livestock. The drivers can leave first thing in the morning.

"Maybe after dinner we can smoke cigarillos, drink that fine oloroso the Don is bottling, and plan the deaths of more coyotes, no?" he asked with a big smile.

"Ramón, you haven't changed since we met in '56. As much as I would like to do all you ask, I have only a few days to get what I need done and then, as always, must be on my way."

"Muy amigo," Ramon said, shrugging and raising his hands in a helpless gesture, "we see you so little and for too short a time when you appear. You should stay here. I have a fine señnorita in mind for you. We should talk."

Ramón's infectious grin was like a balm rubbing away Earl's fatigue. "Well, a nightcap under the stars might be good," he said, managing another smile. "Just show me to my room for now."

Several hours later, Earl and Ramon lounged in hide chairs beneath a starry sky and conversed in Spanish among the items left out for Wilson's party. A bottle and a pack of cigarillos were within reach. The only sign that two people sat in the dark came from the rosy glow that lit their faces each time they had a drag.

Ramon took a puff, tapped the ash, and pointed the tip at a shadowy figure. "Isn't that your nephew crossing the yard?" he asked in a low tone.

"Yes," Earl whispered. "He just went into the storage shed and I think I know why."

"He lit a lantern, muy compadre. Should we go see what he is doing?"

"No, Ramon. We stay here." Earl shifted positions and asked, "Do you believe in sprits?"

"Si."

"Do you honor the dead?"

"Si. Just because I live with gringos, most of whom do not honor the dead, doesn't mean I have given up my traditions. I still believe that, Dia de los Muertos is a most important holiday. Why do you ask?"

Earl took a deep drag, set his cigarillo on an ashtray, and poured more wine. "Then you do not need to look through a window to understand what he's up to in there. You may as well get comfortable because the story I have to tell could take a while."

"Tell me, muy amigo. We've got all night."

CHAPTER 11

Lake Vineyard, San Gabriel, 4 January, 10:30 a.m.

Adam peered over his list at the dandy coming through the wagon shed door. Nodding to a couple of helpers, he gestured to one of the crates with his pencil and made a check. "Good morning, Mr. Wilson," he said folding the sheet and putting it in a coat pocket. He appraised his host as they shook hands.

"Good morning to you. As I told you last night, call me Don Benito if you wish to be formal."

"Fine, Don Benito it is," Adam said with a shrug.

Benjamin Wilson had a slender frame topped by a boyishly handsome face whose smallish eyes seemed to view the world with a penetrating intensity. Adam thought they seemed a little more relaxed than they had been the night before while tallying up the bill Earl put in front of them. He knew Wilson's capacity to pay the bill relied on more than simple posturing. A calculating brain lodged behind those eyes. Adam didn't know much about Benjamin Wilson, but he had heard enough from his uncle to conclude that an especially unflattering trait resided in there as well. Wilson had managed to turn a tendency of his into a socially acceptable art form. Don Benito excelled at exploiting the weaknesses of others while giving the impression he was doing so for the greater good.

Ah, Adam thought, *Wilson is going native today. He's chosen to masquerade as an exceptionally well-dressed Californio! Not wishing to go too far afield, the Don has decked himself out in a trajes suit tailored from a bolt of light* English *wool.*

Adam glanced at the attractive, hand-stitched grapevines that complemented the silk hat band circling Benito's flat-topped sombrero. He lowered his gaze to the string tie and squinted. The aiguillette featured a silver Navajo squash blossom set with a large turquoise stone. A golden vein ran through the beautiful blue gem.

"What have we got here?" Don Benito asked, lifting his lapels and adjusting his jacket. He kicked one of the boxes with the toe of a rattlesnake-hide boot.

"We're about to send in the books and what's left of the artwork," Adam said, gesturing to the open crates. "The Chippendale furniture and the kitchen and dining ware have met with your wife's approval, but the thing that has created a bigger stir among the early arrivals is the sewing machine. Margaret and Mrs. Banning are the envy of the women because they are the only people in Southern California who have them. We left two dozen in Phineas Banning's warehouse. He'll sell them to the highest bidders!"

"Yes, I saw the women admiring the machine," Wilson said. "I'm not sure you have room on your ship to satisfy the orders you'll get for the other item you've neglected to mention—the toilet tissue. Oh, how they enjoy the convenience of having that in the privy!"

Adam offered a companionable smile and changed the subject by waving at the crates. Wilson's library would now have most of the works of Hugo, Stevenson, Dumas, Wordsworth, Coleridge, Talleyrand, and Scott, to name but a few. He and his uncle had stuffed the crates with first edition works of contemporary American authors, including Emerson, Carlyle, Irving, Twain, Thoreau, Longfellow, and Whitman. There was a complete set of the writings of Charles Dickens, and Earl had added as many of the Dickens magazine installments as it had been possible to get prior to sailing from New York. Adam pointed to stacks of past issues of *Harper's Weekly* and *The Atlantic* tied in dated bundles. "You'll find lots of bedtime stories in there."

He reached into one of the crates and removed a signed review copy of Charles Darwin's new book, *On the Origin of Species*. "This is a gift to you from Uncle Earl. He has another copy in his library aboard the Bride. Darwin published the book for distribution last November. We were fortunate to get them through a friend. Darwin's concepts on evolutionary biology will change the way we view the natural world. This is a landmark book," Adam said, passing the copy over to Don Benito.

"Hmm," Wilson said, turning it over in his hands. "I'm familiar with Darwin and his theories. This book could undermine the basic tenets of religion. There are guests arriving who would burn it on sight. I'll read it, but I don't fancy the idea that our ancestors came from lizards. Have you got anything else in there that's controversial?" he asked, dropping the book in the crate.

Keeping his face straight, Adam removed another book. He resisted the urge to mention how he felt about Wilson's *controversial* participation in the massacre of hundreds of defenseless people who objected to white men driving them off lands the Spanish had not yet claimed. Apparently, the cattle barons, of whom Wilson was one, took exception to Indigenous peoples supplementing their diets with beef. That Wilson and his friends had killed off their traditional sources of meat made no difference. As far as they were concerned, a thief was a thief was a thief, including his women and children. *I'd be curious to know how much controversial blood you spilled to get that stone on your string tie*, Adam mused.

Wilson's remark on Darwin's effect on the subject of religion prompted Adam to imagine how the Don could temper his misgivings about the theory of natural selection. Perhaps by extrapolating Darwin's postulates a step further and making it more personal, he might be inclined to favor a science-based evolutionary rationale justifying the extermination of races other than his own. *Be a convenient excuse for cozying up to the secessionists,* Adam thought.

"You'll probably call this one controversial too," he said, handing over Whitman's *Leaves of Grass*. "He's one of my favorite poets. His preference for lying with men doesn't bother me, although I'm sure there are guests who would disagree and like to burn this book too. But those same people would take exception to most of the authors in your library if they knew what was being said between the lines."

Adam saw no change in Wilson's expression, nor did he receive any indication his host could appreciate the ironies he was weaving into their conversation. *The man's a mystery to me. I spent an evening with him and his wife, and I'm no closer to knowing who he is than I was before we arrived. His aimless chatter over dinner might have been easier to bear had he shown any interest in what happened in the Dip. His glib remarks left me with the impression he enjoys playing both sides against the middle, and whichever side comes out on top, that's the one he'll claim he supported all along.*

The dandy carelessly tossed Whitman back among his colleagues. "Are there any other books aboard the Bride?"

"Yes," Adam answered, noticing how the book spun around after a corner of the hard cover gouged Darwin's volume. "We have several libraries. Quite a few topics are covered. In addition to an assortment of books discussing arcane subjects written in numerous languages, there are multiple copies of the contemporary authors represented here. We exchange books with scholars from around the world. We even have ancient manuscripts written on sheepskin, papyrus, and the finest vellum. They're in carefully packed and labeled crates stored in the driest part of the hold." He cleared his throat and adjusted Whitman, so he would lie flat and square. "I find books are more enjoyable to read if their fascicles have not been broken."

Ignoring the bristled reaction, Adam spoke to the men standing nearby. "It's okay to take these into the library now. Put drop cloths on the floor before you set 'em down. A couple more trips, and you can join the party."

Wilson tilted his head and squinted down his narrow nose. "*Okay?*" he asked, clearly miffed by the not-so-subtle scolding he'd just received from an underling. "I've never heard the expression before. What's it mean?" he demanded.

"Okay is a figure of speech people have been using back east for a few years. I think it originally meant 'all correct.' Usually means 'all right.'"

"*Okay*, then, let's see what we have in here." Wilson prodded another crate with his toe.

Adam thought the man's haughty expression revealed more than he wished to say about receiving a lecture from a plebe who acted as if he was the only one who knew what a fascicle was. Not that Wilson knew, because Adam suspected he didn't. *That's it*, Adam thought. *My problem with Wilson is how he intentionally compounds his willful ignorance by acquiring the trappings of knowledge to give the illusion he is wise.*

"Don Benito, are you satisfied with your new acquisitions?" Adam asked, hoping that by changing the subject so abruptly Wilson wouldn't have time to compose himself before the second barb pricked another nerve in the man's vanity.

Wilson winced. "They've cost me a small fortune! I think the person who has the most satisfaction is your Uncle Earl. The sum on the draft I gave him would fund building a husband for the Bride!"

Close, Adam thought. *You'll never know, but you just reimbursed Uncle Earl for the purchase of three perfectly good Donald McKay designed clippers. New ships abandoned by owners and crews the day they arrived in San Francisco.* "All I need now are three reliable skippers," Earl had said after completing the transfers several days before departure.

"Aye," Adam said to the Don, thinking of how his uncle had trained him to keep his equanimity in the presence of such men. "I total up my costs, add a profit margin, and, depending on how annoying the client is, tack on a little extra. Does wonders for my willingness to put up with them. Since you have to interact with them too, I share a portion of the premium with you!"

Tiring of the charade, Adam got busy removing the loose lids from several crates. "These are the Hudson paintings you requested." The Hudson River School paintings by Cole, Bierstadt, Baker, Cropsey, and Durand were stored in slots built into the crates. Adam pulled a couple of paintings out and laid them across the slots. "The grandeur depicted in these scenes attempts to portray a pastoral harmony between people and the natural setting. In all sincerity, I think you live in an environment where that's possible," he said, letting the comment hang between them for a moment.

"Here's a Frederic Church I find interesting." Adam poked around in the slots and removed the cover from a canvas. He leaned the painting on a crate where it could catch the best indirect light. "This one's a bit fanciful. The image at first glance is of a round hill looming over a dark body of calm water. The sky appears to be backlit by a curving aurora borealis. I've no idea if it was Church's intention, but it appears to me the dazzling arc of light is an iris and the perfectly round hill is a person's pupil. Church calls it Self-Reflection," Adam said with a quick glance to the side.

"My, my," Don Benito breathed, rubbing his lips with an index finger. "I suppose great artistry can have multiple interpretations."

Adam managed to keep his eyes from rolling and nodded. *How little you know about the true value of what you spend your money to acquire. You may come to appreciate what we've delivered, but I doubt if you've got it in ya.*

They heard a squeaky squawking sound coming through the door. "Alto saxophone," Adam said. "It went in with the spinet. I think the children have opened the case."

"Saxophone?"

"Yes. We purchased several in Marseilles this past June. They've been around for a few years. A tin knocker in Belgium makes them."

Leading Don Benito to a workbench, he bent over a crate. "We're about to remove the Lar Familiaris, or as you may wish to call it, the Lararium, La-rar-ium." Adam removed a burlap bag filled with coarse grasses. Although he didn't mention it, he thought it fitting the *Familiaris* should arrive in a climate similar to the one it had left.

Two workers removed a large bas-relief and propped it on the bench between two windows. As was often the case in reviewing ancient artifacts, the admirers did not know the original purpose it served, but Adam did. The bronze served to honor the spirits of the dead—another controversial subject he prudently kept to himself. He had no idea what Wilson's thoughts might be on the subject of spirits, and he didn't want to know. All he knew for sure was how reluctant he felt about letting the object go without fully understanding what made it so special.

The relief weighed nearly a hundred pounds and measured four feet on a side. The fine details accentuating the subjects were a testament to the artisanship required to produce such a fine example of bronze casting.

The robed figures of Jupiter and Venus represented revered ancestors housed in a temple whose pediment frieze portrayed an eagle bearing a thunderbolt. Jupiter sat on a throne. Venus wore a myrtle wreath and appeared to be offering him a goblet of wine. He had not reached for the drink and seemed to be gazing sternly at her.

"What a tale you could tell if you could speak," Adam said as his fingers caressed the figures for the last time.

Although he had no way of knowing why, Adam correctly assumed that a third-century Roman commissioned the *Lar Familiaris*. Like many in his day, he may have felt that the villa he built on the Isle of Ibiza would only be complete if he paid familial homage to deceased relatives.

The nobleman moved to an island inhabited by people who had endured the rise and fall of empires whose names littered Mediterranean history— Egyptians, Assyrians, Greeks, Carthaginians, and the greatest of them all, Romans. He chose a housing site within the harbor near a stream on the eastern edge of Eivissa village. The villa outlived him and his bloodline, and eventually his name and devotions faded from memory.

Time passed, and the Roman Empire fell. Moors, English Crusaders, and Spaniards followed, taking turns holding dominion over Ibiza's safe anchorage. Centuries came and went. Title to the property changed as many times. The *Lararium* remained mounted above the central hearth through multiple seasons and owners. It was quite likely that the bronze's admirers came to see it as nothing more than a quaint bas-relief.

Finally, an owner abandoned the site. Tile roofs blew off in storms, and tree roots lifted patios. Lintels and columns collapsed on marble statues. Generations of locals carted off stone stairs and crumbling arches. A few of the more ornate pieces found their way into building facades strung along the shore road. The magnificent home and moorage fell into disrepair and by mid-eighteenth century was a ruin. Eivissa's harbor had become little more than a forgotten backwater by then—unless one was a seafarer who needed a safe anchorage. In a sense, the harbor retained what had attracted early Phoenician traders in the first place.

Adam's uncle knew of Eivissa but never had a reason to go there. A summer storm changed that. The *Bride* arrived one blustery summer day fully laden with cargo. Earl chose to anchor in the harbor rather than contend with the unpredictable winds out on the open sea. The next morning, Earl had a quarter boat lowered and invited Adam to accompany him ashore.

"May as well go," James said. "We'll stay right here until the barometer steadies and the wind makes up its mind on which way it wants to blow."

A hound watched the newcomers from a café. His ears perked up as the boat approached the wharf. Trotting down to the beach and onto the wharf, the dog settled on Earl and Adam as deserving the most attention. He put his nose up close as they prepared to step onto the planks and accepted their presence after taking a good whiff of their hands. Satisfied with his new friends, the animal's springy step preceded them up the walkway.

"I think I saw the dog's ancestors on Egyptian glyphs recently," Adam commented.

Earl nodded and then turned to his men. "I'll have food sent down to you."

The café's exterior walls folded back, exposing the interior. Men dressed in turbans and robes sat and watched. Several women wearing gauzy veils seemed to float among the tables replacing copper *cezves* of hot, thick, dark coffee. The men hardly gave the servers a passing glance. Cups and plates were removed to make room for more cups and dishes laden with *maroo* flatbread, *tabouleh, la ha mishwi, tzatziki, leban, za'atar, judtada, hummus*, and *baklawi*.

The dog lay down by the door and resumed his watch over the beach. Earl and Adam nodded to the dozen or so people. Earl gestured to vacant chairs arranged around a large table. One of several seated men raised a hand indicating the places were available. "Shukran, As-salam alaykum," Earl said. ("Thank you, peace be upon you.")

"Marhabaan bik, wa 'alaykum al-salaam rahmatullah," an old man across from Earl answered. ("You are welcome and unto you, peace.") He smiled, not expecting the infidel before him to know Allah had just made him the recipient of twenty good deeds for being polite. The smug superiority he felt soon dissipated after he heard the respectful response.

"Assalaamu alaykum wa rahatullahi wa barrakatahu." ("Your peace is appreciated.") Earl had just made himself the beneficiary of thirty more good deeds from Allah!

The dog jumped up and stared into the room when everyone laughed at how the older man's smug manner changed from consternation to knowing he'd been had. Earl and Adam maintained their respectful postures but could not hide the twinkle in their eyes.

Regaining his composure, the old man started laughing. "Hal tatakallam al-lughah al-arabiyah?" ("Do you speak Arabic?")

"Na'am qalilan" ("Yes, a little"), Earl said, requesting the old man speak slowly, be patient, and use lots of gestures.

Whatever discomforts the men may have felt with the arrival of strangers, they soon replaced with the easy camaraderie of people sharing an all-too-brief respite from the perils of the tossing sea beyond Ibiza's harbor. They bantered back and forth in Arabic as plates came and went through the morning's easy passage. The women took dishes to the men waiting on the beach by the quarter boat. Earl mentioned the harbor's historic location to the older man.

"Yes," the elder said, pointing to the Roman ruin across the way. He shook his head and said the place had recently changed hands. He went on to say the new owner was going to demolish the remains and planned to build a modern Spanish villa on the property. Curious, Earl dropped enough silver coins in a serving woman's palm to cover everyone's tab and still provide a healthy tip. "Shukran" ("Thank you"), he said to a pair of dark-brown eyes.

"Teslan iidak" ("May God bless your heart"), her soft voice whispered from behind her pink veil.

Earl and Adam walked over to the ruin and introduced themselves to the new owner, who was happy to lead them past workers dismantling the remains. Pointing to a bronze relief mounted on a cracked chimney, he said he had no use for an object covered with such an unsightly verdigris patina. He airily informed them that to make way for the new, this old stained object was about to be tossed into the harbor with the rubble. His condescending manner removed any thoughts Earl might have had in apprizing the man of the Lararium's true value.

Earl arranged to save the builder the trouble of removing the object, and called the boat over. Borrowing a few tools, they got the piece off the chimney and into the boat. Adam knew what was coming and got the words out before his uncle could speak. "Another fool who has more money than brains." The people in the café returned their waves of farewell as Earl and his men hastened to row their treasure out to the *Bride*.

"How did your uncle procure such a valuable object?" Wilson asked.

Adam rubbed his forehead and took a moment to collect his wits before he answered. "Uncle Earl met a Spaniard on the island of Ibiza who wished to part with the Lararium. He was a man of means. A lot like you in many ways."

Wilson straightened and puffed up his chest. "Too bad you and your uncle are unable to purchase such valuable objects for yourselves."

"Yesss," Adam answered, stretching the word with undisguised sadness. "They agreed to terms, and the provenance is included in the list of items we will be leaving with you."

He thought he would give Wilson one more chance to inquire about the relief's provenance. "Time to bring this inside where it can be appreciated for its intended purpose and artistic beauty."

Not expecting a curious response, and getting none, Adam asked himself how in the world it was possible to have a meaningful conversation with a man who put a price on everything but knew the value of nothing. "Don Benito, if I may be so bold, I urge you to leave the protective verdigris in place. It seals the brass and prevents any further deterioration of the piece."

Wilson responded with a noncommittal nod. "I'd rather see polished brass. It's often mistaken for gold."

Adam shrugged and motioned for the men to carry the piece inside where they would mount it above a fireplace. *Uncle said it best,* Adam thought with a resigned sigh, *"Better to be where it's going and misunderstood than forgotten and corroding under broken marble at the bottom of the sea."*

A minute or so later, he was still at the bench. He saw Wilson cross the yard with the men carrying the piece into the house. He shook his head at the sight. "How little you know," he muttered. His uncle was leaning on a porch rail outside the room where the object was about to be hung. Carriages had been dropping guests off for a while, so it was no surprise to see the Bannings and Griffins arrive. The helpers took away the last of the items. Adam made a few ticks, put the list in a coat pocket, and stepped outside to meet the Griffins.

Earl pushed off from the railing and nodded approvingly at Don Benito's choice to build his country house in a meadow overlooking the broad expanse of the San Gabriel Valley. The home was nestled among mature oaks and sycamores and created the impression that the dwelling had been there for years. A breakfast room offered views of vineyards giving way to willow and cottonwood groves along the lake. Stands of stately palms dotted the countryside for miles around.

The valley fell away to the south in tiered rocky outcrops. Los Angeles's plain rolled off to the west, and beyond was the wide expanse of the Pacific Ocean.

Earl thought the house exemplified the standard architectural tastes of those built by prosperous merchants from Boston to Philadelphia: frame construction, white clapboards, broad covered verandas, and large dining and parlor rooms. True to form, the home included multiple bedrooms, a music room, and cozy sitting areas off the library/office. Children's playrooms were in a separate wing.

I wouldn't put it past him to have a carpenter dismantle an east coast cottage and have it rebuilt at the entrance to the harbor. Earl thought with disapproval. *Lots to ponder when it comes to understanding what makes this man tick. Wilson's design preferences supersede the old hacienda's understated elegance, apparently. He's turned the beautiful adobe residence into a barn and has converted the stately wings into storerooms, stables, pigpens, and chicken coops.*

Earl saw the new home as a statement of arrival—an expression of Wilson's effort to live as pretentiously as his elevated station in life could afford. Unable to shake the melancholy he felt toward Wilson and his neocolonial friends, Earl's thoughts honed in on what set him apart from these posers. *How far removed this man is from the spirit of the land he is so determined to shape to his will. I feel as if my efforts to bring an appreciation of the world's wonders to men like him have amounted to no more than an exercise in pandering to the presumptions of sophistication acquired through commercial success. Wilson's guest list is composed of sycophants whose devotions will transform the murderous Don Benito into a benevolent icon whose praises they'll sing for generations to come . . .*

Phineas stepped onto the porch with his wife and saw Earl alone by the railings. She went inside, and Phineas walked over to say hello. He'd seen his teamsters on the way up and been told what happened in the Dip. "Hey there, you still dwelling on what happened yesterday?" he asked by way of greeting.

"Nah, I've found other things to be depressed about. We were a little rough on your coach. I'll pay for the repairs."

"Forget about it. I heard about the holes on my way up here. You're lucky you didn't get shot. I'm going to have to replace two walls and a door. Ralph was sulking on a wagon seat. His left ear is deaf. Says he doesn't like my friends and is quitting. He should be back in San Pedro by lunchtime. That's if he and the wagons toting Benjamin Wilson's wine don't get ambushed along the way. Want to tell me what you and your men did? Sounds gruesome."

Earl didn't get a chance to respond before they heard Margaret Wilson's exclamation coming through a window. "Oh, you men know nothing of women or Roman mythology!" Phineas and Earl glanced at each other with raised eyebrows.

Workers had finished hanging the *Lararium* over the fireplace. Margaret stood in front of the hearth and faced a roomful of guests with her arm in the air. Don Benito, his friends, and Mrs. Banning appeared to be waiting for an explanation from Margaret, who was pointing at the piece. "So many unanswerable questions come to mind," she said waving her hand, "not least of which, who is responsible for portraying Venus wearing a myrtle wreath in Jupiter's presence? A rebel who planned to display it far from Rome, no doubt! Well, we are about as far from Rome as you can get!" she exclaimed. "He's giving her the evil eye because she's challenging the foolish stricture prohibiting her from wearing myrtle in his presence. Good for her, I say! Now let's have a toast, a toast to the rights of women to comport themselves however they see fit!"

Fortunately for Margaret, her exclamation elicited a short, uncomfortable pause. In the spirit of conviviality, her guests completed the awkward toast without much eye contact. Most of the eyes darting from face to face were surreptitiously gauging the level of support for such independent notions. The married men became fascinated with champagne bubbles, grain patterns in the polished floor, and frilly lace curtains, anything to avoid sharing the moment with their wives.

"Well, well, well," Earl said. "Margaret's raising a toast to a woman offering a glass of wine to a grumpy god! Didn't think anyone would notice. She's smarter'n I thought."

"Glad I'm not in there," Phineas said. "I prefer to suffer under my wife's nasty stare in private. Let's take a walk."

Earl followed Phineas down the porch stairs thinking that, if given half a chance, the vicissitudes of life might lead to an enlightened state of mind after all. He turned and grabbed the distracted man's elbow as his heel slipped off a tread.

"Thank you, Earl. The next thing you know, they'll be expecting us to allow them to wear men's pants and vote!"

Earl released the elbow and thought it could be a while before Phineas saw the light. "Do you think the Lararium's original owner might have heard his wife speak up on a similar occasion all those years ago?"

Phineas held his reply until they were away from the windows—and his wife. "Maybe. Are you suggesting that there's any truth in the saying, 'the more things change, the more they remain the same'?"

"Could be," Earl said, ready to drop the subject. He was trying to find his crew in the crowd.

"For what's it's worth, Earl, I think the wife was in cahoots with the sculptor, and as is usually the case in my house, the husband gave in, and she got what she wanted!"

They strolled past guests milling in the bright sunshine or at ease in lawn chairs placed near a shaded banquet table. Stopping to sample the fare, Earl received the expected mix of approving nods and frowns of dismissal. The faces of the guests who whispered among themselves and glanced his way left little doubt in his mind about whose side they supported in the previous day's tussle in the Dip.

Kato was with Tom. They appeared to be watching Mike, who was performing tricks from his seat at a table. Munenori stood beside him. Coins would disappear and return in children's hair, ears, pockets, and hats. Cards came and went to oohs and aahs. No one could keep track of which walnut shell hid the elusive pea.

Earl saw the *Shadow*'s first mate, Dwight Grant, approach with three of his boys and squeezed his hands into fists. "Grant and his crew found a way to get invited too. Where's Horace Buckle, the Shadow's captain?" He could see Bill and Maynard sitting by the wagon barn. The flat expressions on the faces of the men stationed around the perimeter were enough to cause the curious to veer off in another direction. Adam was across the yard with Evelyn having lunch with people he didn't recognize. She was wearing a Mexican-style dress that hugged her waist and lifted her partially exposed breasts. Earl thought she looked good in a pair of trousers too. Phineas saw her also and was half-correct in his assessment of what Earl was thinking.

They heard the clear call of a warbler. "Yellow-rumped," Phineas said.

"Myrtle!" they exclaimed at the same time.

"I think I heard a hermit thrush," Phineas said, leading the way to a leafy grove. "Let's get off by ourselves. I want you to fill me in on what happened yesterday."

Earl and Phineas walked to a knoll overlooking the lake where a group of men talked in a loose circle. One of them had his back to the group. Filling a Ball jar from the contents of an earthen jug, he placed the container on the ground, took a few swigs, turned, and found himself pinned under Earl's gray blues.

Nickie Hale nearly choked. "Ugh!" he burped, loud enough to get the others' attention. The conversation had dwindled into silence by the time Earl and Phineas were within hearing. All eyes turned to the pair.

Unperturbed, Phineas greeted the men he knew by name and introduced himself and Earl to the rest. A couple muttered under their breaths, another found a pebble beneath a foot that needed his immediate attention, and there were a few failed attempts to stare Earl down.

"Hi there, Nickie," Earl said. "Nice to see you again. Is that spring water you have there in your hand? And by the way, thank you for your hospitality yesterday. It was a pleasure meeting you and Almira. I saw her in the parlor a few minutes ago discussing women's rights. You two will have a lot to talk about on the ride home tonight."

Nickie had the harassed appearance of a man who would prefer not to have met Earl Yeaton. The guarded eyes were those of a mournful hound who had seen too many winters and was not relishing the idea of living through another, even if it was to be of the Southern California variety. Nickie's ears flopped out sideways from below his battered Stetson, his jowls hung below the point of his jaw, and his clothes draped over his scarecrow frame. He mumbled a barely audible greeting to Earl and Phineas.

The men Nickie was with had been boasting about how determined they'd been to cut down the Yankees who'd jumped Charlie's crew in the Dip. "We woulda done it too if Almira hadn't a butted in," a tippler said.

Nickie grinned amiably, foolishly nodded to the bravado, took another gulp of courage, and went for a refill. Earl's arrival was enough to make his last swallow of moonshine burn like acid in his suddenly queasy stomach.

After the introductions, Earl met Charlie's blank stare. "I saw you standing on the porch yesterday. I didn't get the pleasure of making your acquaintance, even though I'd heard your name mentioned earlier by one of the corpses we handed over to Ol' Nickie here."

The man with the pebble underfoot stopped moving. The others made sure their hands were visible and shied away from Charlie. Charlie's pasty complexion initially acquired a blotchy purple stain that, by degrees, faded to a greenish-yellow under Earl's calm scrutiny. Charlie's bravery depended upon having the upper hand on his victims, and he wasn't doing too well standing there under the gaze of a man who had demonstrated his capacity to do to him what Charlie had done so often to the defenseless. The sullen defiance in Charlie's restless eyes broke apart and gave way to fear.

Phineas coughed. "Well, it's been a pleasure talking with you all. We'll just mosey on to our next, ah, encounter." He turned and nodded to Earl, who was turning with him. The two walked away. Charlie hadn't uttered a sound.

"I think I should take you up on your offer to give me one of those pea shooters," Phineas blurted when he and Earl were back among the guests. "Might be a good idea to bring one of those along whenever I go anywhere with you!"

"I could give you the one I'm packing under my left arm right now if it'll make you feel any better. We're coming up to our next, ah, encounter." He'd seen Horace Buckle talking with several men.

"Thank you, but not just now," Phineas said with a tremor.

Buckle was the first in his group to notice the approaching pair. Phineas put on a nervous smile and raised an index finger. "Captain Buckle, you know Dr. Yeaton, Captain of the Maine Bride?"

"Yes," Buckle responded, taking offense at the stiff nod he received. He regarded Earl with the same brutish hostility he applied to all the inferior men he'd crushed. Civility in the presence of his betters was not his strong suit, but Mr. Harrington had ordered him to make a go of it. His orders did not include Captain Yeaton, who for an unknown reason had overcome the men sent to kill him. Buckle was a block of bone and muscle. He would much prefer to be standing on a quarterdeck commanding men under full sail. He hated being with a bunch of landlubbers discussing politics and finance. He chafed at having to put on an ill-fitting, out-of-date woolen suit and be polite to Mr. Harrington's allies. He wanted to be done with passing over instructions too sensitive to put on paper. The sooner he got back to San Francisco with their replies, the better. He had three other matters to attend to first: use any means necessary to find out if Yeaton had the bonds, confiscate the Chinese gold, and sink the *Bride*.

Buckle saw a man too comfortable for his own good. Therefore, he needed to be taken down a peg, and Buckle was the man to do it. Earl's calm self-assurance, easy manner, and sophistication were everything Buckle lacked, and he resented it. He knew that feeling might cloud his judgment, but he felt confident it wouldn't be enough to keep him from getting the job done. He hoped that by getting those bonds back and destroying this Maine Yankee, he would advance his employer's goal of securing his bona fides among these naive secessionist fops. Buckle had the nagging suspicion they were all disposable pawns in another of Mr. Harrington's schemes. He hated being party to the political and financial maneuverings his boss's subterfuges entailed. He just wanted to get on with a task more in keeping with his talents: proving his masculinity over a worthy foe.

The man's cruel eyes competed with the attention his busy tongue drew as it passed back and forth over the foul teeth hidden behind his closed lips. His vanity couldn't help but wonder how Yeaton's teeth could be so much cleaner. Earl's dismissive response to Buckle's challenging stare had a disturbing effect. Buckle, used to men quailing under his gaze, found Earl not at all intimidated. Worse, Yeaton actually winked at him!

"Permit me to introduce you to these men, Dr. Yeaton. This is Evelyn Griffin's uncle, Dr. John S. Griffin. These two gentlemen are his brothers-in-law, General Albert Johnston and Judge Benjamin Hayes. I think you're familiar with Sheriff Sanchez and Henry Hancock."

Earl saw a riddle. Griffin had come from Virginia, so Earl could understand his southern sympathies. He knew Griffin traveled overland to California as a physician assigned to General Kearney, so, Earl reasoned, he must be well acquainted with the hardships soldiers commonly faced. Even so, Earl could not understand how Griffin would want the men he campaigned with to choose sides and go into battle against each other. He must have known the number of casualties on both sides would be horrendous. Besides, his tenure in the military had given Griffin many opportunities to observe the lengths to which the federal government was willing to go to maintain sovereignty over the states and territories. Earl also knew Dr. Griffin had been practicing medicine for over twenty years. He must have treated a wide variety of traumas and seen firsthand the horrors of armed conflict. Earl thought it only reasonable to expect that Dr. Griffin would do all he could to spare people the consequences of intentionally inflicted injury. It was an open secret that Dr. Griffin was involved in the efforts to have California secede from the Union. How the man could reconcile within himself the prospect of contributing to the mutilation and death of hundreds of thousands of his fellow citizens in a war his side would surely lose was beyond Earl's capacity to comprehend. He felt sickened to be in the presence of the prestigious Dr. Griffin. As far as Earl was concerned, this paragon of society was the embodiment of evil. It took all of his will to keep his composure and remain civil in the man's presence. His hand twitched at the thought of what he might do to the seditionist if he were holding Kato's sword.

Earl could not shake the feeling there had to be an unrevealed reward men like Griffin received, regardless of the outcome. How else could he and his friends so willingly collude in activities that would cause such monstrous consequences for so many of their fellow citizens? *Do they engage in back-door alliances with their erstwhile foes or sell goods and services to troops assigned to protecting national interests? And if the secessionists win independence, will they confiscate federal lands for the purpose of selling them off to the new state? No matter the outcome, men like Griffin always find a way to profit.* Griffin's smirk suggested he knew what Earl was thinking.

Griffin removed an envelope from his coat pocket and handed it to Earl. "Dr. Yeaton, I heard about your unfortunate encounter in the El Monte Dip. Could have gone either way, I'm told."

"Yes," Earl replied, taking the envelope and peeking at the bank draft to ensure the figures were correct. "The same could be said for your plans for the country. They too could go either way." He waved the envelope before putting it in a breast pocket beside the one he had received from Benjamin Wilson. "Had I known what you were planning, I would have offered to trade Evelyn's travel expenses for the pleasure of seeing you ride up with your friends in the Dip yesterday."

Phineas interrupted the frosty exchange before it went any further. "Earl, this is General Albert Johnston, who, rumor has it, will soon replace General Clarke as commander of the Army's Department of the Pacific."

"Pleased to meet you, General Johnston. You don't provide much of a relief from the distressing thoughts I'm having regarding Dr. Griffin and his cohorts."

"Your point's well taken, Dr. Yeaton," Johnston said, giving Earl a courtesy bow and extending his hand. Earl returned the bow and reached for Johnston's hand.

"I wish we could meet under happier circumstances," Earl said, liking the feel of the general's grip. He knew who General Johnston was and felt it a privilege to meet him. He saw a man who had risen through the ranks to his present position because he had earned his promotions. Albert Johnston had Earl's grudging respect. The man did his duty to the best of his abilities. He was the rare commander who led men into battles they won with minimal casualties. His loyal troops would follow him anywhere. Earl felt inexpressible sadness sweep over him as he held the general's hand. A knowing look passed between them. Albert Johnston had the presence one would expect to see in any classical warrior who accepted the immutability of Fate.

"Are you a religious man, General Johnston?"

"Yes."

"You have two of the characteristics I most admire: loyalty and faith." He felt a squeeze and maintained the grip. "We both know you may join the secessionists, General. I'm sure you've already examined the possibility of losing your life while leading Confederate forces in a grand battle against your West Point classmates. If an epic battle comes to fruition, will you and your former classmates recall being present the day your Greek instructor discussed Eros and Thanatos? Will you clash swords immersed in the ultimate joy of life's existence, while at the same time seeking to plunge yourselves into death's embrace? It grieves me to think that men like Arthur Harrington and Dr. Griffin know these thoughts exist in warriors and use them to prey upon the sentiments of men like you and me."

"I'll try to remember what you said in the future. I'll have no way of telling you what happens." The general let up on his grip.

"True," Earl said, maintaining his pressure. "I'm saddened you're willing to sacrifice your life because you have fallen under the spell of those who adhere to the belief that God's Caucasian children are more equal than the rest. You realize, of course, Dr. Griffin and his friends will be cheering you on from the sidelines. They're unwilling to risk their lives defending their right to profit from the labor of slaves. That's a job for trained professionals. A task they'll assign to men like you. Would you like to know what really galls me, General?" Earl released the man's hand.

"Please tell me."

"They'll be here long after you've given up your life trying to protect their greed."

Earl didn't wait for a reply before extending his hand to Judge Benjamin Hayes. The judge's mild and unpretentious manner was a welcome relief from Earl's exchanges with the others. He shook the hand of a respected jurist who knew his own mind. Frequently asked by his brothers-in-law and his associates to join the secessionists, Hayes declined. Earl told the judge it was a pleasure to meet him. Hayes glanced at the group. "The pleasure's all mine."

"This gentleman," Phineas said with a discernable quaver in his voice, "is Tomas Sanchez, soon to be our new Los Angeles County Sheriff." Earl and Sanchez stared at each other and did not shake hands. The convenient distance served them both well because neither wanted to be in the presence of the other. Earl knew of Tomas Avila Sanchez, a brave officer whose scruples mirrored those of the criminals he pursued. He did have his uses, however. Earl thought of him as a wily guard dog. Sanchez's value depended upon remembering whose dog he was. His current owners permitted Sanchez to pad around the party as a reward for doing what the alpha males running Los Angeles County told him to do. His duties included hounding political and business rivals. They also included staying off the scent of lackeys performing illegal activities too sensitive for there to be any connections drawn between them and the top dogs running the county should their crimes become public knowledge.

Earl broke eye contact as soon as he heard Phineas mention Henry Hancock.

"I believe you know Henry," Phineas said, cringing inside and praying for this encounter to end. *I have to work with these people after Earl is gone!*

"Yes. Hi, Henry, how are you?"

"Fine, thank you. Welcome to Southern California." Henry grinned at Earl, the glint in his eyes barely masking the message in his greeting.

The men exchanged a few more words of small talk before Phineas and Earl excused themselves.

"I'll take that as a compliment," Evelyn said in response to an observation Adam had made about how she'd rejected her uncle's attempt to keep her from being alone with him. They had finished their luncheon with the Griffins and were nearing the stables. "Uncle John may be my father's brother, and I may be a guest in his house, but he does not get to decide who I talk with at parties. He's upset with me because I asked too many questions on the way up here this morning. I'm sorry you had to see that. The fewer questions he answered, the more I wanted to ask. He's angry with you for telling me what happened in Ah Toy's brothel."

"Huh," Adam replied thoughtfully.

"I didn't realize how much danger we were in on the way down here. Do you think Captain Lang would have killed Myra and me if he'd caught up with us on the open ocean?" she asked as they entered the stable.

"We thought so at the time. Are you aware we were attacked in the El Monte Dip yesterday?"

"Yes," she said, approaching a stall. "I'm also aware my uncle met with Captain Buckle and Captain Lang soon after they dropped anchor. He told me it is none of my business after I asked him why he'd meet with the men Arthur Harrington sent to kill you. They met again last night. Their conversations became loud and angry."

"You don't mince words, do you?"

"No," she answered with more conviction than he expected to hear from a woman in her mid-twenties. Most of his women friends were nowhere near this outspoken. "I'm not a fan of prescriptive living. I get to decide what I should and should not do, especially in the presence of men who see me as nothing more than an expendable chattel. We only have today, and if those men sent to kill you get their way, I may never see you again. So, I'm going to tell you what I think while I have the chance." She stopped to stroke a horse's muzzle. "You and the men on your ship treated me like a lady, but more importantly, you treated me like an equal. I do not have time for men who see me as a pretty object to admire or play with and discard. You do not act like that, Adam Yeaton."

She pointed at a short bench. "Can you toss that up on the haymow above the stalls?"

"Yup," he said and threw it up there.

"Good," she said, grabbing a ladder rail. "Up you go."

He climbed the ladder, set the bench a little way back from the edge, sat, and waited. She too climbed the ladder and crossed over to him. Raising her skirts, she straddled his hips and took his head in her hands. "I've wanted to do this since we were laughing in the wheelhouse!" With that she planted a kiss on his lips.

His hands slipped along her thighs and cupped her bottom. "That's much better," she purred, liking the feel of his fingers.

"Do you know which organ is the most sensitive in circumstances like this?" he asked.

"Yes," she replied, beginning to undo his belt.

"Uh-uh," he said, "your ears."

"Ahh, ha, ha," she giggled, then froze at the sound of approaching voices.

"Neither Henry nor you mentioned that you will be traveling over to Rancho La Brea," Phineas said, glad to be away from the icy exchanges he'd just witnessed. "They sure as hell didn't want to talk about what you did to their friends yesterday."

"No and no," Earl said. "Change of plans. I'm sure Buckle and Griffin are responsible for the attack on us yesterday. The incident required advance notice. I'd prefer not to see a repeat before we return to your wharf. Henry is heading back to La Brea tonight. I'll tell him before he leaves that we're coming in the morning. We'll be there in the time it takes to get those skulls and return to San Pedro. I sent a note to James with a teamster. James will inform Ryan of the change in plans. They'll be ready for us when we arrive. The Bride's sailing on the tide tomorrow afternoon. Wilson's casks will be in the hold by the time we get back.

"Thanks again for the use of your wagons and coach. I've come up with a way to repay you. The note instructed James to do one other thing while they're down below. You're getting a twenty-gallon cask of Blandy's Verdelho. The contents have been around the Horn twice. The value of the cask's contents will more than compensate you for the use of the coach, teamsters, wagons, mules, horses, and repairs."

"Thank you for taking me into your confidence," Phineas said as he shook Earl's hand.

"You're welcome, Phineas. You, Henry Hancock, and Benjamin Hayes are the only people I trust in this nest of vipers. Lost Angels, indeed."

As soon as the two were back among the guests, Mike hurried over to Earl. "Adam sent me to find you. He's up at the stables and wants you to join him."

"What's the reason?" Earl asked, not understanding why the boy was so agitated.

"Um . . . um, he's setting Arron's arm," Mike squeaked, hoping Capt'n Earl wouldn't ask if Adam and Evelyn were in the barn before he and Munenori got there.

"Who's Arron?"

"One of the ship's boys aboard the Shadow," Mike answered, trying to get ahead of Earl.

"Tell me the story now," Earl demanded, walking a little faster.

"Arron and two boys started teasing Munenori up at the stables. We were petting a horse's muzzle. They followed us in, and he told Munenori to take his yeller hands off the horse. Arron started making comments about how ugly Munenori is. The others got into the act by calling him a monkey. At first Munenori just laughed them off, so they teased him a little harder. That didn't get the reaction they wanted, either, so they circled Munenori and started shoving him. Munenori laughed and let them push him back and forth until Arron punched him in the kidneys. Munenori doubled over. I horse-collared a boy about to knee Munenori in the face, kicked the legs out from under him, and flung him onto the planks. The other boy tried to grab Munenori. He got a chop in the throat for his trouble. He was still on the floor gasping and squawking when I left to find you, but that's not the reason I left."

Phineas groaned in frustration and made a rolling motion with a hand.

"Arron pulled a knife and lunged at Munenori's stomach. Dumb move. What happened next went by in a blur. Munenori stepped in and slapped Arron's knife hand to the left, where he got a grip on Arron's wrist. Then he hooked his right arm behind Arron's elbow. His elbow was facing up for a little bit before Munenori kicked Arron's feet out from under him. As Arron fell, Munenori brought Arron's arm down across his right knee. Elbow snapped like a dry branch. The moaning, hiccupping, and crying sounded pitiful. Have to say, he had good reason. His arm didn't look too good all loose like that.

"Adam and Evelyn were there right quick. They must have been in the barn too," Mike said, rolling his eyes.

"Hmm," Earl said, his temperature rising. "My nephew." He was still unable to come to grips with the implications of what Adam had told him regarding Evelyn's plans to attend Olivia's wedding in Camden. *What is he getting himself into this time? The last thing I need is to see my nephew involved with a Griffin. This on top of my niece marrying a Harrington! The country is coming apart, and Olivia and Adam are attracted to the offspring of my enemies!*

The three reached the stables and stepped over the sill. A group had gathered around a prone figure on the runway. Adam had rigged a splint on Aaron, who was moaning. Dwight Grant and Horace Buckle watched as Evelyn tied off the splint. Munenori stood off to the side between Kato and Tom.

The *Shadow*'s other boys had come around, sore but no worse for wear. One would have headaches, and the other would have trouble swallowing for a few days.

Grant's mean face turned to Earl, but before he could say anything, Earl spoke. "Stow it, Dwight. If Munenori was lying on the floor, you'd be giving us an excuse for why he deserved to be there. As it is, your boy is lucky Munenori broke his elbow instead of bending it the other way and driving the knife into his throat." Earl stepped closer. "Unlike you, Munenori has the courage to fight with people his own size!"

Adam and Evelyn had finished up with Arron by the time Earl had said his piece. "Take him and the others out of here on a wagon. They're in no shape to get back to the Shadow any other way."

Buckle had put an arm across Grant's chest while Earl talked and stared with all the malevolence he could muster. Earl shrugged him off, expecting Buckle's next comment. "You haven't seen the last of this, Yeaton."

"Figured you'd say as much. Watch what you wish for, Buckle," he answered in the same menacing tone. "Evelyn and Adam, thank you for setting the arm."

Earl glanced at the broken arm and then looked at Arron, "Remember in the coming days that we tried to treat you right. You and your friends should find a way to stay ashore."

Switching to Japanese, Earl spoke to Munenori. "Kare o koroshite inai tame ni kansha imatoki no ken anata wa ienikaeru arimasen." Earl got a dignified bow in return. "In case you're wondering, Buckle, I just thanked my Japanese friend here for not killing your boy."

Buckle's baleful eyes stared back. His eyes shifted to the sobbing boy, and Earl glanced down in time to catch the boy's frightened expression before he turned away. Earl dropped to a knee. "Look at me." The boy's expression fueled Earl's rage. He had the feeling the price of failure was going to cost Arron more than a broken arm. He laid a hand on the boy's shoulder to get his attention. "Whose idea was it to come in here and attack my boys?" Arron didn't have to answer. The glance he darted at his captain told Earl all he needed to know. He squeezed. "I know unsolicited advice often goes unheeded, but I'm willing to take a chance on you. My advice—don't get back on that ship with these men. You and the two with you can stay ashore. What's your last name, Arron? The names of the boys with you?"

"Calhoun," Arron said, watching Earl's expression. He pointed at the other boys. "Preston Brooks and Andrew Butler. They're cousins. You've probably heard the names before too."

"Yeah. South Carolina. Their namesakes enjoy caning defenseless congressmen. Southerners like naming their sons after each other. We do too." Ignoring the threatening grunts coming out of Buckle and Grant, Earl turned to Phineas. "Can you get this boy and his friends admitted to Sister Scholastica's hospital? I'll cover the fees."

"Maybe," Phineas said crossly. "I won't do it unless that boy," he pointed at Arron, "will agree to mend his ways and work off the costs of his hospital stay. Will you agree?" The boy nodded. "Say it," Phineas insisted as Earl helped Arron up.

"I will," Arron said, staring at the other boys. The frightened glances they directed at the *Shadow*'s officers summed up their feelings. Preston, whose throat was going to be sore for a few days, moved over and stood with Phineas. Andrew, whose loyalty to the South appeared to be greater than his good sense, stayed with Buckle and Grant.

"Fine," Phineas said. "One more thing. You pay off the cost of your care by working in the hospital, even if it means cleaning patients and their bedpans. Got it?"

"Yes," the boys said together.

"All right then, you two can ride back with me. But one wrong move and you're on the first ship back to South Carolina."

Earl took a last glance at Buckle, Grant, and Andrew, then led his group out of the stables. They spread out for the walk down to the house. Earl and Phineas were ahead of Mike and Munenori. Arron and Preston were with Kato and Tom. Adam and Evelyn trailed along, whispering to each other. Hearing a snippet of Mike and Munenori's conversation, Earl cast a troubled glance at Phineas. Phineas returned the glance but said nothing. He was too busy thinking about how the last twenty-four hours might affect his business.

Earl didn't think Phineas would want to hear what Mike and Munenori were discussing as they reviewed the various deadly options that had been available to them during the scuffle. Earl realized with a start that the two were speaking in Japanese, and Mike spoke the language better than he did!

"Spartans," he blurted, thinking of what his boys had been through since they'd come ashore. His eyes moved past the flapping awnings and into the distance. His mind envisioned another place, another time, and experienced a detached sense of déjà vu. "The landscape reminds me of Thermopylae," he breathed. He saw battles on land and sea, battles with young warriors at his side, warriors who spoke in uncommon tongues. He pulled himself out of his reverie. "May I interrupt your talk?" he asked in Japanese.

The boys nodded. "Hai."

"Kyo wa masashiku kodo shita, Munenori. Rippana otoka ga inochi o toru sai ni shitte iru toki 1 ni yoyu ga." ("You were correct today, Munenori. You know how honorable men take life and when spare.")

"Arigato" ("Thank you"), Munenori replied, bowing to Earl.

"Do itashi mashite," Earl said with a distracted bow.

CHAPTER 12

Rancho La Brea, 5 January, 6:00 a.m.

Trail's End was an hour behind by the time Earl's outfit topped a low rise and began the decent into Los Angeles' hazy sprawl. The heavens faded from view as the riders slipped beneath the layer of wood smoke and coastal fog that spread a thin gray blanket over the sleeping city.

The group consisted of Earl's coach, a freight wagon loaded with large casks, and his four outriders. The kerosene lantern burning through the bars of a neglected cellblock attracted little more than a passing glance. No sheriff's deputies patrolled Temple's graveled road or walked among the shanties, canvas realty offices, and unpainted sheds sheltering on either side of the forsaken mission's crumbling defenses. Crowing roosters and moaning milkers replaced the incessant bawling of cattle standing in muddy water holes. The riders' flat stares prompted the drunks sitting in the road to roust their fallen comrades and move aside.

Barflies lay strewn around shuttered batwings. Tipplers unable to crawl off to boardinghouses huddled in untidy heaps or fended for themselves in narrow alleys. The more resourceful slept on benches or in wooden armchairs tipped against dusty walls.

Furtive figures slipping around shadowed corners sent hands to holstered triggers. Feral dogs appeared and sniffed still forms lying in the trash scattered between dry goods shops, hardware stores, and second-hand junk dealers.

Shod hooves rounded a corner and entered a maw of cobble-lined blocks offering a toast to Prosperity's architectural cocktail. Rhythmic clicks echoed off hollow masonry shells rising into the pale sky like rows of broken teeth.

128

Rolling past gated federalist mansions mingling with a mix of neoclassical banks and faux haciendas garnished with Moorish minarets, Earl's party could plainly see how the avenue's enterprises stirred finance, beef production, gold, and oil into a distinctive concoction that was ready, willing, and able to slake the exclusionary thirsts of Southern California's newly minted aristocracy.

The police station's gaslights glowed behind office windows long after Phineas Banning's steel tires rumbled past the glare of uniformed coppers walking the beat.

The people, houses, and commercial buildings petered out after the group turned north on La Brea Road. A half hour later, the early morning light caught Earl and his crew emerging from the remnants of a live oak forest. Lookout Mountain and its laurel-filled canyons assumed a more defined shape in the cleaner air. Cultivated fields appeared in the low-lying areas. Cattle grazed on hillsides. Vineyards and orchards lined the roadway. The broad expanse of the Pacific bore an ill-defined smudge under the arc of a milky sky. The far horizon beyond Catalina Island merged with the peculiar cloudbank. The smudge appeared to be slowly advancing out of the northwest.

Rocha had lined the road to his ranch with peach, apricot, and pear orchards. Currents of cool air arrived and blew leaves across the path. Little whirlwinds popped up, only to disappear among the trees. Swallows chased insects stirred up by the breeze. The procession rolled past a small grove of tall palms swaying above the entrance to Rancho La Brea's open gateway.

José Jorge Rocha waited with Henry Hancock beside an old sycamore whose dry leaves rustled in the fitful air.

"Buenos dias, amigo!" Rocha said as Earl stepped out of the coach to shake hands.

"Gracias, Señor." Earl bowed and nodded approvingly at the timeless order of the splendid compound. "Good morning, Henry, thank you for arranging to meet with us at this hour. I apologize for any inconvenience this may have caused."

The day before, Henry stayed behind after Griffin, Buckle, and the men with them said their goodbyes to the Wilsons. Earl had taken Henry aside and told him that he needed to get an early start in the morning. Earl said he wanted to be at the ranchero at sunup. Hancock agreed to the plan and left right away to inform José. As a frequent guest of Señor Rocha, he knew his host would understand the reasons for the change in plans. Hancock knew about the gunfight in the Dip. He'd listened to the rumors surrounding the bonds and the Chinese gold and why Harrington sent his ships to San Pedro. He also knew Earl and his men had another six hours of hard riding ahead of them if they wanted to get back in time to sail on the evening tide.

Hancock, a lawyer, represented José, whose efforts to secure title to his Mexican land grant were proving problematic. His efforts were so troublesome, in fact, that Rocha could no longer afford the legal fees required to petition his case before the courts. Henry was in the process of purchasing Rancho La Brea with gold removed from a placer mine he owned back in the San Gabriels.

Rancho La Brea, located northeast of Los Angles, had so much oil under the ground it was bubbling up to the surface in pools spread over twenty acres. Millions of years before, the area hosted verdant forests inhabited by dinosaurs. The geologic instability of the plain lifted and dropped the land mass in ways that defied description. Long after the disappearance of the dinosaurs, the area's vegetation attracted animals resembling those in existence today. The first humans in the region encountered many of the creatures who eventually found their way into the tar pits. Mastodons, camels, giant sloths, and bears wandered among the palms, live oaks, sycamores, willows, and grasses growing along the waterways and pools in this Ice Age oasis. Dire wolves and the most ferocious beast of all, the sabre-toothed tiger, preyed upon them.

There was much speculation about how thousands of creatures found their way into the unforgiving bitumen muck. But find their way they did, prey and predator alike. That the first creatures to arrive and flourish there would perish in the least-hospitable environment possible struck Earl as exceptionally ironic. The first humans to arrive quickly took advantage of the food sources. This led to the eventual extinction of the prehistoric beasts with which they competed, with one exception—the California grizzly bear. The arrival of the Spanish via Mexico changed that, and the wave of newcomers sweeping over the land were busy killing off the remaining bears. Many of the new arrivals used the same methods to eliminate other inhabitants they saw as a nuisance: native *Tongva-Gabrielinos* and Mexicans. Earl saw the whole panoply of human history playing itself out right there in Southern

California. He had a bad moment every time he stopped to consider what was about to take place on a massive scale as settlers moved west and displaced the tribes and wildlife living between the Mississippi and the Pacific.

Earl knew José's men were constantly on the alert to keep the ranch's livestock away from the tar pits, especially after the rainy season covered the pits with pools of water. The horses and cattle often wandered down for a drink and, unaware of the danger, became stuck in the tar beneath the oily surface. He was less interested in how creatures got in there than he was in the remains of the ones who did. He was particularly interested in the prehistoric skulls. The number of scientists who wanted them outnumbered the supply. Earl was not in the business of satisfying their needs and kept to a minimum the number of skeletons and skulls he chose to distribute.

Hardly the first to puzzle over how best to remove the tarry substance, he found that the best solution was a solution: turpentine, a distillate of pine tar mariners had been using for years as a cleaning solvent, water proofer, and preservative. Earl had delivered a shipment of turpentine the year before and was about to receive bones in return. Although he was primarily interested in skulls, he also requested whole sabre-tooth and dire wolf skeletons. The bones he was collecting were payment for the turpentine. This year's turpentine delivery was in the wagon; part of the balance owed on the shipment of bones he was receiving. Earl handed a sack of gold coins to José, enough to cover the remaining balance.

The ranch foreman directed the wagon over to a warehouse. The teamsters backed the mules and wagon to the loading dock, where José's men untied the casks and rolled them into the warehouse. The mules and horses were led away to be fed and watered. Earl, Adam, José, and Henry talked among themselves while the men placed crates on dollies and rolled them onto the wagon.

José let out a raucous cackle after the last barrel of turpentine rolled into the warehouse. "I bet you are glad to see that disappear, Señor!" he said, puffing into the space created by two hands and miming an explosion.

Earl gave him a weary smile, glad the casks had not been there during the El Monte incident. "Sí, Señor, mucho feliz!" ("Very glad!")

The foreman handed the packing list to José, who passed it to Earl. "The crates are labeled with their contents. I have given you three mastodon skulls whose tusks are closer together, so they will fit through the main hatch. Mucho grande. I itemized the number of sabre-toothed tigers, dire wolves, bears, sloths, and camel skulls. All are packed separately."

"Gracias, amigo," Earl said. "Su hospitalidad es apreciada" ("I appreciate your hospitality").

"Nada, Señor Earl," José replied, giving the sack a satisfying shake.

Earl turned to Hancock. "Thank you for making all of the arrangements and being so understanding about our need for haste and secrecy."

"You're welcome, Earl," Hancock answered. "I want to assure you there are federalists here who not only want to take advantage of what this place has to offer but also plan to improve the lot of all who live here. It's going to be an uphill battle for sure." He handed Earl a bulky manila envelope. "Here is the list of the Californio and Anglo secessionist holdings you requested. I spent the night in the Los Angeles County Clerk's office compiling these documents. Keep them secret. My life depends on it."

Earl nodded and passed the package up to Tom, who stuffed it into Earl's duffel. Munenori sat up there too, holding the reins with one hand and the brake handle with the other.

The men finished tying off the netted crates in the wagon while Maynard tied his mount to the tailgate and climbed onto the seat with Mike.

José's cook sent out jugs of water. His helpers passed around baskets filled with tortillas and fruit for the trip to San Pedro. The time for departure had arrived. José held Earl's eyes "Voy a perder tu amistad, mi amigo" ("Sail soon after you return, my friend").

"Gracias, amigo," Earl said and held the other man's hand firmly in his grasp. He glanced at Henry "Por favor ser amable con este buen hombre" ("Please be kind to this good man").

"Yo lo," Henry said and shook Earl's hand.

Earl climbed aboard and sat across from Adam behind the splintered door. Munenori released the brake and gave the reins a shake. A short while later, Earl's group left La Brea behind, skirted Los Angeles proper, and wound their way south to San Pedro and the sea.

CHAPTER 13

Off Santa Catalina Island, Los Angeles Bay, 5 January, 5:30 p.m.

"Captain Earl," Hopley whispered, shaking Earl's shoulder. "You said to wake you after we cleared Santa Catalina." The boy had been in Earl's position once or twice and could imagine his captain hearing his voice as if it were coming from a great distance. It didn't seem right to be forcing Earl to rise three hours into what should have been a well-deserved ten-hour rest. He nudged Earl a second time and saw his eyelids flutter before they blinked open. Peering with concern at the pale face, Hopley heard a hoarse grunt.

"Thanks. Now go fetch a hot cup of coffee and a few cookies."

The boy returned with a covered tray and saw Earl sitting at the table drinking a glass of water. Smiling with approval, he placed a steaming mug and a plate of oatmeal cookies in front of his captain. Earl had cleaned himself up and made the bed. "Feeling better now, Uncle Earl?"

"Yes. Have a seat, and fill me in on what's been happening." Earl reached for the mug, grabbed a cookie, and raised his eyes.

James's shadow moved past the skylight, and he started barking orders.

"Well, we got underway soon's you hit the rack. The master is adding more canvas now that we're in open water. He says we could be reefing down by full dark if the northwesterlies pick up as he expects. Wind's been rising all day, and the barometer's fallen off quite a bit since this morning. We're in for a blow. The Shadow and Bear are closing in on the weather gauge. They showed up on the starboard quarter south of San Pedro." Squaring his shoulders under Earl's placid gaze, the boy raised his head. "We have a convoy."

"Ah . . . huh." Earl took a large bite out of a cookie and washed it down with more heat than the boy thought he could handle without choking. "You've probably figured out by now what they're doing out there. How're you feeling?"

"Frightened."

"We're all frightened. We'd be fools if we weren't." Smiling through the fatigue dragging at him, Earl finished off the cookie and put the empty mug on the tray. "They didn't do too well in the Dip or in Wilson's barn yesterday. If it'll make you feel any better, I'm sure things aren't going to go too well for them the next time they try harming us."

"Whatcha gonna do, Capt'n Earl?" Hopley asked with a growing sense of confidence. *We're having an adult conversation and Capt'n Earl is letting me in on what he has in mind.* He punctuated each thought with a nod.

"Sink 'em," Earl said, leveling his gaze and nodding in time with the boy. "Yeah," he said rubbing the back of his neck. "Tell James I'll be right up. Please take the tray with you."

Hopley closed the door, crossed the chartroom, and spoke to the silent corridor. "The captain is going to need more than a cup of coffee and a cookie to get him through the next few hours." By the time the boy reached the outer door, he'd moved on to a lesson his father, the frigate captain, had given him two years earlier.

They had spent a week duck hunting in the marshes of Chesapeake Bay. By day six, Hopley was ready to call it quits and refused to get out of bed. He wasn't getting enough sleep to recover from tramping through swamps and was suffering from the effects of trying to keep up. Hopley had burrowed deeper into his bed, grumbling about the awful prospect of slogging through filth getting to a wet blind. "I'm not in the mood to spend another cold day in the rain."

His father listened to Hopley's griping and waited for his turn to speak. "Someday you'll thank me for making you work through your fatigue. Sooner or later, you'll report to a captain who'll be as tired as you are now. You won't know how good an officer he is until you see how well he performs while he's exhausted. Be good for you to know how he feels when that day comes.

Now get up, because he's going to need the fortitude you're going to show me today."

"Today's the day, Dad," Hopley said with a hand on the latch. "I hope I live to tell you how much I've changed," he added before passing through the opening and closing the door with a solid thunk. "I think we're in for more than a dose of heavy weather, and I'm ready to hold up my end of whatever my captain expects of me!"

He heard a cough, rolled his eyes, and saw James leaning over the rail. "Good evening, Sail Master! The captain will be right up!"

Alone again, Earl closed his eyes, released a sigh, and allowed a recurring feeling to flow over him: revulsion over the prospect of having to use deadly force. He rubbed his forehead with both hands. *Time has come for me to accept there are things I cannot change simply by modeling the behaviors I wish to receive. I could get killed trying to set a good example if I'm not careful. Who am I trying to kid? How in hell can I lead men into battle after what I've put them through since we left San Francisco? How in the world am I going to sink two determined foes on three hours' sleep?*

He crossed the room and stared at the bottles lining the liquor cabinet. "So inviting." He closed and locked the cabinet before pressing a panel on the side. He opened a hidden drawer and removed his personal log. He and Adam were the only ones who could read its clipped sentences because he made the entries in modified shorthand.

Earl spent the next few minutes recording Adam's recollections of what he and Evelyn discussed after they set Arron's broken arm. John Griffin sent Evelyn to San Francisco to petition General Clarke to join the secessionists. She had gleaned bits and pieces from the rumors she heard and concluded that Arthur Harrington's men had bungled the attempt to steal the audit instructions and killed Lieutenant Miles. She'd heard her aunt and uncle arguing over how involved Arthur and his friends were in land fraud. She decided to no longer have anything to do with her uncle or the secessionists. Dr. Griffin and Captain Buckle sent a rider to El Monte with instructions to ambush Earl's crew. She would soon be sailing for New York. Appalled by her uncle's treachery, she would share whatever she learned the next time she saw Adam. Earl closed the logbook, put it in with the papers he'd received from Henry Hancock, and snapped the drawer closed.

The shotgun used in El Monte was lying on the bedcovers at the end of the bunk, a parting gift from Phineas. "I think this belongs with you now," he had said. Earl offered it to Tom, who told him to keep it—Phineas had given him one too.

Fully awake now and scratching his stubble, he tried to recollect what had happened on their return to San Pedro. He remembered being willing to let Ryan handle getting the wagon unloaded and storing the bones aboard the *Bride*. He recalled greeting Phineas, who was there to welcome him back, and feeling unprepared to receive his friend's effusive thanks for the wine.

"Do you realize what you've given me, Earl?" Phineas had asked.

"Yes," Earl remembered saying with a tired smile. "You have one of the finest wines ever produced. I hope you are wise enough to leave this Verdelho in the cask for another twenty years before you bottle it."

Earl was in no condition to be giving lessons on how to care for premium vintages. He *was* prepared, however, to do one more turn for a friend whose assistance may well have saved his life. Earl put an arm around Phineas' shoulders and led him aboard. They walked into the captain's cabin, where Earl lifted a trapdoor. He led his guest down stairways into the lowest hold. The light from all three hatches lit the way. With the exception of the main hatch, men had removed the gratings fitted into the box joists beneath the hatches, allowing natural light to pass into the holds. Phineas wanted to pause on each of the three decks because he wanted to know what was stored there.

"I'll tell you on the way. Don't have time to stop and show you everything," Earl said, hurrying down the stairs. "The portion of the hold beneath my cabin contains most of the fine art. Period works share space with contemporary paintings. I've arranged the Old Masters by periods and plan to send nearly all of the paintings ashore once we return to the East Coast. The sculptures, marbles, porcelains, musical instruments, sheet music, and furniture I keep in this area as well." He chose not to mention the vault hidden behind the stacks or the precious gems, gold icons, lyres, urns, and other ancient artifacts he kept out of sight.

Opening another trapdoor, he waved his arm. "The rest of the first hold contains items being commercially transported, like the sewing machines and the toilet tissue the women love so much. There are crates of hardware, machine tools, hand tools, and farming equipment. We're putting the La

Brea fossils in this section because we'll be offloading most of them soon. The ship's water and food supplies are stored in the mid portion of the hold. The windlass and the magazine take up most of the foc's'l area." He said nothing about the crates stenciled with equipment labels containing dozens of rifles and boxes of ammunition. Nor did he mention why the area beneath the aft hatch skylight was clear. Kato and Munenori had been conducting martial arts lessons there for over a year. Most of the crewmembers were now well versed in hand-to-hand, knife, and sword techniques. Earl had been surprised to learn how much Ming and his mates knew. The Japanese form of martial art, jujitsu, had at least one characteristic in common with the Chinese version, kung fu: a devotion to mental discipline transcending its application to combat.

Continuing to talk, Earl went down the stairs two at a time. Phineas was so busy trying to keep up, he missed most of what Earl said next. "The forward section of the second hold is where the sails are stored in lockers. The Bride is capable of carrying a multitude of sails. There are two of each in both summer- and winter-weight canvas. This area has a section set aside for the crew's dunnage. You probably think of that as a packing term, but we loosely use it to mean anything belonging to individual crewmen. I financed the purchase of the Bride by choosing objects I wanted to trade from my own dunnage. We've also stored in here crates of white-oak barrel staves, hoops, and heads. A friend in Belmont, Maine, produces them for me. They're bound for Charles Blandy's warehouses in Funchal, even though he doesn't know they're coming," Earl said, crinkling his tired eyes.

"The midsection of this hold contains the field hospitals and surgical equipment. Here we keep the anesthetics and medicinals, ampoules of morphine, cinchona bark, quinine, atropine, scopolamine, and hyoscyamine, to name a few. Tinctures, powders, ointments, and a host of other mediums for administering remedies sourced from labs and the natural world are labeled and stored in this area." He pointed at rows of crates stacked along each side of the hull and stopped to let Phineas catch his breath. "This is also where we store the libraries. Ancient manuscripts from cultures all around the globe are stored with contemporary authors. A whole section is devoted to maps ranging from the first 1560s Mercator to the most modern." He said nothing about the dozens of mislabeled crates packed with gold destined for Shanghai and Kowloon.

Arriving at the third and final hold, Phineas stared around him at the dozens of casks and crated bottles of wine. Row upon row was strapped to huge ringbolts fastened to the ship's timbers and covered with thick cargo nets. Earl removed a crate holding six bottles of wine labeled D'Oliveiras Sercial 1850. Earl raised his head and called to one of the men working on the weather deck. "Bob Cobb, is that you up there by the aft hatch?"

"Aye, Captain," came the reply from a round, cheerful face peering into the bowels of the ship.

Earl told Bob to lower a small net and stand by to pull it back up. He turned to Phineas. "Take this bottled wine, and save the contents of the cask for later. There are quite a few Madeiras stored in here along with other vintages you would probably recognize."

Phineas eyed a pile of old wooden crates double strapped to the deck. They must have been there for a while because they were covered in dust. "What's this?" he asked, pointing at the stack.

"Well, let's see," Earl replied, reaching for the net. "There are two or three cases of 1789 Courvoisier and Cutler, a few 1795 Brugerolle, and a couple of six-liter Bordeaux jeroboams. The collection supposedly traveled along behind Napoleon while he fought his way through Europe at the turn of the century. Got the whole lot from the son of a warrant officer assigned to their care all those years ago. After the Battle of Waterloo, the officer turned the cart toward home and never looked back." Earl placed the D'Oliveiras in the net and circled a finger. Up went the crate. "You're not getting any of those, sonny. I like you but not that much," Earl said with a grin. He noticed his friend staring off into the length of the hold. "Phineas, do you like brandy?"

"What? Ah, yeah," Earl's dazed companion replied, thinking the wealth contained in this hold would buy most of the rangeland surrounding Los Angeles.

"What do you prefer—sharp, distinctive, smooth and fruity? We have Pomace Grappa, raw, or my favorites, the Champagne region variety—lighter than most cognacs, smooth, and a tad sweeter. I have a standout in here." Earl tried to remember where the cognac was stored. "The one I have in mind comes from the Cognac region, a young one called Croizet Cognac Leonie. Come on, choose. We're short on time."

Phineas held up his hands, bowed, and laughed at his discovery. "I had no idea you were so successful. You choose!"

"Okay," Earl said trying to get his bearings and feeling the weight of the last few days dragging on his willingness to continue. Phineas stopped laughing, cocked his head on hearing *okay* for the first time, and followed along.

They walked in and out of the filtered hatch light, past racks of casks, kegs, and cases of spirits. "I recently heard Dr. Samuel Johnson quoted at the Stanfords' New Year's Eve party," Earl said as they strolled between the stacks. "This excursion reminds me of another Dr. Johnson quote; seems fitting for the occasion: 'Claret is the liquor for boys, port for men; but he who aspires to be a hero must drink brandy!'

"Ah, here we are, a comet vintage," Earl said, receiving another quizzical look. Opening a toolbox fastened to a mast, Earl grabbed a hammer and chisel and removed the lid from a crate labeled A.E. Dor. He removed a squat liter bottle, held it up to the light, and handed it over. He rearranged the straw, replaced the lid, and put away the tools. "This brandy was bottled last spring after sitting in an oak keg for a year. A.E. Dor is a new house located near the best grape-growing area of the Grande Champagne. A dealer in Marseilles sold us a few cases. The flavor is gentle on the palate and it has a delicate aftertaste that lingers pleasantly. Drink it in good health." With a bow, he gestured for Phineas to take the lead back to Earl's cabin.

Phineas turned to go back the way they came, pulled up, and pointed at the floor. "What's down there?"

"The keel. Tons of cobble ballast, rats, and a pipe that goes to the lowest level. The pipe is connected to one of Jacob Edson's new diaphragm bilge pumps we installed the last time we were in Boston." Earl pointed to a piped apparatus mounted on the deck amidships. "We pump the bilge frequently, especially after upping anchor or passing through heavy seas."

"Ahh," Phineas said, thinking of rats.

Once they were back in Earl's cabin, he turned to the captain. "You really do have treasures aboard this ship, don't you?"

"Yes, I do," Earl replied, watching his friend. He could hear Ol' Bud hammering home the hatch covers. Ryan would be ready to cast off soon.

"How do you keep track of everything?" Phineas asked. He was beginning to realize he might be in the presence of the wealthiest man he'd ever met. The treasures aboard this ship would not only be enough to purchase most of the surrounding rangeland but a goodly portion of Los Angeles County as well.

"Not easily! We have lists in ledgers, and all of it's stored in Willard's brain," Earl answered. "I'll tell him of our visit to the hold and what else I'm about to do. Willard can be obsessive about keeping things in order. It distresses me to see him unhappy, so I try to accommodate him whenever possible."

Earl removed two envelopes from his coat. "I have another favor I would like to ask of you." He pulled Benjamin Wilson's bank draft from one of the envelopes and put it in front of Phineas.

"No wonder you're so successful, Earl! That's a lot of money!"

"Yes, it is. I can't cash it where I'm going. Would you mind if I transferred this over to you? You can get it certified at the Wells Fargo Bank in Los Angeles."

"All right."

Earl turned the draft over and wrote on the back: "This check is to be certified and deposited in Wells Fargo San Francisco Branch Account #25-10665 by Phineas Banning Only." Earl put the check back in the envelope. "You can do an interbank transfer, and the money will be safely deposited in San Francisco." He pulled Dr. Griffin's draft out of the other envelope. "I've already signed this over to you."

"I don't want it."

"I knew you'd say that. So, this is what I want you to do with the money. Take your wife with you the next time you go up to San Francisco,. Get a room at the Fairmont Hotel. Have a great dinner, and take her to one of the many Shakespeare plays running at the California Theater. You'll miss Edwin Booth, the best actor in America—he's gone back to New York to get married. His brother, John Wilkes, will deliver the Best Man Speech. He'll have the guests rolling in the aisles! Wish we could be there to see the show!" Earl laughed. "Take in a performance of As You Like It. Be good for you to see a woman in skimpy tights! My treat. I refuse to take no for an answer. Please deposit these checks tomorrow."

Phineas shook his head and put the envelopes in a coat pocket.

Earl moved to the back of the cabin and opened a wide door. Sorting through rows of rifles, boxes of ammunition, and crates strapped on the floor, he found what he was after and pried the lid off a crate. He removed a box, set it on the table, and replaced the lid. Phineas picked up the box and read the label: *Smith & Wesson Revolver Company.*

"Go ahead. Open it," Earl said, having a seat at the table. Phineas sat and opened the box. It contained one of the new .22 revolvers, a hundred rounds, and a webbed shoulder holster rig.

Phineas made a cursory examination of the deadly, shiny object. "Thank you, Earl. Let's strap me in and load this little beauty!"

"Not so fast, young fella. You'll need instruction on how this works before you tote it around."

The two of them went over the gun in detail until Earl was satisfied Phineas could use it properly. Earl stuffed another 200 rounds in Phineas' coat pockets. "There, should do you until I return. It's time to go. The ebb's starting, and there's enough offshore breeze to get us into open water. The westerlies will pick up once we're clear of land. We're leaving now, Phineas."

He led Phineas outside and received a thumbs-up from Ryan. James lifted a hand from the quarterdeck rail and offered a farewell salute to Phineas. Narrowing his eyes at the land forms growing tier upon tier all the way back to the escarpments, Earl sighed and shared a final moment with his friend. "I'll be seeing you, Phineas."

"Yes, you will. Plan to stay with the missus and me for a few days the next time you come this way. Can't wait to hear of the adventures awaiting you. Stay safe, my Yankee friend."

Earl saw Phineas through the entry port, told Ryan to get them underway, and headed for his bunk.

Hours later, Earl heard the squeal of blocks and cracks of canvas over the creak of the mast as more sail was being set. Rain spattered the cabin wall.

"Time for me to see what's going on up there," he said, glancing at what lay at the end of the bunk. "I have a special place reserved for you." He grabbed the shotgun, opened the breach to make sure it was loaded, snapped it shut, set the safeties, and stashed the weapon in a hidden closet. Closing the cabin door on the way out, he asked himself a question for which he had no answer: *What will become of my sense of humanity when I shed revulsion's last constraints and begin ruthlessly taking the lives of those trying to take mine?*

James was no longer barking orders when Earl stepped outside and hurried aft. As expected, he paused at the top of the stairs to view what lay in their wake before he scooted into the wheelhouse. He came out wearing rain gear.

A ragged swath of dark clouds had replaced the milky blue sky over Los Angeles. Bands of rain obscured the view to the north. The foul weather they'd outrun several days earlier had finally caught up with them.

James stayed by the forward rail and waited for Earl to join him. They were wearing sou'westers, sea boots, and weather coats. "Captain," he said, tilting his head to the side. Earl nodded through a yawn and grabbed his hat brim to shield his face from the incoming sheet of spray.

James gave Ryan a sign and pointed at the salon door. He scrunched his head between his shoulders and suffered through the next round of spray to wash over them.

Earl spoke through another yawn. "Wet leaves will be blowing through El Monte's cemetery tonight." He grabbed the wet rail, flexed his hips in time with the plunge of the bows, stretched his neck to take in the set of the sails, and frowned. The late-afternoon sun had given the canvas a worrisome pinkish cast.

Be patient, James said to himself, *that ain't all he's going to notice.* He waited for Earl to shift is attention to the threats cruising off the weather beam.

"I don't like those vessels yonder either, Captain, and I like even less the size these rollers are assuming the farther we get into open water. Northerlies are about to get a boost from the squall. I'm keeping the courses off her for the time being. Jibs, foremast stays'ls, upper tops'ls, reefed t'gallants, and the driver will do in these conditions," he said, raising his voice over the thunder of canvas, rain spatter, wash, and creaking masts. He waved to Ryan and the off-duty crewmen and kept his eyes on them until they were all inside the deckhouse.

"How do you suppose they're faring out there?" Earl asked, his expression darkening. He'd seen what lay beyond the other ships.

James opened his mouth to answer but cut off his reply. The thick purplish-yellow clouds advancing from the southwest were spreading across the sky faster than he anticipated. His answer to Earl's question would have to wait. "Huh. The squall resembles heavily bruised peaches rolling our way!" Lightning flashes backlit the clouds, and the dull thuds of distant thunder sounded like a naval engagement hidden in the fog of war. "Cold fronts're a pair of curtains closing on our position," he said with growing concern. "Ugh, a thunderstorm we don't need. If we get any more static electricity in the air, St. Elmo's fire will be squirting off the masts and spars. My woolen pants are so charged, they're clinging to my legs. So far, so good, but all bets are off if the air turns blue!"

The dying sun's rays had infused the moisture-laden air with a rose-tinted patina and every surface exposed to the feeble light shed a fading red hue until all that remained was a leaking, blood-smeared wound on the belly of the slate-gray overcast. The color leached out of everything soon after the crimson ball sank into the sea.

James stared at the brooding monochromatic panorama left behind and shared an uneasy glance with his captain. He shook himself and hawked up a wad of phlegm. Feigning indifference to their plight, he rolled the slick to the center of his tongue, stepped around Earl, and spat the clammy gob over the lee side. "They put out their tops'ls at the sight of us clearing Santa Catalina. I imagine they're having a rough go of it. Appear to be running as close to the wind as they can. Their rudders'll be slewing around every time they come off a swell. To answer your question, I'd say it's pitch and yaw time out there." He paused to wipe his lips with a wet handkerchief before summing up his report on the perils they faced. "We're running clean, if a little close to the wind. The Bear's staying parallel to us with the Shadow taking up the rear a few cables back. Too close for comfort, if you ask me. Buckle's probably arguing with Grant about whether or not they should put on more sail to keep us in sight after dark. Dicey in these conditions. More sail could cause her to founder once the squall they seem to be ignoring hits. I doubt they'll have any willing hands if they decide to reef in a driving rain. Be tough to keep her upright without masts if they don't get that canvas off her in time."

"How steady's the wind?" Earl asked, his eyes following the speed with which they rose up the next wall of water. The fat raindrops pelting his hat brim seemed to be increasing. He turned aside and got behind James and the mast as a stream of spray blew off an approaching wave. The crest rose above his head before the ship broke through and rolled into the long plunge down the other side.

"Dependable. For the time bein'!" James said, raising his voice. They were gripping halyards over unsteady footing by then. "Out of the west-northwest. Compass heading is due south. Barometer's been falling all day. The fronts will converge in the next hour. Things are about to get really interesting," he added, frowning over Earl's shoulder at what he saw happening in the wheelhouse. Elmer was turning the glass with one hand on the wheel. "Won't be long before we lose sight of those ships between the swells."

"Full dark?"

"Less than an hour. Why? What've you got up your sleeve?" James felt his way to the bell, released the clapper cord, and rang out four bells of the first dogwatch. Distracted by the captain's curt manner, he neglected to hook the cord properly.

"We all done out here?" Earl shouted from across the deck. At James's nod, they headed for the wheelhouse and closed the door just as the squall hit. The rain was coming in sideways.

"How's the heading?" James asked Elmer over the spatter while he and Earl hung up the rain gear and staggered to seats across from each other.

"Due south for the most part," Elmer said, leaning over the compass and tapping the hourglass. He had no idea why James would stare at him the way he was.

James tightened his lips and pointed a stiff finger at the chart. "We're about here. We're doing around twelve knots and will be off San Clemente around the first bell of the middle watch, six or so hours from now. We should be close to Ensenada around the second bell of the morning watch. I doubt if those jackals out there will try to disable us before first light." He took off his spectacles and, giving Earl a nearsighted squint, took his time wiping them off. "What've you got in mind?" he asked again.

Rather than provide a direct answer, Earl asked a question. "How long will it take us to get close to the Shadow? Say a hundred yards out?"

"Fifteen minutes. Drone's running way too close. Three cables away, six hundred yards, give or take. Be nearly full dark. She'll probably start firing at us before then. It'll be a real challenge to get over there. Bride's not designed to be sailing into a headwind producing sixty-foot waves."

"Good."

"Good? What do you mean *good*?" James said, becoming testy. The conversation was moving from the theoretical into the practical far faster than he'd expected. He put his glasses back on and spread his hands on the chart. "Are you planning to ram her, as well?" he asked, his voice dripping with sarcasm.

"I don't think it'll come to that. I plan to sink her," Earl stated with a little more firmness than he would have preferred to use.

"Oh, really? We're not going to get the Bride to scoot across this hellacious chop like so many flickering moonbeams, you know. Did you hear the part about the ship's design? Are you planning to sail over there, quite possibly under cannon fire, and scare them into missing? Your bright idea could tear the sticks off the Bride before we get within cannon range. Are you crazy? Have you been drinking? Are you snorting powders? Not a good idea to be taking your own medicines, Dr. Yeaton. What were you doing all that time alone in your cabin anyway? You've been acting strange lately! I know you've had a tough start to the New Year, but this is too much! Arggh, our first conversation after an assassination attempt turns into an argument!"

Earl tightened his lips.

James raised his arms and pleaded with the ceiling. "Heaven, in your loving grace, save this poor sinner from the ignorant follies of the supremely self-confident residing among us!"

"Oh boy, I thought it might come to this," Earl said, watching James's complexion go from ruddy to dark red.

"What've you got in mind, Earl?" James asked for a third time, using all of the self-control he could muster. "If it isn't one thing with him, it's two!" he said to Elmer.

Elmer put his tongue between his teeth and held it there. *James is right,* he thought. *The captain is acting strangely. He's never holed up in his cabin before. Now this. Two enemies and hurricane-force winds on the way! No wonder the sail master is upset.* Elmer stared at Earl and waited for the answer.

"I intend to alter course. The Bear will run before us and away. Once we've changed our tack, she'll be unable to come about in time to influence what we're going to do to the Shadow. I plan to crowd her more than she's been crowding us."

James grunted, leaned back, and snapped the chart with a parallel ruler. The rain sounded like stewed peas smacking the windows. "Didn't you hear what I just said about the folly of trying that maneuver?"

"Yeah, well," Earl said, raising his voice, "I want us to run on a tack that will intercept the Shadow. Buckle will have a lot to think about when he sees us coming. His gunners are merchant mariners with little experience in naval warfare. Walter Tuttle says they don't even practice running out the cannons, for God's sake. They'll be too rattled to shoot properly. You can get us close enough to put our explosive rounds where they can do the most damage. I'm confident you can do that without dismasting the Bride in the process. We're only going to get one shot at this, James."

James stopped fuming and stared at the wall above Earl's head. Although he hated to admit it, Earl was correct. *The Bride is going to be under fire from two ships come morning. How can we attack the Shadow without getting into more trouble than we're already in? This proposal is fraught with danger. The foc'sl is awash each time the ship plunges into a trough. Opening those ports invites disaster. The gunners are not going to be aligning their shot through an open port. How are we going to time running out the guns? Are they going to close the ports in time to prevent tons of water from flooding the ship and taking us to the bottom?*

Earl spoke before James could move on to other logistical problems. "We'll be mauled by two enemies bent on destroying us if we hold off. I'm not sure how we'd fare in a battle with the two of them. They have the wind gauge, and we have little sea room. I say we peel one of them off now while we still have the element of surprise on our side."

The clapper cord slipped off the hook during the heated exchange. The *ting-ting-ting* of the clapper hitting the bell each time the ship rolled moved from a minor annoyance into the sphere of the unbearable. James cursed and flung the window open. The wet gusts thwarting his attempts to hook the cord increased everyone's tensions by sweeping the chart, compass, divider, and magnifier off the table. That set off a mad scramble to hook the damn cord, close the window, and put everything back where it belonged. It also gave Earl an idea.

He smoothed his hair and rubbed his forehead after he and James sorted out the mess. Earl sat at the end of the table under the forward window.

"Let's settle down and think this through. I'm confident we can deal with the Bear one on one, wind gauge or no. We'll sink her in the morning if need be." He blinked away the images of what had just taken place, took a deep breath, put his elbows on the table, and held his head in the fading light. Everything around him seemed to be swaying, creaking, or sheltering him from the growing gale. *What am I getting us into?*

"We can't wait a moment longer if we're going to do this," he heard James reply.

"No. Put out the fore course?" Earl asked, glancing up and seeing James's color returning to normal.

"We can do that. Probably too wet for the shell packings to set 'er afire. We aren't going to risk putting anybody above the first set of sails in this weather. With any luck, Buckle will see what we're doing and add more sail too. That'd be unfortunate for him if he chooses to do what you hope he does."

"One can only hope. The cannon crews are going to be behind closed ports until it's time to attack Captain Buckle and his boys. I'll get Tom set up while you get busy on the quarterdeck. I'll send Ryan and the crew outside. See you in a bit." That said, Earl bolted out the door and ran back to his cabin before James could change his mind.

He rummaged around in one of the catch-all trunks stored in the back of his closet. "There you are!" he exclaimed. He'd put his hand on a battered old hunter's horn he'd found in a Rockland second-hand store. He opened the trapdoor, went down the stairs, and ran along the deck. A moment later, he ran up the galley stairs and was among the cooks. "Douse the fires, and feed the crew leftovers. Batten everything down. Things are about to get hot!"

He walked around the serving counter, grabbed a large spoon, and filled a bowl with a jalapeno pepper concoction made of stew meat and vegetables. He cut off a large slice of bread and gave instructions to Ryan while he wolfed down his meal. "Call all hands. We're going to sink the Shadow. We need you and your crew on deck. James should be waiting at the rail by the time you get there. We're dropping the fore course. Tom, Hopley, Charlie, and the rest of the cannon crew stay with me. I need Mike."

A few minutes later, he had most of Tom's crew assembled. The gunners, who had been riding out the storm in their hammocks, joined the men sitting around the table.

"Here's what we're going to do," Earl said, grabbing the fiddles and swaying with everyone else as the ship topped another crest. "You're going in the foc'sl now. Hopley and Charlie are going to pass you shells and powder. You're going to load both of the starboard cannons behind closed ports. Get in the foc'sl by way of the galley and magazine stairs." The ship corkscrewed into a trough and they could just imagine how far below the surface the foc'sl was about to go. "You two," Earl said to Hopley and Charlie, "put on cotton slippers; there's static everywhere." He poked Charlie in the chest. "Do it before you go into the magazine."

Earl hung on with the rest of them and waited for the ship to right itself before continuing. "Mike is coming with me. He'll be standing at the base of my cabin stairs listening for the sound of the wheelhouse bell. He'll blow this horn each time he hears the bell." Earl handed Mike the horn. "Give it a blow."

Mike blew the horn. Elmer heard the sound in the wheelhouse.

"That should do it," Earl said. "Now listen carefully. The first blat you hear will be the 'all set' signal. The second will be the signal to open the ports, run out the cannons, and sink the Shadow. You'll have to act fast because you ain't going to get much time to fire and close the ports again. Take a storm lantern with you, Tom. Empty the bowl before you go. The wick will give you all the light you'll need." He started laughing before he finished his next comment. "If I'm wrong and you can't get those ports closed before the kerosene burns off, you'll have a lot more to think about than how to find your way in the dark!" His laughter was as infectious as he had hoped.

Tom and the rest of the men started laughing right along with Earl. "I've had a few wild times, Capt'n, but I've never been squeezed this way. We can either blow up the foc'sl or drown in it! Neither sounds like a good time to me! The boys and I will take the third option and get the job done, thank you very much!

Thirty minutes later, Tom and his crew were riding out the storm behind closed ports. The *Bride* leaped ahead after Ryan's crew sheeted the fore course on the new tack. The sail plan permitted the ship to veer to starboard on the thinnest of margins. The intention to feint a collision put them all at great risk. The sails were set for a south-by-west course versus the westerly heading

Earl was proposing. This heading put them perilously close to plunging through the tall waves head on, losing propulsion, and foundering.

"It's a wonder no one got washed overboard while we were trimming the sails," James muttered as the last man closed the salon door. "Harrumph," he said after Ryan joined him on the quarterdeck. "Hold me against the mast. I want to get a fix on what they're up to over there."

With the first mate squeezing him tight, James raised a telescope and brought the bobbing image to bear on their opponents. "Ayah, just as I thought. The Bear and Shadow are adding more canvas. The Shadow is closing the distance! Trap's set!" he said, wriggling free and heading for the wheelhouse.

Earl and Adam were standing holding handrails. Ryan hung his rain gear and sat facing where the *Shadow* would be in the failing light. Thinking they might be cooped up for a while, Adam raided the ship's stores and returned with a large basket stuffed with dried fruit, cold cuts, biscuits, cups, and a corked jug of water.

"I'll take it from here," James said to Elmer. "Take a seat. You all might want to get a firm grip because it's apt to get a little rough."

James spun the big wheel to starboard. The *Bride* changed her heading and split the first of many rollers coming their way. The bow responded to the addition of the fore course by propelling the ship up the next big wave to come aboard. The added canvas overcame the heading's imperfect trim and used the power of the wind to drive her through the turbulence at a frightening speed. The ship canted alarmingly as she lifted up and over the first in a succession of increasingly tall waves. James felt the wheel go slack as she crested the biggest wave yet and dropped over the other side in an uncontrolled descent into the trough below. So much water came aboard that spume did not form until the surge had smashed against the deck structures. Minutes passed, and the *Bride* plowed forward on a converging tack with an enemy whose location became increasingly uncertain each time the ship slid off the backside of a towering wall. Down, down, down the ship would go until the swell lifted her submerged foc's'l out of the trough. Up, up, up she would rise, sixty or more feet, until she crashed through the top of the next wave. The men in the wheelhouse saw nothing beyond dark, frothing crests, a suggestion of masts, and possibly a t'gallant or two several times before coming up at last to see the *Shadow* much closer than they expected.

"Adam, would you give me a hand holding the wheel? We can give Ol' Elmer here a break," James said, winking at his friend.

"Wouldn't want to be on deck right now," Elmer moaned, feeling a shudder run through the ship as another crest crashed through the rails. No one said anything about how the people in the foc'sl might be doing or commented on how little time they would have to open the ports, run out the cannons, fire, and close the ports before it was too late.

"We're nearly a cable distant and closing fast," James observed. Without thinking, he took his hand off the wheel to turn the glass. "This will go better if Charlie can hear the bell." He was having difficulty guessing where the *Shadow*'s gun ports should be.

The *Shadow* appeared to grow larger as the *Bride* bore down on her. Everyone saw the ports open and the guns run out. A moment later, they saw a flash and waited in dread for the ball to take out the foremast. Nothing. No destructive impact against the *Bride*'s hull, no parting of stays, no snapping of masts, no damage thus far. The second cannon waited too long. The shot clipped a wave and slammed the hull above the waterline. "Take more'n that to smash a nine-pound ball through ten inches of laminated Central Maine oak," Earl said through clenched teeth. The *Shadow*'s ports stayed open while the men struggled with the cannons. "Be mighty tough to pull a ton of cannon up those sloping decks in tossing seas," Earl observed, waiting to see if the second part of his gambit would work.

Adam could feel the keel shearing off to port and spun the wheel to keep the rudder from following suit. He felt resistance.

"Easy, Adam," James said. "Let me feather the rudder. We have to wend our way through this hellish maze with a great deal of care. Let her drift a few degrees more to port."

The *Bride*'s tack placed her less than 200 yards from the point of impact. Gusts from the approaching squall sent streams of water skimming over the surface like plumes of drifting snow. The tips of the *Shadow*'s masts remained visible each time the hull dropped from view. Unless either party altered course, the two storms would converge at about the time the vessels collided.

The men in the wheelhouse had their glasses trained on the *Shadow*'s wheelmen. Next to them stood Buckle and Grant, who were gesticulating at the *Bride*, their cannon, the wheelmen, and the squall in equal measure. James turned the wheel to port at the top of a swell and willed the rudder to remain under water as they tipped over for the long slide to the bottom. The tensions in the wheelhouse rose in proportion to the ship's increasing elevation as she rose on the surge and stalled at the top of the next huge wave. James turned the wheel a little farther to port and made eye contact with Earl. "Let 'er rip."

Earl opened the window enough to reach the cord and banged the clapper against the bell. Mike could hear the racket from his position. He raised the horn to his lips, and the blast mixed with Charlie's yells coming from the bottom of the foc'sl stairs. "I heard the bell! I heard the bell! Get set!"

Tom nodded to his crew, closed the trapdoor, and waited for the next signal. The men holding the cannons in place knew they would have to wait a little longer after the ship tipped and slid off another wall of water. They felt the bow plunge into the trough. The headlong rush slowed as the ship planed off and rose with the swell. No one commented on how long it took the water to stop gurgling above their heads.

Up, up, up the ship rose on the next wave. Charlie heard the bell, and his voice joined the clamor of the horn. Tom and his men were ready. "Open the ports, and run out the guns!"

The ports opened, and he was surprised to see the *Shadow*'s hull looming less than a hundred yards to starboard. The two ships were cresting opposite waves with a common trough between them. Tom pulled his head back. "She's broadside! Now or never, boys! Watch out for the recoil, keep a firm grip on the lines, and mind your feet!" He nodded to the gunner next to him. "Fire!"

They pulled their lanyards at the same time. A flash of red-and-yellow flames lit the greasy expanse, turning each raindrop into a streak of silver. The roar of explosive shells exiting the muzzles drowned out the multitude of other sounds the yelling men were used to hearing. They closed the ports, chocked the cannons, and lashed them to the deck just before the *Bride* tipped to follow her bows into the sea one more time.

The men in the wheelhouse expected the cannons to fire, but the boom jolted them in ways none had expected. Elmer hopped in his seat. Ryan started as if to run. Earl and Adam swiveled their eyes forward as if they were searching for the source of a lightning strike. James tightened his grip on the wheel. Stunned by what he had just made possible, he tried to recall what he had planned to do after he saw the flash and heard the thunder of shells destroying the *Shadow*. Remembering to turn the wheel to port, he hoped to keep the keel even a little bit longer. He was not a religious man per se, but he did pray for Tom to pull the cannons in, lash them, and close the ports before a disaster wiped out his dreams of ever seeing Mrs. Coombs again.

The exploding shells hit the *Shadow* amidships.

"Good God, I didn't know them shells could do that!" Elmer bawled. "That flamin' cavern's big enough to drive a wagon through!" he yelled to his shipmates. They too were shocked at how much damage the shells caused. What didn't go over the side in the initial explosion either collapsed into the hold or set fire to the adjacent structures. The squall's howling winds and driving rains hit the *Shadow*'s courses and extinguished what was left of the burning canvas. Panicked men clung to the useless wheel and stared in awe at the carnage. The crippled ship listed to port and did not top the crest. The cannon crew fled to the weather side and hooked their elbows over the rails. The injured would be the first to go.

The *Bride* slipped ahead of the stricken ship, canted, crashed into the trough, and rose on the same wave that held the *Shadow*. A towering cliff of cascading surge swept over the doomed ship's deck, and before the ship could settle, the space between the remaining survivors widened. The *Shadow* rolled over the next crest first. The *Bride* followed, and from high on the same wall of water, the men in her wheelhouse witnessed the *Shadow*'s tragic passage down the other side. Parting stays popped with the sound of rifle fire. The mainmast snapped off at the trestletree structure, collapsing the top portion onto the foremast. The *Shadow* lost her way as the welter of sails, yards, and cordage fell on helpless crewmen. The loose cannons scurried about the pitching deck like maddened bulldogs seeking refuge in the arms of their masters. Bloody pulps appeared each time a master tried to ward off their affections. What had been an undeniably beautiful menace a few short minutes earlier was now a wallowing hulk that would take the lives of all aboard.

"She's in irons!" Elmer exclaimed.

The *Shadow* would not respond to the helm and was now at the mercy of wind and waves. More chaos appeared aboard the ship as the surge lifted her bows. Men, loose gear, and tons of water in her holds flowed aft. The combined weight drove the stern deep into the following sea. Buckle, Grant, and the helmsmen did not reappear after the vessel rolled into the trough. Earl and Adam exchanged a glance and continued to watch from a hundred yards out.

Surge breaking over the starboard side swept the decks clear of men struggling out of the holds. The men clinging to the rails shared one thing in common with their observers: Everyone had front-row seats for the *Shadow*'s final act. The men in the *Bride*'s wheelhouse stared across the short distance into the terrified eyes of every seaman's worst nightmare. The waterlogged ship foundered in the rising swell, rolled, and keeled over. The crest collapsed on the trough, and all sign that a ship had ever been in the *Bride*'s presence vanished.

James missed most of the last scene. He had his own vessel to spare from a similar fate. Squalls had spelled the end for many fine ships, and as he well knew, the *Bride* could easily join their ranks. The sight of the *Shadow*'s demise nearly unmanned him.

James's shaky voice rose voice over the growing gale. "We'll stay the course! Sou'-sou' west! She's responding to the rudder, and the wash is going over the side. The canvas seems to be holding us upright." He nodded to Adam as if to reassure himself and raised his voice even more. "Steady as she goes, and I think we'll come out on the other side of this sickening sea just fine. Only option is to keep her on this tack for n-n-now," he stuttered, pointing a twitching finger at the compass card. "Hope Tom closed the ports and lashed the guns in time. C-c-can't s-s-see a thing. Everything beyond the windows is a blur. We're sailing blind! Wouldn't want to collide with the Bear about now or go aground on San Clemente Island!" he shrieked, waving a hand at the rain-streaked glass. "For once it'd be nice to be cruising along a lee shore!" he added with a strained laugh that bordered on the maniacal.

Although disconcerting, James's shipmates could easily understand his mad behavior. They too found themselves in a state of fear that bordered on the unbearable. Experience had taught them that the *Bride* had reached the upper limits of her capacity to weather the storm.

James felt Earl's hand on a shoulder. "Easy now, James. We know how you feel. Let's take this one step at a time. So far, so good. We'll get through this. Hard part's over. Thanks to you, we ain't going to be joining Captain Buckle, who expected *us* to be the ones going down with the ship."

"Thanks," James said. "I needed that." He leaned over and took a reading on the compass, then glanced at Elmer. "Please light the binnacle." The man's mottled complexion made it hard to tell where Elmer's face ended and the shadows began. James shook off the spooky image. "God only knows where we are," he muttered. "Soon's the squall passes, we have to get back on a south-by-south heading. Ryan, take my place at the wheel. You're as good at feeling your way through the waves as I'll ever be." He shared a weary nod with Adam and sat on the bench with his head in his hands.

Elmer lit the lamp. Earl tapped the barometer and glanced at the clock. The compass said they were heading southwest. James watched him cross to the log and note the time of the *Shadow*'s passing. Settling into a stolid silence, James and the others paused to review in their still-quailing minds what had transpired over the last short hour. Adam lit the wall and overhead lanterns. James surveyed the group and felt another ferocious breaker send tremors rippling through the seat of his pants. Bending over the basket, he pulled out a napkin, a handful of sliced meat, and a chunk of cheddar. He drank a cup of water, then arranged his dinner on the napkin. "Anybody up for a game of cribbage?"

CHAPTER 14

23°26' N, 21°29' E, Tropic of Cancer,
11 January 1860, 12:30 p.m.

The peal of the afternoon's first bell received an indifferent shrug from the men grouped around the wardroom table. Their attention was focused on the pencil stubs scribbling arcane formulas on notepads arrayed around a chart strewn with timepieces, assorted measuring devices, and little sand bags.

"I know where we are on the globe," James declared. He looked up and saw Bill Hobbs flexing a stay on the other side of a porthole.

He glanced at Willard, the ship's officers and back to Willard, whose eyes were scanning their pocket watches. Except for the second hands, the times were the same.

He then examined the Mercer chronometer housed in an alcove. The clock's hands pointed at 10:30 p.m., Greenwich Mean Time. "How many hours away is Greenwich Tower, Willard?"

Although chronometers were essential to navigation on open water and had been around for close to a hundred years, they retained a mystical aura to those whose lives depended on them. After all, the chronometer was the only thing between its users and oblivion. An hour earlier, Maynard had come down from the crosstrees and said he could smell vegetation for the first time since they'd cleared San Clemente. He also said the boobies and albatrosses they'd seen while making the crossing had been joined by frigate birds, shearwaters, koa'e kea, and other seabirds. Maynard's observations got the men in the chartroom busy with sextants. They shot the sun at noon and rushed below with their findings. Having confirmed where they were on the latitudinal line, their placement on the longitudinal line came next. By calculating how many hours they were from the master chronometer housed in Greenwich, England, they were able to answer a question that had been dogging mariners for centuries: How do we find the ship's position on the intersecting longitudinal line? Willard had the answer as soon as he shot the sun, but, as usual, chose to not upstage his comrades.

"Ten," Willard stated.

"Yes, and I'm quite sure we're right here," James said, placing a divider point over a space in the Tropic of Cancer's dotted line. "This puts us forty-eight hours or so out of Honolulu."

"I agree," Earl said. He gestured to Adam. "We have a small formality to attend to before trying to calculate how far we are from Hawaii. You're to be commended, James. You've guided us nearly two thousand miles over open ocean. We're on course to pass between Molokai and O'ahu tomorrow. Your feat deserves a special toast." Adam crossed the room, removed a towel, and pulled a liter bottle of Veuve Clicquot out of an ice bucket. He removed the foil and wire from the neck and popped the cork. Earl saw him holding the bottle over the bucket and groaned as foaming champagne ran down the bright-yellow label.

"Comet year, Captain?" James asked, cocking his head and peering over his glasses at Willard.

"Yes, 1811 this time. Correct me if I'm wrong, Willard. I think we have eight cases of the liter bottle, a dozen 'piccolo' splits, and a dozen twelve-liter Balthazars packed below." Holding his gaze on the champagne dripping into the bucket, he tried to imagine what it took to produce this legendary Loire Valley wine. He'd been told spring arrived on time that year and the soil received adequate amounts of rain followed by warm, dry airs, which in turn encouraged the grape blossoms to remain open under a full moon during the summer solstice. He wished he could have been there to see the comet's auspicious arrival. Its tail would have added a wondrous enchantment to the starry moonlit nights. Earl was sure the valley's vintners must have known it was going to be a great year for dries as they walked among the vines and heard the vineyards humming to the tune of bees from early dawn until late in the evening. "Ahh," he murmured above the sparkling bubbles, "the proof of this wine's ascendency resides in the pleasure our palates are about to receive from this full-bodied elixir brimming with intoxicating nectar."

"One case is a bottle shy of six," Willard interrupted, waving a finger toward Adam.

"Balthazar, Balthazar," James said. "The name is familiar. Where have I heard Balthazar before?"

"He was one of the three Wise Men who brought gold, frankincense, and myrrh as gifts to the baby Jesus," Willard said with a happy smile. "Oh, how I love being reminded of Christmas!"

"Right. I should have known," James muttered. "I'd love Christmas too if I'd spent them with your mother," he blurted before he could tighten his lips to prevent another disclosure from spilling out.

Adam poured the chilled champagne into crystal glasses. The group toasted James's navigational skills and shared a sip to honor having passed over the line. Ryan pointed his glass at the clock. "Here's to John Harrison, the father of the chronometer. To the H-5, gentlemen." They raised their glasses in a solemn toast to the genius whose perseverance and determination made it possible for mariners to cross the seas in confidence.

James, in a transparent effort to divert their attention, suggested they toast the pocket watches on the chart. "To that Maine Yankee, Arron Dennison, who produced these fine timers in Boston!" They all took a big gulp on that one and emptied the bottle.

Ryan cleared his throat. "Soon as we down the champagne, it might be wise to raise a toast to our good fortune. We could use the cold water in the bucket! I can think of no better way to enjoy our dwindling supply of ice. How far removed we are from the frozen Fraser River. British Columbia sure does seem like a long way and a lifetime ago."

They all laughed at how he'd skipped over the more morbid aspects of what constituted their good fortune. They clinked their sparkling glasses once more after James declared, "And in one piece, by God!" Their hearty laughter carried through the open ports and into the ears of the watch crew working outside.

"The people in there would laugh in the face of the Devil himself," Bill said to the men working with him by the shroud bank. "And make no mistake;

they'd fight their way through hell getting to what awaits us on the other side of the horizon!"

Bill and his crew were reeving new cordage to replace the ropes stretched and frayed by the enormous pressures encountered during the recent storm. Reeving was one thing; getting the proper tension in the running rigging on a ship was quite another. Men like Hobbs, who could properly fine-tune the rigging, were hard to find. "They can have all the champagne stored in the hold," he said, pointing a tarry finger at the weather deck and using it to prod the hairless chest of Danny Rickles. "The best stuff for the likes of us is old Appleton grog. I'll take Jamaican rum any day over fermented grape juice." Bill's bushy eyebrows lifted in anticipation of the treat in store for them. "Today we double up our daily ration at the beginning of the first dog watch." He patted Danny's head. "Should be enough to turn up the heat in there!"

They all laughed along with Danny. The twenty-five-year-old was as bald as a billiard ball and wore a watch cap at all times. "My head feels chilled without it!" he said to anyone who asked. "Captain Earl says I have alopecia. My mother calls it fox mange. Either way, it amounts to the same thing: no hair! I guess I'm going to have to settle down in a place that's hot. And it won't be in Southern Maine eitha!"

Bill cheerfully plucked the shroud they had just reeved to measure its tension. "Not bad for the winds and time of day. We're done here."

He gave a reassuring tug on the thick cords holding the raked masts in place and shuddered at the sight of two people casually swaying back and forth in the tops. Bill's hips and knees flexed eight to ten inches at a time as the deck pitched and rolled beneath them, nothing compared to what was occurring high above. "Ugh," he groaned, as the spar carried the relaxed observers twenty feet forward before the ship's motion swung them off to the side and to the rear for another ten or fifteen feet each time the vessel split an open ocean roller. "Not for me," he mumbled, leading his group to the mainmast shrouds.

Maynard had chosen a perch placing him and Mike as high as possible above the deck. They had climbed beyond the crosstrees after Maynard had made his report to the captain and stopped to have a bite to eat. Their feet were dangling below the skysail yard. The brailed sail, halyards, and foot lines gave them a stellar location from which to enjoy the unobstructed view. Bill had no idea how much they were enjoying sitting in the bright sunshine watching koa'e kea dive into schools of fish disturbed by the bow wave.

"Hey," Mike said pointing at frigate birds plunging into a frothing mass of mahi-mahi forced to the surface by a pack of sharks. The two fell into an easy silence as the ship dipped and weaved its way west-southwest through the seemingly endless ranks of large waves. Below them, Bill and his mates made repairs while the *Bride* glided over an ocean whose welcoming embrace extended for as far as the eye could see.

"Can't take a deep breath, but I can enjoy the smell of land again," Maynard said. "Be good to walk along the beaches of Honolulu for a change. How're *you* feeling today?"

Mike rocked his head from side to side before replying. "So-so. Part of me wants to forget all about what happened back there. Another part keeps telling me to remember I didn't drop the gun. I know I'm not a chicken, so that's good to know, I suppose, but I'm still losing sleep over what I had to do to prove it. I'm a little mixed up. A week or so on the ocean feels like a year has passed since the shooting in the Dip. You know what I mean?"

"Oh, yeah. I do," Maynard agreed, still recovering from having killed a man and getting drilled in the process. "Like Capt'n Earl said, you're doing good. I know, I know . . . you're wondering if I said anything about how you felt in the coach. Don't worry, I haven't told anyone what you said. If Capt'n Earl hadn't 'a winked a second time you might have lost it. Well, you didn't. You shot the bandit, you saved Munenori in the stables, and you sure as hell were part of what got us through the night we sank the Shadow. Be patient with yourself. You'll come around. Time will catch up with you. I'll talk with you whenever you feel like it. No one knows what we talk about up here."

"Thanks. I would rather not go through that again for a while." Mike was quiet for a moment. "You think the Bear is waiting for us in Honolulu?"

Maynard eased his bandages into a more comfortable position and put a hand on his young friend's shoulder. "I don't know. She's the reason Capt'n Earl has had observers up here all day every day since she disappeared the night the Shadow went down. She could be anywhere. One thing's for sure, she's not likely to catch us by surprise today."

They took a gander at the curve of the earth, scanned the vast expanse, and held the halyards a little tighter. Ten days had passed since they had killed off bandits, protected their friends, and sank the *Shadow*.

The day after they crossed the Tropic of Cancer, Maynard leaned forward over the skysail yard trying to get a better view of what lay ahead. A ship's boy had just completed ringing six bells of the morning watch. As the notes faded, Maynard noticed the mottled slopes of Kamakou emerging out of the thinning fog. Land once again became a fixture worthy of note. The islands of Molokai and O'ahu grew out of the western horizon with each passing hour. By late afternoon, O'ahu's Makapu'u Point was a presence off the starboard quarter. Gulls, cormorants, terns, and a variety of shorebirds appeared in greater numbers. Colton Lewis rang in four bells of the second dogwatch and reported seeing a pod of dolphins competing with a flock of frigate birds. They were attacking a school of herring herded to the surface by the dolphins.

The following morning at slack flood tide, the *Bride* sailed past Waikiki beach and the ships at anchor in Honolulu Harbor. The morning light caught her crystal globe and spread a golden pathway over the sparkling ripple. "Deck there!" Maynard called out from aloft. "A ship's tied off on Yeaton Wharf!" His call got the men in the foc'sl busy fishing the anchor. Honolulu anchorage lay dead ahead.

James was with Earl beside the quarterdeck rail. He turned aft at the sound of squealing pulleys and saw Elmer leaning on the wheelhouse wall beneath Old Glory. He and Elmer watched Charlie run up the Yeaton House flag. As soon as the flag hit the stops, Charlie cleated the halyard and scurried off to the foc'sl as fast as his feet could carry him. James was still raising his eyebrows and shaking his head with Elmer when he heard Earl say, "We'll anchor in the roads until we can clear a berth."

"Aye," James replied in a voice strained by what had captured the crew's attention. Young women had rushed to dugouts and were paddling out to greet the boys waving to them from the foc'sl rail. Mike, Hopley, Charlie were pointing at the dugouts they wanted to board.

James shook his head again and had to remind himself that he was young once too. "I'll get this vessel anchored without embarrassing us all," he muttered. He drew his lips tighter and glanced at the pennant. Light airs lifted its length several points to starboard.

He felt the boys' excitement rippling through the crew and had to give credit where credit was due. The men had completed the last of the rigging repairs and deserved the treats awaiting them in Mamala Bay. A small smile broke through when he acknowledged what was bothering him. The boys would be the first ashore! As if reading his thoughts, Earl murmured, "This is the way it should be, James, even if it means you'll have to crack the whip setting the hook!"

Munenori was on duty and rang out two bells of the forenoon watch. Nine o'clock. He ran up the foc'sl stairs to join the boys. Two were sitting on the rail above the anchor. The other two were standing above them holding forestays. Munenori came to a stop by the rail and stared with everyone else.

Excepting the jib and upper tops'ls, the men had furled the rest of the *Bride*'s canvas. There was hardly enough breeze to make way across the water. The morning sun promised a warm day beneath clear tropical skies.

"You realize, of course, the festive atmosphere aboard this ship is going to prevent us from getting any work done," James said.

"Sure. Look around you. The men aren't going to want to have anything to do with the ship for as long as we're at anchor. This is a day they'll prize. After all, they risked life and limb to get here."

"We still have two thousand tons of moving ship to bring to a stop," James grumbled to a captain who was no longer listening.

The land rose in stages away from the sandy beaches to lush green hills clinging to broken craters and volcanic escarpments. The fact that molten lava had pushed its way up from miles beneath the water's surface only added to the appreciation of where they were. The presence of violent primal forces compounded the seductive sensory experience. Honolulu Harbor had several wharfs, a customhouse, chandlers, fish markets, and warehouses on the water's edge. Across the street from the waterfront buildings was the usual assortment of hotels, eateries, laundries, saloons, and the bordellos that drove the Christian Congregationalist missionaries to distraction.

Apart from the neglected fort, the place had little order. The immigrant population called the well-trodden trails *streets*. The lesser trails followed every fold in the earth back into the hills where they petered out or were lost from sight. The sandy gravel foreshore eventually gave way to arable soil. Market gardens and orchards appeared along a streamed winding its way into palm and sandalwood groves lining the hillsides. The land rose rapidly from sparse lower-level vegetation to green-clad volcanic mountains. South of their current location rose the dominant landmark called Diamond Head, so named by British sailors who'd mistaken the calcite deposits for diamonds. The mountain was a volcanic crater and caused the timid to cast wary glances its way long after they'd emerged from its shadow. Less dominant but closer were other craters occupying the approaching foreground.

The *Bride* glided past ships rocking at anchor in the morning light. Several vessels had been there for a while and had awnings stretched across their decks. Gangways were visible on the sides of the larger ships. A pilot boat shoved off from Government Wharf when the *Bride* cleared the headland. The craft resembled a giant water beetle as multiple oars propelled it across the light chop. A man stood in the stern waving a staff attached to a bright-yellow flag.

At James's scowl, Ryan and his mates hustled the gawking men on watch to their places. The crew pried their eyes off the sights and sobered up under James's fixed stare.

"Stay on your toes," Elmer told the helmsman. "This is not the time to disappoint Mr. Marshall."

The sun blinked off numerous telescopes focusing on the *Bride*'s entrance. Many eyes on shore and along the rails of the other ships took the opportunity to witness the same entertaining diversion *they* had experienced—namely, performing an anchor drill under the scrutiny of one's peers. The pilot waved his banner over the spot chosen to drop anchor and moved aside. The eight white oars rose as one as the ship drifted to windward near the anchorage. Like beggars drawn to a banquet, a flock of gulls appeared and circled above the listless pennant. "Let her fall off to starboard another point, Elmer!" The ship turned slightly to the pressure of the rudder.

At a stern nod from James, Ryan called out, "Lee braces! Hands wear ship! Tops'l braces! Tops'l clew lines release and haul!"

James turned to Elmer. "Helm alee!"

The ship swung into the breeze as the way went off her. The men strung out along the tops'l yards gathered the canvas and tied off the sails. The men on the braces quickly balanced them all out, so each horizontal yard was set perpendicular to the hull. *None better*, Earl thought with a sigh of satisfaction.

"Shoo the boys over to the port side!" Ryan called out to the anchor crew. "Let go!"

Free of the dog on the cat's back, the starboard side anchor hit the water with a splash as yards and yards of chain rapidly followed suit. As soon as the anchor hit bottom, the men in the foc's'l allowed the chain to pay out an extra fifty or sixty yards and set the windlass brake.

The young women who got there first shrieked at being drenched. Three of the watching ship's boys were not spellbound for long. Hopley, Mike, and Charlie knew what to do with the enthusiastic maidens. Ryan had already relieved them of watch duty. Tossing their quickly bundled clothes into the waiting arms of the smiling girls, they jumped over the side wearing nothing but their birthday suits. The girls dragged them aboard as soon as they popped to the surface. Once they had the boys in dugouts, the young women started paddling their prizes to the palm-thatched huts lining the sandy shore.

"Six to one," Bob Cobb said with a grin, his words unheard by the men standing with him.

Ryan suspected the two boys left behind were too shy and unsure of what to do in the presence of so much stimulation, so he assigned watch duties to keep them occupied. He felt their introduction to feminine pleasures might need to be a little more gradual and under guided supervision—or so it seemed. He knew there was one thing the reluctant boys shared in common with their brethren: they wanted the tactile to complement the visual. How they wanted to get over their shyness and feel those girls! The glum expressions on Colton and Munenori's dejected faces gave way under the cheerful encouragement of several boatloads of bare-breasted beauties. The boys sought out Ryan and got a smiling nod in return. Off came clothes hastily rolled into untidy bundles and tossed into the ocean. No matter. The boys were soon among the girls. By the time they surfaced, the clothes were in the dugouts. Sputtering and laughing, the boys crawled aboard.

"Sweet mother of God!" Cobb exclaimed, coming out of a daze. "We're in the horn of the Cornucopia!" The men next to him nodded in silent agreement.

"Okay, you idlers," Ryan called, "let's get the boats over the side. Lower the boarding nets and fenders. Come on, there's still lots to do before you get to have the kind of fun the boys are having!"

The *Bride*'s arrival in Honolulu meant shore time in Paradise for everyone. The men who were not engaged in operating the vessel lined the bulwarks and fantasized over the beautiful brown maidens.

Hoys loaded with fruits and vegetables pulled alongside. Nets and money went down, and food came up. Rope ladders with wooden treads hung with the boarding nets. The long boat and both quarter boats went in the water.

Maynard slid down a stay and joined the men on the quarterdeck. He received a nod and heard Earl say, "Take the long boat out later to see how the boys are faring. Bring their side arms and belt knives. Give each a purse of gold flakes. Pack silk, mirrors, soap, bug nets, mosquito repellant, quinine, linens, thread, perfume, tissue, and a couple of sewing machines for the girls. We can deliver kitchen utensils later after we find out what they need." He waved a hand. "What else did you see from up there?"

"The harbor's holding the usual assortment of local, military, and commercial craft. There are approximately fifteen commercial vessels. The Polar Bear's not here. French, Russian, British, and American naval ships're stationed at various strategic locations." Maynard turned and pointed at the one flying a French diplomat's ensign. "The Empire's anchored between the French corvette and Sand Island. There are men standing on her poop holding glasses aimed in our direction. Do you think Mr. Harrington wanted the Empire here in case we made it past the two he sent to intercept us?"

"Definitely," Earl seethed and turned his face away from the *Empire*. "I imagine our arrival is causing quite a stir aboard that vessel. Their concern for the Shadow will turn to alarm if she doesn't show up. They're likely to be full of questions and will become frustrated with us for not telling them anything about her. They can find out what happened from somebody else for all I care, 'cause we're not tellin' 'em."

The *Bride*'s men knew the *Empire* had a new captain whose name was Mathew Stilson. Earl asked if anyone knew more about him, but no one did. "Could get fractious if any of our crew bumps into them ashore," James cautioned with a worried frown. *My captain may be staring at the ship moored to his wharf, but I doubt if he sees it,* James thought.

"Thanks for reminding me. The presence of the Empire's captain and his reasons for being here are a distraction I don't need. Be nice to have fun for a change," Earl griped. "I'd just as soon leave our disagreements right here and hope they're willing to cooperate. My father always said the first sign of a good education is good manners, so we mind our manners and see what transpires." Seeking refuge from this unpleasant turn of events, he let his gaze cross Ala Moana Boulevard and trace the path of Nuuanu Street to a treed plateau below the Punch Bowl.

Unnoticed by Earl, James bit his lip and glared at the anchorage. He half expected to hear Earl put into words what was really upsetting him. This was to have been his final stop as captain of the *Bride* two years ago, a retirement day he had been forced to postpone by the likes of Arthur Harrington and his allies. *Oh, how filled with heartache his last night ashore will be this time around.*

Too preoccupied with his own thoughts to observe James's distress, Earl pushed all thoughts of the *Empire's* captain aside in favor of what awaited him on the plateau. A jab in the ribs put an end to his improving disposition. He lowered his gaze and saw James wiggling a thumb toward the corvette's counter. A quarter boat was coming around her stern.

CHAPTER 15

Queen Emma Kamehameha's Hospital Reception, 5 March 1860, 6:00 p.m.

Mathew Stilson waved a glass of dark rum toward the sparkling harbor. "This has been an entertaining truce, Captain Yeaton."

He and Earl had been admiring the view down Nuuanu Street from the second-floor veranda of Queen Emma's palace. Comfortably seated in a padded wicker chairs, they were enjoying their last evening in Honolulu. Gardenia-scented air enhanced the drowsy feeling of camaraderie they had grown used to whenever they were together.

A two-week stay had stretched into an idyllic seven-week hiatus from the voyage. Guests wandered in and out of the wide French doors. Those who were familiar with the enmity between the Yeatons and Harringtons had given up trying to figure out why Earl and Arthur Harrington's captain got along so well.

Earl had also been in the company of the royals over the preceding weeks. He had given them regular progress reports on what he and his men were doing on their islands. Their activities went well beyond the requirements of a bargain struck the previous year. The *Bride's* men delivered field hospitals to Hawaii, northern O'ahu, Molokai, Maui, and Kauai. Members of the crew traveled to each of the islands with the supplies. Earl and his crew were having so much fun working with the Hawaiians that they decided to stay and assist the carpenters building permanent structures to house the deliveries.

Early one morning a week or so after they had been giving the locals a hand, Bob Cobb and Danny Rickles asked Earl for permission to break open the crates of general hardware items stored in the hold. It wasn't long before boatloads of tools and hardware were sailing off with the hospital supplies. Earl told them to leave everything behind when it was time to go.

"Danny's got his eye on one of the girls," Bob told Earl.

"Easy to see why," Earl grinned. "Hot here."

James suggested the builders might as well add an education room to the hospitals while they were there. Not only would the residents have access to medical attention, they would also get a lending library with a classroom. The idea appealed to Earl, and he gave the okay. James and Willard began gleefully raiding the ship's holds. Crates of books, musical instruments, children's toys, writing materials, and painting supplies were soon piling up in Earl's warehouse. "Fine with me," Earl told the pair, "but you better leave an open aisle to the ton of cinchona bark I put in there. We'll be whipping up batches of quinine in the next few days."

Earl transferred two surgical wards destined for the new hospital to the customs warehouse. In exchange he received title to five acres of land across the road from his wharf on Queen Street. He set a portion of his Honolulu acreage aside and made plans to build a bank since the town didn't have one. He now had a deep-water wharf/warehouse and room to expand into shipping. The new bank and a two-story office were under construction.

Earl and Ming formed the Sino-American Trading Company in late-January. They agreed to a three-way split with a silent third partner drawn from the local population. The next day, Ming introduced Earl to a respected Chinese merchant, Li Ka-Chang, who agreed to become manager of their Hawaiian operations.

The king and queen's appreciation of Earl's contribution to the people of Hawaii came with an unanticipated benefit. Wishing to include Earl in their effort to expand the kingdom's agricultural base, they offered to sell him land suitable for farming and suggested he consider parcels on O'ahu and several of the other islands. Intrigued, Earl asked for and received assurances from them that should he decide to purchase any of the properties, they would have government road access and would include a parcel on the ocean suitable for a wharf.

Earl was familiar with the ruses his American competitors used on the unwary to prevent them from accessing their properties. Unscrupulous landowners used numerous foils to prevent their competitors from profiting from their land purchases. Most of the landlocked property owners who got into trouble did not register easements giving them the right to cross private lands. They chose to avoid paying filing fees by accepting verbal assurances that they would be able to access their property after they paid for it. A day or two after the land transfer; they found "No Trespassing" signs posted on what they thought were their access roads.

Earl had seen a version of this once before. He knew of a hotel owner who sold his hotel numerous times. The method was relatively simple. The owner would find a buyer who had a cash down payment but did not qualify for a bank mortgage. Once they reached a selling price, the hotel owner agreed to transfer title to the hotel in exchange for the cash down payment and a first mortgage. The owner knew the purchaser would be unable to pay the mortgage after deducting operating and living expenses. The purchaser would go into default, and as the mortgage holder, the seller repossessed the hotel, pocketing the down payment and mortgage payments. The last time Earl checked, the hotel had changed hands again. Arthur Harrington had a similar scheme going in California. He too was selling mortgages to people he knew would be unable to service the debt. Earl would not be purchasing properties without registered easements or public road access.

Earl surprised the royals by including Ming as a joint titleholder on all of the land transfers. Not many *haoles* (Caucasians) thought *pakes* (Chinese) were worthy of anything above menial labor. It was unheard of for a haole to collaborate with a pake, a Hawaiian word that may have come from a misunderstanding between one of the first Chinese to arrive and his Hawaiian host. Asked by a Hawaiian who he was, the man answered with his given name, "Pak Tae." From then on, Hawaiians referred to the Chinese as pake. "If you want to share your profits with a pake, go right ahead," they said.

He had been friends with the royal family since he arrived with Captain Pinkham in '36, and much to his dismay, he'd seen how haoles took advantage of the Hawaiian's easygoing manners. Somewhere along the way, the current king and queen had learned haole rhymed with an English word they used to describe many of the newcomers. The not-so-subtle inflections the king employed while pronouncing the double entendre were readily apparent to Earl. The king used the term as a pejorative, the most offensive implication being that although haloes were fond of quoting the Bible, their conduct suggested they misread its essential message.

Queen Emma and King Kamehameha had long ago determined that Earl had the rare quality they valued above all others: a generous soul from which all of his good deeds flowed. Coming from a warrior culture, they respected his willingness to use force to protect that soul.

Earl and Ming viewed several properties and decided to purchase the most attractive. Earl put up the cash, and they formed a subsidiary of their Sino-American partnership, this one focused on land management. Ming became general manager in Sino-American's three-way partnership. As operations manager, Li Ka-Chang reported to Ming.

Li and a group of influential merchants were organizing the Chinese community into a nearly autonomous economic entity within Hawaii. The reason: to circumvent the efforts by racist whites to restrict their right to engage in free and open competition. Well aware of how gwei lo used any means possible to squeeze the Chinese merchants out, Earl financed the infrastructure required to ship building materials, men, goods, and products to and from the Yeaton wharves and warehouses. Ming and Li chose to hire community leaders and distributed bags of gold coins among various trusted Chinese merchants to finance their plans. Ming was particularly interested in employing those who had been coolies before they set up their own shops, men who would be sensitive to the needs of workers. Ming shared his plan to contract and ship more workers from China with the management team. These additional workers would clear the land, put up structures, and plant sugarcane, fields of pineapples, and terraces of rice. They would also grow enough fruit and vegetables to feed Hawaii's Chinese community. Seven weeks of effort produced more than either Earl or Ming anticipated. Now ready to leave, they felt confident Li and the Sino-American Trading Company would be shipping goods to all corners of the globe in a few short years.

"We're going to need the clippers we just bought sooner than I expected," Earl said to Adam over coffee.

"Yes," Adam replied, raising his cup, "and Benjamin Wilson paid the tab!"

Earl released a contented sigh, sat a little straighter, and shifted his gaze from the sparkling water. "Yes, this has been an entertaining truce. Our association has been a pleasant surprise."

Mathew burst out laughing. "You didn't know what to make of me when my quarter boat pulled up and I asked for permission to come aboard!"

Earl laughed. "That's for sure! You made it over before I could mount a swivel gun and track your progress across the harbor. I'm sure there were lots of popping eyeballs on the other end of the telescopes watching us. Be surprised if anyone expected me to permit you to set foot on my deck!" Earl checked to see if anyone was listening and leaned in. "I'd appreciate it if you would continue to keep the reason for our friendship a secret," he whispered. "No one needs to know our past."

"Yes, sir, Capt'n Earl," Mathew smiled.

Stilson was big-boned and muscular. He stood well over six feet and carried the frame of a stevedore. Darkly hirsute, he had a ruggedly handsome head that complemented his engaging disposition. His raven locks and clean teeth framed a pair of emerald eyes that missed nothing.

The day they met, Earl had intended to deny Mathew permission to come aboard. He had ample reason to think Mathew was there for one purpose: Use any means available to determine if the bonds were in Earl's possession and if they were, kill him and the crew to get them. Frowning over the intrusion, Earl had leaned on the rail and, without thinking about it, rubbed his chest. His assessment of the situation was correct, of course, but the way the young man looked at him after they made eye contact caused Earl to change his mind.

"Leave any weapons you're carrying in the boat and come up alone. Your men will have water and a snack sent down." Mathew complied with Earl's request by putting a belt knife on a seat. "Ditch the sea boots. It's a little warm for those today."

Mathew took the boots off and removed the knife strapped to his shin.

Earl narrowed his eyes. "I don't have to reassess my willingness to let you come aboard or ask you to take your clothes off, do I?"

"No," Mathew answered and lowered his head to mask his surprise. He'd recognized Earl, but did not think Earl recognized him. He added two wafer-thin knives he'd hidden in his belt and hat band to the pile. "That's it."

Earl raised a finger. Mathew scaled the ladder and swung himself over the railing. Ryan had Kato go over him to see if Mathew had any more weapons.

"Captain Yeaton," Mathew said, offering his hand. Earl shook it. "Would it be possible for us to speak alone?"

James stepped forward. "If you harm Captain Yeaton, you'll never get off this ship alive. All who are with you will be killed. The Empire will be sunk where she sits, and whoever sent you will be tracked down to share your fate. Now, do you still want to have a talk with the captain?"

"Yes," Mathew replied, undeterred.

James bowed and gestured toward the companionway door.

"Thank you, James. Keep everyone away from the portholes and skylight while we're in my suite. Captain Stilson," Earl said, leading the way.

"May I offer you a drink?" he asked, opening the liquor cabinet and exposing a variety of decanted spirits. Beverage glasses filled slotted pigeonholes stacked inside the doors. Latticed joinery separated crystal bottles. Each decanter had a little chain draped around its neck with the content's name stamped on a golden tab. A row of labeled bottles lined the lower section of the cabinet. They contained Earl's drinks of choice—reds, cognacs, rums, and water.

Mathew noted the quality of the joinery, pursed his lower lip, and nodded with approval at the choice of wood—tiger maple. "Thank you. A glass of rum would be good." He took a seat where he could watch Earl, the door, the skylight, and the portholes. His keen eyes scanned the room while Earl poured their drinks. He soon realized he was sitting in the finest captain's cabin he'd ever seen. *Yes*, he mused, *Captain Yeaton has hidden his secret compartments well. Not a seam out of place.*

Earl poured two glasses of Appleton's Reserve. He also poured two large glasses of water, set the drinks on the table, and sat down. Taking sips, they watched each other over the rims of their glasses.

"You don't recognize me, do you?" Matthew asked.

Earl looked Mathew over while trying to think of a suitable reply. He set the rum aside, leaned back, and slid his water glass from side to side. He kept his face neutral. "You wanted to have this conversation out of the sight and hearing of your crew, didn't you?"

"Yes. I recognized you the moment you started rubbing the spot below your left shoulder."

Earl's eyes narrowed. "You bear a remarkable resemblance to a woman patient I saw seven or eight years ago in Boston. I was at Mass General visiting a friend dying of tuberculosis. A former classmate, Dr. Oliver Holmes, saw me in the ward. He asked me to examine a woman patient who was suffering from an advanced stage of pneumonia. The pleural cavity had filled with so much fluid, her lungs couldn't function properly. She was at death's door." Earl lowered his lids to slits. "I remember now. That was back in '51. The man I went to visit, Clement Yoos, was a draftsman who worked for Samuel Pook, the man who was designing this vessel with me at the time." Memory softened his voice. "I met her by accident. I was one of the few who actually believed it was not only possible to reduce fluid pressure on the lungs but that the intervention could save a patient's life. Many colleagues thought me mad in those days. They laughed at the idea of doing a thoracentesis procedure." Earl wagged his head and sharpened his tone. "They were the same ones who scoffed at the notion of using mineral spirits to sanitize hands and instruments before surgery. Dr. Holmes is of a more pragmatic bent and shares my view on proper medical procedures. Unfortunately, he has been ostracized for being so progressive."

Earl watched Mathew exhale, frown, and take a sip. The pained contraction in the young man's eyes said more than words could express. He was reliving a child's greatest fear—the untimely loss of a loving mother.

The sounds of men moving about the decks passed through the portholes. Mallets pounded wedges off hatch covers. People called to each other as they went about their duties.

Earl had a drink of water. "There were no long needles, called cannulas, in the hospital at the time. I borrowed a horse, raced across the Fens and down Beacon Street to Oliver's Medical Supply. Oliver and I assembled the components of an extraction device on one of his benches. By the time I got back, she was nearly gone. Her husband and their two older children were with her by the bed. She told me to give it a try. I loaded a syringe with an ampoule of morphine and gave her a dose. By the time she was feeling no pain, Dr. Holmes and I had the cannula ready and the collection tube attached to the bottle. His stethoscope found where most of the fluid had accumulated. I stuck the cannula deep into her chest cavity, and pretty soon fluid ran out of the punctured pleura, through the tube, and into the bottle."

Mathew had stopped drinking to palm away tears.

"Her husband's face wasn't much different than yours is now." Giving Mathew a moment to regain his composure, Earl fetched a handkerchief and handed it over. "Thirty minutes later, we'd removed a quart of fluid from around her lungs. Her color came back within an hour. The following week she went home. I hope she's still alive. She had a lot of courage. She's your mother, isn't she? You were the boy standing by the bed, weren't you?" Earl knew by then he had nothing to fear from the man in front of him. "Is she still alive?" he asked before picking up the large man's empty glass and stepping away.

"Yes, she's still alive. You did us another favor after you left, didn't you?"

"Yes. Your father's a draftsman. He replaced Clement Yoos. Is he still working for Samuel?"

"Yep."

"Your sister?"

"Well."

"So everything's good?" Earl asked, pouring refills.

"I think so. There's no way I can do to you what Arthur Harrington has ordered me to do and still be able to live with myself."

Smiling for the first time, Earl glanced at a hidden knife drawer. He put the glasses of rum on the table and decided to put the water pitcher there as well.

"I have to ask," Mathew said. "Why did you do what you did for us? Holmes wouldn't have helped us if he knew how. Our Irish luck musta been what got us through the hospital door. We were destitute at the time. No one would hire my father because—according to the Puritans who run Boston—all Irish are unreliable drunkards."

Earl refilled Mathew's water glass, sat, and resumed rotating his glass between his fingers. "Your observations are correct. The people you encountered in Boston like things ordered to their satisfaction. They show a remarkable facility for getting things done, but for the life of me, I cannot understand why their exclusionary strictures so frequently border on the inhuman. I've observed the pain and suffering this causes all of my adult life, and sad to say, I do not have an effective remedy for the emotional contagion their piety inflicts on the rest of us."

Rubbing a finger on the side of the glass, he decided to set the record straight. "Oliver Holmes is not a bad man. His tenure at Massachusetts General Hospital would have ended long ago if he treated every person his superiors found unworthy." He pointed the finger at Mathew. "Your mother's exceptional beauty is probably what prompted him to act. He did all he could for her once she was inside. You've probably figured out by now that I paid for your mother's care before I left the hospital." Earl took a drink before finishing his thought. "Oliver became disgusted with the inherited sense of moral responsibility his fellow Puritans seem to have over what they so priggishly call 'other people's misbehavior.' He's the one who coined the term 'Boston Brahmins' to describe them. They give him a lot of leeway because he's a brilliant descendant of the Calvinists who comprise Boston's upper crust. He was still the dean of Harvard Medical School the night we treated your mother. The title carries a lot of weight in certain circles.

"As for me, I carve an undistinguished path through life. I'm quite mindful of the Brahmin influences in it. I avoid the Brahmins whenever possible and confront them when I have no other choice. Your mother is a good example of how my choices play out every so often. I helped your family because it was the right thing to do. Oliver and I will never understand how these pious Christians can so blithely do the opposite of what their Lord preached."

Earl sat up and leaned on his elbows. "You must be in your early twenties now. Twenty? Twenty-one?"

"Twenty-two."

"You've done well for yourself, Mathew. I don't know how you came to be the master of the Empire, and I don't expect you to tell me. How you conduct yourself is your affair." Earl paused and thought through what he was going to say next. "Under the circumstances, it could be difficult for us to meet as friends, even though I'm confident we'll be seeing each other socially. Your employer has allies here, and several hail from Boston. They'll report your every move. The children of those parsimonious Brahmins are here and will eventually control the wealth of this place too.

"I do not believe they'll behave any differently here than they did in the Massachusetts Colony." He grimaced and took a sip of rum. "I see no

Algonquin names on any of the Louisburg Square or Beacon Hill addresses. The people living in those houses are descendants of the Pilgrims the natives kept from starving to death after they arrived in New England. All these many years later, the grandchildren of those generous natives don't even have citizenship!"

He lifted the rum in a mock toast before continuing. "I'm sure that a generation from now there'll be no native Hawaiian names on the addresses in Honolulu, either." His laughter held no humor. "I still haven't figured out how the Congregationalists have managed to keep those pesky Jesuits out!"

Mathew had a sip from his water glass, "My father told a similar tale of what the holy fathers and British did in Ireland. I'm interested in what you're telling me." He opened his mouth and closed it again. "I'm also interested in why you rub your shoulder. I saw you doing it in the hospital the night you saved my mother's life. Old wound?"

Earl's hair-raising response to his question gave the young man ample reason to believe he'd overstepped his bounds. Earl became a fiend preparing to leap across the table. A primal wave of naked aggression enveloped Mathew faster than he could recoil from the threat. *Are my eyes playing tricks on me? No!* a voice screamed inside his head. *You forgot to heed Harrington's warning: 'Do not trifle with this man.'*

Earl saw Mathew's shock and asked himself two questions he'd been avoiding for years. *How does your rage serve you, and how much longer are you going to allow this wound to control your behavior?*

Earl pushed himself back into his chair, breathed through his teeth, and addressed his hands before lifting his eyes. "I apologize for my anger. You deserve an honest answer. I rub an unhealed wound. Your question is a reminder of a period in my life that is more painful to bear than the wound itself, and unfortunately, they occurred at the same time."

Mathew lowered his guard and observed the man in front of him with renewed interest. "Thank you, sir. May I say, my family knows many people who suffer from needless pain, and if not for what you did for us, we would still be among them. Please tell me how the good Christians strip people of their lands, their rights, and their dignity."

"I will," Earl said, "but first I want to mention a better reason for why Oliver and I helped your mother. We saw a loving family in need of an act of common decency, and as far as we're concerned, your parents represent the kind of people who make a country strong."

Mathew rubbed his face. "Thank you."

"You're welcome. The assimilation formula is quite simple. It doesn't seem to matter whose missionary group is sent to convert the unwary. Priest or preachers, they're essentially the same. The goal is to convince the pagans to abandon their gods in favor of an all-powerful Christian god.

"The missionaries usually arrive dressed in rags and espouse their devotion to their god while eschewing earthly pleasures. Success is achieved once they've convinced the heathens to become beguiled with a god who could inspire such selfless adoration. The innocents abandon the mean, vengeful gods in favor of a loving god who promises a carefree life after death. Swayed by the pap these evangelicals spew, the converted are duped into accepting a disquieting truth: they're being prepared to participate in an earth destroying event called the Rapture. By the time the preachers get around to serving up *that* poison pill, the steady diet of contradictions the parishioners have been asked to swallow has created so much confusion they've nowhere left to turn for salvation.

"Not to worry, the guiding hand of the Lord is among them. The parish is encouraged to be grateful for having ministers, who, as the arbiters of God's Will, are there to intercede with Him on their behalf while everyone prepares for the inevitable.

"Their new god loves those who share, therefore, the neophytes must give up title to their land, so there may be order among God's children. As luck would have it, there are surveyors and lawyers in the flock who gladly perform the task of divvying up the land and registering ownership. A hollow promise often accompanies these measures: title to the best parcels of ancestral lands shall be set aside for all to enjoy forever.

"As you can imagine, the preachers conclude the 'negotiations' by introducing their militias to any non-believers who wish to impede the application of God's Law.

"Have you noticed how none of the newly converted are deemed worthy of becoming preachers themselves? Indigenous people are seen as inferior beings—human but not quite human enough to correctly interpret the intent of the scriptures. I'm sure they eventually notice the same logic being applied to the wives and daughters of the church leaders. Of course, by the time the converted realize what has happened, they're in the grip of a spiritual contagion steeped in falsehoods. So, in the absence of a viable antidote, the disease infects what's left of the relationship the afflicted have with a land they can no longer call their own.

"Meanwhile, the good Christian lawyers get busy transferring titles over to the senior church members. I'm guessing that in less than a generation, the children of these seemingly penniless missionaries will be the toast of the islands. They have a remarkable facility for smoothly making the transition from devout missionaries to prosperous landed gentry. You just have to spend a few days in Boston to see how it works.

"All I can do is try to ease the suffering these rogues will most surely inflict on everything in their path. I used to think that contending with one enemy at a time would be more than enough. I was wrong. The enemies are multiplying faster than I can keep track of 'em."

Four bells of the forenoon watch rang out. They had been talking in Earl's cabin for nearly an hour. Earl shook himself, tossed back the remainder of his rum, and had a drink of water. He pointed at Mathew's water glass. "Drink up. Time to go." He waited for Mathew to finish his drink. "I'm going to tell you a secret I know I can't compel you to keep. The bonds aren't aboard this ship. You could come up with a way to subdue me, I suppose, and then go on to do unspeakable things to me and the people I care about. I doubt, however, you'd ever find out whether or not we have those bonds. You could tear everything I own apart and still not find them. I can also tell you I would do everything in my power to have you suffer a similar fate were you or anyone else foolish enough to try any of those things. We've gotten off to a better start than I expected, Mathew. Let's tell those who ask that we've called a truce while we're here. We can enjoy ourselves while it's still possible."

Mathew stood, downed his rum, and offered Earl his hand. "Please accept my thanks for saving my mother's life and restoring my father's self-respect. I apologize if I offended you by bringing up a bad memory that still hurts."

Taking Mathew's hand, Earl ignored the apology. "You're welcome. It was the least I could do at the time. There is one last item I want to mention—no confrontations between our crews, either directly or by proxy."

"Agreed. I know you don't have to tell me, but do you know why the *Shadow* isn't at anchor here?"

"Yes, but you'll have to find out why on your own. As far as I know, the Polar Bear is still out there. She could possibly provide you with an insight on the whereabouts of the Shadow. The last time I saw the Bear, she was off Catalina Island in a squall."

Mathew Stilson came aboard expecting to find a self-satisfied prig and went down the ladder wishing he could be half the man he had just met. Arthur Harrington's assessment of Earl Yeaton was shaping up to be the one Mathew would choose to use in describing his employer.

Earl sat up and saw King Kamehameha IV walking on the lawn. The king was conversing with several men dressed in naval uniforms as they strolled in and out of the shadows. Elisha H. Allen, Hawaiian Minister Plenipotentiary to the United States, joined the king's group. Elisha fluttered a hand to get Earl's attention and patted the air.

"What do you suppose that bunch of stuffed shirts are talking about?" Mathew asked. "And who's the man patting the air?"

Earl answered Mathew's second question first. "Elisha Allen. A friend." He laughed and waved at the "stuffed shirts." "The French admiral wants the king to expel all nationalities except his own. The British captain is challenging the Russian to a duel over the right to conquer these islands. The American admiral is about to beg Elisha to get him a private audience with the king in the next five minutes. He wants to discuss the immediate overthrow of the monarchy and American annexation. . ." Earl groaned and pointed at two men walking toward the group. They appeared to be in a heated discussion. They were also snubbing a third person following close behind who seemed to be trying to placate them. "Do you recognize those men, Mathew?"

"No, who are they?"

"Well, the tall, thin one is a meddling Scot by the name of Robert Crichton Wyllie. Robert is a busybody who becomes a familiar pest at everything he sticks his nose into, including medicine, farming, finance, and diplomacy. I think he should stick to diplomacy. His name lends itself well to the requirements of the job." Earl's dark humor caused a little rum to catch in his throat, and he erupted into a fit of coughing.

"Indeed," Mathew wheezed, nearly choking on what was left of his own drink. "Who's the fat one Wyllie seems to be viewing from beneath his narrow nose?"

"James Borden, the American consul to Hawaii. He has the unfortunate distinction of being the ambassador secretary of state Cass sent here. The king knows Cass is pro-slavery. You may have heard that the king holds the United States in disfavor. His hosts treated him rudely while he was on a goodwill trip to the States. Apparently, the pro-slavery people in Washington weren't informed that American interests in Hawaii would be better served if the king were treated as a head of state instead of an escaped slave. King Kamehameha carries a great deal of residual resentment and uses every opportunity to remind Ambassador Borden of it. Wyllie uses this knowledge to hector the long-suffering Borden. Elisha says Ambassador Borden and his buddy, President Buchanan, share a common characteristic. The only reason they get up in the morning is because they need to take a leak."

"I think we need refills," Mathew commented before asking, "Who's the agitated guy trailing behind? They don't seem to be paying any attention to him."

Earl shook his head at the absurd collection of posers. "He's the distinguished Dr. Gerrit P. Judd. He reminds me of another doctor I met recently at a housewarming party in California. Dr. Judd is a Congregationalist physician. He's helping Queen Emma build her new hospital. He's among the scoundrels who have made the miraculous transition from penniless missionaries to joining the upper echelons of the landed class. It only took him twenty years. He's another 'close advisor' of the king. The king has many close advisors who seem to buy a lot of land at ridiculously low prices. Judd bought O'ahu's six-hundred-acre Ka'a'awa Valley nearly ten years ago. He now has a place out there he calls Kualoa Ranch. Six hundred acres are a square mile, and Judd has added more parcels to the property since then. He's really taken advantage of being a court doctor and royal confidant. Judd recently founded a school in the Punahou Valley area north of here. You may have heard of it. The school is solely for the education of the missionary children." Earl paused and finished off his drink. "The cheek."

Mathew scratched behind his ankle, waiting for Earl to continue.

"Affairs of state are wet work." Earl sighed, glanced at Mathew, and watched the double entendre sail right over the young man's head. "Two more glasses of rum are called for, my man. We get to watch the show from balcony seats. Go on with you. I'll save your spot." Mathew hurried inside.

Earl put thoughts of the king's sycophants aside and stopped to appreciate why everyone loved Hawaii so much. Settling more comfortably into his chair, he leaned back and watched leaves bobbing and weaving in the warm air. Tracing the vines of a mandevilla spreading its tendrils out among the branches, his eyes came to rest on a cluster of pink, bell-shaped flowers swaying overhead. Footsteps interrupted thoughts of plants living in harmony.

Mathew returned with two glasses and handed one to Earl. "Tell me more about this school."

Earl nodded his thanks. "Sure, but before I do, I want you to daub this tincture behind your ears and around your ankles." Earl passed a small vial over, sat a little straighter, and had a sip of rum. "You're putting on the best mosquito repellant I've ever used. A medicine woman living on Bunker Hill gave me the recipe last year. The proportions change according to personal preferences, but the ingredients stay the same. I mix lemon, eucalyptus, lavender, and tea tree oils with a witch hazel spirit base. I daub it on and the mosquitos seem to leave me alone. Keep it. I have lots of vials."

Earl put the glass on a side table, wiggled into a more comfortable position, and crossed his ankles. "Back to our discussion of what's going on around here. The purpose of the school pretty much tells the tale. The Christians are teaching their children how to run this place after they subjugate the natives. How the good Dr. Judd can engage in such blatant racism and claim to have a clear conscience is beyond me. I suppose he rationalizes his way out of the moral paradox by a building a similar school for the Hawaiian hierarchy, called the Royal School. The school has nothing Hawaiian about it, with the exception of its students, of course. It's built on a plan the Congregationalists have used on every missionary school from Amherst to Timbuktu. Any references to local customs or architecture are totally absent and not taught by the missionary teachers. May as well call it Uncle Tom's Academy for all the good it's going to do for the Hawaiians."

"You've seen this before, haven't you?"

"Oh, yes," Earl said with a snort. He gestured at Judd and the other two and exchanged a glance with Mathew. They'd seen how fast the three got busy rearranging their faces. All of the men, with the exception of Elisha Allen, wore fawning smiles in the presence of the king.

Mathew laughed and rolled his eyes. "Jesus, Earl, it'd be comical if it weren't so tragic."

Earl raised his eyebrows and nodded in agreement. "I probably know more about the ways of the world than is good for me. I watch as things unfold, contribute where I can, make a few trades here and there, and go on my way." His voice hardened with his last remark, and the eyes returning Mathew's stare assumed a darker tinge in the fading light.

"You sail on the morning tide, Capt'n Earl?" Mathew finished his drink, stood, slipped the vial into a coat pocket, and extended his hand.

Earl rose and shook the offered hand. "Yup, time to go. Seems like the more trips I make around this globe, the smaller it gets. I'll be looking for the cut of your jib each time I see a fresh set of sails."

"Would you like to walk down to the harbor with me?"

"No. Thanks for asking. I'll stay here a little longer. If I don't see you before we shove off, I wish you well. Stay safe."

"Thank you. I have a feeling the next jib you see me commanding won't be under the Harrington pennant. I've done half of what I was sent here to do—keep an eye on you for as long as you stay here and wait for another Harrington ship to arrive before attacking you in open water. I was told to return to San Francisco if help hasn't arrived before you leave. I'll tell Harrington we met, declared a truce, and none the wiser about where the bonds are, saw you get away with the Chinese gold. I'll also be telling him I'm resigning my commission aboard the Empire."

"Well," Earl said with a thoughtful expression before placing a hand on Mathew's forearm. "Send a boat over in the morning. My crewmen will lower a case of tincture. Packed inside will be a letter for you to carry to my warehouse manager in San Francisco. We just might be able to keep you under sail if that's your wish."

"It is my wish," Mathew replied, surprised to be receiving a job offer from Earl Yeaton.

Earl lifted his hand and clapped Mathew on the shoulder. "Remember, Mathew, we all need help every once in a while, especially as we get started in life. There are times, like now, when we're in the right place to receive help. If you decide to sail with me, you'll earn the trust placed in you." Earl liked Mathew's gracious reply and, soon after said his goodbyes. A few minutes later, he watched Mathew's long strides carrying him across the plateau and out of sight down Nuuanu Street.

Earl heard the swish of skirts while trying to decide if he should write a second letter.

"May I join you, Captain Yeaton?" Mary Allen asked. "Elisha said you were up here, and I should sit with you until he can free himself from the king's courtiers."

Earl said yes, stood, and offered Mary the chair Mathew had sat in. He knew Mary from previous visits to Hawaii and enjoyed her company. Her pleasant, easygoing manner suited the friendly, well-arranged face that invariably put people at ease in her presence. She exhibited the same social skills that her father, Fredrick Hobbs, so aptly displayed as a member of the Maine House of Representatives. That she was a cousin of Bill Hobbs added to Earl's pleasure every time he saw her.

Mary completed the picture Earl had been sketching with Mathew as they passed the time waiting for Elisha to join them. Much of what he'd shared with Mathew about the competing interests in Hawaii proved to be true. A little later, he listened to Elisha's perspective over a candlelit dinner served on the veranda. The three friends conversed in muted tones as darkness brought the day to a close.

Earl sat alone after the Allens left and wrote two letters by candlelight. Knowing few people could read, much less identify, shorthand, he had taught Adam, James, Ryan, Willard, and Ward Davis, the wharf manager back in San Francisco, how to read the script. He wrote the letter Mathew would be passing to Ward in shorthand. He wrote *Jane Stanford* across the top of a second letter written in longhand. He folded the letters, addressed them, tipped a candle over the flaps, and sealed the wax with the family crest embossed on his signet ring. He put both letters in a larger envelope, addressed it to Ward, wrote a separate note in shorthand for James, and asked one of the king's nephews to take them out to the *Bride*.

Easing back in the chair, he relaxed. While enjoying a few moments of peace, he noticed the faint scent of jasmine coming through the doorway. He turned in time to see the source of the scent lifting her hands. She bent in close and placed an index finger across his grinning lips before he could finish saying, "Silent partner." Raising his head to her mouth, she gave Earl a warm kiss on the lips, then stepped back. He rose and put his arms around her. "E kipa mai" ("Come to me"), he murmured, bewitched by the elegant beauty of the woman whose body felt like a second skin every time they embraced. His senses were lost in wonder each time he saw her, no matter how long they were apart: "Ho'i hon ke aloha" ("Let us fall in love again"). The woman who held his heart was Lani Keiki (Heavenly Child) La'anui, a cousin of Queen Emma.

Earl and Lani had been lovers for years. She was now a midlife beauty whose grace and infectious manner enchanted him beyond description. He spent every available moment in his all-too-brief visits to Hawaii with her.

He followed her through the palace, said goodnight to the royals and arm in arm they crossed the lawn. She led him to a nearby cottage and guided him through shadowed rooms to her sleeping area. With the exception of the large four-poster, side tables, pillows, mosquito netting, wardrobe, and a few other North American touches, the room was all Hawaiian. Carved masks, shields, woven baskets, tapa mats, and a host of potted plants arranged beneath the pitched roof said *home* to Earl.

Lani lit a candle on her bedside table. He undressed and stood by an open wall facing a pebbled walkway meandering through a high enclosure. A small stream flowed past the various arrangements of native ornamental and medicinal plants growing in her garden. Moths flitted from orchids and hanging fuchsias to Lani Keiki's favorite plant, *pikake* (jasmine). "What would have become of me if not for Lani and the people who nurtured me through my most troubling times?" he murmured while listening to her remove her clothes.

Earl imagined he could see the years falling away from the beautiful form beckoning from the bed. "Eia Au, Eia 'Oe" ("Here I am, here you are"), she whispered.

"I'm still in awe of how my fifty-four-year-old man can so closely resemble an image I once saw of a biblical warrior sculpted out of marble. Yes," she purred in the sputtering candlelight. "My warrior, however, is made of flesh and blood! Pa'ipunahele, nou noka'l'ini" ("Sweetheart, I desire you").

Her lidded eyes gleamed at the sight of her warrior surrendering to the delicious sensations rippling through his body. Slipping an index finger out of the damp recess in her thighs, she savored the wet finger's effect on him. She reveled in how his eyes absorbed every golden contour and shaded promise. Her eyes grew bright for an instant before she licked her thumb and extinguished the candle with a tantalizing sizzle.

CHAPTER 16

Off the Southern Shore of I Wo To, 24° N, 141° E, 18 March, 7:00 a.m.

Mt. Suribachi grew into a drab stain skulking off the starboard quarter. Watchers flanked the bulwarks from bowsprit to poop, and the men who saw darkness in the gray light felt as if the bleak mass were coming toward them instead of the other way around. Sea fog and steady rain made it nearly impossible to distinguish where water, land, and sky met to form the blurred horizon. There was little sense in being aloft as the *Bride* cautiously skirted the last major barrier between her and Japan. The reefs jutting from the splayed claws of the cursed island had torn the keel out of more than one unwary vessel, and the closer they got to Suribachi's southern shoulder, the more the hideous mount resembled an all-too-real black kraken rising out of the sea.

The thick fog swirling around the invisible pennant had dispersed just enough at the surface for the watchers to get a sense of how close they were to what lay ahead. "Rock gives me the crr . . . crr . . . creeps," Hopley spluttered, not liking the way his hand slipped on a slimy forestay.

Maynard kept his reply to a grunt and peered through hooded eyes at the barely visible path beyond the bows. They knew they'd be the first to be blamed if the ship ran aground, so their straining eyes concentrated extra hard on the dangerous task. Ears turned left to right trying to detect the splash of surf over hissing rain.

"Breakers humping shoals," Maynard said, ill at ease. "One hundred yards or so to starboard?"

"Too close for comfort," Hopley said, squinting into the salt-laden spray.

"Too close for us, but we can't go around that monstrous mass if we can't see it."

Foul weather descended on the ship soon after she passed Nishi Fukutoku Seamount the previous afternoon. The favorable winds, which carried her 4,000 sun-drenched miles from Hawaii, veered north-northeast two days earlier than James predicted. The change brought with it a blustery wet drizzle that degenerated into a cold rain. The *Bride* had been sailing under reduced canvas for twenty-four hours. James ordered the upper tops'l and t'gallant yards braced as close to the adverse winds as possible. Maynard and Hopley volunteered to take the last two hours of the morning watch, more to get out of the sail master's irritable presence than to keep the sulfuric menace in sight. "Phew, that thing stinks!" the boy exclaimed. "We could navigate by the stench of the plumes blowing our way," he added before squeezing his damp collar. "Smells dead."

"Aye," Maynard said. "Be a few more hours yet before we can take the northerly heading and take advantage of these winds. They'll take us up the western flank of Suribachi and away from the sense of dread I feel whenever we sail through these waters. We don't have much choice in the matter. The easterlies usually carry us around the southern tip of the island before they deliver us to the north-westerlies. I just hope for all our sakes they continue to veer north once we clear the headland. The master will be fit to be tied if he's forced by these conditions to tack back and forth in the shadow of that evil rock. The cursed slab has a magnetic attraction I find disturbing. I feel as if the thing is capable of drawing us in and tearing us apart."

Lapsing into silence, they wrapped their cloaks a little closer and stared into the gray mist.

Sodden sails, yards, and rigging ran wet with rain. Large drops found their way through the soggy sails and spattered against the wheelhouse windows, smearing the view.

James felt the keel slithering across the current toward the broken shore and told the two men at the wheel to back off a point. The helmsmen glanced at each other, rolled the wheel slightly to starboard, and watched the compass card move one degree west by west—one degree closer to a horrid rock every-one seemed to fear.

Ten hours and several calls to the men on watch to "man the braces and trim the yards" later, the ship was on a northern heading at last. The wind sheared, blew away most of the fog, and assumed a more west-northwest flow. James glanced at the chart, made a few calculations, and decided to run under reduced canvas for the rest of the day and through the night. He noted the course correction in the log.

"Keep the island in sight," he told the helmsman, "and stay several leagues off the starboard side! Do not go near it!" He said nothing about his fervent wish to be back in the open ocean by full dark or how much he wanted to get away from an eerie isle reeking of death.

Soon after the rain let up, he sent observers aloft. They reported seeing the sky begin to lighten in the distance. James spoke with Ryan and insisted he change the observers on the hour until the island receded in their wake. Two bells of the first dogwatch rang out as he left the wheelhouse. Except for going outside to relieve himself, he had been at the conn the whole way around the island's southern flank. He had forced himself to stay put until the watchers reported seeing where the island's northern flats petered out.

"I think it is time for me to get a bite to eat and hit the rack. You boys can take it from here," he said over his shoulder.

"Aye, aye, Master."

Pausing at the top of the aft stairs, he saw Colton walking along the lee side of the forward deckhouse.

The salon was full of seamen. Adam sat with Willard at a weather-side table close to the door. Earl sat in the middle of the room with his back to the lee-side wall. He had eaten a dinner of pork and beans with Tom and Kato. Men pushed plates aside, opened lee-side portholes, and waved lit matches over pipes. Earl was half listening to Roy and Bud banter back and forth from across the room. The two mountain men sat across from him, backs to the wall, their forearms resting on the table between them. They'd been swap-ping hunting yarns with a few of the men. They got Earl's attention when they started making comments about caring for a willful fourteen-year-old while contending with the rigors of prospecting and living off the land. They picked up more listeners after they brought up an encounter Colton had with a she grizzly.

The boy came through the salon door in time to hear his name mentioned. With a resigned sigh, he glanced at Ol' Bud and headed for the serving counter. On the way, he overheard Charlie patiently naming the lima, kidney, and navy beans he was pushing around on his plate. Sitting beside him, Munenori repeated the English names and made up names for them in Japanese. Colton took a helping for himself and sat at the first open spot he saw. He rightly assumed that the tale being told was about to portray him in an unflattering light. He squirmed under the grins he received from the men listening to his tormentors.

James stepped over the coaming just as Colton dug in. Nodding to everyone, he moved to the counter while Bud continued spinning his yarn. He filled his plate, grabbed a slice of fresh bread, and sat within hearing of Colton.

The boy was muttering into his plate. "That bear had me dead to rights." He lifted his head. "What have you told them so far?"

Bud shook his shaggy mane and resumed in his mountain-man patter, "I wuz jest gettin' to the good purt."

"Arggh," Colton groaned.

Bud sucked between his lips and pried a piece of gristle from between his teeth. After rolling it around in his mouth a few times, he blew it onto his plate. "Wal now," he said, pinching two hairy nostrils, "we'd listened to the boy's harpin' about shootin' a b'ar all winter and had tol' him ovah and ovah, the varmints don't come 'round till the berry leaves git to be the size of a mouse's ear. Soon's the snow wuz gone Colton watched them buds for sign. Finally, the day come and we headed out with a couple of double-barrel ten-gauges, much like the ones I heah Tom Flanagan handles so well. The one Colton carried wuz packed with solid shot instead of double-aught. The young'un was loaded for b'ar and rarin' to go that sunny May mawnin.' We stopped at the Coffee Creek trail fork. By then we wuz under the slopes of Kokanee Glacier and smack-dab in the middle of slide country, meanin' winterkills, alder patches, and big b'ars. We wuz standin' thar tryin' to decide which way to go when fifty or sixty yards distant we seen a boar griz cross one of the side trails and entah the triangle made by the fork in them alders.

"The child said, 'Thar's my meat.'" Bud flicked a finger toward the now-smoldering Colton and shook his head. "I patted the pom-pom and scratched my scalp. I tol' him thet he'd have his hands full if'n he went into thet alder patch. Bitin' off a chaw of toback, I tol' him it'd be hard to see the end of the barrel in thar, much less a critter."

Ol' Bud rolled his tongue into the gully behind his cheeks, found what he was after, and chewed the loose morsel. "Arggh, words are often wasted on the young," he said between bites. "The boy pulled his Stetson down 'round his ears, dove in, and wuz outta sight in no time. I got powerful worri'd waitin' for sumthin' to happen. Next thing I know, I heerd a bloodcurdlin' griz roar. Didn' have time to blink b'fore I heerd the even louder roar of both barrels goin' off. Hafta admit, I nearly swallowed my quid." Bud furrowed his straw-colored brows and narrowed his eyes. The sullen eyes gazing back at him held steady while the boy's jaw muscles worked a piece of pork.

Bud shifted his gaze to Tom Flanagan. "As you can imagine, there wuz a respectable pause from the forest critters b'fore the birds and bees started up agin. I wuz mighty oneasy standin' thar in the crotch of the Y. Aftah a while, I noticed alder tops waving my way. I pressed the gun against my hip, aimed 'er at the patch, cocked the hammers, and fingered the trigger guard. A moment later, Colton stepped out. He'd gone white's a sheet. No tremble, I'll give him thet," the old man said, eyeing James. "I asked him what the hell happened in thar. I wuz reminded to carefully scan his trouser leg for any sign of a leak as I lowered the hammers. The boy grunted his reply. He went on to tell me he'd crawed a ways over tangled alders with his head down. Lifted his head an' saw a clear area a few feet away. Two griz wuz in thar facin' him. The boar and a sow were a-humpin' an' a-huffin' with thar eyes closed."

Bud had the attention of the room by now. "Sow opened her eyes and saw Colton. Lettin' out a roar, she charged. Boy said all he could remember of what happened next wuz seein' the griz layin' on the ground at his feet. Said the whole experience wuz a little unnervin' at first. Went on to say he didn't remember raisin' the gun, much less settin' and pullin' the triggers. This had to be a case of instant amnesia if thar ever wuz one. A whole row of the b'ar's upper teeth wuz mowed off and thar wuz a big hole in the back of 'er head whar anothah shot had passed through the roof of 'er mouth. The boar had disappeared inta thin air." Bud scratched his beard "Didn't cross eithah trail."

Colton peered aft and swallowed another bite. "I got my b'ar."

Ol' Bud slapped his knee, saying, "Thet was the first thing ya said aftah I asked what happened in thar!"

"All's well that ends well, I suppose." Colton rose from his seat, bowed to the cooks, and handed his plate over the counter to one of the boys washing dishes. He turned to see James approaching with his hand extended. "What's this?" he asked, taking James's hand.

"I told myself you were a keeper a little while ago. I know what we just heard sounds like a rather long-winded character profile," he said, watching Bud drop a sly wink. "But I must say I'm more convinced than ever you're the kind of man I want aboard this ship." He narrowed his eyes, smiled, and passed his plate and fork over the counter to Hopley. "You may have noticed that I haven't been the easiest person to be around for the past couple of days, and it's a relief to see you taking the ribbing I sorely deserve." He placed an arm around Colton's shoulders and saw the hidden smile reveal itself beneath the youth's cool reserve. He gave the boy a few reassuring pats, skipped past the source of the youth's understandable reserve, and offered a mock salute. James walked out feeling he and Ol' Bud had just moved Colton a step closer to accepting the tragic loss of his father a mere two days after the boy bagged the bear.

The men near Colton shook his hand too, and others laughed at the comments being made about whose bladders would leak first in such a fix. The boys made room for him at their table and started asking questions about life in those distant Rocky Mountains.

Willard, Earl, and Adam, preoccupied with their own thoughts, half listened to the beginning of Bud's tale and enjoyed the ending with everyone else. Willard's expression turned sober. He was pondering a question plucked from the infinitude of thoughts racing about at lightning speed inside his head. His receptivity to this particular thought came from the latest installment in an ongoing discussion on population trends he was having with Earl and Adam. Adam had asked a related question while they were in Earl's cabin preparing lists of what they planned to do after dropping anchor in Edo Harbor. This came on the heels of hearing his uncle say it was a wonder how Japan managed to have such a highly developed closed society. The Japanese had lived in a self-contained kingdom for centuries prior to the arrival of

Caucasians, and with the exception of the Chinese silk trade had managed to adapt the internal economy to accommodate the demands of a growing population. What Earl found most interesting was how they could accomplish this in the absence of the characteristics that plagued other developed societies. "There is a high degree of civil order, a healthy population, little poverty, a reverence for past generations, and a long list of other characteristics I admire about these people." Willard listened to their discussion and twigged on a study he had read years earlier—Malthus's prescient eighteenth-century treatise, *An Essay on the Principle of Population.*

An hour or so later he was sitting in the salon rereading the essay. If asked to describe how he could simultaneously read and participate in what was going on around him, he might have replied that he imagined a clear shutter. Any number of transparent images might appear. These images came out of the ether, scrolled before his mind's eye, and vanished after he viewed them. He could stop the scroll; even examine script or mathematical computations at will, all the while observing what was happening nearby. The writing faded away when he stopped to think about Adam's not-so-rhetorical question regarding how much longer humans could put off the necessity of curbing population growth. His eyes had a trace of sadness as they came to rest on Adam.

Earl had been thinking of literature before he heard Bud say, "There's my meat." Colton's decision to go get the bear reminded Earl of a conversation he'd once had with Ralph Emerson and Oliver Holmes. They had spent the better part of an evening entertaining themselves with examples from writing's four themes, one of which applied here: man against nature. Thinking about it a bit, he speculated on how far into the future he would have to go before acquiring additional examples of "man against man" to share with his friends. Not very far, he concluded, glancing at Adam.

Adam felt Willard's scrutiny and recalled having seen the same expression on his face in Earl's cabin a short while earlier. He lifted an acknowledging hand, gazed through an open porthole, and resumed reminiscing about more pleasant thoughts. He'd been thinking of Hawaii and Uncle Earl's lover, Lani Kiki. *I've never seen him more at ease or rested. He's at peace in Hawaii. So is Danny Rickles. He's so smitten by the one he met, he plans to go back and marry her. Uncle has been fortunate to have two loves in his life, the woman in Boston and Lani Kiki in Honolulu. Will I ever be devoted to one woman?*

He turned away and let his eyes scan the relaxed faces. The crew enjoyed Hawaii and was reluctant to leave—including Willard, who was in demand by those who had met him on previous voyages.

Willard's gifts dissolved societal strictures. "He's the exception that proves the rule," Earl had once said. "The lucky guy willingly sleeps with the most-prized women of many races. And in one or two cultures with women no other white man has a hope in hell of getting close enough to see, much less bed! Never fails—once they find out about him, the fathers, mothers, brothers, and daughters in every port we visit desire to have a little Willard born into their households!"

Adam turned to see Willard staring back at him. "How many children do you suppose you have?" Adam asked. Keeping his face impassive, Willard raised his eyebrows and offered a noncommittal shrug. Adam scratched the side of his neck, cocked his head, and imitated Ol' Bud. "We love the wimmins, we shorely do."

"Yes, we do," Willard agreed, and gazed off toward Asia. "Nothing on earth is more beautiful than the female form."

Adam caught his uncle's eye, glanced at Willard, and raised his eyebrows as if to say, *What can you do?* He received an understanding tilt of the head at about the time Bud started needling Colton.

A scout in the mainmast crosstrees summed up his feelings on how barren the island appeared. "The plants clinging to that dismal rock are stunted and shriveled."

"Yes," the man sitting next to him observed. "And the sooner we clear the headland, the better. This place ain't right. Don't like it heah."

They listened to the laughter coming out of the salon and speculated on who would make the best candidates for the butt of the jokes taking place in there. One of them had no sooner said he thought the grumpy old sail master deserved top billing than he saw James appear and look up. Choking off their laughter, they watched him cross the deck and enter the aft deckhouse. Baffled by his smiling wave, the men resumed their watch.

The rain clouds were petering out and giving way to a high overcast stretching all the way to the horizon. The air pushing them north carried an occasional wisp of sulfur. I Wo To, still a presence off the starboard side, slipped past in their wake. With each roll of the ship, they became increasingly convinced that their apprehensions amounted to nothing more than useless worry.

The hot, rancid breath passing over their unsuspecting shoulders raised the hairs on the backs of their necks and sent cold shivers trickling down their spines. There was no doubt in their superstitious heads about what had happened. Gripping the halyards tighter, the men peered aft and saw surf splashing against a malignant reptile lying across a seamount. They traced the image five miles down the scaly hide to a pair of volcanic nostrils spewing a noxious miasma around Suribachi's misshapen head. The loathsome message contained in the dragon's next putrid discharge caused one of the men to reel and barf a stream of vomit downwind.

The brooding monster had given them a taste of the horrors awaiting those who to dared step onto I Wo To's (Iwo Jima's) ash-strewn shores.

CHAPTER 17

Edo Harbor Anchorage, 36° N, 138° E, 28
March, 8:45 a.m., high slack tide.

The cold, wet snow blowing down Hira Valley from Mt. Fuji's icy peaks pushed aside any thoughts of an easy passage to the *Bride*'s anchorage. Edo Shigetsugu, samurai warlord, had planted his standard in a different place 400 hundred years before the *Bride* arrived. He'd chosen to build his new stronghold beside a sleepy fishing village conveniently located at the end of a fertile valley whose river flowed into a large protected ocean bay. Eventually, the occupants of Shigetsugu's imposing fortress came to rule over Asia's most feared chain of islands.

That first dank morning, the men could neither tell how many ships shared the anchorage nor see what lay beyond the river's mouth. Three thoughts sustained the majority of the weary sailors as they went about their shipboard routines: the prospect of hot baths, hot jugs of sake, and willing women. The crewmen who had been there before cast guarded glances at the massive structure hidden in the mist. What little the *Bride*'s men could see of the largest fortification in the known world seemed to shrink in the gray sleet. The cheerless scene made it hard to believe more people lived in and around its outer walls than existed in all of the New England states combined. The battlements and lake of moats surrounding the magnificent castle may have been invisible most of the time but not the images of what happened to anyone foolish enough to insult the people living there.

Foul weather shelved the much-anticipated drone of bees, a sound that usually accompanied the hum of human activity taking place beneath the valley's cherry trees. Edo's distressed residents viewed the delayed arrival of cherry blossom time as just one of many bad omens. Had they known what was occurring ashore, the *Bride*'s men might have thought twice about how they planned to share the streets with armed samurai. The traders, launderers, and vendors had more to feel dreary about than the weather when quarter boats bumped up against their docks. The tensions radiating out of the castle, plots being whispered about in the Yoshiwara and the overall sense of uncertainty made for a cautious Japanese welcome to the outsiders they called *gai jin*. The residents of Nihon—or Japan, as Westerners preferred to call the kingdom—were on edge. The castle's residents ruled an immensely powerful empire on the verge of collapse. The citizens who encountered the foreigners occupying the city's foreshore were concerned that along with their linens the gai jin would be bringing cannons capable of turning their beloved castle and their homes into burning piles of rubble.

On the eighth and last day of her stay, the *Bride*'s jib boom pointed inland as she rose above her reflection and tugged on her chain in a weak current. Mt. Fuji's snow-capped caldera dominated the blue sky above Edo Castle. Thinning bands of clouds revealed numerous avalanche chutes lining the peak's upper face. Beneath the mountain, the coastal plain carried a gauzy pink overlay spreading down to the water's edge. Nihon's cherry blossoms were out at last and so were her bees.

Kato and Munenori had visited their families and friends. Earl and his men had luxuriated in steaming baths. Clothes and linens had been to the cleaners, sexual appetites had been satisfied in all manner of ways, and the more astute crewmen had traded dunnage pelts for gold and fine art. The weather might not have been cooperating, but the crew managed to find ways to enjoy their first four days in port.

Stationed a safe distance from shore, the *Bride* was ready to up-anchor as soon as the royal barge transferred Kato and Munenori to the ship. Earl and James were leaning on the rail surveying the scene. The crew had been on twenty-four-hour alert for the past four days. Most of the ships at anchor the day the *Bride* arrived were gone.

Earl and James were still recovering from a protracted confrontation James started in the captain's suite four days earlier on the twenty-fourth. James was upset because Earl refused to sail with the others, especially after he got Earl to admit that Japan's sectarian volcano had erupted. "You're putting us all at risk by sticking around," he had fumed. "There's nothing more you can do! It's time for us to leave, damn it!"

"I understand how you feel, but I'm not leaving while I can still make a difference," Earl had answered before smacking a section of paneling beside his bunk. A door popped open revealing a cabinet hidden between the *Bride*'s ribs.

"What've you got in mind?" James asked, becoming alarmed. Earl turned and faced him with a smaller version of a samurai sword, called a *tanto*.

"I'm not telling you." Earl lifted a pant leg, strapped the knife to his shin, and covered it. Then he poked around in the cabinet, grabbed a few other items, including a duffle, and with a flick of the wrist, shut the door.

"How long will it take?" James asked, narrowing his eyes at what was going in the bag.

Earl frowned at a handful of lock picks lying on the bed as if trying to decide whether or not he should bring them along. He glanced at James, grabbed the picks, and hefted them a few times. "Enough," he said and tossed them in with candles and a box of matches. "I don't know. A few days, maybe more. Not sure. I want the ship ready to up-anchor at a moment's notice. Have a quarter boat on standby a hundred yards offshore at all times."

He grunted while stuffing a change of dark clothes in with the medical bag.

"You can still read shorthand, can't you?" he asked, adjusting his jacket over a shoulder rig packed with a loaded .22.

"Yes," James said. He'd seen a short sword go in the bag with a couple of speed loaders.

"I'll send notes if I can." Earl topped the lot off with a box of shells and pulled the drawstring. "That's it," he said, tying the knot.

"Not by a long shot. I want to know where to find you if you're not back here in a couple of days!"

James was still stewing and none the wiser after his captain went over the side.

Earl got back late in the evening three days later. James was in his cabin and heard Earl pass his door. Following along behind, he held his tongue until Earl lit the hanging lantern and placed a sheaf of papers in the liquor cabinet's hidden drawer. Earl closed the panel and held up a hand before James could speak. "I'll tell you what happened another time. Sorry I didn't send a note. We're leaving tomorrow on the ebb. I need sleep. Goodnight."

"Humph," James grumbled, closing the door. "Better sleep on your right side because those stitches are still weeping."

The next day they stood at the rail gazing across the harbor and saw the barge emerge from a large floating barn moored to the government wharf. James knew it was not the time to be pestering Earl with questions regarding how he'd acquired the slashes to his cheek and scalp. The black scabs Earl sported suggested he'd been cut within the last day or so.

James managed to control his emotions while he and his captain had breakfast. He said he'd listen to anything Earl was willing to tell him. The topic of conversation turned to American involvement in Japanese affairs, and by degrees, Earl shared what he had learned while ashore. James reduced the tension even further by agreeing with Earl's assessment of how their fellow citizens were conducting themselves. He reassured Earl that he too was unimpressed with the tenor of the government advisors sent to implement the Harris Treaty and said he felt quite disheartened by what the American representatives revealed. He kept the conversation on an even keel by not asking what, if anything, Earl's orders from Washington directed him to do under the circumstances. James used the opportunity to ask Earl how much he knew about the possible American involvement in precipitating the atrocity that occurred several days earlier.

Adam entered the salon and paused at their table before Earl could answer. "The Americans have closed the consulate."

"They say why?" James asked through tight lips.

"No one's talking," Adam said and hurried off before they could quiz him on how he knew.

"Grr," James growled at Adam's retreating back.

James and Earl had met with American representatives several times in the first few days after they'd dropped anchor. They ate light lunches in the grog shops near the consular offices and had sumptuous dinners at the American delegation. They consumed meals that would have appalled the frugal Japanese, drank spirits unheard of prior to the arrival of the gai jin, and became upset while listening to their boastful compatriots describing their triumphs over the Japanese.

"Our representatives are really good at gaining an advantage over their hosts," James had commented after one of the dinners, "but they have no sense of their new role in this country's history. Worse, they're not sensitive to the festering anger their cultural biases are engendering among the household staff. How they treat the people they think they're allowed to mistreat speaks volumes about their character. Their offensive manners will be reported in the castle and will add to the distrust of the Americans."

Now standing at the rail with Earl, he took a moment to appreciate the beautiful view. "Unfair trade agreements with these brilliantly industrious people won't end well. They have long memories."

"I agree," Earl replied. "I think it'd be prudent to have leadership comprised of negotiators willing to collaborate with their opposites instead of scaring them into submission." He glanced at James. "I find that people get along a lot better when they understand each other."

"Yesss," James said, ascribing Earl's last comment to the disagreement the two had been having over the past few days. He grunted and changed the subject. "I had a word with Adam after breakfast. He admitted to going ashore yesterday, said he had to say goodbye his new lady friend in the Yoshiwara."

"My nephew," Earl hissed; thankful they could talk of other things. "He say how it went?"

"Celestial."

James's grim features remained the same to anyone watching, but Earl was close enough to see the eyes flare behind the thick glasses while he also kept his feelings in check. Earl rolled his shoulders and suppressed a frown.

James thought he had made it extra clear to anyone within hearing: Stay away from the brothels! Adam made it back, unlike several other gai jin, whose dismembered bodies had been removed from the city's dump before feral dogs made them unidentifiable. He gritted his teeth, glanced at Adam, and shook his head at the challenging stare.

The group standing with Adam was keeping a wary eye on their feuding leaders. They were also watching the splendid craft floating across a bay that the Americans were beginning to call Tokyo. Adam had endured James's scolding and asked him if he knew what had happened to his uncle. James shrugged. "You know as much as I do."

"The Japanese have good reason to be fearful of the men who come to their sacred shores," Earl observed as he watched the barge draw closer.

"Yes." James tapped the rail with both hands and said nothing more. Now was not the time to bring up his misgivings about what Earl might have done to the men meddling in Japanese affairs.

They remained where they were and took turns letting their gaze linger on the craft coming toward them. Behind them, Adam, Willard, Ryan, and the cooks continued chatting in the sun near the main hatch.

Men moved to duty stations after the barge crossed the halfway point. Topmen ran up ratlines and strung themselves along the upper yards. Standing at attention with safety lines held behind their backs, they gave their onlookers an appreciative view of the ship's scale, and, more importantly, a sampling of how many men were required to sail and defend a tall ship.

Tom moved closer to his mates by the forecastle's open doors and the four artillery pieces. He went inside and opened the ports. The men on watch became more alert. They covered every approach with four swivel guns. The small cannons, mounted fore and aft, had primers, powder, wads, and canisters placed nearby. They could fire on the deck with ease. Rifles, shotguns, pistols, and swords lay stashed out of sight throughout the length of the ship.

Mike stepped behind the gun crew, grabbed the bell clapper, and rang out two bells of the forenoon watch: 9:00 a.m. He joined the other boys standing a short distance away.

The crew wore uniforms in honor of the occasion. The base color was dark green. Yellow ribbons the width of a thick finger trimmed the outside pant legs. The shirt pockets and sleeves had similar strips sewn on the outer edges. Shirt and jacket pockets bore the Yeaton crest. The hats were also green and accented with a yellow sweatband bearing the ship's name in black letters. The officers wore jackets. Gold braid topped Earl's epaulets. Their hats differed from the crew's in that they had black patent-leather visors. Earl's cap had another gold braid draped over the visor. The officers, with the exception of Willard, carried side-arms.

The *Bride* was cleaned, coiled, and polished. Her beauty was on par with any of the well-appointed homes Earl had ever visited. This thought gave him more than a little satisfaction. That he could have a ship whose quality and finish rivaled the exquisite artistry he saw ashore served him well under the circumstances. His guests expected him to receive them as equals. He had tremendous respect for the people he was about to greet. Until recently, he was comforted to know they held him and his crew in the same high regard.

Now anxious to get under way, he observed how efficiently the barge closed the distance. The numerous white oars rose and fell as one. Opulently dressed women occupied a canopied afterdeck. Men dressed in muted colors flanked them. The riot of colors adorning the clothing, flags, and pennants complemented the pastel backdrop.

"These people have a fondness for pomp and circumstance, don't they, Earl?" James murmured, moving closer to the entry port.

"Yes, they do," Earl answered, watching the vessel's wake with James. Straight as an arrow.

James lifted his eyes and saw a gull hovering above the masthead. The green-and-yellow fabric had started to stir. The bay remained calm, with sparkling ripples here and there caused by errant puffs of loose air flowing down Hira Valley. The gull lost interest and drifted out to sea with the breeze. Letting his eyes linger on the men standing on the yards, James scratched his beard. "Suppose any of those men up there are asking themselves if sailing into this port was such a good idea?"

"Hmm," Earl said flatly, a part of him asking the same thing. "We'll soon find out. We've been lucky so far. A lot can happen in the next few minutes. Could get bad." He took his hat off and hung it over a pin. "Damn thing aggravates my stitches."

The day after the *Bride* dropped anchor, Earl's group paid a visit to Kato's palatial home inside the castle walls. Prior to their arrival, they spent several hours being soaked, washed, and rubbed by masters.

Earl, James, Adam, Willard, and Mike stepped onto a covered porch, removed their footwear, and donned *tabi* sandals. They crossed the threshold, bowed to the servant who closed the door, and left the busy outer world behind.

The subtle cerebral beauty surrounding them gave rise to a sense of ethereal peace and harmony. Pausing at an alcove near the entrance, they bowed respectfully to the *kamidana* shrine set in the wall. The Shinto shrine housed the wandering *kami* spirits of the family ancestors. The family *fuda*, or amulet, did not escape Earl's attention. The *fuda* hung above a shelf festooned with offerings.

Female servants removed the translucent bone-china tea service after the formalities of the tea ceremony. To Willard's delight, they returned with heated sake. Mike and Adam removed items from crates delivered earlier in the day. These they placed on sailcloth spread over the polished floor.

Earl presented the women with button blankets trimmed with ermine and held in place by silver clasps set with argillite stones carved with spirit creature sigils. The men received woolen capes with otter skins sewn across the shoulders and trimmed with pine marten furs. The rabbit-skin caps were a hit. The sabre-toothed tiger, dire wolf, giant sloth, camel, and grizzly bear skulls caught everyone's attention. Kato informed Earl that the collection would soon be on display at the prestigious Kano School of Fine Art. He said the anatomical features would find their way into the fanciful mythical creatures produced in the painting and sculpture studios.

Perhaps it was the sake talking, but Munenori was a little more animated than Mike in describing what happened in the El Monte Dip.

They depended on Willard to do most of the two-way conversing. He provided detailed answers to every question asked over the next few hours in the warm, genteel setting. At intervals in the conversation, they shared gifts. Earl passed out protective *chi* amulets made of gold and silver and set with carved and cut precious stones from around the world. His hosts listened as he told of the places they came from and their intended purposes.

"Last but certainly not least are gifts we have been asked to present to the Kato and Munenori households." Earl gestured for Adam to open two particularly stout chests.

Mike gave Adam a hand lifting bentwood boxes out of their protective cedar-ribbon packing. The carved chests portrayed mythical and identifiable creatures, all bearing the familiar ovoid characteristics found in Haida art.

The beautiful containers had polished brass clasps and slotted hinges made of brushed steel. Earl said he had similar lids and displayed them as wall hangings. Willard's translation of the Haida legends carved into the boxes held everyone's attention. Rummaging around inside each chest, Earl pulled two multicolored Haida clan masks out of their nests of fragrant shavings. Carved into each mask were ancestral eagle and raven totems. Earl handed them to the fathers of the young men in his care. "These are gifts to you from Gwai-Gu-unthin, the hereditary tyee, king of the Haida nation. His people know him as Eda'nsa. Whites have anglicized his name into Chief Edenshaw." Nodding to Adam, he watched as his nephew passed around more Edenshaw gifts: stretched hide rattles, ermine scarves, and beautifully carved argillite totems. Gasps of appreciation accompanied the brightly colored and perfectly preserved antique masks he gave to the wives, sisters, and brothers.

After listening to Willard's description of the Haida longhouses, totems, and cultural practices, Kato's father, Takeru, said Eda'nsa lived the way his ancestors might have lived a thousand years ago. Earl smiled. "I would be happy to carry you on a journey back in time. Let's do it soon because Eda'nsa's not getting any younger!"

Each of the Americans received a silk kimono and finely worked boxes whose joinery would rival the beauty of anything placed within them. They marveled over small tables and fabric panels portraying scenes from Japanese life stitched in colored silk. Each of the men received watercolors on silk cloth and rice paper. The rare paintings depicted pastoral scenes far from Edo.

Takeru and Munenori's father, Hiroshi, led Earl and Adam to a table and, with solemn bows, presented them with Minamoto swords. Each three-piece sword set had a name and a history. Willard filled them in on who had owned the swords.

Satisfied with how their guests paid proper respect to the familial *kamis*, Takeru and Hiroshi gave the Yeatons paintings of their ancestors using the swords in battle. Kano Shosenin, scion of the shogunate artists, had placed his seal on the bottom of each priceless painting. The minutely detailed brushstrokes created a three-dimensional illusion. The brightly colored warriors vanquishing their enemies appeared to be capable of leaping right off the cloth. Admiring the *siu mai* paintings, Earl said the vibrancy displayed in the 2,000-year-old *gong-bi* method could last another two millennia.

Adam received an unanticipated smile of approval from his uncle after Earl saw how the Japanese responded to several paintings Adam passed around. Earl had to admit he was wrong about how much interest their hosts would have in the seventeenth-century genre paintings of Jan Steen. He had gone along with Adam's suggestion that they pack several Steens in with the gifts, saying, "Sure, but I don't think the Japanese will care to see how a Dutch tavern keeper portrays his neighbors going about their daily lives." Quite the contrary. Their hosts *were* interested in how people lived elsewhere in the world. Everyone laughed at Willard's translation of Earl's admission: "I'm going to have to eat crow on this one!"

Earl spread a large map of the world on the floor; a map he hadn't thought was worth bringing along until Adam insisted. Adam produced a collection of picture books that his uncle wanted to leave behind too. It wasn't long before everyone was talking at once about the habits, dress, building styles, and cultural practices of the gai jin.

Earl's group stayed for dinner, admired panels depicting the life of the family in Japan's history, and discussed the rumblings of discontent occurring in both their lands. They parted feeling as if the bonds of friendship were capable of conquering all ills.

The next day, the *Bride* moved to a large Munenori-affiliated dock. Bales of otter, bear, wolf, cougar, seal, beaver, ermine, and skins of other British Columbia furbearers came out of the holds. The hides, purchased from coastal natives and Victoria fur dealers, passed into the adjacent warehouse. Tanners would soon be turning them into supple garment furs. The holds yielded more, including the surgical wards, field hospitals, bales of cinchona bark, sewing machines, rolls of insect screens, and a host of general hardware items.

Wagons were loaded with medical supplies and cases stenciled with farm equipment labels that contain rifles, pistols, and ammunition. Hours later, the wagons wound their way up Fuji's southern flanks and passed under the arches of a remote stronghold brooding high above Edo's castle.

Late in the night, long after the warehousemen had gone home, Earl and his men stowed two dozen chests of gold in the *Bride*'s holds, insurance should the unthinkable occur. Nearly a ton of gold was destined for Earl's bank vaults in New York and Boston.

Earl, Adam, and the merchant representatives of the Kato and Munenori families formed a trading company on 23 March. They had a festive evening that night in the palatial home of Munenori Hiroshi. The gathering was less formal than the one held at the Kato mansion. Earl and his group were in for a surprise. Munenori and Kato presented them with a chest destined for Haida G'wai. Their hosts asked Earl to return the favor on his next visit to Chief Eda'nsa. The beautifully carved Japanese chest contained a variety of Noh masks whose unmistakable ovoid forms bore a strong familial resemblance to the Haida pieces they'd received. Included were bolts of patterned silk bearing the Kato and Munenori family crests, a variety of knives, and, most remarkable of all, several complete sets of the finest Japanese stone and wood-carving tools.

They topped off the evening with a final toast and set the time for sailing: four days hence at high ebb tide.

Much had happened in those four days, and now on the verge of departure, James glanced at Earl and back to the barge, whose occupants he could now identify. "Things could go badly for the Kato and Munenori families if the pro-expulsion faction supporting the imperial emperor gains control of the shogunate. Their heads would join hundreds of others lining the pavement along the Edo Palace walls. The skulls would serve as a warning to any who might choose to question the divine will of the pitiless sun god's heir reigning over a militant Tokugawa Shogunate. A shogunate purportedly set on expelling the barbarian gai jin but secretly conspiring with British and American consular officials, whose government agents and arms dealers will control foreign trade once the Japanese *reluctantly* open their ports."

"Yesss," Earl murmured, watching the way fall of the galley. "The Harringtons and their British allies have once again created enemies where there were none. Fools! All they had to do was act as honest brokers and trade as equals. Not content to let the Japanese sort out their differences on their own, they've aligned themselves with the reactionaries opposed to trade. They're using a tried and true occupation formula: Get the residents fighting among themselves, weaken the government, pounce at the first opportunity, and presto, a new colony! By doing so, they have made enemies out of the people with whom they've agreed to trade." *Must remain patient,*

Earl reminded himself. To keep from touching his head or rubbing his chest, he squeezed the rail and tightened his lips.

James interrupted Earl's thoughts on the steps that he and his Japanese friends were taking to thwart the reactionary coalition trying to weaken Japan's progressives.

"Kato and Munenori could become the last branches on the Minamoto family tree if your plan fails," he said, raising his eyebrows and giving an admiring nod to how well the barge's tiller man guided the craft. The man pretended not to notice.

The oars disappeared as if by magic before the barge cruised to a stop. Men holding landing ropes wore red silk robes nearly identical to the ones worn by the rowers. They tossed fore and aft ropes to the men above and dropped large cylindrical bumpers made of cleverly knotted ropes over the side. Similar bumpers hung off either side the *Bride*'s entry port. The barge crew turned their attention to the gangway and within minutes it was safe to use.

The barge itself had its own contingent of protective samurai who wore bright-red dragon-festooned kimonos. They would remain aboard the barge. An additional dozen armed samurai assembled on the lower gangway and along the barge's deck. They would be the first to come up. Earl and James planned to give them plenty of room. Kato called from the barge and asked for permission to come aboard. Earl and James stepped back to make room for their guests and stood across the deck with Adam and the others.

"Munenori and Kato could well be saying goodbye to their families for the last time," Earl said, "so, let's give them every opportunity to share this moment with dignity. I have no idea how things will go. We haven't seen them since the night of the party, and we've got the bulk of their fortune down below."

James shuffled his feet. "I think we're in the clear. We didn't have anything to do with the death of the tairo. Seems strange that the assassination happened the day after we had our last dinner with these people. The simmering sense of unease we noticed has boiled over into open hostility. There's no such thing as coincidence, Earl."

"Yeah, well, the country's on the brink of civil war and we'll never know if the two are related."

James shrugged and tried to find a common thread in what Earl had revealed while they ate breakfast.

"So much has happened in the four days since the assassination of Ii Naosuke," Earl had said, "I'm having trouble keeping track of everything. Ii was the tairō, whose power is second only to the shogun. At the time of his death, he controlled the current Tokugawa Shogunate. Do you remember what the weather was like that day?"

"Sure," James said over his mug. "Quite a bit different from a day earlier. The cherry trees had put out their first blossoms, only to have them assaulted overnight. The wind was blowing so hard, the wet snowflakes were coming in sideways."

"Well, Ii didn't mind. He was covered in otter robes and sat on a cushion behind drawn curtains. He was riding in a palanquin while his cordon of samurai suffered in silence."

"The rich get all the breaks. Please pass the salt."

Earl gave James the salt and had a sip of coffee. "Um, hmm. Ii was about to enter the castle's Sakuradamon Gate on his way to a conference with the twelve-year-old he'd appointed Shogun. As is the custom, the people on the street went to their knees and bowed in the slush at the approach of Ii's entourage. Custom decreed they remain bowing until Ii passed through the gate. They either bowed or lost their heads. A number of them had no intention to stay bowing for long, apparently. The people who did continue to bow were about to be spattered with blood."

James looked up. "Please, I'm eating."

"You asked me to tell you everything. Well?"

"Okay, okay. Go on."

"All who stayed put were unharmed so long as they kept their heads down. Ii's guards were slain by seventeen ronin led by Arimura Jisaemon, a Satsuma samurai. The attack was over in seconds, according those who dared to peek. Ii barely had time to observe Arimura's objective—lift his head by the hair and with the use of a short sword, cut it off."

"Nasty. What became of the head?"

"Arimura cleaned it and placed it with the others taken from the guards. Then he bowed to the heads and the men with him. Aside from having just secured his place in Japanese history, he knew there was only one thing left to do. Arimura knelt on the wet pavement with a few of his comrades. They removed their arms from the sleeves of their kimonos and folded the fabric below their waists. They may have recited death poems before nodding to the men who acted as kaishkunins, their seconds. Then they drove tanto blades into their abdomens and cut horizontally."

James bit into a slice of bacon. "Seppuku. Must have hurt like hell. You'd never get me to do that."

"Can't imagine you would. The subsequent cut from waist to chest had to have been the most difficult. Soon after Arimura and his men made the decision on whether or not they had it in them to make the second cut, the kaishkunins sliced their heads off perfectly. You may have heard: the Japanese define perfectly in these situations to mean the cut must retain a little flap of skin in front of the Adam's apple. The purpose of the flap is to prevent the head from splashing into the less dignified pile of offal. A quick slice, and the heads were soon arranged with Ii's and his men."

"Have to give the Japanese credit. They like things neat."

"They do. Did you know that a severed head can see, hear, blink, and think until it passes out from lack of oxygen?"

"Good God, Earl. You're beginning to sound like Willard."

"A few of the things I'm told stick," Earl said, spearing a piece of toast with his fork. Using his knife, he loaded the little deck with a gob of egg smothered in Hollandaise. "It pleases my fancy to imagine Ii observing Arimura and his men committing seppuku.

"The ronin who did not join Arimura's passage into the Great Void fled. The red blossoms they left behind were surely not what Ota Dokan, the castle's architect, had in mind when he named the passage Blossom Gate four hundred years ago."

James stared at the barge's occupants and thought about what they must be going through. *The men and women about to come aboard are members of the murdered tairō's bakufu, Japan's ruling elite. Their families are part of the dead tairō's progressive coalition and correctly assume that the shogunate is doomed if it cannot adapt to the changing times.* James let his thoughts drift back to what they talked about while Earl finished his eggs.

"The southern Japanese daimyos whose island fortresses are closest to China, and therefore British influences, are getting the most scrutiny, especially the province called Satsuma. Short of declaring civil war, the country entered the early stages within hours of the assassination."

"There's a lot of civil war talk going around, Earl. Japan, US, China. Have I left anyone out?"

"Probably. Listen to this. Messages sent back and forth through innumerable intermediaries have enlisted the aid of the mysterious ninja. Rumors have it that all negotiations are funneled through influential madams in Edo's Yoshiwara brothel district."

"Good reason to keep our people out of there!"

"Ayah. The task of killing the most well connected bakufu conspirators is left to professionals who, if in the highly unlikely event they get caught, will not know who hired them. Like the merchants, these professionals deal in hard currency."

James shuddered. "Sneaky."

"Yes. One of Ii's captured assassins foolishly kept a Yoshiwara brothel receipt on his person. Bakufu samurai ran to ground the unfortunate brothel owner and all who worked there. They were tortured until they surrendered every scrap of information associated with having housed the collaborators. Their heads line the street in front of the destroyed brothel."

"Need I say more about staying out of the Yoshiwara?" James looked up. "Here comes your nephew."

They finished their breakfast soon after Adam mentioned the consulate and scooted. Earl had more to say while they were doing a last-minute inspection. "Japan is facing an inevitable crisis, James. A host of contradictory forces have finally come together that will overturn two hundred and fifty years of Tokugawa rule.

"Kato told me the former shogun, the Supreme Ruler of Japan, may have been assassinated last fall during the debate over opening Japan to foreign trade. Ii Naosuke, serving as tairō, with the approval of the deceased shogun, had already declared his intentions to open several Japanese ports to international trade. He started by signing the infamous Treaty of Amenity last year. The treaty gave huge trade concessions to the American negotiator, Townsend Harris. The Japanese criticisms have centered on vague wording that cedes American access to Japan in exchange for products and markets yet to be determined. Various interpretations suggest that the Americans will gain unfettered access to the interior of the islands. This is kinji rereta—forbidden! That concession alone, if true, set off a firestorm of indignation among numerous daimyos and may have precipitated the murder of the Shogun. Assassinations have occurred over lesser insults many times over the centuries."

"I don't know what to make of these people, Earl. They have a history of killing each other over the slightest provocation. I've heard of battles that produced over a hundred thousand casualties."

"They are a wonder, and we should be careful dealing with them. Have to admit, they have good reason to be leery of agreements requiring an American presence while Japanese workers manufacture products solely for American consumption. The daimyos became enraged when told the Americans wanted their own managers in the proposed production facilities. Powerful people don't see the agreement as a treaty but as an abdication of national sovereignty and differ wildly on how to respond to the incipient threat."

James scowled. "I'd say our countrymen are trying to compel the Japanese to submit to a form of colonialism."

"That's one way to look at it. Gets worse. The Satsuma daimyos who are suspected of ordering Ii's death could be in cahoots with the British while publicly supporting the imperial court's desire to expel all foreigners. Meanwhile, the French, Russian, and American government negotiators are vying for favor with the ruling secular daimyos. The Jesuits, British traders, and a few of their American allies are playing the secular progressives against the religious reactionaries. Assassinations and weapons sales are doing what nearly two centuries of Jesuit tampering has failed to accomplish—split the shogunate. That's why the Union gave the weapons to the progressives. They wouldn't be able to maintain the balance of power without our aid."

James shook his head. "Many of the things they have in common will ultimately divide them even more."

"Same could be said for what's happening in the United States. Ii Naosuke grossly misread the tealeaves. He went ahead and signed the treaty over the legitimate objections of many daimyos and without the imperial emperor's consent."

"Sounds familiar," James said. "The left hand doesn't know what the right is doing. President Buchanan and his advisors aren't much brighter. Our president is surrounded by yes men who are profiting from his follies, and the only men who aren't are the ones who sent you on this mission."

"Correct. Ii further enraged his supporters by abusing his powers. He began purging any who objected to the treaty, including ordering numerous daimyos and military officials to commit seppuku. Buchanan may not have that power, but his dithering will amount to the same thing. If the president and Congress don't come to a better understanding of how to run the country, it won't be long before they resort to disemboweling each other with cannon fire!

"Ii and Harris wanted to begin trade relations with the exchange of products and services produced in each country. The reactionary opposition vehemently opposes those proposals and sees them as a pretext to permit even greater expansion into Japanese territory. Unfortunately, the Japanese are witness to what the British have been doing to their ancient blood relations in China. Trade by forced consumption, including opium, is abhorrent to the Japanese yet imminently plausible given the military capacity of the British, French, and now the Americans. The Japanese are not as stupid as our trade negotiators would have us believe. They know we have armaments capable of destroying samurai opposition once our armies come ashore." Earl shook his head. "The arrogance of power will only serve to drive reactionary resentments deeper. Who knows when these resentments will surface or in what nationalistic guise? Rest assured, it won't be pretty.

"The dead Ii Naosuke's bakufu supporters know that Harris has a bevy of manufacturers preparing to invade Japan and set up shop. The Americans, led by the likes of Clinton Harrington and his cohorts, are perfectly willing to force the Japanese to trade at the point of a bayonet. They see the often-violent consequences as nothing more than just another cost of doing business. The costs will be borne by American taxpayers whose uniformed sons will die protecting the greed of opportunists. Men who'll flee at the first sign of failure, leaving the taxpayers holding the bag, as usual.

"Ii reasoned that placating the Americans was preferable to the violent alternatives occurring in China. Unfortunately for him and the progressives, they are dealing with unscrupulous people who expect to profit from both sides of any bargain. It'll take generations to overcome the consequences of what our countrymen are setting in motion. Let's hope the Japanese don't strike back before we can undo the harm our countrymen are causing."

Earl watched a crewman open the entry port and then whispered in James's ear. "Time's up. Bakufu samurai caught the fleeing assassins. They're in dark places having the names of the men responsible for the attack pried out of them. I've tried and failed to shut from my mind the unspeakable horrors Ii Naosuke's killers must be going through under the orders of men like the ones you see stepping onto our weather deck."

Too preoccupied to think clearly, he nearly missed Takeru thanking him for being welcomed aboard. "Do itashi mashite," Earl replied, bowing to Kato Takeru. Knowing Takeru meant *warrior*, Earl could imagine how he had earned the name. Takeru was dressed in a utilitarian riding suit cut from a sheet of light-brown leather. His late-seventeenth-century Minamoto swords were among the finest to come from that era. The sheathed swords were worn *daisho* fashion. A leather harness attached to his belt held the fearsome two-handed *katana* near his left elbow. The shorter *wakizashi* resided blade down inside the leather belt. Earl glanced at the tanto strapped to Takeru's outer shin and thought of the one beneath his pant leg.

Takeru was strikingly handsome, tall, perfectly conditioned, and possessed an aura of menace about him. He gave Earl the impression he wanted to leave as soon as it was polite to do so. Earl shared the man's sentiments. They would up-anchor and sail away as soon as the guests departed. Continuing to speak in Japanese, Takeru thanked Earl for welcoming his son aboard for another year. Bowing and stepping back, he gave his brother-in-law, Hiroshi, space to thank Earl for keeping Munenori aboard.

Earl had time to brace himself before facing Hiroshi. He gave the proper bow and made the correct responses. Earl noted that Hiroshi and the armed men who came with him were dressed in similar uniforms. Instead of wearing silk kimonos, they had opted for supple leather jackets, pants, and half boots. The stitching and embroidered reptilian family crests were flawless. These men were dressed to ride horses into battle. Earl also knew "Hiroshi" meant *generous*. The only generosity a person could hope to receive would be having one's head lopped off before suffering through the embarrassment of having any other body parts removed first. Where Earl saw Takeru as menacing, he saw Hiroshi as death. His latent aggression sent shivers through all of those who had the misfortune of being pinned under his hard mahogany eyes. He too, carried valuable swords. Their great worth resided in the ease with which they took lives.

No one mentioned Earl's wounds or his possible connection to the rumors stemming from the American consulate. They suspected Earl had been injured protecting their interests and were not there to ask how well he had done. The only indication Earl received that either man had noticed his injuries was Hiroshi's quick glance at Takeru and a grunt from both.

The mothers and siblings accompanied Kato and Munenori. The women carried tanto daggers pushed into their cushioned bustle sashes. The cousins, dressed for sailing, carried the obligatory two swords in belt sheaths.

"You were dressed differently several days ago," Earl said to the young men, and received the first tentative smiles.

The wives and daughters riveted everyone's attention. The bright kimonos they wore were essentially the same, with a few exceptions. The mothers wore open collars and the single women closed. The quality of the silk was of the highest order. The colors and intricate patterns were enough to dazzle even the most jaded observer. These were women that wise men of any race would find desirable. Their clothing, perfume, makeup, and hairdos enhanced their beauty by subtly capturing the elusive *iki* esthetic. These women were chic, sophisticated, intelligent, and wholly samurai.

Earl relaxed slightly. The keen sensitivities of his observers noted the subtle change and responded in kind. Taking the cue from Earl, the group moved a little more confidently to a side table, filled cups with warm sake, and toasted the *Bride*'s imminent departure.

Eight hours later, Earl invited the ship's officers into his suite after they exited the bay and cleared Kenzaki's headland. They gathered in the cabin while the last bells of the first dogwatch were still ringing.

"I think you people deserve an explanation, and this is as good time as any to give it," Earl said on his way to the liquor cabinet. He poured a glass of brandy for himself and sat in a red leather chair. "Help yourselves," he said, sitting back and crossing his feet on the matching hassock.

James poured a brandy and sat in an identical chair facing Earl. He and the captain sat between the table and the cabinet. Adam sat on the other side of the table with a glass of rum in his hand. Willard poured a glass of red and sat on Earl's end of the table. Ryan took a glass of rum to his seat at the other end.

"I didn't tell you much before I left, and for that I'm sorry. Naosuke's assassination caught me completely off guard. After thinking about it overnight, I decided to satisfy my curiosity. I could have involved you," Earl said, looking at Adam, "but this was one of those times where I felt the fewer people involved, the better. I was wrong, of course. Could've used a hand."

Adam frowned and rotated the glass between his fingers.

"I went ashore before dark, found a room, left my things, and walked to the offices of the American delegation in time to see the staff close up for the night." He nodded at James. "Did you notice the habits of a clerk who attended all of our meetings and dinners?"

James shifted in his chair. "Yes. He didn't say much, drank more than the others, and cast nervous glances at his boss whenever a subordinate emphasized the importance of sticking it to the Japanese negotiators."

"The clerk's name is Orville Cummings. He's the son of a Boston commodities trader who works for Sam Russell Tea Importers."

"They're selling a lot more than tea," James spat.

"Correct. Orville is a career diplomat. His boss is William Staff, Undersecretary for Trade Relations. Willy for short. He's the recipient of a ceremonial role given to the hirelings of President Buchanan's campaign contributors. Willy's father put him here to get him out from underfoot for a few years while he grows up. He'll be rewarded with a prestigious ribbon on his return to the fold. He'll assume the position being prepared for him while he is still glowing from the accolades he'll receive for bravely serving his country in a foreign land. No one will ever know, of course, that the only skills Willy feels worthy of learning around here are taught in the trenches of the Yoshiwara," Earl said, glancing at Adam. The barb turned Adam's frown into a tight line. Earl thought the expression he saw was new.

"Well," Earl said, changing the subject. "I followed the delegation to their favorite watering hole, took a seat in a dark corner, and watched them converse over drinks. After a while the group went their separate ways. Orville went off by himself. I followed him to another tavern where he sat alone drinking. He was still there when I left. Later that evening, I went back to the consulate. A light was on in a window above the offices. I found a spot where I could watch without drawing attention to myself and waited for a glimpse of who put the light out. The street traffic had trickled down to nothing by then. I don't think anyone saw me cross the street and mount the steps. Didn't take long to get the hang of how to open the door with my picks. I returned to my room and spent the next day watching who went in and out of the British consulate. I saw Willy's conniving subordinate pay a visit. I'd seen him the previous night. He sleeps upstairs.

"That evening I was back at the consulate in time to see the group go through the nightly drinking ritual. This time I waited for everyone to leave and followed Orville to his table. I asked if he remembered me. He said sure and invited me to have a drink with him. We sat and talked for over an hour while he got drunk. And talkative. He told me what he knew of the assassination and said there were papers in the consulate's office outlining how Secretary Cass wanted the Harris Treaty to be subverted into serving the needs of a New York trade consortium." Earl paused and asked James, "Do you remember the man who kept encouraging Willy to force the Japanese negotiators into more and more trade concessions?"

James squinted and closed a fist. Earl took that as a yes. "Orville told me about him. Willy's conniving assistant is Roland Hampton, the son of an influential Long Island landowner. Roland's father is an associate of Clinton Harrington. They're descended from Quakers. Roland's ancestors must have spun in their graves every time he whispered in Willy's ear. Orville told me the Harringtons and Hamptons were party to the Satsuma arms transfers, the planned assassination of the tairō, and will join the British once the pro-expulsion faction gets control of the shogunate. Roland, in his role as an in-house lobbyist, kept an eye on things from his rooms above the consulate.

"I nursed a glass of rum listening to Orville pour out his qualms about being party to a fraud culminating in the murder of a foreign leader. I left after he put his head on the table and passed out."

Earl waved his glass and went to the cabinet for a refill. "May as well tell you now because what I am going to say next will show why I shouldn't have been so hasty about going alone." After rubbing a hand over the right side of his face, he cautiously tapped the three stitches on his cheek, then blinked past his thumb. "I didn't know the drunkard had minders," he mumbled.

"Oh, Jesus," James said, sounding peeved. "You got any *more* marks on ya?"

"Couple of contusions here and there," Earl said, lifting his shirt to expose a few welts and bruises. He dropped his shirt after the eyes shifted to the red dimple beside his left armpit.

"Not impressed," James responded. "Dolt. You keep this up, and sooner or later you'll get stuck where it matters."

"Figured you'd say as much. I deserve it."

"What happened after you left the tavern, Uncle?"

"I was followed. Three men jumped me before I got back to my room." Earl took his seat, stared at James, and gathered his thoughts. "I didn't think I was going to get into a scuffle, so I left the short sword in the bag and went armed with the .22, my picks, and a tanto. They clobbered me from behind and knocked me down in an alley. I curled myself into a ball, and they started kicking. Grabbing the tanto, I jammed the blade into an assailant's groin and slashed low on the shin of another. The third guy took a couple of swipes before I could pull my head back. I put the blade up his nose before he could slice me again. The two I cut were begging me not to shoot them by the time I got to my feet. I cut their throats." Earl's tone caused his listeners to break eye contact. "I dragged the bodies farther into the alley and covered 'em with trash."

Except for the sound of chairs scraping, the room went silent for a spell while everyone considered what Earl had said. James emptied his glass and headed for the cabinet. It wasn't long before the comments, questions, and statements were piling up faster than they could be answered, so everyone started finishing each other's sentences in a five-way conversation.

The clamor got to James first. He twirled his fingers. "Finish your sordid tale!"

"Well, *sordid* isn't exactly the word that comes to mind, James."

Willard snorted. "Apt."

Ryan squeezed his lips and pondered the skylight.

"What happened next, Uncle?"

"Well, I wasn't feeling too good as I walked away from what I'd done, I'll tell ya."

James noticed a discernable tremor in Earl's voice and cast a warning glance at Adam. Then he sat and worried, only half listening. *Earl's under too damn much pressure. He sounds like he did the day we collapsed a stack of lumber in his father's yard. Nearly killed ourselves. Must've been six or seven at the time. He's been hiding that dimple from me. Old but not right.* Earl's next words drew his attention back to the conversation.

"I returned to my room, shaved my hair, cleaned out the wounds, and stitched myself up using a mirror. Ever make a repair by doing it backwards? You should try it. Hurts like hell. Have to admit, I was feeling pitiful." He saw James's worried expression, so he sat a little straighter and cleared his throat. "I ate and passed out for a while. I woke up in the dark and realized I had to get a move on if I wanted to get into the consulate without drawing attention to myself. I went inside hoping to get what I wanted and be gone before dawn. Took longer than expected, but I found the incriminating papers in the bottom of a hidden file. Roland walked in and saw me stuffing them into my shirt."

James raised his eyebrows and scratched the back of his head. "Great. Did you wish him a good morning and ask him how well he slept?"

"No, but after I commented on the length of his sword, I suggested he have a seat and discuss what I discovered."

"Did you kill him?" Ryan blurted.

James raised a finger. "Before we get to that, did you bring up the subject of his malfeasance and what you planned to do about it?"

"Yes. He justified it by saying his collaborators had a secret weapon. They were working with Japanese traitors who would do the same to the Americans if things were the other way around. Roland agreed with me when I said they would not only use similar bargaining tactics if they had the upper hand, but by buying those arms, the Satsuma daimyos betrayed the kingdom for personal gain."

James cursed, tossed off his drink, and lowered his eyelids. "Now we know what Carlton Lang and the Polar Bear were doing in Japanese waters. What was it Maynard said off the coast of California?"

"'Alcohol and secrets shouldn't be in the same room together,'" Earl said. "Not so secret now, is it? I might have taken the papers and gone if he'd left it at that. But no, he needed to demonstrate his intellectual superiority by playing the role of suave diplomat wise to the ways of the world. I must admit I found it rather offensive to be accused of being naïve and talked down to by an imperious little prick thirty years my junior. I was past the point of no return by then anyway, so it wouldn't have mattered what he said.

"He stiffened my resolve by claiming to be in league with men using the same divide-and-conquer tactics back in the States. Roland went on to say what he and his friends were doing was beyond the understanding of most people, including me. He said laws governing people like us do not apply to him because he and his colleagues trade on a global scale and therefore see themselves as citizens of every country in which they have investments. His loyalty to America is dependent upon her contribution to his company's bottom line. Roland expressed a sentiment I'd heard before: 'states serve at the pleasure of the ruling classes.'

"He laughed when I said the Framers of the Constitution fought a revolution to rid themselves of people who thought like that. 'Too late,' he said from across the room. 'The momentum is on our side, and we'll rule from the Supreme Court benches.' It was getting light enough to see each other by then, and I was getting tired of listening to his yapping."

Earl shook his head. "I told him Newton's third law is lost on the ignorant. 'What's that supposed to mean,' he asked, lifting his sword. 'The Framers anticipated people like you,' I said. 'That's why they created a republic in the first place. They knew the power of the ballot box is greater than your adherence to the corporate template laid down by your British masters. You may slow the momentum, but you will never stop what the men who signed the Constitution started.'

"He sneered at the notion that anyone could have confidence in the Constitution. He pointed his sword at me and said he was willing to overlook our misunderstanding if I would return the papers and join him in fleecing the Japanese. I'm sure he didn't like my response. I pulled the tanto and waki-zashi out of their sheaths before he could get to me. Foolish man thought the superior length of his sword would pierce my defenses. 'I'm going to enjoy killing you, Captain Yeaton,' he exclaimed. 'En garde!' he shouted and executed a classic fencing lunge."

Earl frowned. "Roland's manner suggested that he assumed the act of killing me was going to be no more dangerous to him than tapping an opponent with the point of his epee. I scissored his sword and pushed. He pulled his head back and glared down his nose in his struggle to get away. His hateful bravado wilted into a mask of fright after I slammed his back against a bookcase. He tried to pull the tanto away from his bulging eyes with his free hand. His resistance fueled my determination to proceed with cutting a thin red line from his temple to the underside of his jawbone. Speaking right into his offended nostrils, I said, 'Too bad you didn't take the opportunity to learn swordplay from a Japanese sensei while you had the chance. He would have taught you how to overcome my advantage. As it is . . .'

"'Stop, stop,' he sniveled as the tip bit. He made water and pleaded for a way to work things out. 'No,' I said, feeling his resistance draining. 'We're beyond negotiating what I have in mind for you. You and the rest of Death's dealers often have a crisis of conscience soon's it's your turn to see what lies under the Grim Reaper's hood. The murders you and your friends so joyfully peddle are about to cost you your life.'

"That said I shoved the blade through everything between the base of his tongue and his crown."

The sudden peal of a bell seemed louder than usual to Earl's listeners. His flat expression shifted to each pair of eyes while his shipmates absorbed his words. He held up a hand before anyone could respond. "I've had all I can take from fellow Americans who think they can get away with anything because no one has the courage to stand up to them. The days of putting up with their treachery are over for me."

Although they might have been interested in hearing him confirm a troubling aspect of the rumors, he still hadn't decided whether or not he should mention it. A day removed from the act, he was still sifting through a realization he had made in the consulate. As for the rumors . . . *To hell with it*, he thought, *they've earned the right to know*. "The rumors are true. I'm the one who tied Roland's corpse in a sitting position and placed the traitor's severed head in his crotch."

"Six months ago I never would have imagined I'd be weighing the implications of what I'm about to tell you. The more experienced I've become at encountering danger, the less fearful I am in its presence. This worries me.

There may come a time when I put you in danger while satisfying my desire to seek and destroy our enemies."

CHAPTER 18

Renji Yi Hospital, British Legation, Shanghai, China, 30 April 1860, 11 a.m.

Earl made room for Adam to rinse his hands in a clean washbasin. "Can't say the blood on your apron becomes you, but I can say you know how to wield the scalpel responsible for getting it there!" They dried their hands and lifted their arms, so interns could remove their bloody aprons. "Well done, nephew."

The group stood near an operating table in a surgical theater. A dozen or so men and women sat on raised benches nearby—the first class of medical students at Shanghai's Renji Yi Hospital. The students had observed Earl and Adam perform an appendectomy on a young woman while Earl described the procedure in Mandarin. Earl bowed to their host, Dr. William Lockhart.

Dr. Lockhart was a British physician and former missionary who had converted a large home on Shantung Road into the first hospital to serve the Chinese community in the territory. Earl and his nephew took a great deal of pleasure in being able to shake hands with a man who, with the assistance of the Western expatriate community, now managed a sixty-bed medical facility that also included an outpatient clinic. Dr. Lockhart was a busy man.

"She should make a full recovery," Earl continued in Mandarin. "She's young, the appendix didn't burst, and the intestinal incision is tied off. The tools and sponges we used are back on the tray." The interns collected the instruments and bloodstained swabs. The appendix was already on its way to an outside incinerator.

"Many of our colleagues don't think it is necessary to use clean cloths to wash her incision. I do. Be sure to daub iodine over the sutures, let it dry, and replace the bandage every day. Wash the used bandages in cold, soapy water, and then wash them again in boiling-hot water. I cannot overemphasize how important it is to keep everything clean and sanitary." Earl reached over and smoothed out a few loose hairs around the woman's face while several students lifted the still-unconscious patient from the operating table and placed her on a wheeled table for transport to the recovery area. "Get her up and walking in a few days. Keep the laudanum dosage to a minimum, and wean her off it as soon as she can get out of bed. Tell her the pain is a reminder she is still alive. Feed her thin soups for the next two weeks."

The students bowed and wheeled the patient away.

"Thank you, Dr. Yeaton. You have been most kind," Lockhart said. "You've been here two days, and you have already saved a life." Earl bowed again to a man who exemplified a side of missionary work that appealed to him. Lockhart saved souls by saving lives, choosing to forgo the former in favor of the latter. Earl believed far too often the two were mutually exclusive.

Earl and his friend shared a passion for the history of medicine that rivaled their commitment to its practice. They spent many hours together in Lockhart's study reading and discussing the works of Hua To, Sun Simiao, and the seminal sixteenth-century pharmacological work of Li Shinzhen, *Syllabus of Medical Herbs*. Earl had been delighted to discover on a previous stay that Lockhart was familiar with Aelius Galen and could read his second-century treatises in Greek. This time around, Earl made sure they took turns reading passages from Galen's work, *That the Best Physician Is Also a Philosopher*, while drinking Chian wine from golden Mycenaean goblets. Earl and his Chinese colleagues fell into fits of laughter as Lockhart tried and failed to perform a running translation in Mandarin.

Occasionally, these same doctors would dine aboard the *Bride*. Their get-togethers ran late on the nights they pored over ancient texts. Finding inspiration, they took turns preparing culinary samplers of the foods consumed by the men whose works they studied and debated. The nights they visited the medical literature of southern China, cases of *huangjin*, a popular cereal wine, extinguished the oral fires produced by the *Szechwan* and *Tien Tsin* pepper-laced cuisine.

Earl also enjoyed sitting in Lockhart's kitchen with contemporary Chinese doctors preparing culinary treats sprinkled with medicinal condiments.

The night Earl arrived in Shanghai they had gathered once again and prepared a variety of marinated meats braised over coals and served with egg sauces poured over basmati rice. Eyes rolled in rapture over sweet-and-sour *kimchi* side dishes accented with slices of pickled Japanese wasabi tuna. The intrepid doctors bravely washed down their portions with warmed *mouti baijiu*, a pure grain firewater distilled from fermented sorghum.

At one point, Earl noticed Lockhart laughing to himself. Two well-intentioned foes had paused during a spirited debate over which of the four pillars of Chinese medicine had precedence. Lockhart held his glass up to the light. "A few more rounds of this, and they'll agree to anything."

Lockhart smiled as if he knew what Earl had been thinking. "I'm impressed by your attention to detail and how well you maintain a hygienic surgical area."

Earl bowed at the compliment. "Next to the tasks we perform, there is no greater contributor to successful outcomes than cleanliness, Dr. Lockhart. Use lots of carbolic soaps and acids in preparing patients for surgery and in cleaning the areas they occupy. I'll talk with some of the Anglos, and we will get a teaching hospital fund started. You can keep the surgical instruments we brought today. We'll have additional surgical wards and the contents of a field hospital sent over, so you will have enough equipment for more surgeries and patient recovery areas."

Earl turned and addressed the students. "I'm aware you are contending with outbreaks of the Plague and the scourge of the Black Death. A recent outbreak in India killed millions. I believe the Black Death is transmitted through the skin of the dead and the breath of the dying." Earl crossed to a board and drew while he talked. "Three hundred years ago, thieves in Europe came up with a concoction made from the essential oils of camphor, rosemary, clove, lemon, and cinnamon. The oil wards off the disease. A sixteenth-century Dutch painter named Hieronymus Bosch included the helmets the thieves wore in many of his paintings. The helmets resembled ravens beaks. They covered holes in the beaks with cloths soaked in these oils. The villains who chose to wear this apparatus while stealing valuables were among the few who did not come down with the disease. I suggest you have these masks made and wear them before coming in contact with the afflicted. I'll have several cases of thieves' oil sent over."

He turned back to Dr. Lockhart. "The recent crush of refugees has put a severe strain on Shanghai's capacity to serve their needs. Even more people will be fleeing into the city if the rumors are true. You will soon need a lot more of the kind of help I'm sending you. I'm concerned there could be a cholera epidemic if the water and sewage services aren't upgraded."

"Yes," Lockhart said with concern, "and there will be no relief. My compatriots and their allies continue to pressure the Qing government to sanction the importation of opium. Despite innumerable objections and several one-sided wars resulting in additional unfair treaties, their smuggling efforts have successfully addicted a substantial proportion of the population. They have created a demand for a consumable commodity over which they have a monopoly. This will further destabilize the country, drive more people into the ranks of the Taiping rebels, and open the way for a European-led invasion. The conceit associated with these diabolical practices defies comprehension."

"Sure does," Earl agreed. "Unfortunately, China is experiencing what the British have done elsewhere. I hear the Foreign Office has presented the Qing government with more punitive demands. These, of course, will compound the folly of the current agreements. It gets worse. Lord Elgin, the High Commissioner for China and Japan, is on his way here. He's a bumbling nabob who had a disastrous stay in Canada as governor general. Three years ago, he oversaw the disgraceful naval bombardment of Guangzhou. You can anticipate a land invasion after that knave arrives. The Prime Minister, Lord Palmerston, has given Elgin a mandate permitting him to order the military to march on Beijing and destroy everything in their path. This will result in the desecration, looting, and destruction of national treasures. China is on the verge of becoming another British colony."

Earl faced the students. "I tell you this because British, French, American, Dutch, German, Russian, Japanese, Taiping, and Qing greed and mismanagement will provide you with opportunities to practice the surgical skills you saw demonstrated here today." Earl's expression summed up how he felt about training surgeons to repair monumental blunders.

Earl and Adam bowed with the students as they rose from their seats. They stayed to answer questions and discussed the students' observations for the remainder of the morning. They accepted Lockhart's invitation to join them for a *gong bao* stir-fry.

An observant male student remained quiet during the meal. Earl raised an eyebrow to Lockhart and glanced at the young man as they cleared the table.

"You're probably wondering why he has been watching you," Lockhart said. "Let me introduce you to Cam Lum, the brother of Sui Mai Lum, the young woman whose life you saved this morning."

Earl and Adam gave Cam a little more attention. Earl had noticed Cam earlier because his rugged North Asian face seemed out of place among the less-defined ovals of his Shanghai classmates. He wore a simple, loose-fitting dun smock and trousers. His firm grip suggested his clothes covered a lean body of medium build. "Hen gaozing renshi ri," Earl and Adam said. ("Pleased to meet you.")

"Wo. Xiexie ri jiule wo de meimei" ("And I thank you for saving my sister"), Cam replied, bowing low.

"Bie keqi" ("You're welcome"), they answered, meeting his bow.

Lockhart watched his guests with a mixture of awe and deep satisfaction. Few Westerners adapted so well to the cultural courtesies expected of them in foreign lands. Earl and Adam were totally at ease, characteristics he and Cam saw at once. *Remarkable*, he thought.

He knew little about Cam, other than that he had arrived soon after the hospital began accepting students. Cam possessed a ready intellect and proved to be an able student in all aspects of his training. *He will make an excellent surgeon*, Lockhart thought as he watched the exchange between his three guests. The timing of Sui Mai Lum's illness and their arrival could not have been better. That everything worked out so well came as no surprise. *Earl Yeaton has been helpful several times in the past few years, so I know what to expect of this learned man. Yet I am still impressed each time I observe him and his nephew. And Earl certainly put his finger on the pulse of what my countrymen are up to*, Lockhart thought with chagrin.

At the conclusion of the surgery, Lockhart had half-expected Cam to request permission to meet with Earl and Adam. He did not expect Cam to extend his request to include talking with them privately after his expressions of gratitude were completed. "Cam has asked that I leave you three to converse by yourselves. Apparently, he wishes to talk with you alone."

Surprised by the request, Earl and Adam followed Dr. Lockhart and Cam to Lockhart's study. Earl entered a room he had been in many times. Books on a wide variety of subjects lined the walls and were stacked like cordwood on the floor. Bright *quohua* paintings competed with dark European oils on the cramped wall spaces. The surface of Lockhart's desk supported a small mountain of papers and journals. The windows behind the desk faced the wide Huangpu River.

Earl suppressed an inclination to ask Lockhart if Qi Baishi's seal was on the gong-bi he'd seen the night before. Instead of interrupting his host, he followed Lockhart to a sitting area—two well-used leather chairs and a matching couch arranged around a lacquered table. The chairs flanked an unlit fireplace.

Cam sat on the couch, and they took seats at the ends of the low table. "I will have tea brought to you. Take as long as you like. Please feel free to start the fire if it suits you." Lockhart closed the door behind him on his way out.

Earl took a moment to glance toward the anchorage and sought new arrivals. The *Bride* floated among a forest of masts scattered along the curving shoreline. Her flapping pennant pointed the way as she swung around her anchor chain. Rain clouds followed the turbulent chop spreading upriver.

He sniffed and experienced a moment of self-deprecation. *Harrumph*, he thought. *It seems I have yet to overcome this instinctual behavior every time I notice a change in the weather.* He let out a small sigh, thinking he might be more primal than he wished to admit. He turned, lowered his expectant blue eyes, and focused on Cam's composed face.

Adam had noticed a red seal on a scroll hanging between two bookcases. Ming To was the reason he knew who created the painting. Ming had been insistent at times during the long instructional hours they spent in the chartroom. "You must learn to recognize the seal of all the great masters, especially those from the four periods of the Song Dynasty," he repeated over and over again. So, Adam had learned how to distinguish the style and seal of the great first-millennium *Sui-Mo* masters. He recognized the distinctive brushstrokes in the *shan-shui*, mountain-river watercolor. *This may well be the seal of the great twelfth-century master, Zhang Zeduan. If so, this priceless painting is seven hundred years old. The tales this masterpiece could tell of its passage through so many chaotic times! How in the world did it end up in this room?* He gave thanks to Ming for making it possible for him to appreciate what he was seeing.

He overheard Earl and Cam conversing in an unfamiliar Mandarin dialect. He caught the gist of what they were discussing and gave his full attention to the two, who, due to the softness of their voices, were reading each other's lips as much as listening to one another. A person standing at the door would not know people were conversing in the hushed space. A light rain spattered the window.

He heard Cam ask Earl if he could understand what he said.

"Yes. You want this conversation to be private, and thanks to many hours of conversing in Mandarin with my second cook, Chin Lo, I'm able to understand most of what you're saying. Court Mandarin has acquired a dialect of its own over the centuries. The nuances have become nearly as convoluted as the palace intrigues surrounding the throne. I will never understand them all."

Cam's lips curled, and holding Earl's eyes with his own, he continued talking.

Dark clouds gradually filled the river basin and released a steadily intensifying rain. Adam noticed the room growing darker and decided to light a few oil lamps. He lit a match and held the flame. Cam had whispered the word *guijian* so faintly he nearly missed it. His uncle leaned further over the table "Guijian? Wo bu mingbai, guijian" ("I do not understand.") Adam blew out the flame and listened.

"Child who is not a child. I am a guijian descendant of Tolui, youngest son of Genghis Khan. My ancestral grandparent was born from one of Tolui's concubines."

"Ah, so," his uncle said in English without thinking. Earl cleared his throat and said in Mandarin, "In English we would say the child was morganatic. These children are usually the offspring of royalty but not heirs. Girls are not included in the family lists. Your ancestor had to be male for you to be so sure of your lineage back to the Great Khan and, as such, was not his child. A child who is not a child."

"Shi."

"And the reason you are telling us this?"

"My yeye (grandfather) needs your attention. He is the last in a long line of archivists charged by Tolui to keep maps and records of the plunder taken from lands conquered by his father, brothers, and son, Kublai Khan. Yeye is in the Old City where our family has preserved the records among those accumulated by the dynasties following the Yuans. We have been keeping archival records in the same building for centuries. "My sister, Sui Mai, my younger brother, Qui Li, and I are orphans. We do not know if we have any other relatives and none of us wish to take his place," Cam said, lowering his eyes in shame.

"Maybe it's time for you to pass the responsibility for preserving your family history to others," Earl replied. "You are making your own contribution by becoming the first surgeon. You'll be known for saving lives instead of preserving the records of those who took them. I'd call that a fair choice. Certainly nothing to be ashamed about."

Adam started lighting lamps and strained to hear the conversation over the smack of rain pelting the windows. Fog accompanied the rain upriver and covered everything in sight. He noticed an eerie orange glow lighting the underside of the fog bank. *Appears to be near the British consulate.* He shrugged and focused on Cam.

"The wendang ku jianshe, our document storage building, is inside the Old City wall next to the Dajing Ge Pavilion, the wall's west gate. Shanghai built the wall in the mid-sixteenth century to protect the city from Japanese pirates. Tolui chose the site ages ago because it would be far away from the seat of power in Beijing. Nomadic ancestors knew the Mongol Empire was just as susceptible to extinction as the empires they conquered. They also knew that dynasties are prone to believing their reigns are superior to whoever came first. My Yuan Dynasty ancestors observed firsthand the selfish tendencies we humans have to accumulate wealth, power, and prestige and the lengths we are willing go to in order to demonstrate our own superiority. The removal of a predecessor's accomplishments becomes part of an effort to rewrite history. Having the historical records far away from Mongolia and Beijing makes that effort difficult."

Adam exchanged a glance with Earl who lifted an index finger, and wiggled it at the fireplace. "So, instead of putting the records of their accomplishments close to their northern Mongolian stronghold, they hid them in the opposite direction."

"Like here, in this remote southern locale," Adam said, placing a lighted match in the kindling.

"Shi." Cam realized he had never had a conversation like this with anyone, much less a gwei lo. Their respectful responses encouraged him to confide in them. "Shanghai was chosen because, until the arrival of the British, it was an unimportant coastal village and therefore of no interest to Beijing. The wealth is upriver in Hangzhou. The building, contents, and caretakers have been alone and ignored for over five hundred years. The Dajing Ge repository holds many valuable historical artifacts dating back to the thirteenth century. The Khans ruled nearly all of Asia back then. Two days ago, it was in the center of a skirmish between Taiping rebels and the government."

He listened as Earl picked up the thread. "Apparently, the rebels are being led by Hong Xiuquan, a Christian fanatic who believes he's the brother of Jesus." He leaned back and rubbed his temple with the pad of a thumb. "Oddly enough, many of the social reforms he wants to implement are consistent with those laid down in our own Constitution. I cannot understand how he can espouse the teachings of Jesus and accomplish his egalitarian goals by so enthusiastically snuffing out the lives of his fellow citizens. I'm told that to gain control of over thirty million Chinese, his armies have slaughtered nearly twenty million. He may end up being responsible for more dead than the British and their French allies."

Cam nodded with approval as Adam crisscrossed a few of the larger sticks in the fireplace, and within seconds, crackling flames accompanied the rainy tattoo.

"Correct." Cam motioned for them to lean forward. "The government may have retaken control of the Old City, but Taiping Small Swords Society loyalists remain and are among the refugees fleeing the fighting. They are an additional cause for concern because they were in the archive two days ago, a day after I brought Sui Mai to the hospital. The loyalists attacked a squad of government troops in the Old City. The soldiers chased them through the streets to the Old West Gate. Unable to get through the gate, the rebels broke into the archive. Fighting ensued within the building. They destroyed cases and documents before the rebels scattered. I hope the escapees report they saw nothing of interest in an old document storage building. The Taipings loot and sell anything of value to help finance their cause. Yeye was trying to stop them, and in the confusion, a storage case toppled onto him. I fear he may be bleeding inside. Would you see what can be done?"

There was a knock on the door before Earl could reply. Adam crossed the room and admitted a young woman. She entered and placed a covered tray on the table. The light from the fire gave her powdered cheeks a rosy glow and danced off the mother-of-pearl barrettes holding her hair away from the fine lines of her neck and ears. The men watched as she placed a large silk trivet in the center of the table. Then she carefully set a steaming translucent teapot on the trivet and surrounded it with matching wafer-thin porcelain cups and saucers. She arranged the cutlery, chopsticks, and red, yellow, and green silk napkins in an attractive pattern. She lifted the lids on two warm dishes and, speaking softly in Chinese-accented English, named each dish as she placed it beside the pot. "Egg rolls, dan juan. Rice and meat dumplings, rou wan." She placed two other dishes on the remaining sides of the trivet. "Prawn crackers, xia pian, and fried bread sticks, you liao." She picked up the empty tray, paused to view the arrangement, bowed, and passed through the door once again.

Cam poured Earl's tea, then Adam's, and finally his own. He placed the pot as he had found it. The scent of oranges and pekoe infused the area. Earl and Adam knew Cam would not touch anything until they had sampled everything.

"There's a lot to admire about China," Earl commented as he reached for his cup.

"Shi," Cam said with a slight smile. "My hope is that after we rid ourselves of the evil sweeping over our land, there will still be remnants of what occurred here in the last few minutes."

Earl nodded and had a sip. "Don't wait for us to taste what is on each of the dishes before you join us. We do not have time for offering, refusal, offering again, and final acceptance," he added with a flinty smile.

A chill ran down Cam's spine as he saw the subtle color changes in Earl's eyes. "Xiexie," he murmured, thinking, *This healer can kill.*

Earl leaned forward again. "Yeye. His name and where he is."

"His name is Wing Wong Lum and is in his quarters with my brother, Qui Li."

Keeping their voices low, and barely able to hear each other over the rain running down the window in rivulets, they discussed how Cam planned to guide the group out of the British sector, through the maze of streets in the French legation, past government patrols, through the Old City walls, and into the damaged repository.

"We're going to be supplied with more than medical equipment on our way out of here," Earl said as he cut the last dan juan into thirds.

"Xiexie," Cam said. "I will go tell Yeye you are coming. We can meet here in three hours."

There was another knock on the door as the three finished the tea and snacks. Adam opened the door as Earl and Cam rose from their seats. Dr. Lockhart stood in the doorway. "One of your men is here. He's in a waiting room and says it's urgent."

CHAPTER 19

Dajing Ge Pavilion, Shanghai, China, 30 April, 6:00 p.m.

Cam Lum had taken Bill, Kato, and Tom ahead to scout the way. Bill returned to give the all clear. "Be dark soon, Capt'n. Archive's around the next corner beside the west gate. Have to say, I don't like being out here in 'no man's land' so far away from help if anything goes wrong. Fog's so thick I can't see the eves. Rain's a blessing though, only an idiot would be up to any mischief in this downpour."

He and Earl were standing under a shop awning with Munenori and Adam. The group huddled beside one of the innumerable lanes running every which way in the ancient quarter of the Old City. Most of the people who were out in the unrelenting rain paid them no mind. The few who did saw the ominous bulges beneath their capes and scurried off.

"Take the lead, Bill. Rai ni me o hanashimasen, Munenori." ("Keep eye on rear.")

Earl shook his head at what little there was to see, settled the collar on his neck, and pulled his sou'wester more firmly down around his ears. "Thank goodness Dr. Lockhart had a spare bed. The nap I had is about to pay dividends."

Dr. Lockhart led Earl and Adam to the waiting room after Cam left to see his grandfather. Chin Lo, the *Bride's* second cook, was in the room. They moved to a far corner after Lockhart closed the door. Earl and Adam cocked their heads to hear Chin's whispered news. "A Harrington clipper, the Falcon, sailed up river at slack tide. She dropped anchor at the mouth of Suzhou

Creek near the British legation. Her anchorage is across a stretch of water near the American legation and within sight of the Bride. I happened to be in the Hongmen safe house on Huqiu Road at the time. Lin Pu, the Falcon's second cook, came in while I was making arrangements to transfer the gold we smuggled out of San Francisco."

Earl and Adam knew of the Hongmen Secret Society safe house. Earl thought it brazen of them to hide an outlawed network's headquarters behind the British consulate.

Chin went on to tell them he had arranged to have the *Bride* moved to a wharf/warehouse owned by a Hongman member. They planned to offload the Shanghai portion of the gold at midnight. "Most of the gold will be on its way to the families whose locations are still known before morning," Chin said. "So many people are fleeing their homes and unaccounted for in the chaos, it may be necessary to spend the remaining gold on food and shelter for the refugees crowding the city."

Adam groaned on hearing this news. "You must be having a difficult time with that thought. The Chinese in California went through a lot to scrape up enough gold to send back to their starving families. I'm sure their belief that the gold would find its way here is what sustained most of them through the horrors they faced." He frowned and shook his head. The set of his jaw and nasty squint said plenty about how he felt about what the white miners and authorities did to Chinese who found gold in abandoned claims or filed legitimate claims and took gold out of gravel the whites said was worthless. Ground the whites dismissed as a waste of time until proven wrong by the hardworking Chinese. The Orientals were then robbed, beaten, and left for dead by claim jumpers brandishing forged claims the authorities were only too willing to verify. "It's a wonder any gold made its way aboard the Bride."

"Zhengque, we will try to find the families and a way to make the best use of the gold so many suffered to produce. We will keep lists of those we find and those we do not. Losing their family members and in all likelihood their connection to their ancestors through the loss of the Family Book will be devastating for many in Golden Mountain," Chin said with a helpless shrug.

He squared his shoulders squinted at Earl with a look that caused his captain lift his head. "But that's not the reason I'm here. Lin came ashore in a longboat with the cooks to buy food. He hurried up to the safe house hoping to pass a message on to me. He said six men left the Falcon in a quarter boat. They were not members of the crew. Arthur Harrington is placing men like them aboard all of his ships. They have been hired to find you, Captain Earl, torture you, find out if you have the bonds, and kill you."

Earl exchanged a hooded scowl with Adam. "We'll see about that."

"No need."

"What?" Earl and Adam exclaimed.

Chin lowered his voice further. "The assassins were followed by one of Lin's cooks to a house in the legation—a house owned by the Harringtons. He ran back and told us where they were. Eight of us killed the qui lo who work there and captured the men sent to kill you. We took them to a place where no one could hear their screams, interrogated them in ways best not described, found out who sent them and why. A boat will dump their weighted bodies in the river after dark. Harrington's house has probably collapsed into the foundation by now. We set it on fire before we left. Do you want us to sink the ship?"

Adam grunted as if he'd been punched in the gut. Earl squeezed his nostrils and scratched the scar above his ear. "Give me a minute to think about it."

Earl's men knew a great deal more than the average ship's crew did about the Chinese people. Nearly all captains were prepared to employ those willing to do tasks too menial for any self-respecting white man. Most captains chose Chinese workers over the less tractable Mexicans and Negros, not knowing they were distributing members of Chinese secret societies throughout the fleets of the world. The gwei lo who hired them had no idea there were scholars among the people for whom they had so little regard; servants who were devoutly religious, highly educated, and soon learned to understand what was said in front of them. Had they known whom they were letting aboard, it is doubtful the captains would have hired servants whose martial arts skills could kill them in the blink of an eye.

Earl became acquainted with a prominent society through Ming. Before he owned the *Bride*, Earl had learned of the obstacles facing the workers who wished to send gold back to their families. He determined that once he had a ship of his own he would assist these long-suffering people, and he would do it without adding the crippling fees other captains charged. Earl approached Ming and asked him if he knew any of the people involved in the perilous task of getting the gold aboard ships destined for China. Ming gave Earl a rare smile- the man's eyes were smiling as much as his mouth. Earl got the impression he'd just passed a test of values.

Ming used the opportunity to provide Earl with an insight into Oriental guile and revealed his Hongmen affiliation.

Adapting to the times and recognizing the global inevitability of Western influences on China, Ming and his comrades spread themselves among the cultures invading their land. They took whatever employment opportunities were open to them, including the most menial. He told Earl he had been smuggling gold back to China in small quantities since he'd come aboard in '54. He also said he had examined his captain with more scrutiny than Earl had exercised in determining Ming's suitability to be his cook! Ming had since discovered that the man who captained the *Bride* knew a great deal more about the ways of the world than he'd ever dreamed possible. Most importantly, he listened and learned.

He and Earl spent many hours discussing subjects of mutual interest. Ming revealed his past, including a closely held secret. He told Earl that Shaolin monks had trained him in the Zen Buddhist tradition of service to families, ancestors, and community. The various sects, including the Hongmen, shared a common goal: the overthrow of the Qing government and the restoration of the Ming Dynasty. The Qings knew this and feared the Shaolin-trained Hongmen.

Late one night, after they'd known each other for a few years, Ming said government troops killed his parents and everyone in his village because they were suspected of aiding the Shaolin. He was a small boy at the time and left for dead. A monk found him among the ruins, adopted the child, and trained him in a hidden temple deep in the Mao'er Mountains. Ming mentioned that he was a Zen master and a Hongman. Most of Ming's backstory was still a mystery to Earl. He had not told Earl or anyone else he was Ah Toy's Old Master.

He *did* tell Earl why the Qing fears were so well founded. The Qing rulers knew the Hongmen counted themselves among those who revered the legendary second-century Han General, Guan Yu, whose construct, the trilateral swords of devotion, loyalty, and patriotism formed the basis of his personal code of conduct. Preferring to quash any opposition to their absolute rule, the Qing outlawed the Hongmen, referring to them as a "triad," and lumped them in with criminal tongs.

The Qings destroyed the remote Shaolin Temple for the last time in 1732. The monks not killed fanned out and continued to teach a form of Buddhism that emphasized spiritual enlightenment, medicine, familial devotion, and self-protection. This last they perfected into an art form called kung fu. Many scholars differed over the origin of the term. One camp believed that a Korean translation, *hard hand*, must be the source of this martial art, while others said the term originated among the Shaolin monks and "all martial arts under heaven came from Shaolin." Whatever the source of the term, there was little doubt that the martial art practices perfected in the lost temple merged the spirit, mind, and body of its practitioners into a lethal weapon if threatened.

Huddled in Lockhart's room with Adam and Chin Lo, Earl repeated an ancient Chinese saying, "Armies protect the emperor; secret societies protect the people." A secret society had just protected him, and he expressed gratitude. He could think of no better way to demonstrate this than by helping an old man who was trying to preserve several hundred years of Chinese history.

Earl stared at the wet cobbles and squinted at the route he and his men had taken to get into the Old City. The narrow street passed through the North Gate's fog-shrouded arch after crossing a bridge that spanned the moat. "The trip has been worth the price of a ticket, so far," he muttered, his eyes tracing the rain-soaked street back into the French legation. The rain did nothing to dampen the spirits of the sailors, traders, pickpockets, remittance men, and western government clerks who jostled each other from the harbor end of Shandong Road to the North Gate. The houses and hovels lining the roadway competed with shops on the first floor and brothels on the second. Catering to the needs of the flesh was the sole purpose of this and the surrounding streets and alleys. Saloons and brothels abounded, serving clientele who ran the gamut from the gritty to the genteel.

The din created by the hawkers, tattooists, soothsayers, and moneylenders vying for attention tried the senses. The crush passed braziers cooking every imaginable edible, from flesh to insects. Fishmongers held their wares over the pandemonium, exposing the wet scales to the multitude of hanging lanterns. Their raucous calls and flaccid wares competed with grocer stalls packed with fruits and vegetables set below hanging carcasses of chickens, piglets, and ducks. Eateries stood out like bollards in the millrace of humanity flowing through the unheeded rain.

Earl nudged Munenori and smiled at the absurdity of being where they were on such a night. "Has to be seen to be believed." He received an indulgent, rain-spattered twist of the lips before turning to follow Bill and Adam. Trudging along, he reviewed the news Chin had delivered four short hours earlier and pondered whether or not assassins had been aboard the *Empire* the day she dropped anchor in Honolulu Harbor. "Too many unanswerable questions," he mumbled and thanked his lucky stars for having saved the life of Mathew Stilson's mother. *Must be doubly vigilant wherever I go now*, he thought, scratching the red welt on his cheek and rolling his shoulder. He had moved on to his sailing itinerary by the time Bill interrupted him.

"Capt'n Earl, Capt'n Earl, we're here."

"Oh," Earl said, bumping into Adam, "I was thinking of other things." He blinked the rain out of his eyes and nodded to the men standing beside a gate attached to a low wall. The squat structure sitting at the other end of a misty path differed little from the single-story buildings lining both sides of the street.

The fog lifted enough for them see what lay atop the Old City wall rising over the building. Perplexed, he and his men stared at the wet scales of a stone dragon. They followed the serpentine body a short way to a malevolent head leering at them from above Dajing Ge Pavilion. Looming over the monster, the fluted tile roof of the gatehouse hung in the shadows like a bat-winged phantom. Bill let out a low moan and groped for the .36 belted to his hip. Everyone had the willies, so they pretended not to notice.

Cam pushed open the gate and stepped onto a stone walkway that led to a thick door built into the archive's masonry walls. The garden was ready for planting. A bed had onion sprouts popping up among the seedlings trampled by the recent conflict.

"Cam, Adam, and I go inside. The rest of you arrange yourselves in a defensive perimeter." Earl motioned for Cam to lead the way.

At Cam's knock on the damaged door, a slot opened to reveal a pair of frightened eyes. Recognizing his brother, Qui Li pulled the door open and let them in.

Cam addressed his brother, who was more interested in getting the door to close than meeting Earl and Adam. "Qui, zehexie si wo gaosuguo ni de ren. Qingwen tamen." ("These are the men I told you about. Please greet them.") Qui Li quit shoving, but he kept his head bowed and appeared reluctant to make eye contact.

Sensing the boy's discomfort, Earl asked Adam to fetch Bill. "Maybe he can repair the door enough to secure it from inside again."

Earl held a finger up to Cam and spoke directly to the black-clad boy. "Qui Li, Qing dai women qui ni yeye" ("Qui Li, take us to your grandfather"). The fourteen-year-old looked at Earl for the first time and let the compassion he saw there overrule his fear.

"Shi." He led the pair through the archive.

Earl followed Cam and Qui Li as they made their way to the living area in the back of the building. Earl estimated that the archive covered an area approximately twenty-five feet wide by fifty feet long. The building was reasonably sound, considering what had taken place in it. Papers lay strewn about the floor. A few cases lay on their sides. The cases left standing were in ordered rows along the walls and floor. A few had solid tops with numerous pigeonholes and drawers built into the sides. Blood was on the floor beside an upturned case in the back.

The living area was all one room. A small fire burned in an open hearth, and a steaming kettle sat on a metal trivet beside the coals. The food preparation area was in a corner of the north wall. The stone counter held a brazier topped with a wok, a sink, and cooking utensils. The table could seat four comfortably. The rest of the furniture consisted of two stuffed leather chairs, a small writing table, and a couple of stools. Prints, paintings, bookcases, and cubbyholes stuffed with scrolls covered the walls. The south wall also held a window and a Dutch door. An outer path led to the well and a privy on the far side of the garden.

The hearth, small oil lamps mounted on the walls and several candles lit the modest room. The windows provided a meager light. The area smelled lived in but clean. A map of China was above a trundle bed by the south wall.

Wing Wong Lum lay on a similar bed beneath a window in a corner of the opposite wall.

The man beneath the blankets appears to be of medium build, like his grandsons, Earl thought. Keeping his eyes on Wing, Earl handed his sou'wester and cape to Qui Li. Cam lifted Earl's duffel off his shoulder and placed it on the table. The bag contained food, medical equipment, dry clothes, matches, and a sack of candles.

Earl bowed before moving over to sit with Wing. *He has the makings of a scholar,* he mused. *Domed cranium, high cheekbones, patrician nose, thin lips, and a well-defined jawline. A handsome man in his youth.*

Wing lay on a straw mattress covered with an old silk quilt folded over his chest. Earl's eyes softened. Wing's head, shoulders, and arms were resting comfortably on a large blue-and-white-striped feather pillow. *I've slept on one of those for as long as I can remember,* he thought. Rearranging the chair beside the bed, Earl patted Wing's hand and felt saddened. The limpid and darkly flecked eyes told him as much as an hour of conversation could ever convey. Taking the elderly man's hand in both of his, Earl nodded his understanding. Without saying so, Wing told Earl he knew he was dying.

Tilting his head toward the duffel, Earl spoke in Mandarin. "We need to see better. Open the bag, and light a bunch of candles."

Adam arrived and gave Qui Li a hand spreading the light around.

Earl turned back to Wing. "Wo keyi jiao ni Yeye?" ("May I call you Yeye?")

"Shi," Wing answered with a slight smile. "Zhiyou wo keyi jiao ni erzi." ("Yes, if I can call you my son.")

Earl bowed and smiled in return. "Wo jiang bushing rongxing. Zai wo zai zheli banzhu ni zai renha fangfa keyi rnang wo, Yeye." ("I would be honored. I am here to help you in any way I can, Grandfather.") Continuing in Mandarin, Earl asked Wing how he was feeling.

"I am in pain here," Wing said, pulling the covers back and pointing to his ribs and abdomen.

Wing allowed Earl to expose the cuts and bruises. Earl saw the indentations of the case in Wing's left side. The deep-purple bruise radiating away from the gash spread outward into a mottled bluish-yellow stain. The case had caught Wing in the lower ribs before glancing off and crushing his abdomen. A corner had pierced his skin, cracked an exposed lower rib, and then slid into his abdomen, tearing a jagged path before coming to rest on a kidney. Qui Li had removed pieces of fabric along with the bone and wood splinters. The wound, although clean, was inflamed.

"Yeye," Earl said to Wing after he saw the extent of the injuries, "these wounds need to be attended to now. I would prefer to do it with you sedated. I have a chloroform inhaler that will put you to sleep while we examine and repair the damage done to you."

Wing nodded his assent.

Adam prepared the inhaler and administered the chloroform while Earl sterilized his hands and instruments. Wing was asleep by the time Earl returned to the bed and peeled back the jagged gash to expose the wound. The peritoneum remained intact. Blood was visible through the membrane where it should have been clear. The lower tip of the spleen appeared to have taken the worst of it. Blood streamed away from Earl's probing fingers, suggesting the spleen was still leaking. Pushing his fingertips into the kidney area, he felt sponginess where it should be firm. He kept his face neutral and cleaned the wound with a stronger concentration of carbolic than he would have used had he been there a day earlier.

"Decision time," he said to Cam and Adam, raising an eyebrow. "What do you think?"

"The lower portion of his spleen is crushed, Uncle. The cracked rib may have pinched the spleen, causing the upper abdominal hemorrhage. My medical school instructors would recommend removing it, or he'll bleed to death. I am not of that opinion. We cannot repair the kidney. Removing it is not an attractive option either. The peritoneum, although bruised, is intact. I would say we'd be doing more damage to him by intervening than if we cleaned the wound and let nature take its course. The risk of infection will go up rapidly if we open the sack. I doubt if he'd recover from the surgery; he'd be in a lot of pain, and I don't think he would live any longer."

"Thank you. What do you think, Cam?"

Cam placed a hand on his grandfather's shoulder and gazed at the old man's face before replying. "I am sorry I put you in so much danger only to have you tell me what my heart refused to accept. Please forgive me. Yeye is old and may not live through our efforts to repair the damage. He will not recover from his injuries. I think we should sew him up and keep him comfortable for as long as possible."

Earl saw Adam nodding in agreement. "All right then. Would you do the honor of cleaning out the wound and suturing your yeye? We'll stand by to assist you. And Cam, one more thing. There is no need to ask for our forgiveness. We're honored to be here."

Cam nodded, poured hot water into a basin, and washed his hands.

Early the next morning, Earl examined Wing. The old man said the pain had lessened. Earl smiled at the laudanum flask. The 200-ml bottle had been full the previous evening. Wing reached for the elixir and shook the dregs. "Should make it till noon. Strange how a drug that has caused so much harm to so many can be helpful if used properly," he said before removing the cork and taking another sip. Earl and the others had decided to let Wing administer his own opium-infused dosages as long as he remained lucid and had an appetite.

"My time may be short, and I do not want to waste it by lying in bed sleeping off draughts of opium. There is plenty of time for sleep where I'm going. Last night while you were sleeping, I decided what I want you to do with me and the contents of this archive after I die." A knot in the hearth popped, and the gas flare lit Wing's eyes. "It is too dangerous for the archive to remain here in China. Chinese nearly destroyed the place fighting among themselves. The British and French would do two things with it if they knew what was here: They would take what they think is of value, not knowing it is all of value, and burn the rest."

Wing asked Earl if it would be possible to transfer the archive to a safe place, preferably away from China. "Yes," Earl assured him, "but only until it can be returned intact. I have a place in mind where it can be stored safely."

"Xiexie," Wing replied. "Cam said you were an honorable man when I gave him permission to bring you here. Now I have seen for myself it is true. You will be relieving me of a great responsibility. Transfer the archive's contents to a secure place. There will come a day when they can be returned to a unified China strong enough to protect its national treasures. Now listen: I want to be buried in an unmarked grave behind this building. Cam can decide for himself where he wishes to live. I want him to stay in China and be a doctor. Qui Li and Sui Mai are to go to America. They are not safe here. Erzi, do you know where my grandchildren can go?"

"Shi. I have friends in San Francisco who will help get Sui Mai settled. They will find a place for her to live, work and go to school, if she wishes. I will take Qui Li with me aboard my ship. He can decide where he wants to live next fall after he sees Sui Mai."

Earl sent Bill and Munenori back to the ship to get several more men. They returned with a wagon loaded with bedding, food, shotguns, pistols, ammunition, ropes, tackle, tarpaulins, and packing cases.

Adam saw to the cataloguing and crating of the archives. Cam shuttled back and forth from the hospital. The third day after Sui Mai's operation, Cam reported she would be up and walking in a day or so.

Qui did the grocery shopping and prepared meals with Earl, who soon realized the boy was a younger version of his grandfather. Earl stayed with Wing day and night. He slept in Wing's trundle bed while the others slept in the archive. He spent many hours talking with the old man, learning all he could of the archive and its contents. He kept notes in shorthand, and he and Adam often sat at the table and cross-referenced everything for later cataloguing.

Earl was surprised to learn the Chinese had not only sailed up the west coast of Africa but had crossed the Pacific and visited California. "After all," Wing said, "we invented the compass and had a fleet of six masted ships."

"Yes, I knew about the compass and the ships. The great fifteenth-century seafarer, Zheng He, who sailed west of here used a compass. His exploits occurred at the same time Europeans explored the northern seas using a similar device. Theirs pointed north whereas Zheng He's compass pointed south. Do you have any records of Chinese ships sailing to North America in here?" Earl asked, waving a hand toward the archives.

"No. The records are not stored here. No one will ever know the extent of Zheng He's achievements. The fifteenth century was a time of transition from the Yuan to the Ming Dynasty. Zheng was a commoner, and worse, a eunuch. He had many enemies at court. The mandarins in the new capital, Beijing, feared Zheng more than they feared another Mongol invasion. Zheng was expanding the empire and growing in stature faster than they could find ways to curb his influence. China's Golden Age came about through increased trade and tributes from the territories conquered by Zheng He. Court nobles and their courtiers convinced the emperors Zhu Gaochi and his successor, Zhu Zhanji, to withdraw support for the sea voyages. Zheng He fell into disfavor, and his astounding achievements were relegated to the recesses of memory."

"Tell me more about the way points on the Silk Road and Kublai's friend, Marco Polo," Earl said, changing the subject. The conversation veered off in another direction, leading to more questions and answers between the two.

Wing said he had been born in the spring of 1764, which made him ninety-six. He said he had lived a simple life and was content to have spent all of his years caring for the archive.

Adam used the three days to pack, crate, and haul the archive to the Hongmen-owned wharf. The *Bride* stayed where she was after unloading the California gold. She would stay there until Earl and his party returned.

The French and British customs officials were amused to see the Americans hauling away dusty, valueless papers and let them pass through the legations unopposed. After all, the British and French wagons returning to their legations were laden with gold, silver, silks, porcelain, furniture, and paintings. The customs officers reserved their smug indulgences for their own looters, people foolish enough to think the heavy bronzes worthy of hauling off.

The officials chose not to poke through the crates again after the first day's close inspections and waved them through. The last load would go out in the morning.

Late at night on the third day, after everyone had gone to sleep, Wing gave his final instructions to Earl. "Wo de, Erzi."

Earl leaned in close to hear the dying man's whispers in the low candle-light. Pointing to the mantle above the hearth, Wing told Earl to remove a stone mortared among the rest. Earl touched the one Wing pointed at and received a nod. He freed the stone and placed it on the mantle. He reached inside the exposed cavity and removed two lambskin sleeves. Putting the stone back, he returned to the bed with the skins.

Wing touched one. "Open this first because what is inside will require explaining. Save the second for later."

Earl removed a rolled map drawn on fine kid. He draped the supple hide over a serving tray and propped it on a chair beside the bed where they could see it. The map depicted the Onon River drainage in Northeast Mongolia.

Earl knew enough of the history of Mongolia to recognize the area from which Wing Wong Lum's ancestors came south in the thirteenth century. The simple map had Chinese writing he could not read. Wing waited while Earl started a new page in his notebook and labored through the task of transcribing Wing's Mandarin translations of Uyghur script into shorthand.

The next hour was exhausting for both men—Earl because he was concentrating so hard on trying to imagine a location he had never seen and Wing because he wanted Earl to identify and record the correct translation behind every word. Earl gained a greater appreciation of Wing's reasons for being so patient in his portrayal of Mongolia's Khentil Province and the Onon River flowing out of the nearly barren Khentil Mountains. The map had long since lost its simplicity.

Wing traced his finger over Ikh Khorig, the Great Taboo wilderness. "You must remember this place. The map does not name it—or this one," he added, moving his finger again while Earl scribbled notes. His finger came to rest on an inset expanding a section of the map. Wing pointed at what appeared to be an inconsequential dot. The location had no reference features or identifying symbols. "This dot is on the fabled Bukhan Khaldun, the most sacred mountain in the Khentils. The inset is incorrect. The east and west flanks of the mountain's southern shoulder are drawn in reverse. The map is useless without this piece of information; you would not be able to identify Bukhan Khaldun without it. Correct interpretation of the map depends on an additional verbal clue. The dot is beneath an escarpment on the mountain's southeast face. The location is visible at dawn on a cloudless day during the summer solstice. The top of the escarpment, then and only then, has the shape of a Mongol helmet. The tomb is located on the plain at the base of the helmet's talus slope."

"Tomb?"

"The Great Khan's." Wing lifted a hand before Earl could respond. "Shh, listen, Erzi. I haven't got much time."

Earl sighed and told himself to pay attention. *And yes, there is room left in my brain for more information. And no, I won't go insane trying to keep track of it along with everything else I've jammed in there.* Forcing himself to calm down, he did as asked.

"The finest treasures from dozens of empires are stored in the Khan's tomb. They are in a network of underground chambers replicating the geographical locations of the conquered lands.

"The tales you have heard are true. Tolui removed all of the people from many valleys and plains before breaking ground on the tomb. The men who built, defended, supplied, and removed any trace of the tomb were slain many li away from the site by his personal guards. These guards he slew close to home. Tolui, being the only one left to know where the tomb was located, gave this map to his youngest guijian, my ancestor. Tolui correctly assumed no one would expect a lowly guijian to bear such knowledge. They spent many long days together arranging for the preservation of the Great Khan's legacy."

"Well, well, well," Earl whispered, "you're telling me where Genghis Khan is buried?"

"Shi, wo de, Erzi. The Great Khan's tomb is on the site's north end. His final resting place is in a chamber shaped and equipped like any common yurt. He is lying on a rush bed dressed in riding leathers. He holds a quirt in one hand and a sword in the other."

"Yeye, why are you telling me this?"

"Erzi, you are the only man I have ever met who will treasure the map more for what it represents than the wealth it contains. You have been with me long enough for me to notice how you revere everything as a Zen Buddhist would. You see life in all that exists—creatures, trees, air, water, soil, and the heavens. I think you were a Mongol in a past life, surely Chinese. You will keep the map secret. My family is not safe with it. I have no one else left to trust. So, by giving it to you, it will remain hidden for as long as there are people in your family like you. I'll go to my grave believing there are as many generations of trustworthy people ahead of you as there are behind me."

Wing lifted a finger. "The other skin contains lists of the treasures buried with the Great Khan. You can read them later. The original lists, compiled by Tolui and written in Uyghur script, are here too. Twenty generations ago, Great-Grandfather Chen Wong Lum translated the list into Mandarin. The two lists have been in the same skin since the fourteen hundreds. I am too tired to go over them with you now.

"Kublai had the archive moved to this place after he united all of China in 1271. He had the foresight to provide enough money to maintain the place.

There are two strongboxes stacked in a crypt beneath the hearthstones. One of those boxes has financed the archive for hundreds of years. The bottom one has an unbroken wax seal embossed with Kublai's chop. Take as much as you want, and put the rest where it can help our grandchildren's grandchildren. You can have the dao jian swords that are in the crypt with the boxes. The inscriptions on the sides will tell you who owned them.

"There is another strongbox beneath the door leading into the archive. There are enough gold coins and gems in there to cover my grandchildren's living expenses for the rest of their lives.

"Give Qui Li the map over his bed. A Zen Buddhist monk, Qingjun, drew it in the fourteenth century on fine silk. It shows the ancient Chinese capitals. There are two more China maps in kid sleeves on the shelf above it. These were drawn by Li Zemin in the same period."

Wing pointed to all the paintings and drawings and again waited while Earl recorded their provenance. Several predated the Yuan Dynasty. Court artists and talented commoners had produced these masterpieces in the Song Dynasty's Hanlin Painting Academy long before Western artists learned to employ the same techniques. Wing nodded toward another painting that he wanted Earl to have, a Guo Xi watercolor mounted beside the chimney. Earl followed the old man's gaze. Then he banked the fire and put out all of the candles except the one by Wing's bed. The time had come to stop.

Wing took one of Earl's hands and nodded weakly toward a watercolor on the wall facing them. "I want you to have my favorite," he whispered. "I saw you viewing this one whenever you wanted to think. I like the trees, the water, the dwelling, and rolling hills beneath tranquil clouds. This was painted in 1163 by Gao Ke-Ming before Song Dynasty realism evolved into a more impressionistic style. Take caa . . . ha."

Earl heard Wing's voice trailing off as he contemplated the pastoral scene. "Xiexie, Yeye. The painting reminds me of a place where I find peace and contentment." Lowering his gaze, Earl shared a final squeeze with his friend just before the old man's hand went limp and his aged eyes closed for the last time.

CHAPTER 20

Kowloon Harbor, China, 12 May, 5:00 a.m.

"Can't imagine the Brits would send a customs cutter out in these conditions," Adam griped from his post by the quarterdeck rail. "Besides, we've got more important things to think about than a cutter pulling alongside," he added as a tremor jarred his footing. "If we don't get that anchor off the bottom soon, she'll rip the chain right through the hawsehole." Shuffling his feet to regain his balance, he shook his head at what little there was to see beyond their anchorage. He glared at the men working on deck and wished that through the sheer force of his will he could get them to move faster. The only reason Adam heard the solid thunk of the entry port slamming shut was because he saw it done. The hiss of spray, rain spatter, squealing blocks, hammering, and other manmade noises were no match for the monsoon sweeping down from the mainland. "Rain's coming in so hard it stings." The urgent need to get the anchor off the bottom aggravated the sense of dread Adam felt about how the job might go. He felt another shudder. "Better to get on with it than stand around waiting to find out if we can free the hook!" he grumbled.

Squinting past the slit in his lashes, he caught a glimpse of Colton standing in the downpour. The boy leaned over the side holding the loose end of a tag line attached to a doubled-up cargo block. Crewmen strung along his side of the deck held the heavy end of a second line running through a series of blocks attached to the mast and yard. Both lines had disappeared into the bobbing hold of a coastal lorcha storm-lashed to the *Bride*. Adam pulled his collar tighter, cast a wary eye into the bleak dawn, and heard a voice rise above the winds and rain.

"Lower, lower . . . easy . . . stop!" Ryan called to the men lowering the last load. Earl and James were with him and didn't like what was happening below any more than Ryan did. The lorcha came close to being upended every time she came down off a roller running along the *Bride*'s hull.

Ol' Bud threw his mallet in a locker and stared over the side at the junk-rigged yawl. "Not much different than the others plying the waterways between the mainland and Hong Kong Island," he said to the boy. "That forty-foot craft is puny from this vantage point, a whale calf seeking her mother's protection in a perfect storm. Hey, what's Ming doing down there?"

Ming had swung into view and lurched into the man beside him. He and the lorcha's captain were bouncing back and forth between the bright-yellow deckhouse and an open hold. The men in the hold were too busy to notice. They were working as fast as possible to release the cargo net, drape sailcloth over the cargo, and strap the works to ring bolts fastened to the pitching deck.

The captain nodded with concern before breaking eye contact with Ming. He cast a nervous glance at Bud and the men strung along the *Bride*'s rail before motioning to the men in the hold and pointing up.

Adam couldn't see the lorcha, but he did see Ryan raise his arm and waggle a finger. Up came the cargo net. Bud gave Colton a hand guiding the net inboard while others swung the yard. Men on the yard lowered the swaying cargo runners to the hands waiting on deck.

The swell gave the two vessels a solid bump. "Shijian qu" ("Time to go"), Ming and the captain said at the same time. The lorcha's master reached inside the deckhouse and handed Ming a rolled bundle. The two bowed to each other and exchanged an arcane gesture. Draping the bundle over a shoulder, Ming stepped across the treacherous gap and climbed the ship's ladder. The lorcha's master raised his voice and gave the order to cast off.

Adam watched his uncle and James cross the shuddering deck, mount the aft stairs, and take their places beside him, while down below, Ryan huddled with his bosuns. He saw Ming climb over the rail, nod to Ol' Bud, and enter the salon with his bundle. Shrugging a little deeper into his coat, Adam resumed his watch and nearly fell with the next violent jerk on the chain. *Get a move on,* he willed Bob and his crew. There wasn't much they could do until the lorcha drifted free of the fenders and ladder.

As soon as she was clear of the ship, the lorcha's master ordered the sails set and, with a wave, leaned on the tiller. He brought her about and passed astern of the *Bride's* counter. The bright-yellow eyes carved into the bows faced northeast. The lorcha, rigged for speed in open water, was soon out of sight. Her flat-bottomed hull was on her way to a clandestine cruise past tidal sandbars and up shallow rivers. The Hongmen smuggler vessel had just placed the last burlap bags of cinchona bark into one of her three watertight holds. The crew had packed the large sacks around a crated field hospital, surgical ward, cases of chloroform, quinine, mineral spirits, thieves' oil, syringes, morphine ampoules, and bug dope. These items were stowed over the main cargo buried deep in the lower portion of each hold: chests of California gold. Two dozen one hundred-pound chests were on their way to Guangzhou Province where so many of the California coolies had come from. Ming had included additional sacks of gold to pay for shipping workers to the Sino-American properties in Hawaii. Buried with the gold were revolvers, rifle cases, and several thousand rounds of ammunition.

Earl shook his head once again at the notion of *coo* meaning *rent* and *lee* meaning *muscle*. The gold acquired through "rented muscle" could well mean the difference between survival and famine for its recipients. *And to think,* he mused with a frown, *the only people trustworthy enough to get the cargo to its destination are outlawed! Not only outlawed; all who aid the smugglers are executed on sight, no questions asked.*

Adam nodded at his uncle and turned to James in time to hear the dreaded order.

"Free the hook!" James called and peered at Adam over rain-dappled lenses. The crew pushing on the spokes started singing a shanty, and the men climbing ratlines picked up the tune as the anchor chain moved inboard once more.

Now we are ready to head for the Horn,
Weigh, ay, roll and go!
Our boots and our clothes, boys, are all in the pawn,
Timme rollickin' Randy Dandy O!

The men spreading along the tops'l yards paused to watch the chain's slow progress through the starboard hawsehole. A few made observations on how the bows seemed to sink deeper into the sea with each turn of the screw.

Roust her up, bullies; the wind's drawin' free,
Weigh, ay, roll and go!
Let's get the glad rags on and drive her to sea,
Timme rollickin' Randy Dandy O!

James took in the run of the rollers, the portside drift of the snapping pennant, and the men singing their way through a perilous maneuver, a maneuver they were required to do while the ship was out of control.

Take your hands from your pockets and don't suck your thumbs,
Weigh, ay, roll and go!
There's work to be done, ye God-fearing bums,
Timme rollickin' Randy Dandy O!

"Anchor's hove up short! Hatches and lockers all battened down!" Ryan hailed to the officers standing on the quarterdeck. The ship was jerking at her chain the way a willful mare tested her bit before the restraining reins allowed her to have her head.

Heave a pawl, oh heave away,
Weigh, ay, roll and go!
The anchor's hove short and there's no time to delay,
Timme rollickin' Randy Dandy O!

"Set the heads'ls!" James called over the roar in his ears.
"On the foc's'l, ease your inner jib, downhaul, haul away the halyard!" Ryan called.
As the men performed each task, others did the same with the outer and flying jibs. The sails flapped and snapped in spite of the tension placed on them by the tightly pulled sheets.
The bosun's cry from forward blew back with the rising headwind. "Break out the anchor! Heave, my beauties, heave!"

Oh, man the stout caps'n and heave with a will,

Weigh, ay, roll and go,
Soon we will be driving 'er through the swill!
Timme rollickin' Randy Dandy O!

"Let go the tops'ls!" James spun an index finger skyward and got what he wanted. "Set your spanker!

The men standing by untied the gaskets furling the sail against the mizzen-snauwmast and the spanker snapped open like a curtain spreading aft over the wheelhouse.

James glanced over his shoulder and saw crewmen watching Charlie hastily showing Kato how to tie off the boom vang. Not liking what he saw, his querulous voice rose over the clamor. "Set the sheet tighter, dammit! She's looser'n an old doxy's trap!" Kato's confused expression turned to laughter at the sight of Charlie's pelvis thrusting into a pair of flapping hands. Laughing mizzen mates reset the sheet after James spun around and called out to Ryan. "Set your lower tops'ls!" James's returning stare reduced the laughter to a few snickers and sent the slackers hurrying for the aft stairs.

The huge sails spread out, and became square white walls plastered against the masts.

"Set your fore and main upper tops'ls!"

The men hauling on the lines pulled the yards as high as the stretching canvas would permit them to go.

"Heave, lads!" Ryan urged the men struggling to maintain their footing while singing above the winds and commands. Pulling the corners tight eased off the wild flapping, but it also added a firmer surface for the winds to attack. "Tops'l sails are set!" could barely be heard over the increasing wail of the wind.

James, nodded. "Fore, man the starboard braces. Main and mizzen, man the port braces. Heave. Brace up main and fore!"

The men at the foremast braces turned the yards to starboard into the wind.

The gale drove the sails against the mast, placing enormous pressure on the foremast, stays, chain hardware, and anchor still hooked to the seabed. The ship tugged at the chain as if she were trying to flee. The relentless winds slamming against the exposed fore sails shifted to port as if trying to tear the bow away from her stout tether.

The main and mizzenmast yards were braced hard 'round to port, letting the wind slip past the loudly flapping canvas. The strain on the masts rotated the keel to starboard. The tipping stalled as the anchor crew countered by turning the capstan in earnest, causing the *Bride* to groan under the strain.

Shove like you mean it; let's get this job done,
Weigh, ay, roll and go,
Time to get this over and go 'ave fun!
Timme rollickin' Randy Dandy O!

The tremendous tension on the chain broke off. "Anchors aweigh!" Charlie yelled from the starboard rail.

Free of the anchor's grip and out of control, the ship drifted backwards. Wind shear caught the heads'ls. The flapping of the inner and outer jibs ceased as they snapped into place with loud cracks. James saw Elmer turning the helm to starboard to increase the drag on the retreating ship's pivot point, the rudder. The bows swung to port, and 200 yards of being out of control later, the ship's backward drift slowed to a halt and she came about. Adam's face summed up everyone's feelings: relief.

"Act lively!" Ryan called to the men straining against the braces as the fore yards tried and failed to follow the course of the wind.

The men at the fore braces hauled the fore yards from starboard to port. The protesting yards came into alignment with the main and mizzen yards. "Sheet the sails home!"

The disconcerting tilt yielded to acceleration as the *Bride* righted herself. The ship was free to run with the wind. James's crew had tamed the wind but not the submerged anchor.

At last we are outward bound for 'Frisco Bay,
Weigh, ay, roll and go,
Get crackin', lads, 'tis a hell o' a way!
Timme rollickin' Randy Dandy O!

The superstitious crew allowed their sense of relief to pass without comment. The last thing anyone wanted was to put a hex on raising an anchor in the future. A fouled anchor in a rising sea with the sails set could have tragic consequences.

The crew got going on another shanty as the capstan continued to go 'round and 'round.

When I was a little lad
My mother told me,
Way, haul away, we'll haul away, Joe,
That if I did not kiss a gal
My lips would grow all moldy,
Way, haul away, we'll haul away, Joe.
Way, haul away, we'll haul for better weather,
Way, haul away, we'll haul away, Joe.

Clank, clank, clank went the capstan's pawls. Up and up came the chain until the anchor rose out of the sea.

"A few more turns, boys!" Henry Oakes, the bosun, said.

The crew stopped turning the capstan as the swinging anchor rose to the cat, a large beam protruding away from the bows above the chain hawsehole whose purpose was to bear the weight of the anchor.

Henry turned in time to see Hopley run down the stairs after setting the chain brake. "Let's be ready to take up the tension soon's the whirling dervish begins banging on the windlass."

A moment later, Hopley was banging away and hollering through two decks, "All set!" No one could hear him, but they did hear the banging, so they took up the tension. Hopley was ready. He lifted the devil's claw chain stopper, jammed the claw between two links, and banged the windlass several times. The chain became doubly secure after the crew backed the tension onto the claw and reset the brake. "Now to the pin," the boy said and disconnected the capstan shaft from the windlass. He arrived back on deck in time to help perform the dangerous task of fishing the anchor.

The crew had turned their attention to the Burton tackle while the boy was below. The men lifted the large multi-pulley, also called a ta'cle, from a ringbolt mounted on the bulkhead. The ta'cle increased the mechanical advantage they had over the two-ton anchor by a factor of ten. A cable was produced that had a closed loop on one end and a hook on the other. Hopley waited for a crewman to slip the loop over the ta'cle's hook. Then he lowered the cable's hooked end over the side. The excited boy threw a leg over the rail and squeezed the cable in his hands. "Time to go anchor fishing!"

A hairy hand the size of an arctic mitt covered his shoulder before he could flip his other leg over the rail. Mervin Albert's hard gray eyes locked onto those of the startled boy. "This is no time for hijinks, young man. Get serious or you don't go down. Ya 'ear?"

Sobering up quickly, the boy nodded. "Yes, sir." Free of the older man's grasp, he went over the side and slid to the swaying anchor. Bow spray and rolling wash greeted him. Bare feet straddling the anchor stocks, he fished the cable's hook through the anchor shackle under the watchful eyes of Merv and Henry. "Rotate!" Hopley called after making sure his toes and fingers were clear of the grinding joints. The crew rotated the Burton's towline and lifted the anchor closer to the cat.

"Next step, Hopley," Merv said from several feet and a lifetime away. Hopley grabbed a hooked chain fastened to the cat, looped it through the anchor shackle and up through a hole in the middle of the huge beam. Merv slipped the hook over a dog mounted on the cat's top. Henry fitted a chock to the dog, securing the hook in place.

"Good job. Now the hard part," Merv reminded the boy over the splash of surf and howling winds. The crew lowered the cable until it transferred the anchor's weight to the cat.

Hopley removed the cable's hook from the shackle and transferred it to the balance band in the middle of the anchor shaft. "Got it," he said to his watchers. He let the cable slip through his fingers while the men on deck raised the anchor. The upper anchor fluke stopped near a chain bolted to the hull. Looping the chain around a fluke, he locked the chain's hook in a link. They lowered the cable until the fluke took the weight. This fastened the anchor to the ship in two places. Hopley disconnected the cable's hook from the balance band and stepped on the hook for the ride back to the rail. "All set!" he yelled and rose with the cable. His head was even with the rails when Merv reached over the side, grabbed the boy under both arms, and hauled him aboard just as a massive roller slammed the hull.

"Enough," he said gruffly to his young friend. "Good job." The men stowing the gear said nothing to the boy about the danger he'd been in. Knowing why they didn't say anything, Hopley kept to himself the thought his famous ancestor had once shared from the warm confines of his parlor in Eastport, Maine: "The only captain worth his salt is the one who has done every task he's willing to ask his men to perform."

Hopley leaned over the rail and smiled, not caring if anyone was listening. "Great-grandpa died on this date in 1812. I wonder if he placed an angelic hand on my backside as I went about my business." He laughed when the bow cleaved an especially large roller and sent spray flying up to drench his face. "Huh," he said to his grandpa's spirit, "a wave that size could've blown me off the anchor while I was down theya!"

Above the boy, the great sails thundered and banged to the hum of shrouds and stays as the men at the helm brought them under control.

The crew sang their way through the more explicitly ribald "Haul Away, Joe" verses and reached a last salute to their leader.

Oh, the cooks are in the galley
Making duff so handy
Way, haul away, we'll haul away, Joe,
The captain's in his cabin
Drinking Napoleon's brandy . . .!

A grinning Bill Hobbs scanned one vibrating cord after another while tying off a coiled line. He dropped the loop over a pin. *I wonder if this feeling of being inside the sound is anything like what a conductor feels. The ship's chorale is composed of caterwauling Maine-iacs. The wind, string, and percussion sections have lost their sheets!* He cackled over his feeble pun. "A body would have to be slightly mad to set sail in a monsoon!" He patted the top of his head. "I'm a sight. My hair is smeared to my skull. My clothes are soaking wet. I'm chilled to the bone. Cold rain is coursing down my body and running off my feet. I feel more like a water rat than a conductor!" He turned to give Bud a hand on a downhaul. "I love the wild winds!" he shouted over the racket.

"Yeah? . . ." Bud rasped as they wrapped the line around a pin and tied off the hitch, "the master says the barometer is about to take a deep six." Bill stared into a pair of hard blue-gray marbles sunk into a ridge of grizzled brows flecked with sea foam. *Poseidon*, he thought, only half listening to Bud.

All along the length of the vessel, Bill's mates completed the sail trim and guided the ship past her sisters and shoals.

Kowloon became an ill-defined smear on the starboard side. Hong Kong harbor and Victoria Peak were dark shadows off the portside rails. The lorcha had become a fading memory. Dawn would last for hours yet.

"We'll keep her on the port tack until we can clear Hong Kong Island," James said. "Should be around four bells of the forenoon watch, Capt'n." He nodded approvingly at the set of the sails, the snapping pennant, the determined helmsmen, the weary off-duty crewmen filing into the salon, and the men at their watch stations scanning the low ceiling.

"Once we clear the shipping, we may set more sail and run south-by-south. Depends on the weather," James added with caution.

Earl raised an appreciative eyebrow and motioned for Adam to lead the way to the lee stairs. Pausing at the top for a survey of his command, he heard laughter coming through an open window and saw James smiling and nodding to Elmer as he scratched out the departure entry in the log. He lifted his head and caught a glimpse of Charlie running in the shelter of the deckhouse after ringing five bells of the morning watch from the foc's'l.

"Be a while before anyone goes forward to do that again. The barometer's falling," he said as he followed Adam down the rain-swept stairs.

Six hours later, Munenori rang out three bells of the afternoon watch from the safety of an open wheelhouse window. The fickle nor'east gale gave way to a stronger easterly after the *Bride* rounded Hong Kong Island and aimed her bow south. Bracing the yards around in the tossing cross chop made for a bumpy ride into the open waters of the South China Sea.

Elmer was at the helm. Adam glanced back and forth from the compass to the chart. Maynard handed Munenori a pair of binoculars and pointed forward. "My eyes need a break."

The rain had let up enough to see four or five cables ahead. The ship would not have much sea room if she had to avoid an obstacle less than a thousand yards away. The biggest obstacle they were trying to avoid now was Hainan Island off the starboard side. Hours later, they would be looking off the port bow for the first reefs, shoals, and sandbars marking their passage past the always-treacherous Paracels.

Earl tapped the barometer. "She's been pretty steady at 28.3 for the past hour."

James nodded. "She'll rise a bit by the time we make our approach to the Paracels. Should pick up favorable winds and have reasonably clear sailing from there to Singapore. I expect the wind to veer southeast by the first dog-watch and the air to clear. You'll be faced with a decision then, Capt'n: to reef or not to reef."

Hour after hour they beat south through seas whipped into towering crests by the last of the spring monsoons. The sky to the north stayed dark and gloomy long after Hong Kong Island dropped beneath the horizon. As usual, James's weather sense was true, and they made the outer Paracels by the end of the second dogwatch. The ragged sky gave way to clear sailing and the sea settled into a more predictable roll. The fifty-knot south easterlies brought open ocean, clear skies, rising temperatures, and the humid smell of vegetation. The barometer rose to 29.6 and held an upper trajectory. James and Earl agreed to have the tops'l yards braced to starboard, set all the stays'ls, and let her run under the full moon.

The strong south easterlies carried them south at a comfortable fifteen-knot clip for the next several days. The crew was able to get into a steady shipboard routine at last and catch up on much-needed rest and reflection. Earl spent evenings in his cabin with James, Ryan, Adam, Willard, his cooks, and a few of the other men. Earl questioned them on what they had heard in the bars and brothels of the two Chinese ports.

Three nights out of Hong Kong, Earl and James were alone in the cap-tain's suite. James had been telling Earl of his experiences in Shanghai while Earl was in the archive with Wing. Earl lit the lamps, sat in a leather chair, adjusted his butt, and crossed his ankles on the hassock. The table was within reach. Small sandbags lay scattered among bowls of crackers, cheeses, nuts, dried fruits, and olives.

James sat in the matching chair. He held a brandy snifter in one hand and traced the table's fiddle with the other. "There are lots of men out there who are taking odds and laying coin on every conceivable aspect of the crisis in Washington. They're wagering on when the conflict will begin, who will be the next president, who will lead the South, which states will secede from the Union, and in what order. You name it, there will be odds on it.

"Jake Delano is the Falcon's captain now. He was in San Francisco the day the Pony Express completed its first cross-country trip. The rider left St. Joseph, Missouri, on April third and arrived in Sacramento, California, ten days later on the thirteenth. The St. Joe's Gazette was included in the pouch slung over the saddle. The paper included several articles on who the abolitionist Republicans were likely to choose as their presidential candidate."

James took a drink and then continued. "The Republicans are having their nomination convention on the eighteenth, by the way. The favorite is the senator from New York, William Seward. His closest challenger is the freshman senator from Illinois, Abe Lincoln. I think Abe's a little wet behind the ears. A bit too soon for him to be running for the presidency, if you ask me. He's on the fence about slavery. Typical politician—he's likely to go whichever way the wind blows. He's prepared himself for the job by memorizing all of Shakespeare's plays and sonnets. He should be able to belt out the next day's headlines and catchphrases with the best of them." James shook his head. "He and his friends are in luck. The way things stand right now, the Republicans could run a donkey against the feckless Democrats and still win by a landslide. The Democrats will trot out a platform intended to please everyone but will end up pleasing no one. Most of them will want the slave laws to stay in place. The people they want to vote for them don't agree, of course. By the time the votes are counted, the Dems will have once again snatched defeat from the jaws of victory." James emptied his glass and slipped its base under one of the bags. Not liking one bag on the base, he arranged a second on the other side.

"Ayah," Earl said and got up. Setting his empty glass under one of the larger sacks, he crossed over to the liquor cabinet and selected a bottle. Removing the cork, he waited until James could hold the snifters in place, poured for both of them, and returned the bottle to the rack. Turning away, he noted how Napoleon's brandy rocked back and forth in time with the ship's motion. "Regular."

He got a mock bow from James when he picked up his glass. "Merci beaucoup, monsieur, et je vous mercie mes ancetres Mercier servi avec Napoléon!" ("Thank you, sir, and my Mercier ancestors who served with Napoleon thank you!")

"Ce n'est rien," ("It's nothing."), Earl snorted. He sat and crossed his legs while cradling the Little General's brandy in a palm. James was familiar with the reason behind Earl's snort. They shared a mutual disgust over the absurd necessity of James's immigrant grandfather having to Anglicize his French-Canadian surname in order to get a job in Waterville. Earl doubted if any of the state's Anglo-Saxon chauvinists knew that France had a province called Maine or that *ville* meant *city* in French. "Salud."

James raised his glass and took a sip. "I bumped into Jake Delano as he was coming out of the Barkley Hotel's dining room. He was with a couple of Harrington traders and Sir Hercules Robinson. Hercules quickly excused himself after the introductions. He gave me the impression that, as governor of Hong Kong, he would have preferred not to have been seen in their company."

"I know Sir Robinson." Earl frowned. "He's one of those political appointees who would eat his own children if he thought it would boost his stature among Queen Victoria's pestiferous lackeys. Whatever he's cooking up with the Harringtons does not bode well for the Chinese or the rest of us. Robinson's stay in Shanghai was brief. Remember, his new appointment will be subject to how little interference he offers to the military and commercial interests flooding China with opium. So, the less he has to do with everyday operations, the longer he will remain at his post. His job is to pass on instructions, get answers, and write reports to Lord Palmerston, period.

"The prime minister's cronies have created a supply line that starts in north central India's poppy fields. Did you know that under the queen's warrant, the factories in Uttar Province produce over six hundred tons of opium per year? They ship the product out of Kolkata and force it on the Chinese at gunpoint. They make the term 'merchants of death' seem trivial. The wealth is contingent upon addicting as many of China's inhabitants as possible.

"They use the silver they take in trade to purchase a number of Chinese goods with little or no capital outlay. The goods, including the most profitable item of all, tea, they ship to London. Then they convert the lucre into titles, seats in Parliament, palatial country estates, and townhouses on Hyde Park furnished with plunder gleaned from Indian and Chinese palaces."

Earl uncrossed his legs. "Any agreements Robinson makes with Harrington's people may as well be written in sand. His role is a ceremonial one at best." He raised his glass for another appreciative sip. "We still have to keep an eye on him though."

James decided to change the subject rather than respond to the not-so-hidden message in Earl's stare. *What has he got in mind?* "Jake and I have known each other for years, so we stayed and had a drink in the bar. He intimated that the disappearance of the men sent ashore to kill you did not bother him at all. Actually, I think he found the trip out here rather distasteful. Jake doesn't like working for people who are constantly pulling the kind of stunts the Harringtons are becoming known for. Jake said the mercenaries sent to kill you must have met people a little more dangerous. He was not prepared to send any of his crew out to find them—not that anyone did. Find them, that is," he said with a squint.

He let his last words float in the air between them. "By the way, I asked him if any assassins were aboard the Empire in Hawaii. Jake said she had sailed before Harrington came up with the idea. I found out later that in addition to bringing men over to harm you, Harrington lawyers were aboard. They were there to lay the groundwork for Asian trade relations with the British Crown once California and the South secede from the Union. They also met with the French who, for once, are in agreement with the British. The lawyers were a little unnerved by what happened after they came ashore. The sight of firefighters pulling their clerks out of what was left of Harrington's Shanghai offices made them ill. Jake said the fire was so hot the building collapsed into the cellar. Nothing left. A few of the lawyers quit on the spot and booked passage aboard the Falcon. Jake said he put boats in the water and had armed guards circling the ship for fear he might get the torch too!"

Earl's relaxed expression didn't change much beyond a slight downturn of his lips.

"Jake confirmed what you said, Earl. There are elements within our own legations and military that are choosing sides and forming back-door alliances in case things go badly for our country."

"The Union has lots of friends," Earl replied, thinking of his Hongmen allies. "I wouldn't want to run afoul of the patriots among them. Those who choose to conspire against us do so at their peril."

James twirled his glass and held it up to the light. "We have friends who could be as ruthless as we're prepared to be."

"Yes. I think it's the reason why so many of them are still aligned with us," Earl answered with a trace of gallows humor.

James cocked his head and let his gaze linger on an Owls Head oil screwed to the wall above the liquor cabinet. The Boudin seascape mounted beside it reminded him of Penobscot Bay, a place he longed to see again. *The sooner the better*, he thought, feeling quite anxious about what he planned to say the next time he shared a cup of tea with a certain lady who lived there. He lowered his gaze.

"The Falcon must be a week or so out of San Francisco by now. Jake was real good about taking the Lum woman aboard. He gave her a cabin and private dining privileges. He'll deliver her to the Stanfords soon's the Falcon's tied up on the Harrington wharf. Didn't seem concerned about the reaction he's likely to get for doing you a favor. Your draft more than covered the shipping expenses associated with her delivery. Jake appreciated the second one made out to him. I told him Sui Mai had been ill and declared fit to travel. The passage this time of year should be a relatively easy one for her. I made sure the letters you prepared for Ah Toy and Jane Stanford's bankers were in a sealed package. Sui Mai has the package. Captain Delano has a separate envelope telling him where to take her after they tie up in San Francisco. He'll meet with Ward and open the letter addressed to the both of them. He'll sign on. Two down. One captain to go."

"Thank you, James. Jake is the maverick in the family and the only one I can trust. His cooks say he is an excellent captain. As for Sui Mai, well, she's in for a bit of a shock when she reaches California. I'm sure a hefty bank balance will help smooth out the path ahead. She's fortunate. She'll find solutions to challenges that are impossible to overcome by most of her countrymen residing in America."

James lowered his voice over the hand swirling his drink. "Jake Delano is a cousin of Warren Delano. Do you know much about Warren?"

"Yeah, I know enough to want to burn his factory in Hong Kong." Earl clucked and glared through narrowed eyes. "Preferably with him in it. He's another American conniver. He came back to Hong Kong several years ago after losing everything in the Crash of '57. As chief of China operations, he's picked up where Robert Forbes left off. He's turned Sam Russell's Boston tea-trading firm into a lucrative exporter of opium. He's also made himself a wealthy man again in the process."

They both knew Robert Bennet Forbes, another ingenious Bostonian. A few years earlier, Forbes had convinced them to separate the topsail into upper and lower sails. The Forbes rig worked to perfection.

"Warren Delano comes from a prominent New York shipping family whose financial web spreads into the quarters occupied by the Harringtons. I went to school with a few of his Massachusetts relatives. The Delanos are friends of the Back Bay Roosevelts," Earl said with displeasure.

"The connivers are piling up, Earl," James observed with a yawn. "Be nice if things in life were a little simpler."

Earl yawned too. "Well, things aren't simple and Warren's not a character the Harringtons would want to annoy over Cousin Jake's indiscretion. Besides, Arthur will have forgotten all about it by the time he and Warren meet again at the Union Club."

Feeling peevish, Earl picked a piece of crumbling cheese off the napkin in his lap and put it back on a dry cracker. "I've had it with blue cheese. Could use a dry red and a fresh Brie or Camembert right about now."

James popped a Spanish olive into his mouth. "Hmm, you've ruined your palate for anything else," he said between bites. "And besides, it's too late to switch to wine. Unless, of course, you want to augment your sour expression with a dash of red vinegar." He finished chewing a piece of pepper and washed it down with a sip of Brugerolle. "Warren met with Harrington's lawyers in the offices over his opium factory in Hong Kong. I'm sure Sidney Harrington provided the lawyers with all of the necessary papers and a step-by-step guide on how to assist Warren in satisfying government procurement requirements. The completed documents are returning to San Francisco aboard the Falcon."

"Right." Earl tilted his head back and wrinkled his nose. James had opened a tin of caviar, and using a finger, smeared a dollop of the delicacy over a cracker covered with Roquefort. "Rather gouache, James. Your manners will not be well received in certain quarters." He sniffed and waved the image away. They both knew to whom Earl was referring. He pointed at the Boudin. "We have a similar one in the hold. Would you like to hang it in your cabin?" He got the wince he anticipated and didn't wait for an answer before picking up where they left off.

"Arthur will review the documents, and then the Falcon's new captain will be bound for Washington with the lawyers who'll deliver them to Sidney in the War Office. Secretary Stanton said Warren is likely to be the sole supplier of morphine to the Union forces once hostilities begin next year. Who knows what promises Warren had to make in return for getting such a windfall."

"That's easy," James, said, waving the concoction in the air between them. "Caviar. The tie that binds." He swallowed the morsel. "Warren buys Sidney's loyalty by shaving a few points off what he charges for the morphine shipments he puts aboard the Harrington clippers bound for Savannah. Harrington adds the vig to his profit margin before he presents the invoice. I doubt if their agreement is duplicitous enough to include billing the Union for the morphine. They'll just have to make as many shipments as possible prior to the declaration of war, paid for in seditionist gold. They'll have the same arrangement on the Union contracts."

Earl's scowl deepened.

Another cracker was on the cutting board beside the cheeses.

"Would you like me to use a spoon this time and make it two?" James smeared caviar over two slices of Gorgonzola and passed one to Earl. "Samuel Colt and a host of northern industrialists are doing the same thing. They're increasing production in anticipation of the orders Sidney's War Office will be sending their way. They're champing at the bit to start producing every-thing necessary to equip and service a modern army."

Earl had a sip of brandy to grease the skids, plopped the cracker in his mouth, chewed, and washed it down while rolling his eyes. "You've redeemed yourself. You'll have your painting in the morning."

"Ah me, the ways of the world—everyone has an agenda." He tipped the glass towards James. "And they use many devices to keep them secret. There is one device I have never used on you, nor discovered you using on me: lying. I may not answer when you ask, but I will not try to deceive you . . . but you've known that for years," Earl said with a thin smile. "I couldn't lie to you if I wanted to. You'd see right through me. I know, I know, there's one thing I've kept from you, and you deserve to be told. Your patience has been remarkable."

James snapped his jaws shut on the treat.

They tapped their glasses and kept eye contact through both bulbs until each had polished off his drink. The story behind how Earl had acquired the scar below his shoulder was a barrier between them both knew would have to be breached in the not-too-distant future. So too was the unmentioned conclusion each had drawn regarding the narrow escapes they'd been experiencing.

Holding his captain's gaze, James experienced a flicker of dismay. He couldn't understand why they hadn't talked about it. "You should know by now that I too can keep secrets, and I'm not the Judas in the ship's company."

Earl nodded, worked his lips from side to side, gazed at the empty bowl and felt at a loss for words.

Weary of all the talk about subterfuges and hidden agendas, James let his eyes linger on Owls Head once again and felt depressed about how far removed they were from the shores of Penobscot Bay.

He thought of mothers, their sons and orphans. Sui Mai and her brother came to mind.

James roused himself and said, "Qui Li has adapted quite well to shipboard life. Couldn't speak a word of English the day we met him. Small wonder he spends most of his time in the galley. He seems to get on well with the ship's boys. They are using a form of pidgin English and a lot of sign language."

"Go on," Earl said, beginning to wonder if his sail master was warming to the idea of having children of his own.

"I like the boy," James added, still thinking of Penobscot Bay and Willard's mother. "Good thing for him the salon is one of Willard's favorite haunts. Willard tells me Qui is a quick learner and a wizard with figures. As far as I'm concerned, the boy can stay with us for as long as he wants."

James misread Earl's scrutiny, closed his eyes, and made room for two more voices inside his head. *All in good time. He'll tell you how he got the scar when he's ready. Not before. Be patient. He needs you now more than ever.*

Yes, the second voice said, *but I need to know what is driving this need of his to recover all he seems to think he has lost.*

Slightly tipsy and wanting James to stay a little longer, Earl splashed a tad of Napoleon's finest into their glasses. "Qui will have plenty of time to decide what he wants to do before we return to San Francisco. If he decides to stay there, I'm sure he'll find plenty of decent Chinese in the community willing to help him.

"I calculated the weight and value of the gold in the chest under the door-sill—came to over three lakhs. I made a proposal to Cam Lum, which he shared with his siblings. They agreed and thought their grandfather would approve. They gave the Hongmen a quarter of the gold to feed and house refugees. They gave another quarter to Dr. Lockhart. He will use the funds to build a new wing to house the field hospitals, surgical wards and medical supplies we gave him."

"The crew gets twenty-five percent of the take. You, Willard, Adam, and I split the rest. I wrote equal bank drafts for each of the Lums. I'll write more checks after we sell the gems in New York. Cam has a large account balance at the Shanghai branch of the Bank of London. Sui Mai and Qui Li will also be in the same position after Jane opens accounts for them at Wells Fargo. Thanks to their grandfather, the three will be set for life.

"I haven't taken the time to open the chests we removed from beneath Wing's hearthstones. I'm not going to open the one with the Khan's wax seal. We'll keep it until an independent Chinese government can open it. I wish you had been there to watch us get them out of the crypt! They probably weigh several hundred pounds each! We had to rig a block and tackle on the chimney and use a horse to lift them out of the hole. It's a wonder the chimney didn't collapse under the strain. Wing got his wish. We wrapped him in his old blanket and placed him in the grave we dug beneath the dragon. Here's to a really good man." Earl raised his glass in a tribute to Wing Lum.

He watched James return the salute and savor a final sip of the one-hundred-year-old brandy. He savored the sound of the water, the creak of rigging, the gentle roll of the deck, and the sense of companionship even more.

He and James put everything away, wished each other a goodnight, visited the heads, and retired to their bunks.

"Deck, there—sails on the weather quarter!"

James and two of the ship's boys lowered their pencils. Colton continued scribbling and piped up with the answer. "We are at latitude north ten degrees, five minutes!"

"Right you are, my boy," James said, checking his numbers again and turning his attention to Maynard, who was sliding down a mainmast backstay. James lifted his nose and sniffed while waiting for Maynard to catch his breath. The current of warm air coming off the coast was heavy with moisture. The humid air also carried with it the strong smell of wetland decay. "Could be in for a squall later. Maynard?"

"There's a squadron of corvettes moving up the coast toward Danang."

"To be expected in these waters. We're due east of Saigon." James pointed shoreward. "The French have been trying to colonize that stretch of jungle for two hundred years. They have little to show for it. There's a lesson for you on the folly of putting effort after foolishness. A year ago, Admiral de Genouilly destroyed the indefensible Citadel of Saigon. Think of the labor they expended a hundred and fifty years ago to build it in the first place. The rice stocks de Genouilly ordered set on fire burned for months after his retreat. Easy to see why the starving Vietnamese hate him so much. The French are going to have even less to show for their efforts now because they've withdrawn their forces to join the Brits in attacking the approaches to Beijing. They'll have to reclaim the abandoned areas. The local resistance is a balloon." James peered through his spectacles at each boy in turn, his fingers squeezing an imaginary balloon in his hands. "Where the French push in one direction the Vietnamese expand in another. The French and their Spanish allies don't have enough men or ships to suppress the area they wish to colonize. The Vietnamese will spread the French forces out thinner than a beggar's purse. Not our fight, thank God." He shook his head at Maynard. "Good work. Keep your eyes peeled. The French may not be the only ones operating in these waters." He turned and stared at his students. "Let's go over the numbers again. Colton, show us how you did it. Follow along, Charlie, because I'm going to ask you to repeat what Colton says when he's done."

Earl and Adam were in the salon having lunch with the off-watch crewmen. They were listening to Roy's description of what had occurred in a bar the last night they were in Shanghai. Roy was telling Bud's side of a confrontation they'd had with a group of American naval officers. Bud, having finished his lunch, pushed is plate aside, and got busy tamping tobacco into his pipe.

Roy frowned at the old-timer. "Bud here asked if any of the men were sailing with Commodore Josiah Tattnall the time he came to the aid of the

Plover during the disastrous British siege of Taku Forts on the Peiho River. One of the petty officers answered, 'Yeah, so what's it too ya?' Bud said he was wondering, is all. The sailor said he'd sail with Tattnall to the gates of hell, American neutrality be damned. The officer went on to say, 'I agree with the commodore, blood's thicker'en water! Them Brits're our kith, and we fired on the fort and offloaded the Plover's crew to save 'em. The commodore wasn't about to stand aside an' let 'em get pounded to matchsticks by Chink shore batteries, dammit.' 'Well now,' says Bud, 'How many of you all think there's a war between the states on the horizon?' He got the expected round of nods from the men. 'How thick's the blood between you Americans who grew up in the South compared to those in the North when it comes to taking up arms against each other? How'll you decide between fighting alongside the men you've served with in the navy and maybe taking up arms against them by joining the rebels? How thick'll your blood be then?'"

Roy watched Bud strike a match. "Those questions put the fox among the chickens. Everyone started talking at once. We got out of there before the riot started."

Ol' Bud appeared to be fussing with his pipe a little more than usual. He alternated tamping the lit tobacco and passing the match over the bowl. The flame went back and forth so many times the men had trouble seeing through the blue cloud he'd created.

Bud scratched his whiskers and spoke around the stem. "I suppose it was probably not a good idea to provoke 'em the way I did, but they sure got my goat with all the sanctimonious talk about white people havin' to stick together. It got confusing, and I lost track of which white people they were talkin' about after a while." He took another drawn-out puff, tossed the spent match onto a plate, and forced two streams of smoke through the thicket growing in his nose. The room went quiet for a spell. The air passing through the open portholes finally got the upper hand on Bud's cloud.

Most of the solemn eyes emerging from the thinning cloudbank were aimed at Earl. "I suppose from time to time a naval officer is permitted to show initiative and do what he thinks is right," he said, "as opposed to what he's been warned against. The men on the Plover were lost if Tattnall refused to come to their aid. He was on his way upriver to meet the delivery date on a treaty. I'm sure he steamed into an untenable situation. He probably substituted the expediency of satisfying the treaty terms with the necessity to save lives. What little I know of the encounter suggests that the Chinese didn't need to utterly destroy the Plover to prove their shore batteries controlled the river. The grounded ships and bodies floating in the current were proof enough of that."

Adam rose from his seat, cleared the plates, and dumped them in the tubs with the silverware. He grabbed a fresh pot of coffee and poured refills while listening to his uncle.

"I think it's unfortunate Tattnall chose to say what he did under the circumstances. I've no idea what he really meant. Seems to me it was a convenient thing to say in justifying why he saved lives. I'm quite sure he wouldn't have hesitated in taking those same lives if the British cannons had been firing at *him*!"

Earl watched Bud fuss with his pipe after he flamed out the tobacco. His eyes softened when he saw the older man knock the dottle out with a knuckle and put it on the side of his plate for disposal.

"Tattnall is from an old Savannah, Georgia, family. He has an ingrained code of conduct bordering on the chivalrous. Maybe that's what prompted him to act," Earl said, letting his voice trail off. The more fatigued men got up and headed for the galley passageway and a few hours' sleep before it was their turn to be back on watch. No one talked, out of respect for Earl and his listeners. "It may not be worth mentioning, but it will bring us back to what we are really talking about—loyalty. Tattnall's career survived defying the official American position on neutrality because he's a capable officer. Naval command ordered him to take over the Powhatan and transport the first Japanese consular delegation to San Francisco. He says that as long as the Union remains united, he will stay at his post. I believe him and respect him for it."

Most of the remaining men had drifted off into their own thoughts while Earl was speaking. They knew the number of unfavorable reports on what was happening back in the States seemed to be increasing. The men examined loyalties fraught with divisive potential as more and more news from home trickled into the ports they visited. The men who knew that today was graduation day at West Point Military Academy didn't mention it. Their captain was soured-up enough already and didn't need any reminders of what awaited him in Camden.

The day the Republicans chose their presidential candidate, the *Bride* faced a sight that chilled every sailor the bone. That the subtropical temperatures were in the mid-seventies made no difference. Maynard's call from the masthead an hour earlier had done little to prepare them for observing one of their greatest fears. Their approach to a clipper burning right down to the waterline miles from shore caused even the stoutest among the crew to cringe inside.

Adam's voice carried to the deck over the creak of rigging and splashing waves. "She's going down soon, and she doesn't appear to have any boats in the water." Nodding to Maynard and Mike, he reached for a backstay and dropped from sight.

Adam took a seat in the wheelhouse facing Earl, James, Ryan, and Elmer. "Gets worse. There's a fleet of junks strung across our path a mile north of here."

A chart of the Malacca Strait covered the table. A pair of brass dividers had been squeezed shut. The tips were pointing at Kuala Lumpur.

James cleared his throat. "I think we're in this vicinity." His stiff finger pointed at Rupat Island.

Earl glanced at the chart, the barometer, and the clock before recording the sightings in the log beside the date, 18 May. "How're the raiders rigged, Adam?" he asked, finding it difficult to push aside morbid thoughts of whether or not he would live to find out who the next president might be.

"Junk-rigged lorchas mostly, a few large sampans and coastal dhows," Adam answered, the image of the burning derelict weighing on his mind. The men in the cabin had not yet seen the vessels Adam was referring to, but they could clearly see the smoke blanketing the ocean off the starboard bow. They would be passing upwind of the wreck within the hour.

James turned the hourglass and eyed the barometer. No one paid any attention to the bell.

"I can see masts and spars off in the distance beyond the smoke now, sir," Elmer said.

The group dispersed to prepare the crew for battle and was back in the wheelhouse less than an hour later.

"We've taken all of the precautions we can, short of turning tail and running back the way we came," Earl said. He was leaning against the lee wall beside Elmer. "There isn't much more we can do under the circumstances. The cannons are loaded behind closed ports. The swivel guns have been mounted on deck, and arms have been placed along the bulkheads." He wondered when to give the next set of orders. They would have to brail up the courses and lower tops'ls to reduce the risk of fire if things got hot. Burning wads blown out of cannons with the charges had a tendency to swirl back and set ships on fire.

They sailed on in a fresh breeze under sunlit skies for the next thirty minutes. The tension among the men rose by degrees the closer they got to the smoldering hulk. The thunk of broken planks grazing the hull only made matters worse. The men strung along the rails saw no survivors clinging to burnt timbers, and no bodies floated among the darting fins. Rafts of barrels bobbed in the litter, a few still burning. Smashed boats floated in the debris field. Ol' Bud pointed his pipe stem at a bunch of splinters. "They prob'ly broke the oars for fun before they crushed the lifeboats."

Earl turned to James. "We'll make for the largest vessel in their fleet under full sail. Brail up the lower sails the moment we open the cannon ports. We'll commence firing from five cables away. Soon as the other vessels begin to converge on us, I want the swivel guns to fire at will."

"Aye, aye, Captain." James had a last look at the wreck in their wake. He saw her roll in the light swell, tip, and begin her plunge to the bottom. Staring ahead through the residual image of a few charred timbers and a small cloud dispersing in the east, he hoped his plan for avoiding a similar fate would work.

As the *Bride* closed the distance, the line of vessels in her path started forming a pinching arc. Earl placed a hand on Adam's shoulder. "Twenty minutes from now, we're going to be in the thick of a tale that today's survivors will be telling for years."

Ryan saw Ming exit the salon and run along the deck and up the aft stairs where he joined Earl, Adam, and James by the rail. James was about to give his sail instructions when he stopped to stare at Ming, who was dressed in his finest silk. This seemed odder than the fact that he rarely if ever stood where the group was gathered. He was carrying the bundle he'd brought aboard in Kowloon. He bowed to Earl. "May I speak freely?"

Earl nodded. "Zong." ("Always.")

"The lorcha's master gave me a flag he says will get us through pirates loyal to the rebels. I hid it in the galley where no Qing or British naval officers could find it. I did not tell you about it because any who possess the flag are subject to immediate hanging if caught by either government."

"We can talk about what you did later. What would you have us do? We're running out of time."

"I would like to take the flag forward and run it out on the flying jib stay. I will stand near the flag on the forward rail where they can see me. I'll probably be the first killed if I'm wrong."

Earl scratched the scar on his cheek. "I think that's a task we should do together. Belay the order to set more sail, James. We may have to parley, in which case I want you to be prepared to heave to. I'll tell Ryan to keep the men close to their guns behind closed ports. Adam, you'll come with us. James . . .get Charlie to run out Old Glory and the house flag."

"Will do." James walked with Earl to the top of the aft stairs and took his hand. "Don't be a hero."

"Not my style. I'm paying a visit to the foc'sl. Keep the cannons lined up on the pirate ship's quarterdeck. Tom pulls the lanyards the second they start shooting." Earl clapped James on the shoulder. "See you in Valhalla if we don't make it through the next fifteen minutes."

"Go on with ya," James grunted and gave Earl a light shove down the stairs. He returned to his place by the quarterdeck rail. "Can't fool me," he murmured to the retreating figure. "You were wearing the same mask when you said farewell to Lani Kiki on the dock in Honolulu."

The three made their way forward, and after a brief chat with Tom, mounted the foc'sl stairs. They removed the rebel flag from its sleeve and did as Ming suggested by running the large black-bordered red triangle out on a stay. Chinese characters sewn into the fabric spelled out *Tiandihui*, heaven (*tian*) and earth (*di*) society (*hui*) after the branches' founders in Guangdong Province.

Ming To climbed onto the rail, grabbed a stay, and stood beneath the flag in full sunlight. His red-and-gold raiment gave him a singular appearance never seen before by those who thought they knew him. Ming had the regal bearing of a dour emperor surveying his minions from the prow of his ship.

Earl and Adam leaned on the rail and had the same thought: *There is a great deal more to Ming To than meets the eye*. "The stage is set, and we get to see the show from a lowly orchestra pit, nephew."

The *Bride* glided over the sun-dappled water, her bowsprit aimed directly at the largest sampan in the fleet. Sunlight glinted off numerous lenses. The space between the ships shrank to a few cables, and Earl braced himself for the now-or-never moment. A collision would become unavoidable if the distance became much shorter. Less than two cables away, the huge sampan veered to starboard, exposing her stern to the *Bride*'s cannons. As the vessel completed her turn, a black flag festooned with red chops and gold streamers rose above armed men standing by the counter.

Elmer brought the *Bride* a few degrees to port and filled the passage between the sampan and another large vessel less than a hundred yards away.

Ming made eye contact with the captain of the pirate fleet and resumed his pose above the *Bride*'s glowing orb as the ships closed to within hailing distance.

The Yeatons witnessed the exchange of formal bows, and by all accounts, the fleet master and the men with him bowed significantly lower than Ming To.

CHAPTER 21

Kolkata, India, 24 May, four bells of the morning watch (10:00 a.m.)

"I'm impressed, James," Earl said to the man seated beside him. They sat on a quarter boat facing the broad delta whose fertile soil nourished one of the oldest continuously inhabited cities on Earth.

James ignored the compliment. "The wind's holding from the southwest and should keep us on station until the tug gets here. I'll feel a lot better once we're moored to the wharf over yonder."

Earl nodded with understanding and clapped James on a shoulder. "You did well. It'll be nice to see the ship come to a stop for the first time since we raised anchor off Kowloon twelve days ago. You'll feel better after you've had a bite to eat."

"Thanks." There were few things more harrowing in James's estimation than navigating a ship the size of the *Bride* thirty-five miles up a congested river. The number of times he'd had the crew cross-brace the sails in order to maneuver around the tightest bends caused his head to ache. He'd been on the conn for over seven hours and was in no mood for small talk.

Earl was the first to set foot on the government wharf and greet the British officials waiting there. He accompanied them to the customs house and went through the usual rigmarole: the purpose of his visit, how long he expected to stay, what he was leaving, and what he planned to take away with him.

Back at the wharf, he and Ryan exchanged a sheaf of papers for a sack of Indian silver currency. Earl shook the sack and led a few of his men to a livery barn a short distance away. They returned with six saddled horses and eight mules drawing two freight wagons. Earl and the men going overland with him had an early lunch while Ryan supervised the loading of the wagons. An hour or so later, the horses bore Bill, Kato, Colton, Munenori, Qui Li, and Maynard. Tom lounged beside the lead wagon waiting for Earl. Willard and Adam were on the second wagon. They were dressed in tan ranger clothes. Bill, Maynard, Colton, and Tom wore battered Stetsons. Kato, Munenori, and Qui Li wore conical hats made of woven reeds. Earl, Adam, and Willard sported the relatively new British Foreign Service helmets made of pressed pith covered with lightweight canvas. They were all wearing leather half boots. Willard, as usual, went unarmed. Qi Li carried a tanto. The rest chose to carry a combination of swords, knives, shotguns, and pistols.

Tarpaulins covered tall mounds held in place by cargo nets. Duffels, shotguns, and medical bags competed for space behind the seats. Several cases of surgical gear, syringes, morphine, chloroform, mineral spirits, quinine, mosquito repellant, French perfumes, toilet tissue, spices, and extra boxes of ammunition were stowed on top.

Ryan had the men place two crates stenciled with iron crosses up against the headboards of both wagon beds. The rifles in these crates carried scopes attached to their barrels. They packed several thousand rounds of matching ammunition beside the rifles. The crew buried the German rifles and ammunition under a dozen cases stenciled with farm equipment labels. The cases contained Spencer repeating rifles and three thousand rounds of ammunition.

Crates of wood and stone-carving tools—mostly consisting of an assortment of hammers, chisels, wedges, sandpapers, and gouges—were packed among kegs of nails, screws, drivers, latches, hinges, sewing machines, scissors, garden tools, rolls of screen material, salt blocks, bolts of silk, linens, and insect netting.

Adam's wagon carried a crated John Deere steel plow covered with sacks of cinchona bark. The crated harrow sat on top of an assortment of rifle, revolver, shotgun, and ammunition cases. These they buried under a pile of leather-bound chests filled with illustrated books, playing cards, board games, and toys, including spinning tops and climbing bears. Other chests held pastel Conte sticks, pencils, boxes filled with multicolored Lemercier crayons, bound drawing books, globes, and colorful maps. The works of Dickens and

Hugo vied for space in a separate chest. These they tightly packed among the rest of the miscellaneous items Earl tossed in at the last minute.

"That should do it," Earl said, taking his seat on the box beside Tom, who by then was holding the reins in one hand and the brake lever in the other. "We'll be back in a week to ten days."

Peering toward where Bud's bushy eyebrows ought to be in the cloud of smoke wreathing the older man's head, he said, "Watch your topknots."

"Watch your'n," came the mumbled reply from behind the clay pipe's stem.

James and Ryan shook their heads at the parting shots and waved Earl's party on their way. The wagon wheels rumbled over the wharf's planks and turned north on the Strand. The three boys left behind gathered along the rail feeling lost and alone as Earl's party rolled out of sight.

Earl left Ryan and James with the task of arranging to trade spices, cotton, silk, and hardware for bales of jute, denim, indigo, Oriental rugs, and sacks of nutmeg. The trades completed, they were to anchor the *Bride* in deeper water for safekeeping. There was plenty to keep the crew busy. The *Bride* would remain at the wharf and spend the next three days switching from winter to summer-weight canvas while they completed the trades. More bags of Earl's silver would find its way into the markets. Fifty people ate a lot of meat, vegetables, citrus fruit, grains, nuts, and seeds. The boys would clean out the water tank and take on fresh water from lines running out of the city reservoir. Off to the laundries would go the clothes and linens. The high tops and rigging were about to receive new cordage.

Glancing at the dejected boys left behind, James gave up his nap and cleared his throat. "Ryan tells me that on the way upriver, you two reached down the head's throat and scraped the crap off the flappers real well. I'm pleased with you." Mike and Charlie squinted at fingernails scrubbed clean with carbolic soap and rinsed in mineral spirits. Hopley snickered. The boys had good reason to examine their hands. They had just completed their turn to make sure the heads smoothly discharged the crew's bowel movements. The flapper flipped out on its hinges from inside the discharge vent and backed against a stop if surge came up the vent hole. Cleaning the heads was arguably the foulest chore aboard ship.

James rubbed his hands together. "So, let's get cracking and batten this vessel down. We should go have a peek at what's cooking in the bazaar! I'm still hungry! My treat. Hop to it, boys. I want to rub shoulders with those pretty Indian lasses before my whiskers get any grayer!"

Several hours later, Earl and his men rolled past the last of the settlement buildings. The city's outskirts had given way to open countryside hosting palatial estates and cultivated acreages. Temples, both majestic and forlorn, blended into the pastoral landscape. The trunk road followed the curve of the Hooghly River as it meandered through mangrove swamps, grasslands, and acreages sown with jute. Every rise and fold in the living green carpet supported a wide variety of plants and animals. They passed under flowering dhak trees whose discarded petals turned their path into a tangerine ribbon. The road wound through groves of Indian coral trees housing colonies of baya weavers peering out of scrotal nests swaying in the gentle afternoon breeze. The air resonated with the sound of insects. Flashes of multicolored plumage accented birdsongs. The sharp cries of hunting kites were hard to ignore.

"This place must have been a Garden of Eden before the first humans arrived several thousand years ago," Earl commented.

Tom nodded. "Ayah. We humans sure do know how to make the most of a good thing. The ruins we've been passing must have been here while the natives were spreading out across North America. Come to think of it, the place we call home was once a garden too."

Tom held the reins in his right hand most of the time. He let the left loosely take up the slack while he rested his forearms on his thighs. Earl glanced at the bulge of the tanto strapped to Tom's calf. Attached to Earl's leg was the tanto that killed Roland Hampton in Tokyo. The coach gun nestled between them in a rice sack placed on the padded leather seat.

Tom's small eyes accented his bony features and weathered skin, giving him a boyish look. The hands holding the reins were strong and wiry, like the rest of him. He and Kato spent many hours together below the aft hatch learning and practicing self-defense techniques. The incident in El Monte taught Tom a great deal about the merits of including Kato in the ship's company. Tom learned jujitsu and taught Kato how to handle firearms and overcome his fear of heights.

"We'll be pulling into Sahibzada Muhammad Mardan's palace before sundown. His lands stretch as far as the eye can see in any direction," Earl said, scanning the ruins for signs of movement.

"Tell me again, Capt'n Earl, how you came to know the people we're about to visit."

Earl rubbed his nose and thanked his lucky stars. The man he sat beside was no longer the boy he had taken aboard several years ago as a favor to a friend. He glanced at the shotgun again, and the brave young man who may well have saved his life. "I met Sahibzada in the winter of '48. I was working aboard an American trading vessel at the time."

Tom kept his eyes between the heads of the lead mules. He knew most of Earl's family history but next to nothing about his reasons for going to sea instead of practicing medicine closer to home. Tom's father had said Earl could teach the boy a lot if he could keep his temper in check. Tom had seen Earl lose his temper and was glad *he* hadn't been on the receiving end.

"We'd dropped anchor in Kolkata," Earl continued. "I went ashore to check out the hospital and got to talking with an East India Company medical officer. One thing led to another, and he asked me to examine a wounded military commander at their station north of here in Barrackpore. Captain Pinkham thought it would be good politics to let me go." Earl shrugged. "The Brits gave me a tall black that had been up there a few times. I put a change of clothes in the saddlebags with my medical gear, gave the horse his head, and rode off to lend a hand.

"I didn't know much about what was happening in the rest of the world back then, Tom. I was a country boy who had made it through a difficult time. I wasn't paying much attention and had only a vague understanding of what the Brits were doing in this part of the world. I've learned a lot since those days. I've also learned whose side I'm on, and it doesn't seem to matter what race they come from. I seek the company of people who are stewards of the lands sustaining them. Had I known what I know now, I probably would have lent a hand anyway. Sick people need help no matter whose side they're on. It grieves me to think the weapons we'll be delivering to Sahibzada and his friends will be used to put men in the same beds I saw years ago." His voice turned hard again. "I would much rather see those rifles used on the people responsible for putting those soldiers in harm's way."

He crossed his arms and stared into the shadows. "A few miles beyond what turned out to be the palace road I came around a curve and saw a coach flipped on its side in a drainage ditch. The large tiger tracks beside the red stain going into the elephant grass left little doubt about what had caused the crash and became of the driver. The wheels were still turning. I pulled the horse to a stop and rushed over. The horses had regained their feet and stood shivering in a tangled mass of harness gear. I tied their heads down with a pair of loose reins and climbed the wreck. A man and two women were struggling in three or four feet of water. They had welts on their heads and were helpless. I dropped into the ruined cabin and got them out of there before they drowned. They were more dead than alive by the time I spread 'em out on what was left of the cushions.

"I used the horses to pull the coach back onto its wheels. Took a while, but I got it on the road and the team back in the traces. I loaded the people inside, tied the black to the boot, and drove them up the side road I'd seen earlier. Arriving at the palace, I discovered I'd saved the lives of the owner of the estate and two of his wives. Sahibzada insisted I stay. Since their injuries were not serious, I said no, but I did ask if I could stop by on my way back. Several days later, I returned. Our relationship has blossomed into a friendship that has lasted a dozen or so years. I hardly ever see his wives, and when I do, they're wearing veils.

"I visit the palace each time we sail this way. I wanted to bring Adam with me last year, but he had to stay behind and tend to Bob's broken arm. James usually sits where you are. He and I like to come up together. We bring a wagon loaded with things Sahibzada can't buy here. I usually travel with fewer people. This year I've added another wagon and armed outriders. I decided to make this a special trip because who knows when we'll be back? The situation at home is pretty bleak, and I may be needed if those fools in Washington don't stop bickering.

"We have more men with us this time for another reason. Hostile incidents directed at Westerners remain a constant threat even though the Indian Rebellion ended a year ago in April. There's still a strong undercurrent of resentment toward the British, despite the Crown's dissolving of the East India Company two years ago. Adding insult to injury, the pompous asses have labeled their occupation of India the British Raj, which means 'rule' in Hindi." Earl darted a glance at Tom and shook his head. "The damn fools accentuate the power of their dominion by stuffing objecting kings down thirty-two-pound cannon muzzles. A red mist is the last thing the women and children see of their lord before the balls arrive."

Tom's eyes popped open, and he started wondering if Earl could tell friend from foe in these parts. He was quite sure Sahibzada knew the difference and would have no qualms about using the weapons they were delivering to prove it.

"I'll rest a lot easier knowing James is back there caring for the Bride." Clapping a hand on Tom's sturdy shoulder, Earl smiled. "Besides, I need the kind of protection you so ably provide if things get out of hand while we're here."

Tom responded with a nervous smile. "Aye, aye." He tightened his grip on the reins and thought of what Mike had told him after they left El Monte behind. *"Adam has a feeling Harrington's people are being tipped off on our plans."*

"Can I ask you a personal question, Captain?"

"Sure. But I get to decide if I want to answer it."

"How come you said James was back there instead of Ryan, and why did you leave Mr. Marshall at the ship in San Pedro instead of bringing him to Wilson's ranch?"

"You risked your life saving mine, Tom, so I think you have earned the right to ask those questions. I don't have a good answer right now, except to say James Marshall is my most trusted friend, and I want him protecting the Bride if I can't be there to do it myself."

Tom nodded. "Thanks. And there's more, isn't there?"

"Yes. Our enemies may have an ally in our company, and from what I've seen so far, it could be anyone but you, Adam, James, Willard, and me. I don't know about Ryan. He hasn't done anything to draw suspicion. Until he gives me reason to think otherwise, I'm going to continue to trust him, but not enough to be alone with the ship. Does that answer your questions?"

"It does." He was silent as they had rolled up the road a ways. "So, who is this Sahibzada, if you don't mind my asking?"

Earl smiled despite the worries Tom's questions triggered. "I don't mind. You've earned the right to ask me just about anything! Sahibzada is a subject of the British Crown. His family are members of the former ruling Mughal Dynasty. He can trace his ancestry hundreds of years back to the period when the Persian and Mongol descendants of Genghis Khan formed the last dynasty to rule India. He's also a nawab, their word for king, who presides over a vast stretch of arable land. The land and the treasures handed down over the generations by his ancestors are the source of his wealth. His great-grandfather, Mir Mardan, died in 1757 at the Battle of Plassey defending Siraj ud-Daulah, the last supreme nawab who ruled here. We've anglicized the pronunciation of nawab into nabob, by the way.

"At the time of the Mughal defeat, Robert Clive, the East India Company's military commander, conspired with several Mughal kings. They betrayed Siraj at a pivotal time in the battle. Clive's forces routed Siraj's armies, ending the Mughal reign in India and, in effect, paved the way for a hundred years of East India Company rule here. The sonsabitches are using the same tactics on our friends in Japan." Earl's utterance held more vehemence than Tom was used to hearing from his captain. "May as well mention it while I'm on the subject of betrayal—we have people doing the same damn thing with the Brits at home!"

Earl dropped his hands to the seat, sat up a little straighter, and narrowed his eyes at an innocent copse of trees. "Many of the nawabs, including Sahibzada's ancestors, signed off on their loyalty to the Mughal Dynasty and became subjects of the British Crown. They get to keep their palaces, manage their estates, and pay an annual remittance to the Crown in silver currency at uniformly fixed rates of exchange.

"Many nawabs have lost their fortunes and their estates. You'll see their former palaces occupied by protégés of the British Crown. Numerous owners did nothing to displease their new masters other than occupy a space desired by their current rulers. I'm sure similar confiscations took place right here many hundreds of years ago after people formed tribes for mutual protection and the defense of their food sources. Through guile, negotiation, or outright theft, armed groups expropriated lands occupied by others and held them by force until subjugated by a stronger rival."

Clearing his throat, Earl brought up a subject the Yeatons had not yet come to grips with. "Our Native American Indians were doing the same thing to each other until the Europeans arrived, and now white settlers are driving the natives off their lands." Shaking his head, Earl got back on track.

"Sahibzada says there are ruins on his property dating back to the Baro-Bhuiyan semi-feudal period. In those days, independent princes who called themselves rajas occupied the region. Bowing to pressure from the Sultanate of Delhi, the Baros joined the Lodi Dynasty.

"Sahibzada's great-grandfather, General Utpalendu ud-din Mardan, assumed control over this principality as his reward for participating in an epic battle two hundred years ago. The battle put an end to the Lodi rulers."

Earl rubbed his jawline. "Tom, a part of me wants to be detached from the things I see humans doing to each other. I know history has a way of repeating itself, and I also know the wrongs I see will not be fixed in my lifetime. I try to do what I can to improve the lives of people like you and our friends." His voice turned hard again. "And make a difference for the *worse* in the lives of the people spreading hate and self-interest. My goal is to make the lives I touch a little bit better, but I'm realistic enough to know the changes I would prefer to see will rarely, if ever, occur because I'll never be able to eliminate all the greedy people going about their evil ways. I feel that by remaining detached and dispassionate I can maintain a semblance of sanity." Earl laughed. "I'll let you be the judge on whether or not I'm successful!"

Tom thought about the mixed feelings he'd seen in Earl's eyes back in the El Monte Dip. *"The Harringtons will have a lot to answer for when I catch up with them,"* Earl had said after they'd tied the last body across a saddle and patted a horse's flank on the way around. *"None of us seek to kill people, but we are going to have to if we're faced with having to decide between killing or being killed."*

"This may sound odd, Tom, but I actually enjoy a few of the beneficiaries of all the conflict and turmoil. I'm far less interested in their wealth and prestige, which unquestionably have their attractions, than I am in the content of their character. The people whose company I enjoy, I keep as friends. I've come to the conclusion that wealth is only one aspect of who a person is. I don't subscribe to the notion that these fortunate people are by definition societal parasites. I think the parasitic turn of mind is an acquired trait."

Tom shifted the reins and waited for what was coming next. He'd heard the charge in his captain's voice before.

"And you know what I think should be done about parasites."

"I sure do," the young man said with conviction, "and I'd chase them across the Great Plains if you told me to!"

"How a person *manages* wealth is a much better indicator of their character," Earl said. "It ain't about the money. It's about the way they live. Sahibzada is one of the few people I know who actually nurtures his land and the inhabitants of his vast estate. That is the reason I like him. It is also why I'm shipping the arms in those crates back there." He thumbed the load. "I'm helping him protect his way of life. Sahibzada will be hosting a gathering while we're here. The arms he and his friends are receiving will be used to attack the opium convoys coming south from Indian and Afghani poppy plantations. His guests will be taking more than full stomachs home with them." He reached for a drink of water and took a long pull before passing the jug to Tom.

"Sahibzada emulates a Mughal ruler whose reign I admire: Akbar the Great. Akbar was a learned scholar, inclusive, and he organized the military and civil service to run on a meritocracy that encouraged religious diversity. Over the course of his reign, the wealth of the country rose through trade and diplomacy. His armies were the strongest on the continent because they had the strength of the people supporting them. He ushered in the Golden Age of the Mughal Dynasty. This world could use more people like him.

"Out of the hundreds of rulers to walk over this continent, only two leaders stand out for me: Akbar the Great and Genghis Khan. I shudder to think about the punishments they inflicted on the emperors and citizens of the empires that displeased them. Akbar was the kind of ruler his distant ancestor, Genghis Khan, would become in a later life. I doubt even he and the Khan would have stooped to conquer a whole race of people in order to grow a substance intended to poison another race of people. They may have been ruthless, but they were not evil!"

Earl had been observing the multitude of butterflies flitting from one group of colorful blossoms to another. Try as he might, he couldn't find his favorite from among the differing color combinations: the iridescent orange-striped awl. The strain of being on guard and getting hungry was taking its toll. He became drowsy in the late-afternoon sun and would have nodded off if he hadn't glanced ahead. "Ahh," he said, sitting up. "We're almost there. Let's pull over at the turn off. We'll take a leak before we get to the palace."

He lifted a hand to point at a break in the trees up ahead, glanced at Tom's restless eyes, and rallied.

"I told Sahibzada about Willard a few years ago. He felt offended to think I would keep such an important secret from him. He insisted on meeting Willard immediately. He got his grooms to hitch his fastest team to a well-sprung curricle, and taking the reins himself, raced us back to the Bride. Willard was happy to return with us. He sat in the middle and conversed with Sahibzada while those Arabians ate up the miles. It was hard for me to follow their conversation because their sentences were punctuated with English, French, Arabic, Hindi, Chinese, and Farsi words. Didn't take long for Willard to figure out why he was being fetched. Sahibzada told Willard he was to spend four days in the harem with four different concubines. Sahibzada became serious. I could have told him that he was wasting his breath trying to impress upon Willard the honor being bestowed upon him. You know that guests are to stay away from certain areas in the palace. One of them is the women's quarters where the nawab's harem resides—the special women, his wives and concubines. I have never been within a corridor of the entrance to the harem, but I have heard Willard's descriptions. The most luxurious balconied apartments are there.

"Sahibzada has extraordinary views on the roles we have in each other's lives. He calls how we have come to know each other kismet. The Hindus and Buddhists call it karma. Most of us Westerners refer to it as chance but hasten to add that we don't believe in coincidence. Arggh, I suppose every culture has its inherent contradictions. Just part of what makes us human, I guess. Sahibzada values intelligence above all other characteristics, and Willard is the most intelligent person I have ever met, which is why Sahibzada was so insistent on giving Willard a chance to produce another one like him!"

Tom nodded and relaxed the bridle reins running through the harness's ivory hoops. "How in the world did you meet Willard?"

"How in the world is right. I met him by accident. He was supposed to be in school. People had noticed his language skills and suggested his mother take him to Bowdoin College, where a professor introduced him to another language prodigy, L. Joshua Chamberlain. They suggested he go to the Boston Latin School. He wasn't there for more than a few weeks.

"Said he didn't like being treated like a lab specimen and returned home. One of the ways he passed the time included humoring his mother's suitors.

They'd ask him to demonstrate his knowledge of winds and tides by estimating sailing times over familiar trade routes. He readily supplied answers to any nautical distance questions requiring advanced Cartesian coordinate theory computations.

"A Coombs family friend approached me in '55, thinking that Willard's capacities might be useful. Have to admit, I was skeptical at first. I felt quite sure that an unusual individual with no seafaring experience, of slight build, unique social skills, and compulsive reading habits would require more attention than could be justified by the merits of his mental capacities. As a physician, I'd heard of savants. I understood them to be oddities of nature whose gift of amassing trivia served little purpose, but on a hunch, I agreed to meet with Willard.

"As expected, I found myself in the presence of a walking encyclopedia. I did not expect Willard's engaging disposition and eccentricities to appeal so strongly to my own inquisitive nature. The longer we talked, the more I realized Willard would fit right in with all of the other personalities lodged aboard the ship. Admitting to myself that I could be wrong, I suggested he might like the idea of being the ship's purser. He *did* like the idea.

"Willard and his mother met with the ship's officers the next day. Mrs. Coombs paid particular attention to the courtly manners of the sail master and invited him over for tea.

"Several days later, she saw Willard to the Bride, got him settled in his cabin, and went happily on her way, but not before having a private word with Mr. Marshall."

"What?" Tom asked, having difficulty imaging her attraction to the sail master.

They both laughed. "You wouldn't know it to look at him, Tom, but James can be a charmer!"

Reducing their laughter to smiles, they rolled up the road toward the palace turnoff and became part of the scenery—a group of wagons and outriders wending their way through light beginning to cast longer shadows.

Earl gave voice to another thought they were entertaining. "Tom, I'm telling you the truth. I didn't see Willard for four days after Sahibzada raced us back to the palace. Willard said that he felt like he was in a dream state the whole time. He awoke each morning with a different woman at his side. They spent the day entertaining each other with cerebral exercises, including chess, backgammon, and Parcheesi. Sahibzada's women have a wide variety of skill sets, apparently. They ate delicious meals lasting for hours and after sunset slept together. As soon as he was asleep, another woman replaced the one with whom he had spent the previous twenty-four hours.

"On the fifth day, Willard was placed in a coach with his things—the clothes he had worn and gifts the women had given him—and returned to the ship. This is the fifth year in a row he's been invited back. He's memorized the contents of several tantric sex treatises and claims to be quite adept at pleasing the women. He won't discuss who he sees or what they do together, with one exception.

"Several children have been born since Willard's first year here, but it's too early to tell if they got the desired results. The chances of that happening—and here Willard can give you an exact number—are less than one in ten thousand.

"I hear a certain wistful quality in his voice when he says his favorite number is four, if that means anything." Earl paused for a moment. "I think he might be spending the night with more than one woman at a time.

"He did mention a favorite concubine. Her name is Uma Alakananda, a descendant of Himavat, king of the Himalayas. Her side of the family is renowned for their knowledge of ancient languages. Willard says he and Uma pass the time seeking a linguistic thread common to all languages. They are also engaged in working out a theory on how language becomes writing. He says they have been poring over tomes in Sahibzada's library and are close to deciphering how ancient linguists converted sounds into each language's unique script."

Earl lifted a hand and pointed at a break in the trees. "Here we are, Tom. The palace road is up there on the right. They know we're coming, so we should be able to drive right past the marble columns, arches, and steel gates. The peacocks will let you know how close we are to the palace. Much prefer hearing *them* announcing our arrival. Can't stand barking dogs. Two other guests often stay with us while we're here. I should tell you about them."

Earl and Tom continued to talk as the wagon rolled along toward the open gates.

The mules drawing Willard's wagon made the turn onto the palace road after he and the rest of the crew took their break. Seated and relaxed, he resumed his preoccupation with the beautiful panorama. For the past hour or so, he had been absorbing all of the sights and sounds as his mind listened to a concert he'd once heard performed at Bowdoin. He smiled after passing under the arch's beautifully carved glyphs and tilted his head to the fading strings. "Four days will quickly steep themselves into night," he murmured, "four nights will quickly dream away the time."

Sobered by another line in Shakespeare's play, he stopped to consider what was in store for Queen Victoria's opium trains and sighed. "Oh, what fools these mortals be."

Adam was far too preoccupied to hear Willard recite Hippolyta's opening lines or notice his fingers tapping out the final notes of Mendelssohn's companion piece to *A Midsummer Night's Dream*.

He would say he noticed a change in the atmosphere from the moment he stepped onto the wharf. The air felt different.

An unfamiliar sense of peace seemed to envelop him. He recognized feelings he would usually ignore and perceived an elevated sense of detachment accompanied by an intense sense of belonging. The mutually exclusive feelings seemed to enhance a growing appreciation of the sensory awareness associated with being *present*. Shrugging his shoulders, he tried to chalk up these inklings of heightened awareness to a good night's sleep and a tasty lunch. That explanation only went so far, however, because he had the vague sense he was part of an undefined quality greater than himself. Concluding that India was having an effect on him, he couldn't shake the feeling he'd been there before.

Adam's sense of déjà vu felt stronger the closer he got to the palace. Passing a spot where the forest grew thick, the feeling became intense. No road or trail led into the undergrowth. He glanced at the receding verge just before the road made a wide turn and wondered why the feeling was so intense right there. He recalled having a similar feeling every time he came near the *Lar Familiaris*.

Staring ahead, he became distracted and nearly missed hearing the peacocks announcing their arrival.

CHAPTER 22

Sahibzada Muhammad Mardan Palace, 25 May, 6:00 p.m.

Still feeling preoccupied, Adam paused by the entrance to the grand hall and saw a floating ceiling. He thought he'd passed into a world where the laws of physics didn't apply. "This can't be true," he quavered, staring at the underside of a freestanding balcony. The sweeping curve held his attention until he cleared the edge and transferred his wonder to the domed rotunda whose tinted plate-glass windows infused the hall with a soothing honey-toned glow. "Too much to take in at once," he murmured.

He blinked and saw corridors running off in all directions from arched openings in the curved walls. Multicolored Qajar oils, Tanjore cloth paintings, banners, tapestries, rugs, and runners accented the marble floors, columns, and stairs. He was too enthralled to recall being told that many of the pieces portrayed events of importance to the palace's heirs.

A colorful woolen carpet lay over a large area of the open floor. He'd soon discover that the mezzanine rail was the best place from which to view the rug, because he would then have the benefit of seeing how the colors joined to form a map of the Orient. He followed his uncle across the carpet's sandy Mediterranean shores and gazed upon a sampling of the finest artistic treasures ever produced in the lands over which they strolled.

He heard Tom comment on two large *kalamkari* tapestries facing each other from opposite sides of the hall and saw his uncle's raised brow. "Well done, Tom. You listened to what I said and recognize scenes from the events we were talking about on the way here. The one on the right is our host's distant grandfather kneeling with General Munium Khan before Akbar the

Great after the Battle of Tukaroi. He's the patriarch of the Mughals who've managed this estate ever since that day. The kalamkari on the left is of the First Battle of Panipat. The great Mughal nawab, Zahir ud-din Babar, defeated the Lodi Sultan, Ibrahim, in this battle. Babar was a direct descendant of the Great Khan and the Persian conqueror, Timur. Our host is a descendant of Babar. Sahibzada says Sultan Ibrahim's ancestors were members of the ancient Afghani Pashtun tribes. These tribes continue to occupy the Khyber Pass region, the gateway to Asia and China." He pointed to another painting. "The kalamkari hanging off the balcony is a fanciful portrayal of what this area may have been like during the reign of the Baro-Bhuiyan rajas."

A smiling major-domo and his servants appeared while Earl was talking. They relieved the men of their duffels and invited them to follow. Tom and his crew walked to rooms strung along a corridor near the servants' sleeping and dining areas. Willard headed off to familiar lodgings while Earl and Adam followed their guide up a wide set of stairs and down a long corridor. A side of the corridor eventually opened onto a balconied apartment wing built around a central courtyard. Their apartments were across from each other. Two adjoining apartments at the end of the wing completed the raised enclosure. Their garments were taken away to be washed while they bathed. An hour or so later, Earl and his men changed into clean clothes, had a late dinner, and for the first time in weeks, slept in beds that were not rocking.

Well after sunrise the next morning, Earl woke to the sound of laughter coming from one of the apartments at the end of the court. He visited the *socalaya* room, whose bowl-shaped depression in the tiled floor had a vent hole over which he squatted and washed after he relieved himself. "Not much different from what we do aboard the Bride," he commented, pouring a bucket of water down the hole after using damp towels to wipe his hands and privates. He draped the cloths inside a reed hamper and laughed. *As soon as Sahibzada's wives hear about water closets, they'll be asking me to bring them in here by the cartload!*

Standing at a marble-top dresser, he glanced in the attached mirror and ran his fingers through the wavy dark hair covering his wide brow. Hair had grown over the scar on his scalp. The knife cut on his cheek had healed into a thin red line. The clear blue eyes looking back at him with such good humor went well with the handsome face, even though his eyes noted how the crow's feet seemed to be a little longer each time he returned to this spot and saw his reflection. Removing a towel draped over a pitcher, he poured warm water into a basin and washed his hands with strong soap. He lathered, shaved, brushed his teeth, combed his hair, and dumped the wastewater down the socalaya. Daubing bug dope on his feet, he smeared a little behind his ears and reached for a light change of clothes. He donned a pair of beige shalwar pants. *I like the cut,* he thought. *The loose cotton balloons away from my legs and keeps me as cool as I'm going to get around here, and the tapered ankles discourage mosquitoes from flying up the pant legs. Nice.* He slipped a rose-colored kameez shift over his shoulders and combed his hair again in the mirror.

Crossing to the balcony, he felt heat gathering in the courtyard. Adam's door was open. Walking barefoot over the cool tiles, he stood at the door to the apartment from which the laughter was coming. "Hallo," he called, his voice carrying to those seated on an outside balcony. He heard chairs moving and subdued mumbling converted into more laughter followed by a boisterous, "Apaka svagata hai, hailo, hailo, you Ol' drifter! Welcome and hello, etcetera!" The speaker emerged from the bedroom twirling an outstretched hand over his baldpate. His tall companion was laughing too. Earl delighted in the image the two elderly men conjured; a pair of corpulent cherubs sired by Father Time. *They may be yogis*, he thought, *but they are not ascetic!* The two men rushed in and took turns giving Earl a bear hug. The next moment they were all hugging each other while unabated tears of joy flowed from their dancing eyes.

"Apa ghara a ga e haim" ("You have come home"), the shorter one said, holding Earl.

Smiling and easing off the pressure, Earl answered in broken Hindi. "Dila hai, jaham ghara hai" ("Home is where heart is").

They released Earl and exclaimed, "Apane ghara hamare dila mem hai!" ("Your home is in our hearts!") The shorter of the two switched to English. "Have you eaten? It's time for breakfast. Let's all go down to the kitchens and see what Sahibzada's cooks have on the stoves. Will your stethoscope be able to hear anything through this?" he asked, rubbing a fond hand over his abdominal bulge.

The three walked along the balcony and made the turn onto the wide hallway. They strolled over a corridor lined with more rooms, sitting areas, priceless silk runners, Zand period oils, watercolors, mirrors, *torans*, and vibrant tapestries. Birdsongs and peacock calls accompanied their stroll through the palace halls. Earl passed a balcony and thought of Adam. The opening gave him an expansive view of the forests and fields he'd traversed to get there. He would have been alarmed had he seen what his nephew was doing in the forest.

The night before, Adam had dinner with the crew, said his good nights, and was sound asleep before his head hit the pillow. He fell into a dream state, and the deeper into sleep he went, the more any sense of the present gave way to images rising out of the past. The tenuous thread holding his consciousness to the present parted as his mind's eye liberated itself from his body and passed into a realm of times past. Letting the last of his conscious constraints go he dreamt that his spirit rose out of his body, exited through an apartment window, and hovered over the palace lawn. He watched a thick vapor envelop his disembodied spirit and begin spinning. The vapors peeled back the years and eventually dispersed, revealing the palace grounds as they appeared ages ago. His spirit saw a disconsolate young man step out of the palace and start walking down the road. Adam's dream self knew he was observing the conflicted son of a Baro-Bhuiyan raja who, against his father's wishes, was in love with the daughter of a neighboring raja. Their parents had betrothed them to others and denied their repeated pleas to marry. The star-crossed lovers were caught in a web from which neither could be released.

Adam's body wriggled under the covers while his mind wrestled with the sorrow, pain, and loss the young lovers had experienced hundreds of years in the past. The distraught young man walked around a curve in the palace road, pushed aside the underbrush, and crossed to the location of a temple he had built to Mohini, the Hindu goddess of love. Swearing the best sculptor in the kingdom to secrecy, the prince had the image of the princess serve as the model for a bronze Mohini. Housing the image in the clandestine temple, he prayed to the goddess, hoping she would intervene and free him to marry the love of his life. He placed before the goddess all the treasures he would have given his lost love had they been allowed to be together. The prince continued to visit the shrine years after he and the princess married the spouses their parents had arranged for them. His father eventually discovered the hidden temple and in a fit of rage had an impenetrable outer shell built around the structure.

Finally accepting his lot in life, the prince no longer visited the source of so much anguish. He became a dutiful husband to his wife, had children, and prospered on the lands where he was born. Fearful of the dire consequences if caught in each other's company, the two lovers lived out their lives with the spouses chosen by their parents.

Seasons came and went; creepers twisted around the abandoned temple's shell. Grasses grew over the flagstones and dead leaves. Decay soon followed. The site eventually assumed the appearance of so many other neglected relics as the years wore on.

The prince and princess raised their separate families, attended palatial ceremonies held at the dozen or so estates in the small kingdom, and kept their distance from each other. The few times they dared draw close, they could plainly see how the passage of time had changed their appearance but could not age the bittersweet love of their youth. By the time they had outlived their parents and spouses, there was no one left to remember they were once lovers, and now *a raja,* he visited her as she lay dying. Left alone in her chambers, they gazed at each other in loving peace knowing they would soon be free of earthly constraints. He lay down beside her, and, holding hands, they entered the realm of the dead, yet not dead, finally liberated from having to endure one of those sorrows that did not bear thinking about for long.

Opalescent wisps rose out of the lovers' brows and spun into shimmering spheres answering the call of the stars. Unseen forces drew the orbs faster and faster into dark space until they were lost to the mind's eye in a wide span of flickering specks drifting away into the galaxy's great mandala.

Years passed. Adam saw their spirits descend from the heavens to be reborn, live, and die in different places and in different times over the course of the following centuries.

Adam felt his spirit returning in the early morning light and imagined he saw a glimpse of her through his third eye. Her puzzled expression suggested she was trying to make sense of what she saw. The more conscious he became, the more her image faded. Rising out of the depths of his dream, he felt the bond of entwined destinies receding into his unconscious. The sense of loss made his soul ache with a painful desire to be with her. Feeling as if a gauzy curtain was separating him from the love of his life, he reached out and tried to remove the barrier before she was totally lost from sight. Unable to reach the curtain, his arms dropped to his sides. Returning to wakefulness, he saw her perplexed expression disappearing behind the gray mesh of the mosquito netting. Their eyes locked, and she was gone. He awoke with the mind-numbing realization that his eyes had been open the whole time.

Rubbing his temples, he swung his legs over the side of the bed and placed his feet on the floor. "Ahh," he groaned and stared at the tiles with his head in his hands. "Waking up is taking longer than usual."

After a while he forced himself to get on with his morning routine. He used the socalaya, washed, shaved, brushed his teeth, and combed his hair by habit. He put on the Indian clothes without knowing he had done so until he saw himself in a mirror. *I'm too dazed to appreciate that today is going to be another beautiful one. What's happening to me? My inner turmoil is preventing me from appreciating the birdsongs, scents, and warm breezes. I don't know if I'm coming or going or what to do next. I feel as if I'm in the land of spirits.*

Adam had always known spirits influenced his life but had not given much thought to the idea he might be in their presence. His previous experiences had occurred at séances, and he occasionally communicated with his ancestors this way or was with others who were in communication with their own dead kin. "Is it possible my spirit has returned to a land where I was born, lived, grew old, died, and was buried, freeing my spirit to be reborn into other bodies over and over until I became me?"

A voice in his head answered. *It's possible, I suppose, and if it is, then you need to go find what you saw in your dream.* He squeezed his temples between his palms. "Arggh, I feel like I have two personalities now."

Yes, you do, the voice said. *And you know where to find what we are talking about, so put on clothes more suitable for walking in the bush. One other thing: You should get a bite to eat before you go. This could take a while.*

He changed his clothes and stuffed a few matches in his pants pocket on the chance they might come in handy.

The estate workers greeted a young man taking an early morning walk. If they observed a pair of leather gloves sticking out of his back pocket, the Bowie knife clipped to his gun belt, or the water skin on a string, they said he was wise to take precautions and had nothing further to add regarding his activities or appearance.

Adam was leaping over the ditch at about the time his uncle was passing by the balcony overlooking the forests and fields.

The elder of Earl's two friends was Asima Jnanda, a Hindi scholar. Asima said he did not know his exact age. Earl had seen centenarians, so he was familiar with the signs of advanced old age. The man he walked beside had the casual stride of a younger man and the wit of a jokester, and he wore his years well. Asima had once told Earl he could recall hearing of Robert Clive's victory over Siraj ud-Daulah. He might have been ten at the time. Earl figured Asima was around a 113 years old. Earl had examined him the year before and declared him to be in perfect health. Asima stood over six feet tall. His movements were deliberate, graceful, and elegant. He wore his beautifully tailored shalwar, kameez, and modi kurta vest with the regal bearing of a Brahmin, India's highest social class. He wore no jewelry. His dark patrician facial features were as arresting as the impression one got from observing him at a distance. The man had a natural charisma that drew others to him. Asima's dark cheeks had the rosy under glow of a man who ate well or perhaps a little too well. A thin cotton loop held his hair away from his face. Wavy white strands hung past his shoulders and covered part of his upper back and chest. A curly beard grew below his sternum. Full lips covered an ordered row of teeth that reminded Earl of old ivory. Asima's hawkish nose, although lined with small veins, resided quite comfortably between the most arresting features of all: a pair of sharp, clear, penetrating almond eyes set beneath thick black eyebrows. Asima possessed the certitude found in people who have taken their own measure and found themselves to be worthy of high self-esteem.

Vinamra Adami was different. He wore a cotton robe dyed with turmeric, as opposed to the more costly saffron dye made from crocuses. His egalitarian robe enhanced the unassuming tranquility surrounding him. He had been born in the Himalayas and wouldn't discuss who his parents were or their lineage, although, he too came from a family of Brahmins. Vinamra said a person's pedigree was far less important to him than the character residing in the body's current incarnation. His manners, obvious good nature, genuine interest in the people he was with at any given time, and his insights into human nature spoke well of whoever sired him and set him free to follow his unique path to enlightenment. He shaved his head each day. Earl thought Vinamra might be bald because he also claimed to be over one hundred years old. His face had soft folds around his mouth, eyes, and ears. Gentle light-brown eyes peeped out of their folds each time he smiled.

Earl thought Vinamra resembled the fair-skinned Nepalese Lumbini he had met years earlier on a trip to India with a group of Harvard Transcendentalists. They were visiting the holiest of Indian cities, Varanasi.

Vinamra stood a lot closer to five feet than six feet tall. His round body reminded Earl of the Buddha statues he'd seen. His jovial temperament was a primary reason why Earl returned to this place time after time; he basked in the light of the man's presence. He felt a strong kinship with Vinamra and was willing to go to any lengths to protect him. He chose not to reveal this combative trait to Vinamra, although he could never be sure how much the yogi already knew.

Adam trudged along until he arrived at the spot where his feelings peaked the previous day. Stopping by the side of the road, he turned and saw no sign of the palace or any indication of how far he had walked. "In for a penny, in for a pound," he said, putting on his gloves. The undergrowth, although thick, let him through. Paying little heed to the multitude of sounds, bright greens, and fragrant scents, he hopped over the ditch. The roadside vegetation thinned out before he needed to clear a path with his Bowie. A hundred feet or so from the road, the tree canopy muted the available light and limited the forest ground cover to short grasses and occasional vines. Tying strips torn from his bedsheet to branches where he could see them on his return, he walked in a forested cathedral whose pillars were tall sal trees, the species Gautama Buddha claimed to have been born under 2,000 years before. The deeper he walked into the forest, the quieter it became. The ground had begun a gradual rise soon after he'd left the roadside. He would not have known how to find his way back without the markers.

He had been walking for ten or fifteen minutes when he saw what he thought might be a vine-covered erratic, a huge boulder deposited by an ancient glacier. The closer he got to the object, the more he realized it was a circular stone structure. Vines had attached themselves to the building and covered much of its surface. Dead leaves littered the domed roof, walls, and foundation. He straightened his shoulders. "Let's see where this dream takes me," he said in a low voice.

The structure's solemn dignity overshadowed the rustic decay. The one-story building was composed of quarried blocks. Heavy fitted stone slabs sealed the roof. Circling the twenty-foot diameter, he could find no visible way to get in without compromising the structure and causing the building to collapse. He touched the wall and imagined he could feel tremors passing through the polished stone. He'd felt a similar sensation placing his hand on a horse's withers and feeling the muscles quivering beneath the hair.

He came to a stop by the wall's eastern face, where the most light fell. Touching the wall with the tip of a finger, he felt cool stone. *Huh*, he thought, *I think this is where I get in.* He pushed, but nothing happened. "Grr. . . too many vines," he grumbled, and for the next twenty minutes he hacked and tore his way through the growth until he had exposed a wide section of wall. He tried pushing again. This time he put his weight behind the push and got the same result. *The stone feels like a muscular horse*, he thought, pulling his hand back and feeling his frustration growing. *What's going on here? Well, I've come too far to turn back now.*

He placed his hands on a stone he would have designated as the key if he were the builder. "I am the rightful heir to this temple and have returned to claim this shrine," he said. He shoved with all of his might. The stone slid into the hole it created and dropped inside the wall. "That's more like it." He pulled another stone out and spent the next hour pushing and pulling stones. The process went on until there was a space beneath the roof's lintel large enough for him to walk through. He'd seen two stout wooden doors built into another circular wall as he worked. "Yes." He wiped the sweat off his brow. *There's a structure within a structure, just like the ones I saw in my dream.*

He stepped in and swung both doors open. Stale air greeted him. His desire to get inside was greater than his willingness to wait for the air to change, so he walked right in, fished matches out of a pocket, and lit the candles lining the wall. Adjusting to the wan morning light filtering into the room, he saw a raised dais supporting a life-size female figure. She was smiling at him. Adam recognized the mythical enchantress Mohini, the curvaceous avatar of Vishnu, the Hindu god. A jeweled belt was the only article of clothing she wore. Her beguiling face and luscious body may have been a millennium removed from the young prince who'd placed her image in the shrine, but that fact did nothing to alter her allure. She aroused in Adam a desire to get closer to her. He glanced down to avoid treading on the precious objects spilling off the dais.

The hairs on his body rose as a shiver ran through him. His eyes locked on the extended fangs of a dead cobra lying on the pile scattered about the idol's feet. Horrid fascination replaced awe. He felt an irrational impulse to test the sharpness of the fangs on his palm. They pierced his skin faster than he could come to his senses and change his mind. "Ouch!" he exclaimed, tossing the snake aside. Examining the punctures, he poured water over them, had a drink, and made sure the room did not contain any more unpleasant surprises. *What have I gotten myself into this time?* he asked himself, wrapping torn cloth around his palm.

"Let's see what we have here," he said, peering inside chests filled with jewelry boxes and poking through the open bags of gold and silver coins littering the floor. The closer to the figure he got, the more valuable the offerings. *Whoever chased this bronze goddess did so with great care. Her exquisite facial features, ample breasts, slim waist, perfect tummy, smooth hips, round bottom, and legs are those of a beautiful woman.* Mohini stood with her legs apart, hips akimbo, left palm resting on her upper hip. Her right arm held her hand out, the raised index finger encouraging Adam to come closer. *Now I know how Pygmalion felt after falling in love with the marble woman he created. Mohini is in a class of her own.*

She wore on her crown a beaten gold *Damin* studded with diamonds, rubies, emeralds, jade figures, sapphires, cat's eyes, onyx, lapis lazuli, turquoise, and many other stones Adam could not identify. A matched pair of fire opals dangled off the *Damin* beside each of her temples. A polished gold ammonite fossil hung over her third eye: the sacred *Shalagrama-shila* stone of Nepal's revered Gandaki River basin.

Studying her face and body on his walk around the sculpture, he saw gold and jewels on every surface capable of holding them in place. Her fingers and toes bore rings of every description. Her beckoning hand wore a *panchangala* whose fine gold chains connected the gem-studded bracelet to her finger rings. The elaborate *chandra* fastened to her slim waist held a jade knife in an elephant hide sheath threaded in gold and studded with rubies, emeralds, and royal blue sapphires. The beautifully carved katan dagger rested on her upper hip beside jeweled amulets and silver mesh purses filled with moonstones.

So much jewelry covered the dais that her feet seemed to be standing in a glittering puddle of treasure. Betel-nut boxes overflowed with strings of black and white pearls. Crystal mirrors propped this way and that caught the flickering candlelight. Bracelets dripping with ferret-tooth pearls spilled out of a sandalwood box. Slipping a string of these unique pearls over the extended index finger, he spotted an attractive gold necklace interwoven with several others bearing pendants of great beauty. "Ah ha, Navaratnas!" Moving a collection of gold and pearl necklaces aside, he exposed a large pendant lying close to her heart. "This one is exceptional," he said, lifting the jewel-encrusted medallion.

Adam spent the next hour rummaging through the treasures in Mohini's temple. "This place is wonderful, but it has not been mine for a thousand years." He had a last walk around the chamber, put out the candles, closed the doors, and retraced his way back to the road.

He had not yet recovered his wits by the time he came around the last curve in the road, and he was much too preoccupied to give a proper greeting to the people standing in groups near the porte cochere. Weaving his way through the guests chatting over items removed from the wagons, he noticed another group standing a short distance away. They clustered around several men holding hooded falcons. Adam shrugged and headed for the palace entrance, his vacant smile ignoring the laughing children who ran among the adults passing through the wide-open doors.

He passed men who were dressed in a variety of earth-toned suits. They wore matching turbans adorned with exotic multipiece sarpeches or stylized aigrettes set with pigeon's blood rubies. The aigrettes had elaborate feathered arrangements composed of fluffy down. Others carried fanned rows of iridescent wings slipped into minute silver sleeves.

The women wore similar sleeves on sarpech tiaras, maang tikka and shinka head ornaments. Feathers and flowers bobbed above sparkling gems. Scaly mother-of-pearl cobras woven into long tresses extended all the way to the dimples on their exposed hips. The women's garments came in a wide variety of colored silk, muslin, and satin fabrics. Saris, sarongs, shalwar kurtas, Ghaghara pleated skirts, and cholis blouses bore a multitude of pattern combinations. The more daring of the beautiful women wore sheer silk midriff-exposing cholis whose fitted stitching accented every sensuous curve of their upper bodies. Jewels chosen to enhance their attractiveness glittered every time the women moved. Diaphanous headdresses added a seductive veiled allure to the maidens and the more desirable wives. Sparkling gems studded the barrettes holding the light fabric in place.

Young unmarried men circled the women with a great deal of caution. Woe to any suitor foolish enough to approach them; the penalties for doing so without the permission of the nawabs who owned them were severe.

Oblivious to the beauty surrounding him, Adam watched flocks of strutting peacocks flee before the children's madcap advance across the wide yard.

The children's charge came to a halt beside Kato and several falcons jessed to perches. One of the handlers lifted a hooded falcon up and down, causing the bird to flap its wings. The children stopped and stared as the stranger and one of Sahibzada's sons examined the pennaceous flight feathers each time the bird extended its wings. The children were not the only ones intrigued by the tall man dressed in a red silk kimono printed with golden dragons. It was the first time any of them had seen a Japanese person. The older men standing with the falconers were surprised and confused by how well Kato blended into the unfamiliar setting. Kato's attire, his knowledge of falcons, and the two priceless swords he wore at his waist reinforced the whispers his observers had heard: they were in the presence of a man whose royal status rivaled their own.

Lifting a disinterested hand toward the men standing with Kato, Adam walked past rows of hardware and farm implements. He nodded at Maynard, who was standing over an open crate watching a carpenter flex a spring-loaded hinge. *The crew must have been up early this morning getting this stuff organized,* Adam thought.

Several of Sahibzada's field supervisors and guests were in a loose circle near Bill, who, with the assistance of an interpreter, was explaining how to use the John Deere plow and harrow. Scribes were recording his instructions with the new pencils and drawing books he had given them. Bill's voice dwindled to a murmur and stilled at the sight of Adam. He cocked his head and spun a confused finger at the sight of Adam's soiled clothes and weapons. Adam swatted his pant legs for effect and kept going.

By the time he got to the steps of the porte cochere, he was having second thoughts about going into the palace. The crush of unfamiliar faces in the entry hall only exacerbated his growing unease. He stopped beneath the balcony. "I'm not ready to be in the presence of so many people," he murmured. While trying to decide what to do, he heard a child's plaintive squeal rise above the babble, and before he could find the source, a mature toddler emerged from the press and came running toward him. The child was leading a group holding up streamers and waving small national flags attached to dowels. Adam heard tinkling and felt a small boy bump into his thigh. The child would have fallen if Adam hadn't reached out to steady him. The toddler wriggled his nose before regaining his balance and running outside with his troupe. Several pairs of little feet wearing slippers with silver bells hanging off curly toes trailed along behind. Adam shook his head and saw the squealing child running across a raised dais and into the waiting arms of a woman.

Feeling out of place and not sure what he should do, he noticed that the great continental carpet had been replaced by crates taken from the wagons. People were milling about in small groups or standing alone examining his uncle's gifts. He saw his uncle talking with a group of adults across the room. They were standing in front of a raised dais, and Adam caught a glimpse of his host for the first time.

Sahibzada Muhammad Mardan sat on a throne sharing the dais with his children, wives, and concubines. He might have been facing the entryway and a roomful of neighboring kings and queens, but his pinched eyes were on a slipper tapping a leather hassock. His glance at a veiled wife was not having the desired effect. The distressed child in her arms refused to be comforted and was becoming more agitated with each step the young Japanese guest took in their direction. Sahibzada dearly wished he could send them back to the harem without creating an even bigger fuss. The wives in chairs knew enough to pretend not to notice and envied the lessor wives lounging nearby on oversized multicolored pillows. Several of these women held children who were flipping through illustrated children's books.

The older children seated on the carpet had stopped taking turns spinning a globe and stared at the stranger bearing a fearsome *wakizashi*. Their mothers' stern eyes tracked Munenori's path to the hiccupping child. This was the first time they too had seen a Japanese person up close. Munenori's straight black hair, beautiful facial features, and self-confidence became inconsequential once they saw the pattern on his blue silk kimono. The women, who knew about these things, were aware that Munenori's golden cranes standing in a rice paddy could only mean one thing. Their Japanese guest was a prince. "He moves like a cat," a young wife murmured in Hindi. The wives within hearing had moved beyond such trivial observations. An older wife summed up their sentiments with a snort. "I prefer to sleep with a cat whose claws are not razor sharp! You can have him!"

Munenori had been sitting with a group of children and young adults going through the contents of a chest filled with toys and games. Opening a deck of cards, he performed a few of the magic tricks Mike had taught him. Munenori's tricks had progressed to the point where he was making coins and small objects disappear off a cushion. An overconfident three-year-old approached the outsider, placed his prized ruby sarpech on the cushion, and dared Munenori to make an object so big go away. Munenori waved a finger over the clasp indicating the boy should take it back. Not believing Munenori could make it disappear, the child pointed at the object. Taking exception to the child's imperious manner, Munenori waved his hand again. The second the sarpech vanished, the child ran howling to his mother.

Following the child to the dais, Munenori rubbed his hands together in front of the huffing boy and closed his fists, "Sentaku," he said ("Choose"). The petulant boy grudgingly pointed at Munenori's right hand. A moment later, his eyes grew big, and he snatched his cherished ruby.

The child's joy was short-lived. The tensions Munenori's antics and sword aroused around the dais were about to be overshadowed. The spoiled child and his mother were the last to see another armed stranger crossing the hall, and this one was coming their way too.

Adam's attire and apparent aloofness sent a ripple of fear through all who saw him and caused a palpable decline in the festive atmosphere. The other mothers on the dais felt the uneasiness spreading through the hall. They sat up straighter, hushed the children, and watched Adam approach.

Asima, Vinamra, Qui Li, and Willard stopped listening to Earl. They'd seen Sahibzada stiffen and stare over their shoulders. They turned in time to see a handsome young man of medium build walking past crates stenciled in German script. The hall grew quiet, and much to the relief of those closest to the erect figure, saw him glance at the rifles with no interest. The disquiet he created gave Adam more to think about than temple treasures, firearms, and children with toe bells. Up until he realized he'd become the center of attention, he'd been forcing himself to show up in order to avoid embarrassing his uncle and offending his host.

Now halfway across the hall, he saw Sahibzada staring at him too. Thinking it might be appropriate to do so, Adam removed his hat, bowed, and twirled a hand, not knowing he'd just exposed a crown of curly auburn locks plastered to his skull. Raising his eyes to his host, he received a solemn wink in front of an audience who had no idea what to make of the peculiar young man bowing with respect before the palace's nawab.

He stumbled into Asima coming to a stop beside Earl. "Excuse me. Uncle."

"Nephew," Earl sniffed, giving Adam's sweat stains a quick glance. "Nice of you to join us. How are you?"

"A little worse for wear, but I'll be okay. I could use a glass of water."

"Ahem," Earl answered while motioning to Munenori, who got the drift and went off to satisfy Adam's request. "He'll be right back with your drink. I want you to meet the man you just bumped into. Asima Jnanda."

Adam took Asima's outstretched hand and felt a current spreading up his arm. The current passed through everything between his hand and his eyes before crossing the distance between him and the most penetrating gaze he had ever seen. Feeling his hold on reality being stretched to the limit, he could not be sure if a part of his sentience was fusing with what he saw residing behind Asima's dark pupils. Released from the grip, Adam heard the last part of Earl's second introduction, ". . . Vinamra Adami."

"Ahh," Adam said, feeling numb and finding it difficult to concentrate on Vinamra's lips.

"You exhibit the behaviors common to acolytes who have returned to the present after experiencing their first meditative state and are still under the influence of a profound encounter."

"So it would appear," Earl said interrupting Vinamra, who was about to tell Asima to give the young man a chance to recover before pressing him any further. Earl cleared his throat. "Please greet our host. Sahibzada Mardan, this is my nephew, Adam Yeaton."

Adam turned and bowed to the man clothed in simple robes. With the exception of a plumed silver aigrette set with cat's eyes pinned to his wheat-colored turban, his host wore no other jewelry. Sahibzada held up his hand and cut off Adam's attempt to apologize for his appearance. "You've been outside all morning and into the afternoon. There's time enough for you to tell us the reason you dressed this way, where you have been, and what happened while you were there."

Adam had no idea how the glass got in his hand. He drank all the water while gazing into a pair of hazel eyes identical to his own. He became aware of a clean-shaven face whose appealing self-confidence helped steady him. The man's sculpted temples suggested that the turban covered a high cranium. Adam felt the presence of a broad intellect residing behind a pair of eyes that revealed an unguarded inkling of concern. He watched Sahibzada rise from his seat, step down from the dais, shake his hand, and lay an arm across his shoulders. He half expected his host to scold him for leaving the palace without an escort. Instead, to his astonishment and that of everyone else, Sahibzada released his hand and embraced him. "You must be hungry. Food has been prepared, and we are about to go the dining hall for dinner. Be my guest and sit with me while we eat." Adam glanced at his uncle and then gave himself over to a man whose manners soothed him.

Munenori moved away from the dais and spoke within hearing of the startled child. "Kara wa watashi ni kidzukimasendeshita" ("Adam did not notice me"). He lowered his eyes to the empty glass and could not fathom how it got there.

The women next to Tom lost interest in learning how to operate a treadle sewing machine and turned to follow their host. Colton stared at Adam from across the room. Forgotten for the moment was a guest's son who set aside the book on venomous creatures they'd been discussing.

Murmurs had turned into conversations by the time Sahibzada steered the procession to the dining hall. His gesture toward Adam had its desired effect, and the celebration was back in full swing.

The hall's glittering chandeliers, opulent ceiling, fabric walls, and matching furnishings eclipsed any Adam had ever seen in America. Entourage in tow, Adam followed Sahibzada to the middle of a U-shaped table whose wings extended back to the entrance. Earl, the two yogis, the kings, and their most favored wives spread out and took their places in the reserved seating. Sixty diners faced each other over narrow tables laden with meat and vegetable dishes running down the center of a serving aisle. Liveried male and female servants appeared and attended to the menu choices of each guest. Adam sat in the place of honor on Sahibzada's right and received every courtesy. His awareness increased with each serving of oven-cooked tandoori he consumed. *Aha*, he thought, watching a servant remove a plate, *Sahibzada knew I would not be listening to all he's telling me until I've eaten, so he's engaging me in light conversation and including me in the discussions taking place with the other guests.*

Calmed by the reassuring voice at his side, Adam half listened to his host's descriptions of the diners. Warming to Sahibzada's improvisations on what the people at the other ends of the table might be saying to one another, Adam became increasingly aware of the honor being bestowed upon him. Sahibzada spared no one, including his wives, children, Earl, or the other guests. *Hmm,* Adam mused, *he's doing more than leading me through subjects of little or no importance. He's giving me a glimpse of the man behind the title.*

Adam continued to eat long after his appetite was satisfied. He was in no hurry to deprive his palate of the delicious flavors produced by the lamb, chicken, fish, and prawn tikka served on small mounds of turmeric-laced basmati. The lamb seeka kebabs served with an Indian tzatziki called *raita* and eaten with maroo flatbread made him wonder if Sahibzada's ancestors may have shared the same meal with Phoenicians on patios overlooking the Mediterranean. By the time Adam tasted the honey-mustard dressing on the palak salad, his equilibrium had returned. Wishing to continue savoring the flavors in his mouth, he refused Sahibzada's offer of coffee and dessert. Adam saw the lips curl, not knowing that Sahibzada had just locked away another favorable impression of his guest. Watching a servant remove the last plate from the table, Adam thanked Sahibzada. "You've been patient with me. I'm ready to answer any questions you may have about what I did today."

Sahibzada glanced at Adam's Bowie and stood. "I have a feeling the story you have to tell would best be recounted with a smaller audience. I will listen to you in the presence of your uncle and our learned friends. We will hear what you have to tell us after we excuse ourselves from the table and see the guests out the door. I have just the place."

Adam watched Sahibzada walk the length of the table, have a pleasant word here and there, whisper into the ears of the three he wanted to hear Adam's tale, and brought the dinner to a hospitable close.

Soon after Sahibzada excused himself to say his goodbyes, Adam returned to his rooms, bathed, slept for over an hour, changed, and descended the marble stairs in a much better frame of mind. Walking among servants sorting out the containers, he stood aside as they hauled away the empties and carted Earl's gifts to rooms where they would be stored or used. He noticed several servants taking the time to flip through Dickens's illustrated *A Christmas Carol*, *Tom Thumb's Picture Alphabet*, back issues of *Godey's Lady's Book*, Cousin Sarah's *Stories for Children*, and Lewis Carroll's version of *Aesop's Fables* with illustrations by the venerable John Tenniel. "This may be the first time you have seen images from another culture," he said over the shoulder of a man who didn't understand a word he said. After receiving a confused grunt, Adam walked off to join his uncle and the two yogis. They happened to be reviewing a copy of *Episodes of Insect Life* by Acheta Domestica, or "House Cricket," the nom de plume of L.M. Budgen, a writer whose work the publishers would have rejected had they known the author was a woman.

Adam glanced up as the palace major-domo appeared from a side hall. The man approached, bowed, and gestured, "Is traaph se aao" ("Come this way").

Their guide led the group down a corridor they hadn't seen before and asked them to stop beside a wide door. Inserting a large brass key, he released the lock, opened the door, and ushered them into a room that exceeded their expectations. "Mere newaabon ka garbhagrh" ("My nawab's inner sanctum"). The major-domo stood aside as the spellbound guests gave themselves over to the splendor surrounding them. He watched them disperse into a large drawing room whose north-facing wall opened onto a fountained courtyard. He lingered long enough to see them gravitate to the sculptures, oil paintings, and bookcases filled with ancient and modern tomes. Then, unnoticed, he bowed and closed the door behind him on the way out.

Children's laughter rose over the tall wall. "The sounds they produce are among the most pleasing in nature," Vinamra murmured while a hand caressed the face of a 200-year-old sculpture- a life-sized bronze of Sonan Gyatso, the first Dalai Lama.

Earl replied with an absent nod as he stood near a bookcase. He ran a hand along the spines and tapped the volumes he had given Sahibzada.

Adam bent over a glass case and tried to imagine who the figures might be in the golden sculpture. Had he been able to read the Aramaic inscription carved into the plinth he would have been astounded. The sixth-century Persian archer who rode with a teamster on a chariot drawn by three horses was a distant relative of his host.

Asima's mind was elsewhere. He was lost in thought before a painting of Lord Vishnu, King of the Cosmos. The seated Blue King was addressing Black Yama, the Hindi god of Death.

Servants carrying trays and pushing a wheeled service fitted with plates, cups, silver, and napkins interrupted their musings. Veiled maidens laid out serving dishes bearing folded *lobongo latika, pati shapta crepes*, deep-fried *shor bhaja,* and *khur kadam* pastries. They left behind a caddy laden with steaming pots of coffee and aromatic teas. Asima and Vinamra led the way to ample helpings of the desserts. Adam and his uncle exchanged amused glances over their coffees. "Must be tea time," Adam said quietly.

The group moved to a circle of chairs and couches. Asima and Vinamra sat on a leather couch and set their tea and dessert plates on a low table in front of them. Earl sat across from them in the middle of another couch. Adam sat in a chair at one end of the sandalwood table. Sahibzada arrived and took the seat facing Adam. The afternoon sun lit the back of the courtyard. The soft reflection would give the cooler drawing room natural light for a while yet.

Adam knew what they expected of him, so he began by telling of his experiences in Kolkata. He took his time, leaving nothing out, and noted how his words affected his listeners. During the explanation of how he had felt on the wharf, Sahibzada lowered his eyelids, sat a little straighter, and folded his hands in his lap. Several times during Adam's description of his dream, he saw his uncle watching the yogis. Asima pursed his lips, stared off into space, and drew little circles on his cushion with an index finger. Vinamra gazed at the young man with heartfelt understanding. Adam told of his experiences in the shrine and apologized for not having recovered by the time he returned to the palace.

Earl got up, poured glasses of water, and set them on coasters. Everyone took the opportunity to digest what Adam had said thus far. Sahibzada thanked Earl, then took a sip. "Has anything like this happened to your nephew before?"

"No," Earl replied and shifted his eyes back to Adam.

"Most unusual," Sahibzada said, eyeing the yogis.

Asima cleared his throat and thought about what Adam had said in the context of how he spent most of his time exploring the relationships between past, current, and future selves. Hearing Adam's descriptions of what had taken place in his rooms and within Mohini's temple came as no surprise. He saw Vinamra raise a hand before he could speak, checked himself, and waited to hear what his friend had to say.

Vinamra fluttered a hand at Adam. "You've had time to think about what happened. Do you still feel you were once the young prince?"

"Yes, as fantastic as it sounds," Adam responded. "I felt it most strongly coming out of my dream. I became aware that I could possibly repeat the prince's suffering and felt despair. I relived the anguish of the past over again and felt I could be destined to have a sorrowful life. It was painful to be so close to her, only to see her fade away as I awoke."

Sal trees beyond the courtyard filtered the late afternoon light, causing shadows to spread into the room. Children's laughter had passed from hearing. Peacock calls became infrequent. Birdsongs ceased altogether. The fountain seemed to quiet. Servants appeared, lit corner lamps, and removed used cups and dishes. They left behind fresh coffee and tea.

Vinamra poured a cup of coffee for Adam and pointed at a khur kadam. "Please," Adam said, and Vinamra placed the food and drink within reach. "Thanks. Buddha said we spend a large portion of our lives in states of unnecessary suffering. I understand what he meant. Even so, I still feel 'tis better to have loved and lost than to have never loved at all."

Vinamra lowered his eyelids to mere slits. Asima cleared his throat again and studied the grain pattern in the tabletop. Earl continued to regard his nephew with an expectant expression. Sahibzada rubbed the stubble forming on his jawline, and waited with the others for the young man to resume his story.

Adam flipped a hand. "I know in my heart of hearts, our spirits will meet again. Our suffering has only served to confirm our attraction for one another." His gesture had exposed the punctures in his palm.

Earl sat up with the others and told Adam to rest his hand on the table. Earl studied the inflammation, and before he could ask, Adam said, "There has been no change in the past four hours." Vinamra wanted to know if they hurt. "A bit."

Sahibzada leaned back, drew a finger across his lips, and glanced at each of his guests.

"You have had quite the twenty-four hours," Asima said. "Few of us ever become acquainted with our karma by observing our past selves. I have chosen to live this long because I want to visit my past selves as many times as possible in this life. Our present selves are the link to our past and future karma, so it is important we understand how we conducted ourselves in previous lives. You have been through a window into your past few can achieve in multiple lifetimes. Use the knowledge you have gained to improve your understanding of who you are." That said, he laid a hand over Adam's forearm and felt his pulse with three fingers. Asima closed his eyes and listened to the murmuring spirit residing in Adam's being.

Adam closed his eyes and willed himself to remain calm.

Asima sat back a minute or two later. "You have a pure heart. You strive to interpret your experiences, are willing to learn how to do this, accept that you may never know everything, and are receptive to gaining the insights contained therein. You are shrewd enough to know these traits will influence the degree to which you mature in this life. You have an intuitive grasp of the three most important *pramanas*: *pratyaksa* (perception), *arumana* (inference), and *upamana* (analogical comparisons)." He turned to Vinamra. "Is it safe to say Adam is well on his way to attaining the enlightenment described in the Eightfold Path?"

Vinamra rubbed his forehead before answering and directed his reply to Adam, who by then was under the impression that the spirits of these two men could pass through his eyes and communicate directly with the consciousness residing in his being. "You exemplify many of the concepts contained in the

Eightfold Path," Vinamra said, peering at Adam. The round man hitched himself into a more comfortable position. "You do not subscribe to the belief that all things in life have an unsatisfactory basis though, do you?"

"No," Adam heard himself say, recognizing the sense of detachment he felt on the wharf. "I do not. I'm responsible for how I feel about my existence at any given time. Circumstances play a major role in how I perceive my experiences, but ultimately, I'm the final arbiter of my feelings. I try to address the sources of unsatisfactory feelings in my life and if possible change the behaviors engendering them. I know I will never be completely satisfied. I accept it as a condition of residing in a human body, a body whose mind is often preoccupied with the concept of time. We humans have decided that time is the means by which we measure our actions. The measure only has meaning if it is finite. So much of how we feel about who we are is dependent on our interpretation of how we spend our time. I believe my spirit is free of time constraints, and if I could remember to practice an awareness of this freedom, I would be less driven to get things done and more likely to find satisfaction in whatever I accomplish."

Asima raised an eyebrow at Vinamra and then directed a question to Adam. "Do you believe in the permanence of a soul or spirit?"

"I believe each individual has a spirit, or, for lack of a better word, a soul. They mean the same to me. I have no idea how long my spirit will exist. I do know I have a duty to nourish it. Buddha and Vishnu offer many insights into how I can conduct myself to that end."

Adam paused. "I have never felt more alert than I am now." He turned to face Asima. "I may be foolish, but I want to experience a wide range of human interactions and feelings each time I inhabit a body."

"You know the impermanence of your lifespan could cause it to become cluttered with cravings, desires, and useless acquisitions?" Vinamra asked.

"Yes, I know. Being receptive to so much stimulation may inhibit the path to a truer understanding of others and me. I suppose a part of being continuously reborn may have to do with not having learned how to better conduct myself each time around." He reached for his cup and chose to have a drink of water instead. His stomach felt hollow, yet he had no interest in coffee or desert.

"I want to be continuously reborn. Let's say I die and go to a place where I am to face an all-powerful god, if one exists. We review how I have conducted myself, and I prove to have attained an acceptable level of consciousness. I'm free to choose what will become of my spirit. The choices may include a void free of consciousness, for example, or a spirit world full of consciousness embracing all religions, or I could choose to become a sentient being on a far-off planet too distant to comprehend, inhabited by fantastic creatures. I would choose to be sent back to Earth as a human. I cannot conceive of any place in the Milky Way more exquisite than the planet my spirit calls home." Asima exchanged an understanding nod with Vinamra and glanced at Earl, whose flat stare revealed nothing of what he was thinking. Sahibzada sat and listened.

Vinamra drank and waved his empty cup at Adam. "You could enter a state free of all earthly passions, desires, unfulfilled dreams, and disappointing outcomes by purging all bodily constraints."

"Yes, but I've no wish to experience enlightenment and give myself up to an all-encompassing Nirvana if it means abandoning my spirit. I admit to finding this flawed world unbearably disturbing more often than I would wish. I try to see the flaws for what they are—undesirable aspects of what I love about the tactile and cerebral sensations associated with being sentient.

"I believe there are millions of worlds in conflict with each other, where goodness and evil exist side by contentious side. I could spend the rest of my life puzzling over why such states exist and be no closer than I am now to knowing the answer."

Adam thought of the women in Ah Toy's brothel and squinted. "No, Vinamra, I am not a masochist, even though I'm liable to feel I am on the days I subject myself to repairing the damage my fellow humans inflict on the innocent.

"I'm grateful for my existence. I believe I have a reincarnating spirit that can withstand inevitable suffering and reach fulfilling heights of joyous rapture over and over again. Like you, but nowhere near to the degree you do, Vinamra, I venerate Buddha and seek to live in the grace of his teachings.

"Asima. I believe the deities you call gods are spirits that inhabit the ethers, and once in a while they reveal themselves to us in recognizable forms.

"I'm pantheistic. I think everything is God, from the core of the Earth to the most distant stars and everything in between. I'm attracted to Zen Buddhists who, I am given to understand, revere all that exists equally. The Chinese Shaolin monks exhibit a branch of Buddhism I find appealing. Their practices are the most compatible with my views on the subject of religion.

"I believe our sentience, although confined to the present, is attached to a greater whole. With the exception of our consciousness, and quite possibly that too, we could be part of an infinite mosaic held together by a unified continuum whose algorithms for time and space a person like Willard will dissect and define."

Sahibzada made an unintelligible utterance and readjusted himself at the mention of algorithms. Lapsing back into silence, he regarded Adam with an intensity the young man hadn't seen in his host until then.

Feeling fatigued, Adam wrapped up his thoughts. "I believe existence stretches back into the past and forward into the future. Everything is connected. What occurs in one place has an influence on what occurs elsewhere. I think the Milky Way is a living organism. The proofs are beyond my ken, but I would wager that Willard, or a person like him, will prove me correct by finding a replicating pattern in all of nature. This, of course, will lead the more inquisitive among us to scientifically prove what you and other yogis hear each time you enter the highest states of consciousness: the pulse of the universe."

Sahibzada was about to speak and stopped. Adam had pulled the shrine's stunning Navaratna out of a pant pocket and was offering it to him. "I believe this is yours, Sahibzada."

Sahibzada sat up and glanced at the Navaratna resting beside Adam's punctures, then shifted his eyes to the flawless gems. *I will never forget this moment for as long as I live or how much these people have come to mean to me. This young man and his uncle are the only Westerners who have the courage to provide us nawabs with the means to rid ourselves of the pestilent British and their opium trains.* He looked into Adam's hazel eyes. *These too I will recall the first time my new rifle's crosshairs come to rest on a British officer's black heart.*

He pointed at the Navaratna. "The nine stones in this pendant are exceptional. They pay homage to the planets they represent. This is a sacred object to which its intended recipient will be forever drawn." He closed Adam's hand over the Navaratna and squeezed. "Yes, the treasure is on my land, and I can claim it, but I will not. I have enough wealth. There are things in life more important than treasure. The time I spend with you and my friends is worth more to me than what you found in Mohini's temple. Keep it. You are the rightful owner of this medallion, including the contents of the shrine. Go find the woman to whom you have dedicated this Navaratna, and give it to her."

CHAPTER 23

Off the Coast of South Africa, 7 June, daybreak

The anemic mist parted enough to reveal an empty space on the fore royal yard where the frigate bird usually roosted for the night. The bird had been with them since they'd passed through Ceylon's Palk Strait the previous week.

"Ahh," Mike Stanley said from his perch above the deserted yard. "He's gone. Why do you suppose he's flown away?"

"Who knows? Last time I saw him was yesterday afternoon. He was diving for herring off the starboard bow." Maynard grinned. "Cheer up. The bird had good reason to fly the coop! Probably knows about the coming changes in temperatures and wind directions. He'll be miles away to the north of us by now in search of sunny skies, warm temperatures, and willin' hens!"

Mike wasn't ready to shake off his sober mood just yet. "He paid me a visit after you went to supper. Glided right in and flew beside me for the longest time. Had the feeling he was trying to tell me somethin' before he sheared off and became a speck in the late-afternoon sun."

They were the only ones aboard who were out of the dense fog keeping pace with them as they cruised over the Southern Indian Ocean. Much to the dismay of the sail master, the fog had begun appearing late in the middle watch a day out of Mozambique Channel. The impenetrable surface layer the *Bride* shared with the steady breeze would not be with them much longer. The southerlies would soon be giving way to cooler westerlies blowing across the Cape of Good Hope.

No moon illuminated rocky shores or reflected off rolling crests. Absent were any visual references to mark their progress. Several miles southwest of their current heading, the arc of the starry sky merged with the dark mountainous tip of the African continent. The stars on the eastern horizon were about to give way to another shrouded dawn.

A week or so earlier, the warm, humid air flowing out of India had delivered them to the strong south easterlies coursing out of the Arabian Sea, opening the way for clear twenty-four-hour sailing. The arid winds produced perfect sailing conditions and enabled Earl to justify leaving all of the *Bride*'s canvas out for days on end. The same airs that had carried her to South Africa now coursed over cooler ocean currents rising up from Antarctica. Mixing the warm southerlies with the cool humid air produced a thick surface fog that could last for hours.

Although the watchers seated on the crosstrees often felt as if they were riding on a magic carpet, they were there to keep an eye out for another set of masts heading toward them through the murk. The ship and fog were traveling at the same speed and attracted no more interest than they gave to the ever-present pull of gravity. Below them, the watch crew had assembled beneath dripping rigging. The men were in the early stages of preparing to add more sail.

Two bells of the morning watch rang out from the foc'sl.

Earl sat beneath a swaying lantern in the wheelhouse with the master and his first mate. The three were discussing how best to navigate their way around the Cape, whose approaches they'd be entering in the next several hours. Ryan sat beside Earl and kept his mouth shut. He'd been listening to Earl describe the route he wished to take around the treacherous reefs, and didn't like his captain's plan any more than James did.

Oblivious to what was taking place a short distance away, Willard sat in a stuffed leather chair with a book. His reading lamp pushed away the morning chill and added a homey glow to the suite's blond woods. A hot cup of coffee and a muffin were on a side table. Placing slippered feet on a hassock, he adjusted the robe over his ankles and opened a book James had picked up while strolling through an outdoor market in Kolkata. "The bookseller tossed this anthology in without charge," James had said as he handed it over. "He didn't think much of the contributors and called them 'spasmodic poets.'" Taking a bite of muffin and a sip, Willard licked a finger and flipped a page. A poem's cadence brought to mind the opening chords of "Pachelbel's Canon." Reading along, he tried to time the poem's beat with the canon's notes. Anyone passing by would only hear the rhythmic creak of the mizzen trunk and the sluice of water splashing the hull. They'd never know that on the other side of the door, the cabin's occupant was basking in a lighthearted wall of sound.

After a while he finished his coffee and put the book aside. The ship's motion had started to change and he decided to get on with his day. He went off to use the head reciting a stanza that appealed to him.

I would I could adopt your will,
See with your eyes, and set my heart
Beating by yours, and drink my fill
At your soul's springs—your part my part
In life, for good and ill . . .

Willard chose to have breakfast instead of paying a visit to the wheelhouse so he missed the abrasives James was about to heap on the captain.

Up in the wheelhouse, James was having difficulty keeping his mounting frustrations in check. Earl's reckless sailing practices were piling up and James had reached the upper limits of his patience. Earl's plan to race headlong through the nastiest offshore waters on earth were about to get a strong rebuke from the *Bride*'s sail master. He was primed for a confrontation. They had been getting along fine until Earl decided to sail all night under full canvas. His refusal to explain why had added fuel to what James intended to say if the issue ever came to a boil. There was a reason he hadn't blown his top already: the scary practice was working. They hadn't seen any vessels since clearing the Indian coast and had been able to maintain a steady eighteen knots around the clock. At times the sustained breezes brought her up to twenty knots for most of the day. He forced himself to control his misgivings so long as the north westerlies blew from the starboard quarter day and night. The only concession James managed to squeeze out of the captain was reefing the studding and stays'ls at night. They had been flying over the ocean this way for the last ten days.

There had been no alarming periods in the predawn hours until three days ago. Since then streams of surface-level fog accompanied the prevailing winds in the early hours. James hated sailing blind and said so. He ground his teeth every time Earl countered by saying, "I know how you feel. It is unpleasant not being able to see the water or the upper masts, but the men in the tops are in the clear, so we're not really sailing blind." Earl further infuriated his sail master by refusing to slow down and sail under reduced canvas during the morning watch. Dawn found them in the wheelhouse with Earl adding insult to James's injured self-esteem. The captain was showing his senior officers how he planned to save a day's sailing by passing *over* the Cape's reefs at high tide!

On this day, as he had done the previous day, James made sure his two best sentinels were above the fog at daybreak. The fog usually burned off shortly after the sun came up—a time prudent mariners chose to add more sail. He did not care to know how the two passed the time or how much they had to say, but he cared a great deal about how much attention they gave to what was in the ship's path.

An hour earlier, after they came on watch and climbed aloft, Maynard returned to a topic he and Mike had been discussing off and on since they'd left Kolkata. "Asima told Earl there are whole galaxies out in the universe," he said, pointing at the fading band of the Milky Way.

"Never would've guessed," Mike said, turning his eyes heavenward and adjusting his backside on the thick crosspiece.

"Asima says the Milky Way is just one of millions scattered throughout Creation. Capt'n Earl shook his head on that one. He said the best Western astronomers hadn't twigged on the idea." Maynard lowered his gaze and peered forward a little more closely. "Earth has a moon spinning around it, just like our sun has Earth and a bunch of planets doing the same thing. Asima says what we call stars are whole clusters of suns with millions of planets spinning around them. They are just too far away for us to tell them apart."

Mike shook his head. "I guess. The more I'm told, the less I think I'll ever know."

"Asima says many of those planets have creatures on 'em like us. Others have creatures unlike us—more primitive—and others so advanced they've traveled through space and visited us. Can you believe it?" Maynard shifted his eyes and tilted his head, hoping to get a fix on what he thought he'd seen.

Unnoticed by Maynard, Mike's doubtful expression turned to dismay. "I don't know what to believe anymore," the boy said before noticing the space on the fore royal yard and commenting on the frigate bird's absence.

Maynard lost interest in the whereabouts of frigate birds and tried to find what he thought he'd seen while they were discussing what might or might not be in outer space. He and Mike held on as the bow dipped into a large trough, rolled to port, and swung them back on an even keel once again. The rollers were becoming less predictable and more susceptible to the influences of intersecting currents. No longer comfortable sitting, they got to their feet and tried to identify what Maynard thought he'd seen in the growing light.

Morning broke, and the sun's horizontal rays spread over the horizon. The thinning fog turned into a giant prism, infusing the mast with a translucent violet hue. Blue, green, and yellow shadings descended to the forecastle's pinkish beak. The rainbow disappeared as soon as the bow poked through the dispersing fog.

Miles away off the starboard quarter, golden cliffs beckoned unwary mariners. Mike filled the pause with a barely audible revelation whose content Maynard nearly missed.

Maynard was only half listening. He was far more interested in peering through the streaming mist for whatever it was he had glimpsed.

"As a kid, I remember being confused by how unfamiliar the colors were," Mike said. Immersed in how the sun's rays amplified the violet hues, his gaze turned inward for a moment. "I thought I was in an unfamiliar body when I was little," he murmured, "especially since the colors I thought I was used to seeing started at violet."

Maynard gave Mike a quizzical frown and placed a hand on the boy, silencing him. Mike would have quieted anyway. He turned at the touch and was startled to see Maynard's dazzling blue eyes turning violet in the filtered light. Maynard was too preoccupied to notice Mike's expression. "Hold on,

I had a feeling this spell was too good to last. Hand me the signals telescope you've got strapped over your shoulder, and stand in front of the mast."

Maynard was raising the telescope at about the time Adam said good morning to the men in the wheelhouse. His sea sense had noticed the changes in the ship's motion and woke him. He was carrying a covered tray bearing several mugs of strong coffee and a basket of hot raisin muffins. "I saw the water on the way up here. Fog's lifting."

James rolled the chart while Adam waited to set the tray down. It was light enough to see by, so Ryan turned out the lamps. They were chatting and taking bites between sips when Maynard's hail came from aloft.

"Deck, there! Three sets of sails!"

James spilled coffee into his beard and, with a curse, was the first outside. "Where away?" he asked, giving Earl a withering I-told-you-so look.

Earl just raised an eyebrow and leaned on the doorjamb. He finished his muffin and topped it off with the last of his coffee.

"Dead ahead, a thousand yards, three vessels converging!" came Maynard's delayed response. "Two on a cripple!"

James made for the deckhouse stairs and turned to Adam. "Take a pair of binoculars, and go see what's out there!"

Adam was on his way to the mainmast shrouds when he heard Maynard's next call. "Deck, there, cannon fire!"

James whirled at the top of the stairs and glared at Earl with a fierce scowl.

Earl squinted up at his antagonist. "James, I must say, you have remarkable agility for someone shaped like an acorn!"

Keeping an eye on James, Earl used a different tone with Ryan. "Call all hands. Belay the order to set more sail. Man the clews, sheets, and braces. Brail up the courses and lower tops'ls." He turned and pinned Ryan under a hard stare. "Keep going forward once you relay the message to the bosuns. Have the gun crew prepare to engage. I'm going to make a notation in the log, and James will be giving orders to your bosuns by the time I join him at the rail."

The rumble of cannon fire caused confusion among the milling watch crew. The off-watch crew had heard the cannons too. They came on deck in time to hear Ryan passing orders to the bosuns on his way forward. The experienced men raised their eyes toward the pennant and saw sails emerging in the daylight spreading across the sea.

Less than a minute later, the *Bride*'s golden globe led her hull out of the haze, while high above her tan summer-weight canvas glistened against the receding fog bank.

Adam climbed into the crosstrees and found the two observers standing against the mast. Mike stood with his back to the topmast gripping a halyard, the thick end of a telescope resting on his shoulder. Maynard was staring through the other end with one arm clamped around the trunk. "Easy, easy, gotcha!" Maynard said between his teeth as they crested another roller. "Thank you, Mike. We can get a little more comfortable now. Good morning, Adam," he said, hooking an elbow around a futtock shroud. "The three-masted schooner under attack is the Helene out of Bremen. The two brigs harassing her are unknown to me. They have no flags or names. The men on the quarterdeck are white. British built. New. Beautiful and expensive."

They watched as the *Helene* and one of the brigs began turning in circles in an effort to avoid exposing their unprotected sterns. Maynard pointed at a swaying spar. "I think the Helene was replacing a main t'gallant yard before the attack. The smaller two-masted brig is holding off for now. It'll attack after it has the wind gauge and its partner out of the line of fire."

"Keep your eye on 'em," Adam said and grabbed a weather stay. He turned to Mike. "Happy birthday."

Mike brightened. "Thank you, I feel different." He scratched the fuzz on his chin. "Does this mean I'm an adult now?"

Adam laughed despite the danger they faced and said the first thing that came to mind on his way down, "Half human!"

Earl and James listened to Adam's report while staring through telescopes. The sullen boom of cannon fire followed the darting red and yellow flames leaping out of the combatant's ports. They watched holes appear in the *Helene*'s fore course. The holes became rents that turned the sail into tattered sheets.

The attacking brig had sustained damage to her lee bulkhead. Two of the ten cannons mounted on deck were lying on their sides. The wash leaking through the scuppers carried a red stain, suggesting the ship itself was bleeding.

"We'll be within shooting range in a couple of minutes. What do you want to do now?" James asked, lowering the glass. He was burning inside to mention what could have happened had they plowed into the *Helene* an hour earlier while she was making repairs in the fog. Cannon fire continued to rise over the sounds of the thumping canvas, shifting winds, and hissing surge.

Willard sat alone in the salon watching Ming and his helpers put out the cooking fires and secure loose items. Having no interest in observing conflict, he finished eating his breakfast beside a sunny porthole and listened to Tchaikovsky's *1812 Overture*. His imagination was finding it impossible to find a pattern in the cannon fire and could not transpose the blasts into the piece's percussive salvos. Too random, he decided, waving his fork to the tune and accenting each exchange with a flick of the wrist. Pushing the plate aside, he smiled to a pleasing diversion.

"Zaoshang hao iaoshi," Qui Li said. ("Good morning, teacher.") The boy took a seat opposite Willard and laid a worn deck of cards beside the cribbage board he placed between them.

The men working the *Bride* knew they too would soon be in range of the brigs' cannons. "We have friends aboard the Helene," Earl said, gripping the rail a little tighter and dropping with the stern. "You've met Karl Nimitz, her captain. We're going to prevent those other vessels from doing any more damage to her," he added, lifting a hand to Ryan, who nodded in acknowledgment. Ryan was standing with Tom and the gun crew by the open foc'sl doors. Earl waved and pointed to the larboard side. Tom and his men started shoving loads into the port cannons. "We'll take the outrider first and give Captain Nimitz a hand with the other one later. Keep the wind gauge. We'll engage with the port-side pieces first," he said pointing at the row of enemy cannons being run out.

"Aye, aye, Captain," James said, noticing how the water's brassy sheen was giving way to sparkling silver crests and not liking how fast they were closing the distance between the ships.

"What do we do now?" Mike asked Maynard, a part of him wanting to know what the odds were on living through his sixteenth birthday.

"We stay here. We're going to be needed," Maynard said, lifting his chin at the flaming tongues erupting from the smaller brig. Holes appeared in the fore and main upper topsails. Loud bangs thumped against the *Bride's* hull, and a snapping backstay sliced Danny Rickles in half. "Let's make ourselves useful," Maynard said, pointing at the ripping tops'l. "Come on, let's get the torn rag off her."

The young men in the crosstrees may not have seen what happened to Danny, but Earl and Adam did. They hurried down the aft stairs and nearly fell coming to a stop among loose entrails. Earl ran to a locker and pulled out a length of rope with a section of sailcloth. "Steady on, Adam!" he exclaimed. Adam was turning in circles and jabbering about the things Danny would never get to do. "I share your pain! We can talk about it later! There's work to be done! Here, put your foot on this corner and help me roll Danny's shoulders onto the cloth. You'll feel better if you stay busy. There, now grab his legs and I'll take what's left of his midsection." Adam lent a hand, and they trussed up Danny's corpse. They placed the wet bundle beside the deckhouse. Straightening up, Earl put bloody hands on Adam's shoulders. "How're you doing?"

"I'm good now. Thanks. I'll open the medical room and prepare the table. A clean shirt will have to wait."

"That's better. I'll drop by the salon. See you in a bit."

James waved an agitated finger over his head at the helmsman and clenched his fist. The ports were parallel with the other vessel. "Fire at will, boys," he said, willing his eyes to stare past Danny's leaking bundle.

Blood spattering a hand caused his shoulders to slump and his head to droop. *Now what?* Forcing himself to respond, he glanced up and saw the pulverized remains of Ernold Corson's upended body swaying in the tangled lines.

Having learned how loud it could get in the covered area, the men tied strips of padded cloth around their heads to protect their ears. "We look like a bunch of pirates," Charlie shouted to Tom from the bottom of the stairs while passing a powder canister. Hopley came out of the magazine with an exploding shell. "What'd you say?"

The thunder of waves pounding the hull and hiss of spray washing over the starboard rail seemed louder than usual in the foc'sls confined space. Tom forced himself to restrain a growing sense of urgency. Giving the order to open the larboard ports exposed a dreadful sight. Three hundred yards out, more flaming tongues erupted from the other ship. "Run out the cannons!" a shaken gunner's mate howled. "Run out the cannons!"

"Not yet, dammit!" Tom yelled into the confusion. "Ram the shell home and brace for impact!" A nine-inch ball blew out the bulkhead aft of the foc'sl stairs, and a series of loud thumps shook the hull beneath their feet. "*Now* run out the cannons, goddammit!" he cursed over the screams, flying splinters, and shattered blocks showering the men running to make repairs.

A man lay dying at Tom's feet and several more lay writhing beneath the loose blocks swaying over the men left standing.

"On the up-roll, boys! Fire!"

Belching flame, the cannons roared and sent their missiles across the water. The men holding the tackles checked the recoil, sponged out the muzzles, and prepared to ram home another shell. Tom said, "Stop! She's done." Not daring to question the tone of Tom's voice, they did as he said. "Secure the guns, close the ports and get ready to switch to the other side. One more to go!"

Tom had seen the forward shell blow apart the brig's midsection. The second shell had smashed the quarterdeck. The first shell must have hit the brig's magazine because the nearly simultaneous explosions were far greater than anyone had seen before. He turned and saw Bob rushing to the aid of an injured seaman and stopping to gawk through the hole in the *Bride*'s side.

"Motha lovah," Bob said. This was the first time he'd seen what the ship's explosive shells could do. "We'd be dead if they had a row of our cannons!" he exclaimed as the brig's weather deck spun away in a welter of collapsing masts, sails, and rigging. Bob threw the injured man's good arm over his shoulder and half dragged, half carried him across the deck, his mind filled with images of how the wind and waves would soon be tearing apart what was left of the burning hulk. Greeting Earl at the salon door, he grimaced. "I hope the sharks get the men clinging to the wreckage."

"Not to worry," Earl seethed, helping Bob carry the seaman through the door, "we ain't taking survivors today."

They exited the salon intending to go forward and assess the damage. Rounding the corner, they nearly bumped into the men laying Ernold's corpse beside Danny's bundle.

They made it to the foc'sl in time to witness the last breath of an old friend. "Help me, Capt'n Earl," Bob faltered. "It's Merv Albert." Merv lay on his side beneath a pile of broken planks and torn stay sails. They cleared the debris and rolled him over. Bob held him close and, taking Merv's hands in theirs, they heard the old man's last words. "Oh, the things I've seen," he said, coughing blood, "pink sails cruising over pharaoh's sands, a mother's loving gaze, children laughing in the sea . . ." He hiccupped and moaned through blood-stained lips. "If a younger me had a second chance . . . so different, so diff . . ."

"Merv's gone!" Bob cried, choking in his anguish. "Help me lay him beside the deckhouse with the others, Capt'n. There's so much to do. Please make it right for Merv's sake!"

Ryan stepped in front of Earl before he could remember what he planned to do next. "I sent men below. There are no leaks in the hull. Cladding is splintered where the balls hit, but there's no structural damage. We can do a temporary fix on the bulkhead. The masts will remain upright so long as we don't get into rougher seas or encounter a gale."

"Thank you, Ryan." Earl gestured to the corpses. "Cover the dead."

James did not have time to watch the brig go down. He had a far more pressing need: get the ship on a new tack. Pointing at Bill's deck crew, he gave the signal for the helmsmen to spin the wheel and shuddered. The men in the tops were releasing torn sails and splicing and reconnecting damaged stays on masts held in place by frayed threads. "Must bring the Bride about for the next salvo!" he said as the bow swung around and the ship healed on her new tack.

"Oh, you know what's coming," James said across the water. Having seen his sister ship destroyed, the brig's captain had broken contact with the *Helene* and was trying to flee. "Not so fast," James grunted through stiff lips as the *Bride* rolled and Tom pulled both lanyards.

Everyone stopped what they were doing and watched the charges demolish the fleeing brig's stern. No magazine exploded this time, but it didn't matter because the shells blew out the keel. Hard eyes watched the brig's bows lift clear of the water and the after-portion settle into the sea. Slowly at first, then with increasing speed, the hull, loose cannons, broken masts, torn rigging, and clinging survivors slid into the swell. The air trapped in the foc'sl created a froth no one could swim within as the vessel slipped beneath the waves. The triangular fins slicing through the carnage darted back and forth in the red froth blowing away with the spindrift.

James cleared his throat, spat over the side and called to Ryan. "We'll stay on this tack for now! Be prepared to heave-to after we've cleared the debris field!"

"Aye, aye, Master!" Ryan lowered his voice as he turned away. "Just in case you hadn't noticed Mr. Marshall, I've got more jobs to do than hands to do them."

Earl, Adam, and Ming stood together by the salon door discussing the injured. Several men were lying on sailcloth spread over tables. Others sat and stared. The cooks got the fires going again as Willard and Qui Li moved among the wounded.

"No bad injuries in here. Three dead?" Ming asked, sharing the rage in his captain's eyes.

"No and no, five dead," Earl stated, still recovering. "Thank you, Ming." He pointed at an injured seaman. "Willard, give Adam a hand taking this man into the medical room. I have to see how our friends across the way are faring. I'll be back."

Stopping with his hand on the door, Earl turned and bowed to his cook. "Quing yuanliang wo. Wo zhidas nikeneg youpenguou women sha. Feichang baoqian." ("Please forgive me. I know we may have killed a few of your friends. So sorry.")

Ming bowed in return. "Wo yuanliang ni wo de pengyou." ("I forgive you.")

"We'll keep the Helene in our lee," James said once Earl joined him by the rail. He gauged the distance between the two ships. "I suggest we drift down on her until we can get within hailing distance. I'll get you in as close as I can." They grabbed the rail with both hands as the swell tilted the *Bride* at an alarming angle. "This is no place to be idle." James frowned over the unsteady footing. "The ship can act as a temporary breakwater. I don't want to be hove to for long in a rising sea because our ships are going to drift apart. The wind and tide are carrying us south of Port Elizabeth. Mossel Bay is where things will get even messier. Winds're going to be changing direction soon, and the currents will be raising hell with the cross chop. Whoever goes over is in for a rough ride. There's debris out there. Don't be gone long! We need all hands to make repairs!"

The *Helene* was also preparing to heave to. Sails flapped against the men strung out along the yards. Fisting the rebellious canvas out of the wind was taking longer than usual. The *Helene*'s fore course was on the deck as the two ships drifted to within hailing distance. Earl saw men tossing broken rigging, a ruined quarter boat, and woodwork over the *Helene*'s starboard rail. Carpenters were already replacing the gaps in the weather bulkheads and smashed deckhouses. The ship slowed and began to roll.

Earl held a speaking trumpet to his mouth and called across the water. "Kaptain Nimitz, guten morgen. Wie geht's? Sie hilfe benotigen?" ("Good morning. How are you? Do you need help?")

The German who called back gave Earl the impression he could have removed the threat to his ship without the *Bride*. Just the same, the man dressed in a naval officer's uniform exhibited the manners of a man who appreciated Earl's gesture. "Guten morgen, Kaptain Yeaton. Ja, wir hilfe benotigen" ("Yes, I could use help"), the man replied from beneath his black patent-leather visor.

"Lower the starboard quarter boat over the side!" Earl called to Ryan. He raised the trumpet. "Ich komme!" ("I'm coming!") He turned to James, who was frowning at the turbulence. "You have the conn, Mr. Marshall. I'll be back as quick as I can."

Earl ran to the salon and spoke to Ming. "I need you to cover for Adam in the medical room. We're needed on the Helene."

Earl grunted as the seat smacked his tailbone. "We're in danger of capsizing, and we haven't even left the shelter of the Bride," he said between gasps.

"No rest for the weary," Adam responded, not daring to touch the shipside gunnel for fear of mashing his fingers against the looming hull.

Bob pushed off and the eight-man crew rowed through waters that threatened to swamp them. Bob had the tiller.

"Better start making ourselves useful," Earl said as wave after wave splashed over the side. He and Adam were soon bailing in earnest beside men nearly toppling onto one another whenever the oars lost their purchase in the unpredictable swells. His head was down, and he was battling a bout of nausea when he overheard Bob say he saw a floating man.

"What?" Earl said, lifting his eyes to a wall of water. Neither ship was in sight. Nor was the man he thought he'd heard Bob mention.

"He's coming."

Sure enough, a moment later the little boat nearly crushed the man lying across a section of decking. The swell pulled them apart again.

"He's not going to make it, Uncle." Adam watched the oars dipping closer and closer to the evasive scrap. The wounded man appeared to be clutching a weatherproof pouch.

"Up oars," Earl said, leaning over the side and yanking the bag from the man's hands. He tossed it at Bob's feet. "Stuff it under your seat."

He and Adam nearly upset the lot of them while trying to drag the castaway off his makeshift raft. Blood was leaking out of several holes in the lacerated body. Adam peeled back a closed eyelid. "The light's pretty dim, Uncle." The man groaned and vomited bloody seawater.

"Well, not much we can do here. Getting a little crowded, eh, chappy?" Earl asked Bob as another swell threatened to upset them. Cobb didn't have time to think of a reply before his captain spoke again.

"Ah, we're here," Earl said, cringing at the sight of the shifting hull and swaying hooks. "Keep the sack out of sight, Bob. No one touches it but you. I'm guessing it contains the brig's log. Could be wrong again. We picked up a survivor after I said we wouldn't, didn't we?"

Bob was too busy fishing boarding hooks to think of a suitable reply.

The *Helene* hoisted Earl's party over the side, and everyone stayed put until strong hands lashed the quarter boat to ring bolts. Earl left his seat with a better understanding of why James looked so worried. The trip across could have been their last. The unseen currents were worse than he expected, and the swaying ride up the *Helene*'s side was as dangerous as the crossing.

Earl surrendered his hand to Captain Karl Nimitz's iron fist as he greeted a friend he had seen on and off for over twenty years. *Solid as a block of Harz granite*, he thought. The man Earl gazed upon was of average height, impeccably dressed, and chiseled. Nimitz's closely cropped beard accented his deep-gray eyes and darkly shaded skin. He had the bearing of a man whose family had been sailing to all corners of the world for over a hundred years. How one of them could have given up the sea and moved to Texas was a puzzle Earl would have to solve another time.

"I see you picked up a passenger on your way over," Nimitz said, peering at the body. "Would you like a few of my men to find out what he knows before we toss him back?"

"That would be good," Earl replied, meeting the flinty stare.

"Please come this way." Nimitz stopped and pointed to one of his men and then at the castaway. "Find out what he knows."

Leading Earl and Adam to a set of stairs, he turned. "Thank you for coming over, Captain Yeaton. We came around the Cape last night. We saw their sails last evening. We might have avoided them if we hadn't slowed to make repairs. The yard was no match for yesterday's currents and winds. The brigs attacked while we were lowering the yard." Nimitz pointed at a cracked spar two men were tossing over the side with the wreckage. "Our casualties are limited to a few broken bones and minor splinters, with one exception. You know him—Prince Oskar Henneberg. He has a broken shaft embedded in his side beneath his heart. I think you are better equipped to treat his injuries than we are."

"Let's go see him," Earl answered and motioned for Captain Nimitz to lead the way to Oskar Henneberg's cabin.

Oskar was propped on the outer edge of his bunk and would have no relief until either he died or they removed the source of his discomfort. The sliver was the size of an axe handle split along the grain. The shaft passed between two ribs several inches below and to the side of Oskar's left nipple. He had been standing by the wheel when a cannon ball crashed into the bulkhead rail. The impact sent a hail of shards flying across the deck. One of the larger fragments lanced Oskar's side as he was turning to check the attacker's position. If he hadn't turned, the splinter would have pierced his heart from the back.

The helpless patient was a far cry from the dapper man about town Adam had spent a week with in Monte Carlo the previous summer. The auburn hair with the golden highlights hung limply from Oskar's damp forehead. After giving the Yeatons a pained flicker of recognition, he rolled his eyes and stared at the teak shaft piercing his chest.

"Lange nicht gesehen" ("Long time no see"), Adam said, using his stethoscope to take soundings from various places on Oskar's upper body. Try as he might to concentrate on listening to Oskar's heart and lungs, Adam couldn't block out memories of evenings spent playing roulette with Oskar and his lady friends. A moment later, he nodded to Earl, who unraveled the cotton strip looped around the object in Oskar's side.

"Guten morgen, Oskar," Earl said, offering a reassuring wink to the man's frightened eyes and mopping Oskar's sweaty brow with a damp cloth. "What have we got here?"

Earl got down on his knees and saw several inches of thumb-sized shaft exiting Oskar's back. Blood oozed out of both punctures and dripped onto a blood-spattered piece of sailcloth. "The blood is red, but not too red. I'd be surprised if the splinter punctured the pleural cavity and nicked the lung." He straightened "Pass me the shirt and jacket Oskar was wearing." Adam gave him a hand flattening out the rips to see if there was any missing fabric. "The rips match, so there's no fabric inside Oskar."

Adam placed a hand on Oskar's knee to get his attention. "Your heart and lungs are clear. We can remove the splinter now and leave you to your own devices or bring you aboard the Bride where we would be more comfortable treating you. There is the possibility of infection once this is removed," he said, pointing at the jagged wooden object. "We're bound for the Mediterranean, and you're headed there too, if you decide to be treated by us. Twice is too many times to be making crossings today," he added, becoming worried about Oskar's shallow breathing. *Shock is right around the corner*, he thought.

Oskar gritted his teeth against the searing pain and grimaced with the first wave of nausea. Swallowing vomit, he let Adam lift him long enough to get his queasy stomach back under control. Holding a metal cup to Oskar's lips, Adam gave him a drink to wash the foul taste out of his mouth. He smiled before Oskar could thank him. "Hell of a way for us to share a drink."

Earl met Oskar in the summer of 1857. Oskar was living with an uncle in Suhl, Germany. His uncle, Count Henneberg, was hosting a reception in his castle the day they met. The Henneberg's were the ancestral heirs to one of the world's finest deposits of low-carbon iron. Steel from Suhl's mills had been producing weapons of exceptional quality for centuries.

Earl was at the reception as a guest of J.P. Sauer of the Sauer and Sohn arms manufacturers. Earl's invitation had come by chance. He was in Suhl to pick up a special order of Sauer sporting rifles. Sauer's gunsmiths had hammered gold wire into etchings carved into the receiver plates of several rifles and shotguns. The gold inlays highlighted scenes from a client's hunting experiences.

Earl brought Adam with him in the summer of 1859, a year after Adam graduated from medical school. They were there to take delivery on the scoped sniper rifles they had recently passed on to their friends in Asia. Oskar and Adam hit it off right away. One thing led to another, and before they knew it, they were in Monte Carlo while Earl made a business trip to Marseille.

Oskar was twenty-eight at the time, well educated, independently wealthy, had the body of an athlete, and was popular in the company of both sexes. He had chosen to go into finance and worked out of the Count's bank in Lichtenstein. He tailored his interests to structuring arms sales in foreign markets. He was aboard the *Helene* for that purpose.

Oskar's clear blue eyes blinked their long blond lashes in appreciation for the sip and returned Adam's gaze. "You're a long way from home, my friend," Adam said, lowering Oskar back on the mattress. "You may as well come with us because you'll have to postpone the mountaineering trip you were talking about last year. The Eiger will be covered in sleet by the time you're healed."

A fierce knot of pain radiated out of Oskar's wound as he opened his mouth to speak. Well aware that the Yeatons were risking their lives and those of their crewmen to save his and hardly daring to breathe out the words, he grimaced through his teeth, "Thank you for offering to take me with you. I think my health is more important than selling a shipload of weapons. Please stuff my checkbook in the sea bag with my clothes, Karl."

"Okay," Adam said, "let's see if we can get you on your feet."

Oskar was in rough shape by the time they got him on deck.

Earl stood with Captain Nimitz while Bob and his men propped Oskar beside Adam in the cramped quarter boat. They wrapped Oskar's bag in sailcloth and stuffed it into the bow while listening to what Nimitz's men had pried out of the castaway before he died.

Nimitz's deckhand spoke in a dialect Earl was unable to understand. He was able to deduce one fact, however. The body had already gone over the side with the trash. Nimitz grunted his thanks and turned his stony glare on Earl.

"Those two ships were sent here to wait for you, Captain Yeaton. They've been here for months. You must be carrying a cargo of exceptional value for the ships' owners to have gone to all of the time and expense of placing them here, yes?"

"Yes."

"The man said they had disabled, robbed, and sunk several trading vessels. A lot of merchandise sank with them. He said it was pocket change compared to what you are carrying."

"Did he mention my missing brother?" Earl asked and closed his eyes against the answer he knew he would eventually hear.

"No."

Less than an hour later, they boarded the *Bride* with their new guest. Bob removed the brig's damp log from the pouch and went off to hang it above the stove in the galley.

Oskar never complained or groaned on the way over. The hardest part was keeping him conscious. The wound stiffened, and the nausea had returned by the time they got back. Several men lifted Oskar out of the quarter boat and carried him to the medical room. They placed him on an operating table bolted to the floor. Earl and Adam scrubbed as soon as the chloroform put Oskar to sleep. Tom and Colton came in and cleaned up too. They were there to give the doctors a hand positioning and restraining the patient. Propping Oskar up with rolled towels, they placed a pillow under his head and stood by to help in any way they could. The sound of James's tread came through the room's ceiling as the *Bride* made way once again. The motion, if not ideal, was certainly better than the nauseating pitch and yaw that came with drifting. Adam wiped his hands. "I saw the pain on your face after Captain

Nimitz answered your question regarding Uncle Nathan. He hasn't been seen in months, has he?"

"No." Earl put a towel down. "He was supposed to be in San Francisco in early December. Never showed up. I've asked about him in every port we've been in since January. No one has seen him."

"Are you all right doing this surgery, Uncle?"

"Yes. I came to the conclusion that we would never see Nathan again before we left San Francisco. It's the reason I stayed in my cabin on the way to San Pedro. I did all of my grieving back there. My brother's probably dead, Adam, and so are many of my dreams for the future," Earl said, not caring if Tom and Colton heard him. "Arthur Harrington said as much at the Stanfords. Nathan was asking questions in places with no exits, and I think the Harringtons killed him. Solving the mystery of what happened to him is one of the reasons I'm in a hurry to get back. I have a question I intend to put to Arthur Harrington: what do we have that he is so willing to risk his life to take away from us?"

Working together, they made the incision and shoved the spreader's tongs between Oskar's ribs. "Okay, Adam, open him up, and let's see what we have in there." Adam rotated the spreader's turn screws and opened the chest cavity. Once the spreader moved the ribs far enough apart to expose the splinter, Earl daubed away the blood and probed for strands of nervous and arterial tissue lining the inside of Oskar's ribs. A frayed strand of nervous tissue lay across the splinter. "Mustn't sever that. A few ruptured blood vessels are running along the surface of the peritoneum and will require tying off once we remove the splinter. The lateral intercostal artery is intact. There's a little hydrostatic shock damage we'll have to suction. Open him up a little more. Be nice to be able to back that shaft out of there."

They managed to slip the object out of Oskar's body without doing any more damage. They tied off the broken blood vessels, removed the jellied soft tissues, and daubed away most of the blood in the cavity. Finally, with everyone holding him down, they washed out the wound with pure ethanol, the only true sterilizer available. Keeping a firm grip on Oskar's twitching shoulders, Earl used a fat syringe to squirt the astringent into the weeping areas one last time before they dried and closed the cavity. Tom watched and smacked his lips. "Mind givin' me a taste, Capt'n? I could use a dose of that medicine. This is dry work."

Earl's lips stayed firm while his bloody fingers dried the wound with a clean towel. "That's easy for you to say," he harrumphed before raising the syringe and squirting a shot into Tom's mouth. Colton held Oskar's hips and watched.

"Finest kind! Made from Macks! Where'd you get it, Capt'n?"

"Huh?" Earl said, wiping his hands. "Okay, Adam, you can remove the spreader. I get the ethanol from uncles and cousins, Tom. There's no shortage of Macks on the family farms." He started threading a needle.

Tom held Oskar's shoulders while Adam backed the spreader's screws off. "What's their favorite way of doing it?"

Earl finished threading the needle and spoke while waiting for Adam to close the cavity. "Well, the process they use is quite simple. Uncle Ralph Hilton prefers to call ethanol 'alcohol.' He lets apple juice ferment in a stout oak keg long enough to produce a hard cider. Usually takes a couple of months. He leaves the keg in a shed until the coldest days of February have been around for a few weeks."

Adam removed the spreader "Give me the needle. I've got this. Keep talking."

"Sure." Earl handed over the needle. "As the temperatures drop into the minus forties, the alcohol, having a much lower freezing point than water, migrates to the center of the keg. Uncle Ralph says this is the fun part. He loves drilling through the frozen water to tap the pool of alcohol. He inserts a bung in the keg to plug the tap and turns the keg on its side. Opening the bung releases the alcohol into a funnel sitting on a receptive jug." Earl daubed the wound while Adam sutured the slit. "Tom, do you know what happens to overeager imbibers?"

"Yeeup. Most of the people who take large swallows right out of the jug don't do too good."

"No, they don't. Hard to breathe through an Adam's apple that's been flash frozen!"

By six bells of the forenoon watch, Oskar was stitched, wrapped, and groggy. They moved him to the guest suite Evelyn had occupied. Adam pointed at a tincture of scopolamine on a side table. "You may want to use this as a mild anesthetic and to ward off the effects of motion sickness."

He returned to the medical room after seeing Oskar tucked away. He and his uncle shook hands after cleaning up and getting the space ready for whatever might come next. "That's all we can do for now, Uncle. I arranged for a boy to be with Oskar at all times. He may require a few shots of morphine to see him through the next few days."

After making sure the room was shipshape, the pair left. They stepped over the coaming, checked the drift of the stiffly flapping pennant, crossed the weather deck, and headed for the salon. Getting their first bite to eat since having coffee and muffins in the wheelhouse six hours earlier would have to wait. They had to check on the injured first.

Another hour went by before Earl could stand by the stove with bowl of stew in one hand while the other probed between the pages of the recovered log. He decided to let it dry out a bit before taking it to this cabin and thumbing through its damning notations.

The crew spent the next six hours repairing the damage, clearing the decks, washing away the stains, and getting the ship back on course. The southern tip of Africa was off the starboard bow, and night would fall before they rounded the Cape. James got his wish to avoid the reefs. Oskar was sound asleep in his bunk. Three of the injured men couldn't lie in their hammocks, so they were moved to bunks in suites near the medical room. Colton volunteered to be the first to watch over Oskar and the men.

Late in the afternoon, Earl stood on the quarterdeck with Adam and James. The rest of the crew arranged themselves in a loose circle below the rail. Five sailcloth shrouds lay on planks beside the lee scuppers. Cobbles sewn into the bottom of the shrouds guaranteed a feet-first plunge to the sea floor.

"We lost five good men today in a battle none of us saw coming," Earl said. "I know I speak for all of us in saying their loss will affect us for a long time. I'm sorry this happened. I wish there was more time for us to give them a proper burial. The seas are far too rough for that. We'll be putting ourselves at risk if we take any longer. You know what to do after I say their names. We commit Merv Albert, Danny Rickles, Ernold Corson, Mike Plouard, and Eddy Loftstrom to the sea."

Robert Joseph

Four men lifted each board and tipped the dead over the side.

CHAPTER 24

Blandy's Wharf, Port of Funchal, Madeira,
20 June, first bell of the dog watch

"Almost there," Bob said to the boy maintaining the tension on a tag line. He and Colton flanked a weight-bearing line depositing a netted wine cask into the lower hold. The line passed through an overhead pulley shackled to the swing arm of a gantry mounted on the wharf. Squinting into the ship's bowels, Bob twirled his portside hand in a downward spiral until he heard Hopley squeak, "Stop!" Clenching his fist, he glanced up to make sure the men on the wharf got the message and halted the horses harnessed to the other end of the line. Bob leaned over the hole and waited for the signal to raise the net.

Charlie squatted beside Bob and stared into the hold. "What's taking you so long down theya?"

Hopley's muffled voice rose out of the darkness. "Why don't you come on down if you think you can lash fifteen hundredweight to the stack any quickah!"

"Okay!" Charlie grabbed the line, wrapped his feet around the rope, and dropped out of sight.

Bob caught Colton's eye. "Glad he's not my brother," Colton muttered.

Ten minutes later, an empty net hung over the hole. The men on deck removed it and the tag line from the block. Bob gave the signal to swing the gantry away and shared a smile with Ol' Bud. They'd been watching Colton putting gear in a storage locker. "That's it. You and the boys can secure the hatch."

Bob crossed the deck and leaned on the rail beside James and Ryan. They'd been watching Colton too and thinking the same thing. "Boy's a natural leader," James stated. "I don't know what to do about Charlie."

"Go easy on him," Bob said. "He means well, and he's a willing worker. He shows up on time and works until he's told to stop. And there's another reason, if you care to hear it."

"I'm all ears."

"Everybody likes him."

They leaned on the rail watching the men on the wharf. The wagon that delivered the last cask pulled ahead to make room for another. James turned away and let his gaze linger for a moment on the sea haze obscuring the path they sailed to get there. "Tide's about to ebb, and the wind is in our favor. I'm going to take a stroll on the wharf while we wait for the captain. And Bob?"

"Yeah?"

"I stand corrected. You're right. He is a good kid," James said as he slowed to let Ming and the watch crew precede him through the entry port.

He peeled off after Ming's group approached the last wagon. The teamster removed a tarpaulin placed over covered serving dishes, pots, steaming kettles, several sides of roast beef, and jeroboams filled with fresh spring water. Most of the hot food and water went into the galley. The rest and several cases of bottled wine headed for the captain's suite.

James knew the Blandys were not the first to discover the ideal growing conditions on the island; they were the most successful, however. Charles Ridpath Blandy exhibited the same uncanny business acumen his gifted father possessed. He knew exactly what to do after the disastrous oidium fungal infestation destroyed most of the island's vines in 1851: he bought as many pre-1851 casks from his depressed competitors as the family finances would permit. The Blandy's were now in the enviable position of having the world's largest private collection of premier wines. The characteristic that set these wines apart from most of the finest European vintages, of which there were many, was that Madeira's had the unique quality of improving with age while the other great wines were turning into vinegar.

James walked to the end of the wharf where he could see the *Bride*'s figurehead. He took a moment to marvel over her beauty, the thousands of miles they'd traveled together and asked a question Earl refused to answer. *Who is the woman he chose to model the ship's figurehead after?*

"Please lead the way home, dear lady," he whispered. "Your ship has never been more deserving of a refit."

Although a fresh coat of paint covered most of the repairs, the scars would be there for a while yet. "She's going into dry dock soon's we get to Rockland, James. We'll tidy her up then," Earl had said after they'd cleared the Cape and made sea repairs.

Resting his eyes on the distant haze, James thought about what had transpired since they'd brought Oskar aboard off South Africa's Grue Banks. Not caring whether he was overheard, he spoke to the spirit of his silent companion. "Have to admit, the young man has plenty of pluck. His first twenty-four hours with us were nearly as hairy as the last one he endured aboard the Helene. His predicament had plenty to do with the discomfort associated with our ill-timed passage through those often-disastrous waters. Stopping to assist him contributed significantly to missing the early morning winds and favorable tides that would have made everyone's trip around the Cape far more pleasant. Got to give it to him, though. He never complained, took his medicine, and refused shots of morphine. Tough enough to be up and walking once we reached the more predictable winds off Africa's west coast."

Oskar proved to be more than an unobtrusive patient and passenger. He dined with the men and shared tales in the wheelhouse, and unlike most guests who boarded the *Bride*, he'd offered to stand watch. He stayed out of the way, and the crew enjoyed his company. By the time they cruised past the Gulf of Guinea, he had become an accepted member of the ship's complement. Fair winds, clear skies, and a hearty appetite did wonders for him. Still sporting a nasty red scar over his mottled ribs, he showed no signs of infection. His breathing appeared to be normal even though twelve inches of highly sensitive intercostal muscles were trying to knit while he breathed. The signs of strain around his eyes revealed more about how his wound felt than he would ever admit. "That young man is welcome to stay for as long as he can stand us," James had said to Earl.

"You're going to get a chance to find out," Earl replied, "because he's going to be with us longer than expected. He has friends in New York he wants to see."

James thought again of what had occurred at Sahibzada's palace. Sahibzada encouraged Earl to return to the *Bride* with his men right after he told Adam to keep the treasure. "News of this nature travels fast, Earl. The road to Kolkata is lined with traps. You should leave right after we load the treasure onto the wagons. Even I cannot assure you safe passage to Kolkata. Bandits, always a problem, have multiplied since the British arrived and brought wholesale banditry with them. It's becoming increasingly difficult to know who I can trust anymore." Taking Sahibzada's advice to heart, Earl abandoned thoughts of pleasant dinners, nightly visits by nubile maidens, falconry, tiger hunts, and rides through planted acreages. Sahibzada sent a rider to Kolkata bearing a letter written in shorthand. The letter instructed James to have the *Bride* moored to the wharf and ready to sail. Fortunately, she was still at the wharf taking on supplies and completing the switch to summer-weight canvas.

Dozens of farm workers assisted in the effort to get Earl's group on their way. Working through the night, they managed to pack the whole kit and caboodle before sunrise. Opening bales of jute, the workers' clever hands created hidden cavities into which they stuffed the statue, chests of jewels, and precious objects. Sahibzada sent an armed guard to accompany Earl and his men as far as Kolkata's Strand. The riders turned back before the customs house inspectors knew they were there. Earl declared the cargo of jute, loaded the bales, and departed before noon.

James had known the Yeatons since childhood. He'd attended séances at Yeaton family reunions and was well acquainted with their spiritual practices. Still, Adam's dream had no parallel in a lifetime of experiences with this family. There was no mistaking the sad expression he'd seen on Adam's face as the river's current swept them away. "This is the second time on this voyage I've felt as if I am leaving a part of myself behind."

James traced the hull's sleek lines and let his mind drift over the recent acquisitions and the effort required to keep track of them. Earl, Adam, and Willard spent many hours together cataloguing the contents of the shrine and chests they pulled out of the crypt in Shanghai. With the exception of Mohini's statue, the Navaratnas, and samples of the more colloquial jewelry, the objects in each collection were strikingly similar. Most of the artistry associated with the treasures had come from the desert lands of the Middle East, quite likely from as far away as Egypt and Greece.

The Navaratnas, of which there were several, fascinated James. The nine gemstones, selected by a trained astrologer, and set in gold by a skilled artisan, supposedly produced a sacred relationship between the intended recipient and the cosmological forces summoned by each stone. Earl told him India's residents had been revering the priceless pendants for centuries. The Navaratnas were composed of flawless rubies, pearls, red coral, emeralds, yellow sapphires, diamonds, blue sapphires, moonstones, and cat's eyes. Sahibzada told Adam that many Indians believed that once the Navaratnas were no longer with the original owner, whoever possessed them would do well to be cautious in the presence of such unified cosmic influences.

"Huh," James said, staring at the water, "perhaps that's why Sahibzada refused to touch the pendant." He tilted his head to the side. "They don't seem to bother Adam."

His face sobered when he thought of a relic Earl had placed on the table in his cabin one evening. It had come out of the unsealed chest they'd removed from Wing Lum's archive. The supple leather-bound tome written in Aramaic was indecipherable to Earl. Willard refused to try to translate the book, stating what everyone in the cabin could feel in its presence. "This is evil," was all he said. Willard had summed up their sentiments, and Earl returned the book to the chest stored on the deck below. James shivered every time he recalled what Earl had said when he got back. "I share your suspicions about the book's contents. Strange as it may seem, the leather has the feel of a living person's skin."

James moved on to other intriguing artifacts removed from the Khan's chest. Greek goblets studded with rubies and emeralds, jade ceremonial flasks, and daggers from Persia. He liked the feel of a thin Mesopotamian helmet sporting a red horsehair plume. He was wondering if Alexander the Great might have worn the golden helmet when he noticed a Zeno's petrel skimming over the light chop. He followed the bird's flight past the wharf until it was lost among the warehouses, shops, and stuccoed villas lining the shore. "Ah, there they are," he said to a woman whose name he did not know.

Earl and Adam were walking toward the entry port with Charles Blandy. Ryan had seen them also and had men standing by to cast off. James waited for the three to shake hands and say their goodbyes. He then walked to the entry port, said "Adieu," and hopped aboard.

Long after the sun had set over Madeira's purple ridges, Earl, Adam, James, Willard, and Oskar sat at ease in the captain's suite feeling inebriated and drowsy from the food and wine they'd consumed. Several of the ship's boys slouched in chairs or nodded off beside the bottles, plates and serving dishes scattered across the chart table. Ryan, whose turn it was to be on watch, had fallen asleep in the wheelhouse.

The dinner started with an announcement. Earl tapped a glass with a silver spoon. "To wit," he declared, waving a hand over steaming platters brimming with *cotelettes d'agneau, porc,* and *veau*; a bowl of vermicelli swimming in Hollandaise; and another bowl of double-egged spagettini sprinkled with dashes of *espagnole* sauce. He gestured to the chart room table and pointed at strips of sliced roast, *truffs Marengo, Coquilles St. Jacques,* and sautéed vegetables. A selection of cheeses and bowls of fruit filled a nearby tray. "We're going to sample every varietal of note produced on Madeira," Earl said. "You are about to have a dinner worthy of why Charles and his friends expended so much effort to produce these wines in the first place."

The silver service, polished woods, and cut-crystal decanters gleamed in the horizontal rays of the setting sun. Each place setting had several wine glasses. Earl urged his guests to drink each vintage from a separate glass and not mix them. "Ship's boys are standing by with clean replacements for those who forget which is which. The jeroboams of fresh spring water are here to provide ample fluid. Cleanse your palates frequently if you want to taste the subtleties in the fare.

"Charles has generously provided us with samples from his family's cellar. He has given us two additional vintages to complement the four classic Madeiras: Sercial, Verdelho, Bual, and Malvasia. The first of the two extra varietals is an 1836 Blandy Tinta Negra, the only red produced on the island. The second, which I am truly humbled to offer, is a 1761 Borges Terrantez. This," he said, pointing to the bottle, "should only be tasted with a sharp cheese if it is to be accompanied by anything at all. Charles was also kind enough to sell me a case of Barbeito's 1795 Terrantez. We'll save it for another time.

"I had a great deal of difficulty convincing him to satisfy my request that the following vintages come from specific years—a 1761 F.F. Ferraz Sercial, a 1789 Abudarham Verdelho, an 1822 Blandy Bual, and an 1832 D'Oliveriras Malvasia. As you can see on the labels, Charles managed to satisfy my request, although I would not tell him why," Earl said to Willard, who grinned at him and then laughed.

"Blandy knew," Willard said, "and he was probably beside himself fetching a selection of the most prized bottles in his cellar. The reason he went along is because he is indebted to you for keeping two dozen of his precious six-hundred-liter pipes in the Bride's hold for over two years! The amount of money he'll make adding the 'vina de roda' label to his bottles will surely surpass the premium he could charge on the vintages we are about to drink." Willard neglected to mention that in exchange for stowing additional casks, Earl got to keep a pipe of each of the four classics. The shipment of oak barrel components that Earl provided gratis softened Blandy's reluctance to give Earl the four pipes, and sealed the deal.

"Ich verstehe nicht. Warum jene jahre?" ("I do not understand. Why those years?") Oskar asked.

"Comet years," Earl answered, observing how well Hopley poured the dark Tinta Negra into a carafe. "Wines produced in comet years have a near mystical reputation among oenophiles. Have to admit though, I can't tell the difference."

Their luck changed forty-eight hours later.

Gibraltar's towering cliffs protected them from most of the winds blowing over Spain from the Bay of Biscay. The torrential rains these winds carried swept down on the ship as she made the Mediterranean course correction. After the first twenty-four hours of reefing and trimming sails in the cold rain, most of the crewmen were ready to hide in their berths, drop anchor anywhere, and ride out the storm—anything to avoid having to go back out every time they heard the call, "All hands! All hands!" The rough treatment they received crossing the Gulf of Lion had most of the crew in the mood to abandon ship once they sighted the Rhone River estuary off Marseille. The rain came in sideways most of the time, and everyone's clothes were beginning to smell musty.

Earl rejected James's suggestion that they weather the storm in Ibiza's protected harbor. Aggrieved once again, James felt they were back where they had been before the naval engagement off the coast of South Africa. "I'm not required to tell you the reasons behind my decisions every time you ask," Earl said after listening to James's complaints.

Four days out of Madeira, the retreating fog exposed the tall watchtower above Saint Jean's citadel. Dark clouds moved east and left behind thin streamers releasing a parting drizzle on the fort's signal gunners.

Fading echoes accompanied the *Bride's* passage as she rounded the point and sailed into Marseille beneath the welcome rays of a warm sun. Vaporous tendrils rising off every surface might have given her observers the impression that a fire ship would soon be among them. The steam coming off their clothing made the watch crew look more like wraiths than seamen. James stood at the rail giving Charlie the sternest scowl he could muster. The boy grinned back, correctly rang out eight bells of the morning watch, hooked the clapper, and ran the length of the ship.

The clogged harbor held craft of every description. Massive ships of the line were anchored in the most desirable positions, their ports open to reveal row upon row of cannons. Three tiers of gun decks gleamed in the growing light and heat. Trading vessels from all corners of the globe competed for space in the massed wharf area. Freighters whose cargos needed immediate transfer were moored three deep with gangplanks crossing several ships.

The tide of human occupation rose from the sea and spread up the sloping plain. Golden domes and bell towers sat atop cathedrals and churches accenting the high points of the granite escarpments surrounding the ancient city.

Charlie put out the American and Yeaton house flags long before the patrolling pilot boat could wave its bright-yellow flag over where it wanted the *Bride* to drop anchor. James turned to Elmer. "Bring her head into the wind."

The men in the pilot boat gazed with indifference at the well-executed maneuver as the ship lost her way and shrugged off how fast the new arrival's sails disappeared.

Men in the foc'sl found other tasks to do after prepping the anchor for free fall.

"Okay, Hopley, you have the honor of knocking the hook off the dog's back," HC said after removing the chock and handing the hammer over to the boy. Peering into the sun's reflected glare, Hopley made sure the chain running through the anchor shackle ran true. The swinging black anchor cast a dim shadow on the sun-dappled hull. He tightened the hammer's thong around his wrist, leaned over the cat, and with a firm grip on the handle, gave the hook a solid ringing whack. Freed of the shackle, the *Bride*'s steel tether dragged the squealing anchor chain to the seabed. The boy ran below and hooked the devil's claw on the windlass while the tide swung the ship's stern toward Old Town's busy foreshore. The backward drift came to a stop a few cables from the wharves lining the cobbled Quai Du Port, and the *Bride* became one of many vessels drifting over their reflections.

Lighters laden with fresh water, fruits, vegetables, live chickens, and cuts of meat arrived and began vying for Ming's attention. With the assistance of a French-Canadian crewman, Ming bartered for enough food to feed the crew for several weeks. This would be the *Bride*'s last stop before crossing the Atlantic.

Boarding nets and fenders went over the side. Men climbed onto the galley roof, turned the longboat over, packed the oars, and rigged the tackle. The men on deck raised the boat while those at the braces swung the yards and lowered the boat over the light ripple. Men followed and climbed aboard as soon as the boat hit the water. Earl, Adam, James, Tom, Kato, and Munenori came next. They were all wearing ranger clothes and the dependable half boots. Bob stood in the rear by the tiller. Charlie jumped over the rail, scrambled down the net, placed a foot on the foreword gunnel, and shoved. The oars soon had the boat carrying Earl's group across the crowded bay.

Earl, James, and Adam sat near the stern of the longboat. Earl and Adam carried pistols and pouches stuffed with rolls of hundred-franc Napoleons. Tom, Kato, and Munenori took seats between the men rowing the boat to shore. James and Tom had .22 caliber pistols hanging from their hips. The Japanese cousins wore their swords openly. The wakizashis were on their belts; the katatas hung from sheaths between their shoulder blades. Tom held a duffle bearing a cut-off version of his favored defender, the coach gun.

The warm sun felt good on Earl's shoulders—for the moment. He smiled at Cobb. "Not quite as hot as the swing around the Gulf of Guinea, eh, chappy?"

"No, sir," Bob murmured. They both knew it would be hard to tell the difference in a few hours. "Raise oars!"

"Now listen, Bob, we're going to make this visit short and sweet. Wait out here in sight of the wharf until you see us coming down Rue Pytheas on the other side of the quay. Might take a couple of hours," Earl said as the boat bumped up against the landing.

Earl led his group to the first of several stops he had planned for their brief visit in Marseille. Their entrance into the front offices of Freres Berube Wine Exporters caused quite a stir among the busy staff, who mistakenly assumed they were about to be robbed.

Michel Berube came out of his office with the intention of giving the bandits anything they wanted. His rosy complexion turned pasty at the sight of Earl Yeaton and armed men standing there instead. Michel appeared to be more than a little surprised to see them and held his hands up in mock surrender. "Je suis à votre merci! Ah, bonjour Capitaine Yeaton. Comment allez-vous? Bienvenue!" ("I am at your mercy! Good day. How are you? Welcome!")

"Bonjour, mon ami. Quez-vous recu mon lettre?" ("Good day, my friend. Did you get my letter?") Earl asked.

"Oui," Michel replied. Switching to heavily accented English, he went on to tell Earl the vintages he ordered were in the warehouse.

"Tres bien."

Showing the way to a corner of his cavernous warehouse, Michel removed a tarp draped over a large stack of cases. He pointed at the names stenciled on the crates: Latour, Margaux, Haut-Brion, the pink Loudenne, and several other chateaus of note surrounding Pauillac village in Bordeaux's legendary Medoc region. "I have tried to satisfy your request to procure the best vintages produced by these houses in the past thirty years. You will find in here the most exquisite merlots, Cabernet Sauvignons, and Pinot Noirs. There are no better Pinot Grigios, Chardonnays, and Sauvignon Blancs than the ones you have before you. I know of your fondness for comet years, so I took the liberty of including two cases of Chassagne-le-Haut, an 1832 Chardonnay, and an 1845 Pinot Noir," he said, rubbing sweaty hands on his pant legs and darting nervous glances at the pistol hanging beside Earl's pouches. "The cheese you ordered is in my cold room. There are eight of each in four-kilo rounds: Roquefort, Bleu d'Auvergne, and Gorgonzola. You also have ten kilos each of Brie and Camembert."

"Merci beaucoup," Earl said. "Can you have the lot taken out to my ship as soon as we settle on a price? Adam will pay you."

Shrugging in misery, Michel nodded. "Mais oui. Immediatement."

The bill paid, Earl halted where the group could hide within sight of Berube's loading dock. "Tom and Adam, I want you to watch the office and warehouse doors. Follow anyone who leaves in a hurry." Earl drew a street sketch of where he planned to stop before he returned to the quay. "Here's the route we plan to use. The only deviation would be to retrace our steps if we can't take the direct route along Rue Saint-Saëns and Cours Jean Ballard. If possible, follow our wine and cheese purchase to the wharf. Make sure a barge takes everything out to the ship. This ain't right, so be careful. Go now, if it's not too late," he said, staring at the two and pushing them on their way.

A few minutes later, Earl and his three companions approached a shabby building on Rue Haxo. The shop's flyspecked windows had not been cleaned in ages. The only indications that the premises might house a business were several dust-covered paintings placed on indifferent display behind the dirty glass. No sign hung over the door. "Okay," Earl said to James, Kato, and Munenori. "We're about to enter Emile Lautrec's framing studio. He's a member of the French nobility. He's sensitive about this, so you must do as I say once we're inside. There's another thing I have to mention," he said, raising a finger, "his parents are first cousins, and his grandmothers were sisters." The two Japanese, not much given to overt expression, instantly sucked air through their teeth, shocked.

"I know," Earl said. "There's more. As you might expect to happen from such unions, he has congenital aberrations and is eccentric."

The language skills of the two Japanese had not progressed to the point where they could understand everything said, but they certainly knew enough *not* to expect to be meeting an average person once they were inside. They had heard of similar unions taking place among relatives of the Japanese emperor.

Earl spoke slowly, so they could understand what he said next. "Two things are worth noting. The first: although he is small and a little misshapen, he has a great deal of vitality, ah, energy, especially for an old guy in his late seventies. Oddly, the second makes up for the first: he has an encyclopedic mind when it comes to painting . . . and money." Earl mimed a big brain and rubbed his thumbs and forefingers. "Emile's studio is a favorite of Europe's finest contemporary artists. Most prefer to mount their own paintings, but the more accomplished artists know their works fetch better prices if a master mounts them. Oh, yes, I almost forgot: Emile never uses his name and does not want anybody to use his or their own in his presence. So, no introductions or acting like you've never seen him before. He wants you to act the way you do with people you already know. Other than what I have told you, he's relatively normal," Earl said with a smile and rolled his eyeballs.

They came to a stop at the studio door. Earl knew if he turned the knob, the door wouldn't open, so he bent over and removed a key from under a pot.

A bell tinkled over the door on their way in. No one appeared to be within hearing. Holding his hand up for the men to stay where they were, Earl stepped around the counter and disappeared in the back. The three left behind stood away from the dusty counter, rickety chairs, and empty shelving. Flies buzzed against grimy windows while down below, others sought nourishment in the carcasses of their dead brethren.

"Come on back," Earl called after a few minutes. James and the cousins shuffled around the counter to a corridor that led to a high-ceilinged workshop filled with paintings. A clean skylight lit the large room. Everything there was dry and dust free. The riot of colors and multitude of paintings stored in floor-to-ceiling racks stood in bright contrast to the slovenly disorder found in front. James emerged from the hall just in time to see his captain wink and slip a folded envelope into his back pocket. *What in hell is he up to now?* James wondered. *Whatever it is, I'll bet there's a dollar sign attached to it. Or a list of collaborators. Or both.*

Earl stood at a bench with a wizened old man who was putting the finishing touches on an oil painting he had just mounted. His beard brushed the bench as he peered at the brads holding the picture in place. Emile's wrinkled face reminded Munenori of a dried plum. The oversized head turned on the boy and caught him staring. The wily intelligence in the rheumy eyes staring back made Munenori wish he had stayed in the front. The eyes flicked to Kato. Munenori suppressed a shiver as the colorless old eyes shifted back to him, and he knew they'd noticed identical eyebrows and noses. Emile sniffed and turned back to what lay on the bench. He flipped the frame over and held the picture up to the light. "Ce bon, nes pas?" he asked.

"Oui," Earl said, continuing in French. "This is the first time I've seen plein aire captured this way." He took his eyes off the tranquil lily pond and peered at the signature. "Who is this Claude Monet? I've never heard of him. He has talent."

"Oui," the old prune said. "A young man with promise, I would say. Eugene Boudin gave me this painting. You have several Boudin seascapes. I know because I sold them to you. Monet was eighteen when he painted this one in Eugene's studio two years ago. You can have it if you take the Boudin you keep looking at," the old geezer rasped, unable to keep his eyes from darting to Earl's waist. "You might like this compositional study done in the same style by Edouard Manet," he said, waving a hand over a group of nude bathers having a picnic on the edge of a wood. Earl scratched his chin.

"Here, these are my favorites," Emile said, removing more paintings from his racks and arranging them along the bench. The oils had a luminescent, ethereal quality about them and, contrary to conventional realism, suggested the artists were more intent on conveying impressions of what they were seeing rather than drafting an accurate portrayal of the subject matter. "These paintings by Boudin and his Flemish friend, Johan Jongkind, were rejected by the Salon De Paris," the elderly man said. "I'm not sure Jongkind will ever recover from the insult." He waved a liver-spotted hand while gazing at the collection of pastorals, seascapes, portraits, and still lifes. "The judges dismissed these paintings and said they were unworthy of being placed among the recent masterpieces produced by Corot, LaRoche, Dupré, Rousseau, and others." Emile stroked his beard. "They declared these paintings to be immature and grossly incomplete!" he cried with contempt. "Mon dieu!" he cackled. "The artists were so discouraged by their reception that they nearly threw these treasures away. I bought them for the price of a café meal and a handful of sous. You would have thought I was treating them to lunch at Le Grand Vefor and paying a king's ransom! If possible, I would buy all of the paintings produced by these young geniuses. Which ones do you want, Captain?"

"I think I know where I can get a wagon. Let's talk about prices," Earl said, patting his pouch. He decided to give the canny collector an extra roll of coins after they agreed on a price. He felt quite confident they could find a mutually agreeable way to purchase additional paintings.

A short while later, Earl veered off Rue Saint-Saëns and led the way into a cobbled alley near the opera house. They passed a wagon shed and the heads of two draft horses leaning out of a stall. Earl stopped and pounded on the back door of an aging depot. No answer. He pounded harder a second time.

"Allez! Allez!" (Go away! Go away!) came the reply from deep inside the building.

Earl pounded harder and harder. "Ouvrir, vous vieille voleur!" ("Open up, you old thief!")

The men standing with Earl were exchanging nervous glances when a shotgun barrel poked through a crack in the door. The head of a large man followed. Fierce black eyes gave way to awe at the sight of Earl. James and the cousins kept their hands away from their weapons and waited for what would happen next.

"Mon dieu, est-ce vous, Earl Yeaton?" ("My God, is that you?")

"Oui, ce qui reste de moi!" ("Yes, what is left of me!") Earl said, allowing himself to be crushed against the man's huge chest.

The deadly object was a child's toy in the giant's massive fist. James retreated from the waving weapon.

Passing an appraising glance over Earl's men, the giant shifted his eyes up and down the alley, waved the group inside, and bolted the door.

Armand de Pape, otherwise known as *Le Pape* (The Pope) stood much closer to seven feet tall than to six. Munenori imagined the man must have had a prodigious appetite to maintain such a huge body. Armand wore a shaggy cotton shift, which did nothing to impede the waves of vitality emanating from him. His grin rivaled James's, whom he immediately recognized as a fellow Frenchman. He placed an arm the size of a small tree across James's shoulders and led the way to a collection of artifacts gleaned from the civilizations lining Mediterranean shores. Although dwarfed by the strength and size of his guide, James was soon conversing with Le Pape as an equal.

Over the course of the next hour or so, Kato and Munenori loaded a freight wagon pretty much by themselves. They wrapped each item in muslin, straw, discarded tapestries, and twine. They stowed a medium-sized granite bust of Ramses III; a faience statuette of Anahita, the Persian mother goddess; a full-size Greek marble statue of Athena absconded from a place that Le Pape refused to identify; and marbles of the twin Hittite divinities, Teshub and Hepat. Le Pape said he'd dug the pair out of the ground at Tell-el-Halaf, Syria. Pretending to be reluctant to see her go, he allowed Earl to purchase a golden nude of a Minoan woman on a swing. Not expecting Earl to believe him, Armand claimed to have removed this precious artifact from a tomb on Knossos. Earl declined the offer to procure a couple of mummified heads ostensibly belonging to the Pharaoh Sekenre and Nebtu, a wife of Tuthmosis III.

Earl, James, and Le Pape wandered around the warehouse selecting items and left the cousins to stow each purchase in the wagon box. The wanderers stopped beside a mixed collection of late-eighteenth-century items carelessly scattered in a corner. Armand said he had sold off most of the valuables. He said they were looking at all that remained of Renard Menou's possessions. Feigning sadness, he told them that Renard was a descendant of Jacques-Francois Menou, the Napoleonic general who had ordered the French retreat from Alexandria in 1800.

James lifted his head and gazed down the bridge of his patrician nose. Not wishing to offend his host, he kept to himself the thought that the source of Le Pape's sadness was more likely rooted in the dreary prospect of having to find a place to dump this worthless junk.

While poking through dismal pieces of damaged furniture, tools, common military hardware, and cracked pottery, Earl noticed a brassbound leather-covered chest buried in the pile. Wrinkling his nose at the water stains, he inquired about its contents. Le Pape opened the chest and pulled out a moth-eaten officers' uniform, a few Egyptian campaign ribbons, a broken sword, and a cavalry bridle. He asked Earl if he wanted the trunk because it was the only thing of value, such as it was.

Earl ignored James's disapproving frown. "Sure, throw it on the wagon. I have a few odds and ends I can put in it." Armand swept up the battered old box and passed it to the two lackeys in the wagon.

"Packrat's collect junk too," James said, peering into the cavity created by the trunk.

"Cela devrait le faire" ("That should do it"), Earl said, handing over a substantial number of coins.

"Oui, c'est bon" ("Yes, it is good"). Le Pape nodded with a broad grin.

James had noticed a twenty-gallon cask buried under a pile of horse harnesses and assorted stable tack. Pushing the stiff leather aside, he read the crude lettering on the barrelhead: "Aha—Barbeito, Terrantez, 1795. I heard about this year recently," he said in what he hoped was a bored, offhand tone.

"Ah, vous avez trouve mon petit precieux," ("You have found my little precious.") Le Pape said before his smile turned into a grimace. The belt surrounding James's ample waist held nothing more than a puny gun.

Earl noticed the grimace. "Donnez-moi un nombre, Armand. Nous sommes à court de temps." ("Give me a number. We're running out of time.")

They haggled over the dusty maltreated cask while the sweating workers standing in the wagon grew impatient with the gai jin. Le Pape finally threw hands the size of small hams into the air, and cried, "Allez! Combien avez-vous laisse dans les poches?" ("Enough! How much have you got left in those pouches?") They put a price on the barrel before Earl agreed to hand over any more coins. Le Pape turned the barrel on its head, and within seconds the cask bore a pile of hundred-franc Napoleons. Earl counted out the francs as he dropped them into a leather sack Le Pape held open. The solid clink of gold coins piling on top of each other carried over the sound of shallow breathing, the swish of horsetails, the occasional snort, and twittering of sparrows.

The transactions completed and the cask in the wagon, Earl was about to thank Kato and Munenori for their patience when Le Pape interrupted. "Un moment, s'il vous plait." ("A moment, please.") "Perhaps you could do me a favor before you go."

The giant was in his office before Earl and James could exchange puzzled glances. Le Pape dropped the sack on his desk and pawed around in a tangled pile of lace curtains and worn wall coverings. He returned holding a chest the size of a small suitcase. "I want you to take this with you. Gratis," he said before Earl could object. "A defrocked priest working in the Vatican archives secreted this chest out of the vast storehouse below the Church of Saint Peter. The priest ran afoul of the administrators for refusing to falsify records in support of an embezzlement scheme run out of the Vatican. He stole the chest before they dismissed him. He fled to Marseille fearing for his life, came here, and asked me to keep it hidden. He said he would be back in two days to take it away. He left behind a sack of Spanish doubloons. I have not seen him since. The chest has been with me for over a year. I attract enough attention getting the items I sell. This one has the feel of a danger I am unwilling to bear. I have not opened it. Take it." And with that, Le Pape removed a thong bearing a key from around his neck and slipped it over Earl's head. He handed the chest up to Kato, and with Earl translating, the chest was hidden in the load.

Earl sat beside James on the crowded wagon seat after they swung by Emile's studio to pick up the paintings. Armand drove them down to the quay. Kato and Munenori opted to walk rather than sit on a load rumbling over cobbles. Earl bought a dozen falafels and several dry reds from street vendors on their way through the Old City's busy streets. They crossed the quay, and Le Pape delivered them to the wharf, where a barge crew was waiting to offload the wagon and float the purchases out to the ship. Earl thanked Le Pape and saw him ride off munching on a falafel. Jammed between his feet was a nearly empty bottle of wine.

Adam and Tom sat on a bench with Earl. They were sharing a bottle, eating, and talking about the wine dealer. Earl's eyes were on the barge weaving its way through the water traffic. James, Kato, and Munenori were sitting in the sun. Their eyes were on the women taking a stroll on the quay.

"Berube hurried up the street after you left, Uncle. He went to the offices of Franco-American Exporters."

"Figures," Earl said, taking a sip of wine and handing the bottle to Adam. "They're Harrington's Marseille shipping agents."

"Well, soon after Berube walked inside, a man ran down the wharf and sailed away aboard a sloop." Adam had a gulp from the bottle and nearly choked when he saw the hostility in his uncle's eyes.

Earl patted Adam on the back and turned his attention to Tom. Adam passed the bottle. Tom nodded his thanks, swallowed a last mouthful of falafel, and took a swig. "Berube was the only one who ran off. I decided to check in the back. The boys in the warehouse seemed to be taking a little longer than is usually the case among the Latins, so I walked over and encouraged them to get a move on," he said stroking the shotgun. "The goods are aboard the Bride, Captain."

"Uh-huh," Earl said. "It appears we have unfinished business with Mr. Berube."

Earl called to James and pointed at Kato and Munenori. "Get over here." He explained what he wanted done once they reached Berube's shop. Before they left, he called to Bob and told him to bring the boat in and be ready to leave on a moment's notice.

Adam had a glimpse of his uncle's anger the night they'd assisted the women in Ah Toy's brothel. He saw it again on the trip to San Pedro while discussing Earl's New Year's Eve confrontation with Arthur Harrington. Subsequent events had revealed a side of his uncle he'd never known existed. If Earl had a strategy on how to deal with the Harringtons, Adam was unaware of what it might entail. Whatever it was, he intended to help execute the plan. Mr. Berube was in his uncle's crosshairs now, and he had no idea what would happen next. *One thing is for sure*, Adam thought, *Uncle Earl has been pushed to the point where he is capable of committing murder.*

The wine merchant's treachery cut deeper than Earl would have guessed possible. He had cultivated his relationship with Michel over many years and felt their friendship was a stronger bond between them than the profits they earned selling rare wines. Things were amiss with Michel, and he intended to find the underlying cause before he killed the man.

He sent Tom and Kato around the back. Tom's shotgun and Kato's wakizashi were enough to persuade the warehouse workers to sit in the middle of the floor. Earl, Adam, and Munenori entered the shop with their weapons drawn. James closed and locked the door. Adam herded the workers into a corner and motioned for them to sit.

Earl was holding Munenori's katata when he closed Michel's office door. "Stay seated, and keep your hands on the desk. You're going to tell me everything, and you are going to tell me now," he seethed, pinning the sword to Michel's cravat. The tip came to rest between his collarbones. "Have I got your attention now?" Earl asked, shoving the tip into the startled man's jugular notch. "I'm going to press, and the only way you're going to get me to ease off is to start telling me a story that makes sense. You move, and I'll shove until I hit the bones in the back of your throat. Speak." Earl pushed until he saw the tip turn red.

Michel's pasty face talked to the sword. "Carlton Lang was here a week ago." The tip backed off. "He had a letter from Arthur Harrington telling me to meet their demands or I would never see my family again. I told Lang you had written and were overdue- you were supposed to be here by ten June. Lang smirked and told me if you did not arrive by yesterday, you would not be here. He asked what I planned to charge you for the order. I told him, and he gave me enough gold to cover the bill two times over. Then he told me how to send word if you arrived. I think you know how I sent word."

Earl eased off the pressure, but the tip stayed in the notch.

"He told me to mind my own business the first time I asked him what he meant when he said you would not be here. I overheard a clerk in the shipping office say you must have slipped past the two vessels sent south to intercept you." Seeing Earl's eyes waver, Michel pared the blade away with a letter opener. Maintaining eye contact, he opened a desk drawer and removed an envelope and sack of gold. He placed them on the desk and pushed them toward Earl. "This is Harrington money. Use it to remove the threat to both of us. I know I will never regain your trust, but I want you to know I never meant you harm. I'm sorry for being forced to put my family's interests above yours."

Earl placed the wet tip of the sword on the envelope and regarded Michel. "I walked in here with the intention of killing you. Glad I had the good sense to keep my passions from getting ahead of my capacity to control them, because if I hadn't, I would have turned you into a victim two times over. I'm the one who should be sorry. If I'd killed you and found this letter, I never would have forgiven myself.

"Your honesty saved your life, Michel. I would do well to remember that.

"You love your family more than the money you receive from our relationship. I could never fault you for making such an obvious choice, and for what it's worth, you've committed a forgivable betrayal."

The tip left a blood smear on Harrington's scrawl when Earl moved it to the sack. "I want you to keep this. Use half to buy me another shipment of premium wine. What you do with the rest is up to you. Please accept my apology for getting you mixed up in my affairs. As far as I'm concerned, Michel, we're still friends. May I see the cut?"

CHAPTER 25

Open Ocean south of Cadiz, Spain, 30 June, four bells of the forenoon watch

Earl and his nephew knelt under the aft hatch skylight going through the contents of Le Pape's ratty old trunk. The contents lay in a pathetic array on a piece of sailcloth spread over the grating. "Not much of value here, Uncle." Adam stuffed lint back into an empty pocket of the faded waistcoat and dropped it on the pile. "Buttons might be worth saving."

"Oh well," Earl said, using a corner of the chest to push himself up. "We'll find a use for the trunk after we air it out." He turned to Le Pape's small chest and produced the key. "Let's open this."

"Hold on," Adam said, rapping the lower sides of the trunk with a knuckle. "I think the bottom is higher on the inside than on the outside." The tone changed after he rapped the side five or six inches above the base. They rapped the interior and pushed on the bottom. Peeling wallpaper lined the chest. Ripping apart the loose paper exposed two holes. Fingering them, they pulled the trunk's bottom right out of the box. Setting it aside, they exchanged glances.

"Whoever packed those things did so with a great deal of care. They filled the whole space. They stuffed waxed rags around the boxes and lambskin sleeve. No mildew," Earl said with a sniff. "Go ahead, you found 'em, you get to open 'em."

Pushing the trash out of the way to get the most light, they arranged the compartment's contents on the deck. "I think we should start with the boxes and work our way up to the sleeve." Adam picked up a long rectangular tin coated with candle wax and popped the lid. They gasped. Scarabs fashioned out of all manner of materials ranging from gold, ivory, lapis lazuli, jasper, amethyst, and carnelian shared the space with a steatite collection covered in colorful faience glazes. The find included amulets, seals, and commemorative scarabs. They spent the next ten minutes passing the pieces around before packing them back together and turning to an intriguing wooden container. Adam removed an ebony box carved with glyphs and arcane symbols. He slid the lid along channels fashioned into the sides and exposed a gold cartouche covered with hieroglyphs.

"There's a message in the glyphs," Earl whispered. "Maybe Willard can tell us what it says," he added, watching how carefully Adam handled the unique container. Several other wooden boxes contained Aramaic scrolls tied with hemp. Adam put the lids back on and set them aside.

He hefted a large square box. "This one is heavy for its size," he said, sliding the ancient lid along its channel.

"Ahh," Earl said. "Do you know what this is, Nephew?"

Adam extracted a brass instrument with gears resembling those found in clocks. The brass discs held rows of script, the sun, moon, and planetary images. "Yup," he replied, "an astrolabe. Although there are many more improved and modern examples, this may be a third-century version. The people who knew how to use it could determine latitude and the positions of astrological bodies for years to come. Skilled users could predict the passing of seasons, planting schedules, and due dates of astral bodies, including comets.

"I'm holding a treasure from antiquity used during the height of Alexandria's Golden Age. The place must have been incredible before Cyril, the Bishop of Alexandria, unleashed his fanatics on one of humanity's crowning achievements. Cyril encouraged his followers to ransack the earth's greatest temple of learning, the Library of Alexandria. Not content to destroy the vast accumulation of knowledge, he sanctioned the murder of the incomparable Hypatia. She had one of the greatest minds in human history. His rabble desecrated temples, burned scrolls, and killed 'pagan' scholars. They dragged Hypatia out of a carriage, flayed, and dismembered her. Then they burned her corpse. I can think of no act of depravity that could possibly exceed the dimensions of this craven display of barbarism. I'm quite sure the person in whose name Cyril sanctioned these horrors would not have approved. Yes, Uncle, I know what this is. I'm deeply concerned for the future of a species so prone to performing such acts on the most intelligent among them. I've come to the conclusion that if Jesus were alive today, he would renounce his divinity and declare himself an atheist if he thought by doing so he could spare the life of any child about to be murdered in his name!"

Adam placed the astrolabe back in its box and replaced the lid. "I'm disheartened by how otherwise rational people become fixated on so many destructive behaviors. They spend their lives chasing the hollow rewards of personal advantage, tribal membership, and greed. How they can justify following leaders incapable of giving them a good dose of common sense is beyond me. Followers, who by the time they understand the consequences of what they have allowed to happen, will have moved humanity a step closer to destroying Earth's capacity to recover from their willful ignorance. I'm not at all sure how much longer Jesus's Father can be expected to forgive them for not knowing what they do."

Adam failed to see the tightening around Earl's eyes, but he did hear his uncle express an inner conflict he could no longer restrain. "You just put your finger on a question that's been plaguing me all year. What role am I playing in the scheme of human activities, which, if not brought under control, will probably lead to our eventual extinction?" Earl toed the broken sword. "If we don't start putting controls on our rampant consumption, the refuse we produce will wash away the blue. There are too damn many of us. I think Arthur Harrington and his cohorts know this, and I think it's one of the reasons they are so avid in their pursuit of getting all they can while the getting is good. I don't think they care about their children's future."

"People like us are a major impediment to them, aren't we, Uncle? That's why they're trying to destroy us."

"Yes," Earl said, his eyes scanning the hold, the trash, the trunk, Le Pape's Vatican chest, and the boxes filled with Egyptian artifacts. He stared into the dark recesses and imagined a tunnel in time going back millennia, the walls lined with animated scenes portraying the original owners handling the treasures carried aboard his ship.

"We're in a battle over who controls destiny. Harrington and his friends see us as nothing more than an inconvenience. They're confident they can dispense with us by force. They're uninterested in our view that there is more to life than the fruits of blind greed. They could care less about how we frame the conflict between good and evil, beauty versus ruthless consumption, consent against tyranny, cooperation over compulsion, or virtue over violence. Our opponents don't really care about the issues of importance to us. They're perfectly willing to foul everyone's nest if it means they can get more of what they want because they can always afford to build new nests for themselves on unspoiled terrain. They want to destroy us because we object to the notion that they are the rightful heirs to power, and any who trade with them must lose.

"They detest the fact that we have become wealthy by *cooperating* with the people we meet. The only thing we have in common with the Harringtons and their ilk is how we keep track of our transactions. We use the same book-keeping methods."

"There is another thing we have in common, Uncle Earl. We're willing to fight if they threaten us."

"Yes. Until we started pushing back, they saw our willingness to cooperate as a sign of weakness. Arthur said as much the night he and I were in the Stanfords' drawing room. Once he found out we differed, he mistook my calmness for pacifism. His dismissive manner suggested he expected me to resign myself to living in a world where resistance is futile. He would prefer that I accept this as fact, and if I don't wish to be devoured, enjoy life for its own sake, and not swim in the waters he occupies. I'm sure he feels differently now, so we must be extra vigilant. I may not act like it, but I agree with the pacifists. War destroys. Only love can conquer hate. Will we learn to put a clamp on the influence peddlers before it's too late? Peddlers agitating politicians on behalf of profiteers who like nothing better than financing their puppet's congressional campaigns!"

Adam had untied the lambskin while Earl was talking. He removed the sheath, and they gasped again. Adam held the cylinder up to the light and stared spellbound as he turned the gem-studded piece. Greek and Egyptian symbols carved into the sides told a tale he could not read. He rubbed his palm on the stallion prancing on a golden knoll atop the scepter. The call came from the crosstrees before he could guess who the horse might be.

"Deck, there! Cannon fire! Take cover!"

"Not again! What is it this time?" Earl asked, dropping his head.

"Ambush!"

A groan went through the ship as chain shot tumbled through shrouds, stays, and sail rigging. They put everything back in the trunk, tied the works to a couple of ringbolts, and ran up Earl's cabin stairs. Through the skylight they heard the whip cracks of parting stays over the sounds of running feet. Rushing along the corridor, Earl shouted to Willard and Oskar. "Give a hand in the salon!"

Adam opened the medical room and laid out the surgical tools.

Earl's pained eyes saw chaos when he opened the deckhouse door. Men raced up ratlines and gathered the torn sails. The foc'sl doors were open. Tom and Hopley bent over cannons. Blood spattered the longboat and ran in streams down the salon walls. Body parts hung from twisted lines, and scattered remains lay in windrows strewn along the bulkheads and deckhouses. Blocks that had not landed on the deck banged off masts, spars, and unwary noggins. Earl rushed across the deck and flung open the salon door. Ming and his helpers were once again throwing sailcloth over tables and bringing in the wounded. "I'll join you as soon as we can assess the threat," he said, bumping into Bud. "You could use a hand." He lifted blood-spattered legs and followed Bud to a table.

"Can you patch him up, Doc? My nephew's havin' a real bad spell."

"Yup. Could be a while. I need to get rid of what's causing this calamity. Hold a cloth on the gash until we can cut off the bleeding." Earl didn't recognize Roy at first. Blood was pouring out of a gash that crossed his crown and ran down his temple to a patch of skin attached to his flapping left ear. Roy's bloody lips started babbling about how much he missed his mother. One eye pleaded with Earl. The other stared at Bud. "I'll be back," Earl said and closed the door on an image that followed him all the way aft.

He ran up the quarterdeck stairs in time to see his two lookouts land on the poop with heavy thuds. Maynard hurried to join the men by the rail. "We saw the flash coming out of the fog bank off the starboard quarter," he said. "They've had time to reload and fire by now." Another orange glow lit up the thinning fog bank. "Deck, there! Take cover!" he shouted and hit the deck. The starboard rail and upper portion of the bulkhead blew apart. One of the men standing by the rail took the full force of the blow and became a wet sack slapped against the midship deckhouse. The concussion blew the men with him off their feet. Flying splinters pierced arms, legs, and torsos. Pools of blood spread beneath open wounds. Qui Li, Kato, and Munenori appeared and hauled away the injured.

A ball struck the side beneath the men on the quarterdeck. Earl shook his head "We can't be together, especially this close to the boats. Get back aloft, Maynard. Mike, give Ming a hand. Ryan, you know what needs doing. I'll get that battery in action. James, direct the helm, and sail plan from the lee stairs. Get those ports aimed at our attacker!"

Earl's shadow fell across the cannons before Tom and his busy crew knew their captain was among them. Tom stopped urging a gunner to drive home the last shell, "That's good, Jake. A few degrees to port, and we can let 'er rip." Tom turned and saw Hopley struggling up the stairs with another shell. "Where's Charlie?" he asked, taking the weight.

"Don't know. We got separated in the confusion. Hi, Capt'n. Looks like we might be in for a bad spell."

"So I hear. You boys ready to join the ball?" Earl twisted his head toward the source of a howl running through his crew and saw towering topgallants.

The white hull of the *Polar Bear* emerged out of the mist, detached, impersonal, threatening.

Earl pressed a hand on the nearest cannon and spoke to the men. Tom felt as if he was in the presence of a stranger. "We'll sink the Bear this time. Apparently, they didn't get the message to leave us alone last January! No mercy!" he fumed, pointing through the open port toward their adversary and grinding his message into the eyes of each man in turn. "You do not stop firing until one of us goes down!" he yelled. "Get to work!"

Earl started aft on bloodstained planks and caught a glimpse of Adam carrying the lower half of an injured seaman into the aft deckhouse. "One for the butcher's table." Another salvo passed overhead. The balls poked holes in the exposed tops'ls and cut a man in two. One moment the man was standing on the Flemish Horse reeving a clew line, and the next his innards were showering Earl and the men below. The horrifying sight of his severed torso tumbling off the yard added a nearly frantic sense of urgency to the men trying to avoid a similar fate. The spume and blood smears made it nearly impossible for the men to get any traction on the wet debris.

Shudders went through the hull as two balls bounced off the *Bride*'s side at the waterline. "Get a grip on yourself, man," Earl's bloodstained face whirled on a confused seaman. He shook the man and pointed through the shattered bulkhead. "Captain Lang'll have to be a lot closer if he expects his balls to get him out of this alive. His cowardly choice to ambush us from the safety of a fog bank is going to cost him his life! He doesn't know it's child's play for our rifled cannon to deliver exploding shells right where he's standing! You need to hold fast, Witham. Can I count on you?" He didn't wait for an answer before he was gone.

Earl's tortured mind fixed on one ferocious thought as his feet hurried aft through the gore. "Yes," he yelled, raising a fist to the heavens. "We'll overcome this tragedy and bring to account the knaves responsible for so much suffering."

Those who saw the smoldering gray eyes staring through the holes in their once beautiful ship took heart at the sight of their captain's defiance. The men still at their posts saw a leader striding with fierce determination across his command and only got to see the half of it.

Their leader had crossed retribution's maddened borders and had gone beyond pain's fearful outer limits. His grim expression unmasked the vow rising through the primal tremors of rage and hurt tearing at his mind. "You've created a mortal enemy, Arthur Harrington! You and I are going to have a final accounting, and the sums I intend to charge will stagger you. We're going to settle up, and I can't wait to see the look in your eyes the day I take payment in full!"

Tom stared through a porthole while the sail master guided them around in the freshening breeze. "We have to make these shots count!" he yelled across his cannon's breach, his strident voice competing with the slapping boom of waves crashing against the bow. "Gather the tackle lines, and stand away from the recoil," Tom said to both crews as he pulled the slack out of his lanyard. "On my word," he said to Hopley, who insisted on holding the second lanyard. "Come this way a bit! You're in the path of the recoil! Better! Wait . . . wait . . . wait . . . *fire!*"

The first salvo hit the *Bear* high, blowing away her fore and mainmast tops. The parting stays and falling sails did a slow pirouette as the topgallants twisted and fell on the men operating the cannons. The sails rapidly filled with seawater, creating a giant sea anchor, stalling the *Bear*'s advance. Men with axes appeared at the rails and chopped the lines in an effort to clear the side. The *Bride*'s second salvo hit the *Bear*'s foc'sl and main deck. The shells sheared away the shrouds and set decks and sails aflame. Swaying drunkenly with the motion of the ship, the shattered timbers splintered box joists, steps, and keelsons, until they finally tore free and crashed on the burning men chasing the tangled tops into the sea. Survivors dropped their axes and began tossing damaged boats over the side.

"We're aiming this next salvo for the quarterdeck," Tom said. "We're going to take out the wheel, kill Captain Lang, and sink her!"

As if reading his thoughts, James swung the bows a few degrees to starboard.

Ryan was standing by the main hatch directing repairs and winced. Earl had grabbed his elbow and yanked him around. "How long before we can put her into the wind and take the weather gauge on the Bear?" Earl said on the way by.

Chilled by the unexpected blast of cold rage, Ryan flexed nerveless fingers and scanned the damage. "Be awhile. We're manning the ship with a skeleton crew just now!"

"Arggh!" Earl said, moving away. "The carpenters can repair the woodwork later. I want every hand busy getting our rigging repaired or replacing sails. I intend to get around behind that coward before he can retreat!"

"Aye, aye, Captain," Ryan said to Earl's back. "Soon's I can get to it. Right now though I intend to do what needs to be done to keep us afloat." The bosuns had returned from a survey of the wreckage and stood within hearing. He stopped flexing his sore elbow. "There's only one direction the Bear's going, and that happens to be straight down."

Tom nodded in agreement when he saw where James wanted the shells to go next. They pulled the lanyards, and the *Bear*'s quarterdeck blew apart in a shower of burning planks, mutilated corpses, and tattered sailcloth. A shell hit the mizzen ten feet or so above the poop. A broken stump was all that was left of the stern features after she received another salvo. The wheel and all the men who had been standing around it were gone.

"The mast's glowing stump looks like a smoldering cigar," one of the gunners said. "Not much left to blow apaht."

"We're going to keep firing until I tell you to stop," Tom replied as he slipped another shell into his cannon's muzzle and watched the rammer drive it home. "Load your gun!"

James brought them back to port, and the next salvo hit the *Bear* amidships. The main and aft decks blew apart and accelerated the fires caused by the first shells. Orchestrating the orientation of the vessel from his familiar spot, James kept the men in the foc'sl lined on their target. Knowing that Tom intended to sink the enemy, James prudently kept them away from the doomed wreck.

The exhausted men making repairs paused to stare at the burning *Bear*. The frantic sense of urgency they had been experiencing was changing into a dull awareness that what they were witnessing could well have been them. The watchers had a clear view of what happened next. Spreading fires ignited the magazine.

Enveloped in a red-hot cloud of expanding gases, the scorched hulk vomited an array of flying body parts, hatch covers, hardware, and flaming ribbons. Slowly at first and with gathering speed, she keeled over on what was left of her port side. A crashing rumble thundered over the crackle of burning timbers as her bow pitched deeper into the steaming water. The cobble ballast shifted into an avalanche of cascading stones funneling into the shattered bows. What satisfaction the *Bride*'s crew might have felt in preventing the *Bear* from inflicting any more damage to their own ship faded after the stricken hulk turned turtle and slipped beneath the waves.

Feeling unnerved by what he had just witnessed, Ryan turned away and spoke to a stunned bosun. "Get a grip, Sidney. Now listen," he said. "Look me in the eye. That's better. Tell Maynard to stay in the tops. We're in no condition to weather another surprise ambush right now. We can rig for running with the wind and begin making repairs. Attend to the bulkhead first. Last thing we need is a gap in the rail if we get hit with another squall."

Ming and his helpers had taken control of the situation by the time Earl regained his composure and opened the salon door. Ming had arranged the wounded according the severity of their injuries. He was in the process of figuring out the ones in need of surgery and in what order. He tossed Earl a damp towel. "Wipe your face."

Earl's brief appearance reassured the injured, who knew they were getting the best treatment possible under the circumstances. Earl exchanged an understanding nod with Bud, who also knew his captain had no time to walk among the injured and have a quick word before he left the area. His presence was required elsewhere.

Adam and Colton were bending over the patient when Earl closed the medical room door. Pausing to glance at the table on his way to the washbasin, he nearly fainted. Charlie was lying on his right side. He was staring at Adam's bloody hands.

Earl gripped the counter and nodded with approval as Adam finished adjusting a tourniquet. His eyes shifted from the forearm's mangled stump to a splinter the size of a marlinspike protruding from Charlie's shoulder.

"You scrub, Colton?"

"Yes."

"Remove the shirt," Earl said, dipping his hands in soapy water and scrubbing rapidly.

Colton cut away the tattered shift and bit his lip.

"Captain Earl," Charlie said in a small voice. "Don't look too good, do I?"

"No, you do not," Earl answered, reaching for a towel. "I would say your right hand is going to have to work overtime with the ladies from now on."

"My privates are still in place, aren't they?" the boy asked with a grunt as Colton peeled torn fabric out of an open gash.

"Yup, and I'm sure you'll play the sympathy card to perfection the first chance you get to flush your plumbing," Earl said, pouring ethanol into a cupped hand. "Or you can play the hero and tell the girls you were mauled by a polar bear and lived to tell the tale."

"Could be worse, right, Captain?" the boy said with hardly enough courage to speak.

"Truer words were never spoken," Earl answered, rubbing his hands and giving Adam the signal to put the chloroform inhaler over the boy's face. "And if it's any comfort to ya, the Bride's taking you home."

"Charlie has another question for you, Capt'n," Colton said.

Adam held the inhaler away, so Charlie could whisper through his pain. "The boys and I have been asking the older crewmen what the Bride's name is. No one knew. Would you mind telling me?"

"Who thought to ask that question?"

"Me."

Earl curled a finger at the inhaler. "The Bride's name, my brave young friend, is Hope."

ABOUT THE AUTHOR

Robert J. Joseph was born in Waterville, Maine in 1948. After driving tractors on a haying crew at the age of ten, he has since earned his keep at a variety of jobs, including cleaning hen houses, digging ditches, patching dams, and bar tending to name a few. He worked his way through college, eventually earning a bachelor's degree in Psychology (Springfield College) and two masters degrees in Education (University of Maine and Boston College). He taught visually impaired and special needs children, sold real estate, and owned two companies, one of which he gave to his employees. He was Board Chair of the Kootenay Coop Natural Food Store the year it was cited by a trade publication as "the best natural food store in the Pacific Northwest." He is currently president of the Whitehead Water District, which services forty-six homes. He and Early Evans, his wife of forty-plus years, live on their twenty-acre homestead on a mountain near Nelson, BC.

9 781525 561207